## *The Price of a Dream*

Bronstein leaned closer, drifting above the asteroid's surface until he was less than a meter away from the probe.

Chisak felt a little nervous, watching him like that. "Miroslav. Don't you think you'd better move back?"

A moment later, the probe hopped—not fast, of course, but Bronstein's faceplate was only thirty centimeters away. Chisak heard the clank through his earphones, and felt a cold sweat bead onto his face. "Jesus, Slava! I *told* you . . ."

"I . . . hear a hissing sound." Bronstein's voice was flat, the same voice you heard from pilots as the ground rose up to kill them.

Also available from Bantam Spectra:

*Iris* by William Barton and Michael Capobianco
*Burster* by Michael Capobianco

# FELLOW TRAVELER
## СПУТНИК МИРА

*A Science Fiction Novel*

# William Barton
# and
# Michael Capobianco

BANTAM BOOKS

NEW YORK · TORONTO · LONDON · SYDNEY · AUCKLAND

FELLOW TRAVELER

*A Bantam Spectra Book/July 1991*

ISBN 0-553-29115-7

*Published simultaneously in the United States and Canada*

PRINTED IN THE UNITED STATES OF AMERICA

OPM     0 9 8 7 6 5 4 3 2 1

*Dedication:*

Sergei P. Korolyov
and
Wernher von Braun


*Acknowledgement:*

A substantially shorter and simpler
version of Appendix 1 appeared in
the November 1989 issue of *Ad Astra*
magazine, the official publication
of the National Space Society.

**Sputnik** (Russ., *fellow traveler*)
1. the first artificial Earth satellite, launched by the USSR in 1957;
2. a nonmember who sympathizes with the Communist party;
3. companion, friend.

> "Where there is no vision,
> the people perish."
> —Proverbs 29:18

> "Beauty is the shining of the Idea
> through Matter."
> —Georg Wilhelm Hegel

# Caveatski

*Fellow Traveler* is a work of fiction, and all the characters in it are wholly invented. Although in several cases the names of actual Soviet cosmonauts, technicians, and program managers have been used, all incidents, dialogue, and opinions expressed are drawn from the imaginations of the authors and should not be construed as portraying real individuals.

The sole exception is Mikhail Sergeevich Gorbachev, whose character is a matter of public record. The authors wish to congratulate Mr. Gorbachev for appearing on the stage of history at such an opportune moment. Perhaps he will, in reality, see the true value of the Soviet manned space effort and help see it through to the maturity portrayed in *Fellow Traveler*. If not, then his economic reforms may be wasted.

As this is being written, it is late 1989. Tumultuous changes are occurring throughout the Communist world, and it is impossible to predict what will happen in the Soviet Union and Eastern Europe. Though some are forecasting the end of communism, the authors take a more conservative view, assuming that Gorbachev's policies of *glasnost* and *perestroika* will ultimately succeed. The alternative is not pleasant to contemplate.

The status of various national and international space programs is optimized for dramatic effect. It is assumed that the Soviets will use items already displayed by the year 1990 to their best effect, something not at all inconsistent with their history. On the other hand, the authors are assuming that the United States will, in fact, build every major piece of hardware now under serious consideration.

This is not very likely, given the events of the past thirty-five years.

The Soviet Union may not be gearing up for a manned lunar landing ten years from now. But it seems quite conceivable that by the year 2001, Americans will be grounded forever.

This novel may, unfortunately, represent the best future we can possibly expect. As it stands now, the Luddites are winning.

William Barton
Michael Capobianco
December 31, 1989

# PROLOGUE
## *December 14, 1994*

The timer was beeping madly, a thin noise like a fly's scream. Georgia Paar, an attractive woman with penetrating blue eyes, a great horsetail of blond hair hanging to the small of her back, made the twenty-step journey to the machinery, which wasn't supposed to act this way, the snapping of her low heels echoing in the vast pavilion housing Palomar's Big Schmidt telescope. She looked up at the streamlined milk bottle, set low to see into the inner solar system, that contained the 122-centimeter mirror and its related optics. It was dark and cold in the dome, and through the slim, curving rectangle of the opening, blinding Venus dominated the sky.

Every setback that lost precious telescope time was an aggravation. Being part of that small clique of astronomers interested in finding out about the near-Earth asteroids, tiny bits of debris trapped near and inside the orbit of the Earth, meant that her projects were invariably given low priority. The stars, after all, were what astronomy was *really* about. At one time she'd fantasized about taking money from her college professor's salary to finance the project.

She punched the reset button and slid onto the observing stool, sighing as the columns of sequential pointing objectives appeared on the monitor. The idea behind the Computerized Optical Search Interface was its autonomy—it was supposed to conduct its survey without any human interference. There was nothing wrong with the pointing. What did that leave? Absolutely nothing. She broke out of COSI, loaded her editor, then read in the source code for the last version of the program. Yep. It was, of course, right where she'd made the last modification, in the subroutine that exited search mode to follow a particularly quick-moving object that hadn't registered on enough pixels to get a good plot. She shook her head and took out the extra bracket that had screwed up the program. A voice from just behind her shoulder spoke, "So. What's up?"

"Maarten! I wish you wouldn't do that! I swear I'm going to put tacks in your crepe soles so I can hear you coming."

Maarten Hakluyt, a mouselike presence behind heavy glasses and gray-streaked, black Vandyke, smiled compactly. "You won't catch me that easily, Georgia." The Dutch accent was a slight, inappropriate intonation. He put a hand on her shoulder and craned to look at the monitor. "What's up?"

"Just a minor bug. Introduced by yours truly, I'm afraid. What are you doing here?"

"I might ask the same of you, my dear. Neither of us is being paid to monitor our friend COSI. We should be preparing exams for the little stargazers. My excuse is that I was going over Saturday night's results and I found something I wanted to check out."

Georgia restarted COSI and chose the analysis section of the program. "Which one?"

Hakluyt drew out a pad from under his sweater and consulted it. "Object four. Time 2449700.49."

She panned through the 112 objects found so far. Day seven, number four was not particularly unusual, absolute mag 17.9, moving three pixels per integration. "Okay," she said, "here it is."

"Doesn't look like much, does it?" Hakluyt gave her a second to nod. "These preliminary calculations put it on a collision course with Earth, give or take half a million kilometers."

Georgia stared hard at the chartreuse numbers on her screen. "Well, well, well. An Aten, I suppose. What's the inclination?"

"Close to zero. But I don't want to prejudice anything. . . . We need to refine these figures before we have any right to get excited."

They heeled the telescope over a hard two degrees and switched over to a real-time image from the CCD. They would need to watch Object 7-4 until it was lost in the glare of Vista and Oceanside to refine its orbital parameters sufficiently.

Later that evening, after they'd faxed the discovery circumstances and preliminary orbit to the Minor Planet Center, Paar and Hakluyt sat in the fake-stucco-façaded Taco Borracho not far from the base of the mountain. They were drinking coffee at one of the sparkle-impregnated tables. Georgia picked at the remains of her nachos and laughed. "No death asteroid, at least. Even at a third of a kilometer, it would make a heck of a crater."

Maarten looked at her and wished for the hundredth time that their relationship were not professional. This was the first time they had been "out" together, and there were too many other things to talk about. She was married, divorced, and married again, anyway. "If we handle this correctly, we won't have to worry about NASA renewing the grant. I hate to say it, but I think we should contact the media, and let them know about Object 7-4."

The woman shuddered. "I gave an interview to *Find Out About It* during the Baja eclipse, Maarten. What a fiasco! I don't care to go through that kind of thing again."

"Too bad, Georgia. You're the kind of photogenic astronomer that they want. You know they 'tested' me for that spot, too. . . . Didn't quite make a dramatic impact, I suppose. But sure, you don't have to appear."

"So what do we do?"

"It's easy. I just give a call to the International Press Service. Everyone, CTN, Cable News, the newspapers, they all get their copy."

"Will you mislead them?"

"Don't have to. Just tell them it will come close—they'll do the rest. Look, I don't like it any more than you. We were lucky enough to get the Big Schmidt for as long as we did. If we want to get the time and money for a thorough survey, we have to throw ourselves to the wolves."

Georgia Paar looked deep into the indeterminate eyes of her coworker. There wasn't much to see. "The wolves . . ." she laughed.

Lyle Marlowe sat behind a big, blotter-crowned desk, sorting through sheaves of paper, selecting the story he would use for the final segment. This was his first night as anchor of the CTN Evening News, unexpectedly replacing

Todd Bormann, who'd had a nervous breakdown at lunch, during the content conference. The sight of the Prince of News picking up his salad and squashing it into Schlossberg's face was unforgettable. They'd never get the vinaigrette out of the old man's tie. Now Bormann was in the hospital, Marlowe sat in his chair, and Schlossberg was still in charge. Things seemed to be going well.

He looked up from the desk to see that the on-line director was giving him a thumbs-up sign. Sixty seconds. This business of letting the anchors pick from a selection of stories as the broadcast progressed, riding behind the trough of a ninety-second live-time delay, was inspired and seemed to have given CTN the edge over its competitors.

A brace of HDTV cameras swung down to point at him, yellow warning lights winking above lens batteries. The director held up a hand with thumb, index, and middle fingers extended, then dropped them in cadence.

Three. Two. One.

The red light popped on.

Lyle Marlowe had dark brown hair and chestnut eyes, scientifically determined to look "convincing" on an HDTV fast-frame screen. His features were bland and regular, with just the right mix of beauty and masculinity. His skin was absolutely clear and smooth, the skin of a man who'd never known the meaning of the word pimple.

People at home, that eighteen percent of the viewing audience with HDTV, saw a complex image, a holistic montage that mixed his face with imagery from the words he was reading in the news report. Viewers with old-fashioned televisions had to see a sequential montage, constructed *ex post facto* by a flex-script program that could recognize what reports were being used.

"For our final segment tonight we have a story from the world of science. Astronomers from Mount Palomar Observatory today disclosed the discovery of a new asteroid whose orbit brings it unusually close to the earth. . . ."

The montage constructed itself behind him, a spherical Disney asteroid rolling through space, hot red cinders glowing in the fissures of its craterless surface. In the distance, blue against a spare, starry sky, the Earth was a mottled and substantial sphere. The sun twinkled against its limb, yet the face of the planet was fully illuminated. The picture of Earth was reconstructed and enhanced from a photo taken by moonbound astronauts twenty-five years earlier. It grew as the asteroid rumbled onward.

"The asteroid, as yet unnamed, will swing by the earth, making a perilously close approach to our world in the spring of 2002, a mere eight years from now. . . ." Scenes of the asteroid whipping through the clouds, making a whooshing sound as it passed low above the New York skyline.

"Older viewers may recall a similar event when, in 1968, the Earth suffered a close call with the approach of the asteroid Icarus. At that time, panic was widespread and many scientists believed that a catastrophe was virtually certain. . . ." Scenes of hippies trekking toward the mountains, montage clips of Woodstock, concerned looking men in white lab coats giving lectures to college classes.

"At the time, studies were made which indicated that the nation's military would have been able to shoot down Icarus, had it come too close. . . ." Scenes of *Apollo 17* lifting off in the only lunar night launch, followed by a computer-enhanced clip of a large thermonuclear weapon being tested in 1954.

"That's all we have for you today. When there's news, CTN is there, because we think you ought to know. . . ." The director sliced a hand across his throat. Cut. And the red light blinked out.

As the credits rolled across stock footage they'd shot forty-five minutes ago, CTN News Director Moe Schlossberg strolled across the studio, pushing a substantial stomach before him. "Good work, Lyle. The job is yours. Weekly preview conference is in my office. Ten minutes." He turned and walked away.

Lyle stood up and stretched. *The CTN Evening News with Lyle Marlowe.* Too bad about Todd Bormann, though. Too fucking bad.

# CHAPTER 1
## *October 21, 2001*

Mikhail Sergeevich Gorbachev dropped the thick document to his desk, riffled through it once more, and sank back into the leather of the most comfortable chair in the USSR. His gaze traveled, as it often did, to a portrait of Lenin, in an exhorting posture, on the far wall. Vladimir Ilyich wouldn't recognize his fatherland any more. He'd died so soon, only seven years after the Revolution. Before all the horror and ignorance; before Dzhugashvili and his pernicious evil. Before mankind invented the means to wipe itself from the planet. And now I've been in the hot seat seven*teen* years! It hardly seemed more than an instant.

Where will it end for me? he mused. Nothing had gone according to plan. After his selection as general secretary, he'd instituted the reforms he and his friends dreamed of, established a powerful presidency, and taken it on. He had brought the Soviet Union back from beyond the brink, but there had been so many compromises. . . . Ten years should have been enough! Maybe no mortal span of time was enough, propped before the implacable bulldozer that was human perversity. Now Yeltsin, of all people, was president, making him general secretary again, of a Communist party that had been stripped down, barely allowed to function in domestic matters. Even though the successes of the party had stopped the erosion of respect, and even restored many of the ideas and goals of the country to their former prestige, things were very different than he had hoped for. Trying to stem the floodtide of bullshit with such a little shovel. Academician Derzhavin was a madman, of course. The whole thing was a fantasy, nothing more. And yet . . .

The space program had never been one of his highest priorities. He'd always seen the benefits that accrued from sending men into space in rather human terms—how to unify the Soviet people behind a long-term, exciting quest, how to increase Soviet technological know-how without giving full rein to the military, how to maintain the pride that the USSR rightly felt about its accomplishments since 1917. These goals were nebulous indeed.

He sighed meditatively. Seventeen years at the top hadn't made these decisions any less difficult. He distrusted any plan that could solve so many problems at once, yet he remembered the bold step in agriculture that had propelled him so quickly into the Politburo. The irony was that mass harvesting didn't really work all that well. Since *perestroika* that type of upper-level fiat had become unacceptable. After the near anarchy of the early nineties, the distasteful "market economy" had kicked in surprisingly quickly. Now domestic matters followed their own improbable course, and the government, for the most part, sat back and watched. In fact, with the coming of the successful *samfabi* four years ago, even military production *apparatchiki* were increasingly relegated to mere tinkering. It was just as well. On the other hand, boldness did have its rewards. He'd been looking for something with which to commemorate the fiftieth anniversary of Stalin's death, the "New Beginning" he often cited in his speeches of late. This plan was bold if it was anything.

Still, he distrusted it. If he hadn't read Glavkosmos's disturbing report of "anomalies" in the Interim Lunar Lander's ascent engine, he would have dismissed the thing out of hand. Reanalysis of recent tests showed that cosmonauts *might* be stranded on the Moon. . . . Might. Estimates of one chance in seventy-eight. Very remote. So *now* what do we do? *Oryol,* with the offending engine, was already in orbit, coupled to *Serpachek,* ready for departure. *Molotochek* and six brave cosmonauts were already in lunar orbit, docked to *Mechta.* A billion dollars already spent. So? Send them anyway? Cosmonauts die. It's their job to take these risks. And yet, we'd look *very* bad if anything happened and then the truth came out, as it eventually would.

Now *this* bizarre proposal: A trip to an asteroid would be one thing—but bringing it back? Although he regarded

himself as a scientist of sorts—political philosophy being as
rigorous as any field that dealt with humans could be—the
concepts involved were almost beyond his powers of com-
prehension.

The astonishing thing about Derzhavin's report was how
*easy* it would be. They would hardly have to revamp
*Molotochek* for the journey, and the recently concluded
tests to determine the practicability of using tactical nuclear weapons for engineering showed clearly that they
could mount and detonate a charge of the correct magnitude. Sinuhe was even now approaching a position that
made it a perfect target. And it was made of iron and nickel
—materials that were the cornerstone of any industrial
economy.

He smiled and excitement surged through his body. And
the Americans! What will it do to them to see this monstrous boulder come hurling down from space? He could
barely restrain himself. Those damned Republicans and
their Star Wars would think twice about using weapons in
space after they saw this! What could they do but stand idly
by and let the USSR pull such a coup? It would be worth it
just to see the expression on that fool Wren's face!

What of unexpected dangers? Cosmonauts were already
sick, maybe dying, from exposure to solar radiation. *That*
had been fixed; but who knew what other dangers might
lurk outside the orbit of the Moon? Send cosmonauts off on
a wild goose chase and they might die. *Then* how would we
look?

You old fool. You're just afraid you'll look bad in the
history books. Hell with it. Historians make everyone look
bad, sooner or later. What will they say if you *don't* do it?
Look at the things they say about Carter. Gorbachev stood
and stepped over to the window, where the midautumn sun
was already hidden behind the Troitskaya Tower. He
folded his hands behind his back and looked up into the
clear silvery sky. He had decided.

Space Station *Mechta,* Dream, had been turning in lunar
polar orbit for eighteen months now, sweeping along a
slowly precessing six-hundred-kilometer orbit that traversed every point on the battered globe. In that time,
*Mechta* had seen three crews come and go. The first had
been a brief set-up team, there solely to start the station's

subsystems and put this new house in order. Though they stayed for a mere four weeks, it was this crew which had gotten all the international attention and Kremlin accolades, for these were the first Soviets in lunar orbit, setting aside, finally, the humiliation of 1968.

The next crew stayed for half a year. Though intended as a selenographic team, they were in fact the first human beings to spend a significant amount of time outside Earth's magnetic shield. Even now, those six cosmonauts were very sick men, one of them not expected to survive. The third crew was a construction team, come to prepare *Mechta* for the lunar landing attempt of 2001. They stayed for eight weeks, and the first thing they added was a large water tank in which a cramped solar flare shelter lay embedded.

The core of the station was a *Mir*-class base module, a stepped cylinder slightly more than four meters in diameter. From its sides projected a pair of large L-shaped solar panels, which generated some twenty kilowatts of power. To this base station had been added four necessary components. The flare shelter had been coupled to the aft docking port. It was nothing more than a cylindrical water tank with a through tunnel, barricaded by "floodable" airlocks. At its forward end, *Mechta* sported a spherical docking adapter with five docking ports and a remote manipulator. Two bell-shaped utility modules were already docked: moonward, a "kvant"-class science module sprouted a battery of instruments and telescopic cameras; on the dorsal side, an engineering module housing a vacuum machine shop/airlock and two Cosmonaut Maneuvering Units completed the T.

Aft, beyond the flare shelter, the only part crucial to a lunar landing was docked at the main resupply port. Surrounded by an open framework of girders and struts lay the "service station" module, another cylinder, narrower than *Mechta* itself, about which were clustered several spherical dewars containing extra fuel and oxidizer for the Lunar Landing Vehicles to come. Within an assortment of unpressurized bins, spare parts and special materials of all kinds were stocked.

In late October of the year 2001, not many weeks before the eighty-fourth anniversary of the Revolution, space station *Mechta* circled the Moon in active mode, unmanned, awaiting its next cosmonaut crew. The signal came: space-craft inward bound.

The tiny speck that was Lunar Transfer Vehicle *Molotochek* fell around the north limb of the Moon, accelerating toward two and a third kilometers per second. The LTV was really little more than a flying fuel tank: a glossy sixty-five-meter cylinder a touch over eight meters in diameter, surmounted by a solar-panel-winged command module itself not much different from a *Mir* base station. The tank section of the propulsion module was painted dark green to match the thermal blanketing of the command module, and down one side the name *Molotochek*—Little Hammer—was painted in Cyrillic lettering. This was bracketed by the clashing flag decal of the USSR and the institutional logos of IKI, Vernadskii, and Glavkosmos.

By the time the ship was at periselenion, midway across the farside and out of touch with ground controllers, the crew had turned the craft around, pointing the propulsion assembly forward into the direction of travel. If all went well, the six men aboard *Molotochek* would join a meager forty-two others who had circled the Moon over the past thirty-three years. And in less than a week, the roll of moonwalkers might rise from twelve to fifteen.

The moment came. A button was pressed and, after a split second of ignition, the engines lit. The two powerful hydrogen engines pushed a globe of transparent fire ahead of *Molotochek,* spending delta-V, shedding velocity. When it was over, the ship lay in a six hundred by twelve hundred-kilometer polar orbit, ahead of their destination but following the same meridian. *Mechta,* lower and faster, crawled around the Moon after the manned ship until, two orbits later, following a brief phasing burn, they were ready for rendezvous.

The two spacecraft flew in tandem, co-orbiting a few hundred meters apart, while final checks were made. Then, with *Molotochek* assuming a stable position, the OAMS thrusters of *Mechta,* operated by remote control, began to close the gap. It made sense to do it that way. With a 200,000-kilogram fuel load still on board, the LTV was by far the more massive object. The ships swept together at a slow walk and met with a barely perceptible internal crunch. After a brief pause, while a few little sensors made a status check, there was a faint jiggling motion as the androgynous docking rings rotated into a secure hard dock. There were tense smiles as green lights lit both in space and on Earth. This took some getting used to. But they *were* getting used to it.

Vladimir Alekseevich Manarov, Volodya to his friends and family, floated in the dimly lit airlock of *Molotochek,* carefully inspecting a rack of dials set in the bulkhead by the forward hatch. Clad in the green, gold, and red flight uniform of Glavkosmos, Volodya came close to matching the media-generated profile of a Soviet cosmonaut-hero. His face was square and handsome, with a thin nose that was just long enough. He had pale skin, light-blue eyes, and copper-colored hair that he combed straight back, revealing a slight widow's peak. Though a little taller than average, he was nonetheless compact and muscular. Like most Russians, he had a tendency to put on weight from a fatty, starchy diet, but the physical training required of all cosmonauts kept it under control.

He methodically read his way through the dials, which showed the pressure, temperature, humidity, and general composition of the gas on the other side of the door. It was air, as opposed to vaporized hydraulic fluid or some such, at standard values. He keyed his headset. "LTV Flight Engineer. Conditions are nominal in the transfer tunnel. Permission is requested to release the hatch." It was, he supposed, a little ridiculous, since the propulsion control room was within earshot, only a few meters away. But on this historic flight, protocols would be followed to the letter. He smiled. Forty-one years old, he thought, and here I am, almost on the Moon for the second time! Almost. The smile took on a wry twist. Maybe his plan would work and maybe not. He was trading glory for experience, but. . . . So I won't be the thirteenth man to set foot on the Moon, nor even the twentieth. I'll be more than fifty when we go to Mars. But if I get to go, I'll be commander. And the commander steps out first. . . . Maybe.

"LTV Commander. Permission granted." In accordance with regulations, Miroslav Ilyich Bronstein, age forty-five, colonel in the Strategic Rocket Forces of the USSR, was wearing an in-ship pressure suit. They'd been doing things this way since Volkov, Patsaev, and Dobrovolski died, way back in 1971. For decades, during flight maneuvers, every Soviet cosmonaut had had to suit up. Now, those regulations were beginning to relax a little. The pilot still had to wear one, because if something went wrong they needed someone to close valves, make repairs, and, most important, bring back some kind of an explanation. There wasn't much danger here. In the worst possible accident only Manarov, trapped in the airlock, might die. But these regulations made eminent sense. The idea was to succeed in the mission, not display childish courage.

Through the open faceplate of his helmet, only Bronstein's face could be seen. It was heavy and flat, skeptical, with dark-brown eyes under blond brows. Whatever his nose had once looked like, it had been broken and was now slightly pushed in and bent to one side. A good plastic surgeon could have fixed this thing in half an hour, but the pugnacious look it gave him had served in good stead more than once. Despite the suit, you could see that he was short and muscular. And his internal passport read Volga-German. It was his mother's nationality, of course, and a poor sort of choice, but much to be preferred over the alternative. He watched as the pressures equalized on his own readouts; then, to the four men seated in the back of the room, he said, "We are docked with *Mechta*. Flight maneuver protocol is ended."

The two men in the middeck space turned to exchange a knowing smile. Artyukhin, the Lunar Landing Vehicle pilot, and Zarkov, the LLV flight engineer, knew their moment of glory would come in only a few days, as they set *Oryol* down on the dusty floor of the crater Schrödinger. This business of getting into lunar orbit was secondary to them.

In his acceleration cot against the port side of the room's rear bulkhead, flight surgeon Lev Mikhailovich Chishak, forty-two years old, relaxed and began to undo the straps that held him in place. He was a tall, thin, somewhat stooped man, with curly brown hair and pale hazel eyes. Come, Lyova, he told himself, for you this isn't a flight to the Moon at all. You're here to observe these busy men and keep them in condition. Almost a passive role: to monitor and observe. If you can make some headway with the current-induction device, it will be a bonus. You might as well be aboard *Mir*, just a few hundred kilometers up in the sky. As he unclipped the snap-lock buckles, his hard, professional stare softened. Shorn of expression, Chishak's face was horsey, with big teeth set in a definite muzzle and a nose entirely too long and thin. He looked like a man who should wear glasses, and the spidery lines of Fyodorov surgery could be made out on his eyes.

On the starboard side of the hatch, Anton Antonovich Serebryakov could taste his triumph like a sip of freezing vodka evaporating off his tongue. Finally, the beginning of his rich harvest had come. It would be worth all the hardships, the discomfort. He grinned suddenly. At thirty-six years of age, he was about to become the first planetologist to set foot on another world. True, that American geologist Schmitt had gone to the Moon, but in 1972 there had been no such thing as planetary science. The whole field was a product of the seventies and eighties, and his would be the first *in situ* research.

He moved his head slowly, feeling the dark hair rise above his head slightly and wave around. He was a friendly-looking man, boyish, with a high forehead and finely-drawn straight eyebrows over almond-shaped brown eyes. His nose was not exceptionally large but fleshy in the Russian manner. The whole effect was somewhat Asiatic, which caused some to assume he came from the Far East, but his chin and jaw, shaven five hours before, had a distinctly unoriental beard shadow. He let his smile fade, watching the men who would ferry him down framing the forward hatch expectantly, waiting for the grand reentrance, trading jokes with Bronstein. Good men, he thought. My name will be linked with theirs. He began to unfasten his safety harness, thinking of the things that still needed to be done.

In the airlock, Volodya Manarov unlocked the handle that would let him into the docking adapter and *Mechta*. Slipping his feet under two bracing straps attached to the "floor," he began working the lever that would retract the hatch's locking mechanism. Once again. The door decoupled with a slight pop and swung open, letting a lifetime of dreams flood in.

Second unit homework finished at last, Volodya stood on the roof of his apartment block, looking down on the dark and snowy streets of Arkhangelsk. Though the family's evening meal was hours away yet, the sky above was already a dark and starry mystery. The solstice was only a few weeks gone, the days steely dim, the nights long and fatally crisp. Volodya hated the cold and fantasized about the deserts of Uzbekistan they studied in school, but when it was dark and cold, he often came here, just to watch. The dry, frozen air was stable and there was no high-altitude haze. Perfect weather. It seemed as though a billion stars wheeled about Polaris. And, as he waited, the Arctic night's one real benefit was there: a dim yellow curtain appeared against Ursa Major, spreading upward almost to the zenith, surrounded by subdued coruscations as though the atmosphere itself were quaking. Aurora. He said the word to himself. It was a special treat.

The view of the ground from the roof of the tall building was of a different world. Billowing clouds of habitation fog cloaked the streets, making the headlights of the few cars seem eerie, wraiths moving through an alien dimension. The fog rose perhaps a dozen meters from the ground and, when the Moon was up, you could see it being produced, sliding from the concrete façades of the buildings, dropping from the windows to build yet more darkness.

Volodya shivered, pulling the down comforter that he wore like a shawl more closely about his shoulders, glad for the snug fit of his expensive fur hat. He liked to stand up here, freezing cold or no, and watch for the lights of his father's car to come crawling up the street through the mist. When he got out of the car, heavy shouldered in Red Fleet greatcoat and cap, it was a warming sight. A. N. Manarov wasn't a naval officer, just a civilian engineer. But a *Kandidat*-class engineer was still a rarity in the Soviet Union of 1970 and his carefully honed skills meant privilege for the man and his family. The lappets of Volodya's hat were lined with ermine. The family apartment had a private bathroom and the boy slept in a room of his own.

It would be a while yet before the car came home. Volodya turned away from the street and looked back at the Arctic sky. Stars, thousands of them, and Volodya was beginning to learn their names. The odd Arabic and Latin designations had a romantic ring, in tune with the Turkish names of the Central Asian cities that he longed for. Just as names, Merak and Dubhe seemed as warm and beckoning as Tashkent or Dushanbe. And who knew what might lie there? The science fiction writers said fantastic things.

And then there was reality. The "troika" mission of

*Soyuz 6, 7,* and *8,* with its horsey emblem on the news shows for a week, was only a few months gone . . . but the Americans had been to the Moon four times already. Landed on it twice! On the night *Apollo 12* touched down, he'd overheard his father talking with another naval architect. What, they wondered, was Comrade Eyebrow playing at? Since *Sputnik,* since Gagarin, the Soviet Union had been first in space for a decade. Now, it seemed, they went in circles. For a while, in the appalling spring of 1969, there had been rumors that Cosmonaut Belyaev, commander of *Voskhod 2,* would fly alone to the Moon in an experimental spaceship, snatching up the prize at the last moment, but nothing had come of it. His father's friend said there were rumors of a giant booster exploding at Baikonur in July, only weeks before *Apollo 11* took off, killing hundreds of technicians and destroying the lunar launch complex.

It was inexcusable, said his father, and, in a hushed voice, too bad the leadership couldn't be held to proper account. Khrushchev had been such a crude old peasant, embarrassing on the world scene and, in the end, cowed by a handsome American boy. But, like Mussolini, he seemed to have the knack of making things work. Maybe that was important.

Volodya looked at the sky and wondered what would come of it all. Maybe the Americans would fly off to Mars, taking all their hates and greeds away with them forever. Or maybe they would put a giant battleship in the sky, a floating island loaded with hydrogen bombs with which to terrorize innocent humanity. It was a frightening thought to a boy living on the Arctic coast of Fortress Russia; a boy whose father built the nuclear attack submarines that would slip out in a war to sink American aircraft carriers and hunt down enemy missile subs. His teachers said that a confrontation was inevitable.

A light on the southern horizon caught his eye. What? He squinted as it emerged from the masking fog, a bright, flickering pinpoint that brightened and took on a definite shape as it rose. An aircraft? No. That would have been a steady, moving light, maybe flashing if it had one of the new xenon safety beacons. This thing was irregular, like a candle flame.

The object went higher yet in the sky, reaching a maximum brightness and then beginning to grow dim, taking on a disklike shape. He thought for a moment of the UFO crazes that continued to sweep the Soviet citizenry at regular intervals, but the scientific attitudes his father had given him dismissed the notion outright.

The firelike dot grew smaller and dimmer, then, suddenly, seemed to extinguish. No, it was still there, but very pale now. There was a flicker-flash in the air about the object, clearly defined tongues of white flame for half a second, then there were two objects, one bright and continuing to climb, the other all but invisible, a falling glow against the night sky.

He had read enough to know what it was. A small satellite launch vehicle taking off from Plesetsk Cosmodrome only a few hundred kilometers to the south. Even as he watched, it was streaking across European Russia, dropping its first stage into some Ukrainian wheat field, driving on toward polar orbit. A northward launch would have been safer, dropping that heavy booster onto the uninhabited icepack somewhere near Novaya Zemlya, but just across the North Pole lay America. And if some trigger-happy general thought he saw an ICBM, it might mean the end of the world. Better to risk hitting some innocent farmer than to bring on the accidental death of all humanity. . . . The light in the sky winked out.

Volodya shook his head slowly, lost in a sea of stars. *I wonder,* he thought, *what it must be like to sit in a tiny cabin on top of a tall, powerful rocket and fly away into the sky?* TV sometimes showed cosmonauts in training, usually crushed, with distorted faces, in the torture chair of a centrifuge. Maybe it was like that. And what if the rocket exploded? What if the ejector system failed to work? There'd be nothing left of such a cosmonaut, nothing to put in the Kremlin wall.

He supposed they were unafraid. Cosmonauts did die, after all. Vladimir Komarov, first Russian to fly in space twice, had been smashed to his death trying to land *Soyuz 1.* And Yuri Gagarin, forcing his copilot to eject, had ridden a failing jet into the ground, deliberately crashing in a successful bid to avoid hitting a schoolyard full of children. He supposed that was what made them heroes. But, just maybe, when they sat atop some giant rocket, waiting for the thud of ignition, they were just a little bit nervous?

The dull slam of a car door forced him back into the cold

night. His father had driven up undetected and was even now striding into the building foyer, trailing a long plume of condensed breath. Volodya turned and went into the building himself, running for the stairs, down to his family's apartment.

When he got there, his parents were embracing in a toasty kitchen full of cooking smells, two little girls jumping against their legs, grabbing at their clothes. His father released his mother and tossed his cap across the room, his ruddy, windburned face wrinkled by a broad smile. He beckoned to the boy. "I've been promoted, Volodya," he said. "We're going to Leningrad."

"This meeting of the Political Bureau of the Communist party of the Union of Soviet Socialist Republics, October 21, 2002, will come to order." General Secretary Gorbachev glanced down at the backlit LCD monitor embedded in the wood before him and pressed the acoustic-wave touch screen on the outline processor option, then chose the files containing his notes for tonight's meeting.

He looked around him, smiling ingratiatingly. Although the Politburo was finally up to its full strength again, the members were old, almost as old as they had been during Brezhnev's last days, when he was a young upstart fresh from Stavropol *Krai*. Even the best politician starts to stiffen up after seventy, he thought, even me. But the Sinuhe thing. . . . This would be an interesting meeting, if nothing else.

"Comrades, I have asked Academician Akhmatov of the Vernadskii Institute to attend this meeting because his group is responsible for an outstanding proposal that I wish to bring before you tonight. Comrade Akhmatov is the recipient of three Lenin awards for his contributions to our country." Akhmatov, a tall, wiry man with a fish-face and a goatee, looked completely uncomfortable acknowledging the looks from the others. "The project to put cosmonauts on the Moon is experiencing some difficulties. We do not have full confidence in the interim lander, which is an extremely important component of the mission. I needn't tell any of you how unfortunate it would be to have three of our boys stranded on the Moon, with no hope of rescue."

Aleksei Guptev, a dazed-looking, poodlelike Ukrainian with two great tufts of white hair, interrupted. "The *Oryol* is on its way to rendezvous with *Mechta* as we speak, is it not?"

Gorbachev sighed. "Well, no. The landing vehicle is still in Earth-orbit. *Molotochek* is now in lunar orbit awaiting the lander. This will make cancellation all the more unseemly. Unless . . ." He paused for effect, then said, "Unless, comrades, we implement a new mission, a spectacular mission that will make even a return to the Moon seem insignificant."

He could tell that he had gotten their attention. "Few of you are specialists in the realms of astronomy and physics. I don't know how much of a preamble to make. Even if we all remembered the bulk of what we were taught in school, it might not help, because many of those things were wrong.

"You no doubt know about the asteroid belt, a region where many tiny planets circle. It is beyond the orbit of Mars, our now familiar brother planet. We have all been briefed about the importance of Mars to the future of Communism, and many times we have had reports about our successes and failures as we move toward putting men on that beautiful world. The advantage that we have over our capitalist rivals is patience—and relentless progress toward goals that have no place in their ephemeral society."

Guptev made an impatient gesture, fearing the beginning of one of Gorbachev's interminable speeches. What *could* the old bastard be getting at? "Mars is far enough, Comrade General Secretary, the asteroids you speak of are fine —but they are even further away. You must—"

Gorbachev smiled. *"Those* asteroids are not the only ones, my friend. Not so long ago, it was believed that the region close to Earth contained only a few, fairly large asteroids and those in orbits that made them quite inaccessible. We know now that this is not the case. As the search intensified, and devices with higher resolutions were used, the number of nearby asteroids has increased logarithmically. Since the Americans have started a computerized search, literally hundreds of these things, some no bigger than a Zil, have been discovered."

Akhmatov showed his teeth in a strange imitation of a smile. "Two thousand, eight hundred and sixty-nine at last count, Comrade Gorbachev."

Another smile, perhaps a bit thinner. "Thousands, then.

I will get to the point. Academician Derzhavin has presented a very interesting paper concerning one of these asteroids. It is called Sinuhe, after the ancient Egyptian writer. He has computed the round-trip for one of our Lunar Transfer Vehicles and his calculations show that it is quite an easy thing to accomplish. In fact, a mission leaving in May of next year would be well within rating limits for a manned rendezvous and return."

Many of these old men had, as old men will, come to the conclusion that nothing new was being proposed. So. A mission to a space Zil—so what else is new? They were surreptitiously poking their screens, accessing unrelated data when they thought he wasn't looking.

"Comrades, Academician Derzhavin has gone beyond merely computing the mathematics for a hypothetical space journey. He has shown indisputably that, by carrying a cargo of tactical nuclear weapons, the LTV can bring the asteroid back with it." He had said it casually, almost merrily. And the slower ones did not respond immediately. The Politburo took a full thirty seconds to react—and it reacted with ten versions of the same horrified/amazed look. Some of them, Blok especially, were staring at him so intently he wondered if they thought him mad. No one personally remembered what it had been like in Stalin's Politburo but they had read history. It was not a pleasant thought.

"No, comrades, I have not gone mad. And I *have* thought out the consequences, both internally and globally. Let me simply say that this mission elegantly accomplishes a number of entirely unrelated goals, all of them greatly to the advantage of the Soviet Union. I am going to turn the meeting over to Comrade Akhmatov, who can answer your questions better than I."

Guptev gave the middle-aged scientist a hard, probing stare. These fools will spend us to death, or worse. . . . "You are capable of judging this thing better than any of us, with your mastery of numbers and physics. Do you feel that it can be done?"

Akhmatov ran his fingers through his lank black hair and tried to get comfortable, squirming, imperceptibly, he hoped, against the creaking plastic of the chair. He ended up in an even more untenable position. He cleared his throat and tried another smile. "It is clear from

Derzhavin's calculations that such a mission is possible. The total strain on the craft would be slight."

Vladimir Semyonovich Ponomarev, head of Strategic Rocket Forces, held up a hand and pursed his thin lips. He was a burly man, by far the largest in the room, and had a full head of auburn hair despite his seventy years. "Yes, yes, Academician. The controversial part of this idea is the part about bringing the asteroid back. Is this then a possibility?"

Akhmatov, unable to control the cramping in his back, reclined uncontrollably, and the chair accommodated him, lowering his head half a foot below any of the others'. He knew of Ponomarev's reputation, and did not want to cross the man. "Over the past few years, Comrade Ponomarev, the technical designs of the Lev- and Lebed-class explosives have been quantified to a remarkable degree. There is no theoretical reason why a series of these weapons, placed strategically and ignited serially, could not modify the orbit of a small asteroid so as to bring it into orbit around the earth. However . . ."

Gorbachev was looking at him expectantly. "However what?"

"My original specialty is cosmic radiation, which is very much removed from this idea. However, in my position as head of the Vernadskii Institute, I have had many years in an administrative position, overseeing all types of astronomical and astrophysical projects. I feel that it is too soon to attempt a project this ambitious."

There was a moment of silence. Everyone seemed confused by this tack from someone who evidently had been produced to boost the project. Gorbachev was scribbling something with a stylus, which made a barely audible squeak.

Frowning ominously, Ponomarev said, "You admit that it is technically possible and presents no insurmountable obstacles. Why then are you opposed?"

Akhmatov cleared his throat again. Damn those fried *pirozhki*! he thought. "Firstly, it goes against the slow and steady course our space program has taken from the very beginning. The window for launching a craft to Sinuhe ends May twenty-second of next year. This seems to me too hasty. Secondly, the makeup of small asteroids such as Sinuhe is still too poorly known to make quantitative assessments of explosive propulsion. Very thorough gravimetric and compositional testing would have to take place before we would understand the nature of a body such as this. Thirdly, it might destabilize the relationship between the U.S. and the USSR. Asteroids such as Sinuhe could easily be turned into weapons of mass destruction."

Gorbachev smiled at him benignly. "It is for us to make international policy, not for scientists such as you."

Suddenly unnerved, Akhmatov looked from the head of the table back to Ponomarev. The man's bearlike eyes seemed to be glittering deep under the heavy brows. "That is true. I was invited here to speak my mind. I have done so."

The head of Strategic Rocket Forces suddenly seemed to relax. He leaned back and folded his hands on the table. "Hegel would be proud of you, Academician. I think you can go now." As the door closed behind him, Akhmatov thought that he heard eleven voices sounding at once.

After days of hard preparation, they were finally going on an EVA to erect a new radiotelescope for *Mechta*'s science module. Floating in the dimly lit science module airlock of *Mechta*, Volodya carefully inspected the monitor of the systems-check computer before him. The letters were bright blue against a black background, and they told a satisfactory tale. His suit was holding pressure perfectly in the airlock, which had been evacuated to the exterior environment. Two columns of data matched point for point, his suit's function and the parameters of nominal function. Joint integrity. Electronics. Life support. Temperature. Water circulation. Air/power time-on-line. Egress release lever secure and locked. He smiled wryly to himself. Be very embarrassing to accidentally exit the suit during an EVA. He reached out and punched a function key on the wall-mounted console. His column of data was replaced by information on Serebryakov's suit. Similarly nominal.

"Okay, Anton. Disconnect." He reached out and unplugged the unit's data cable from the connector on his chest. The cable automatically reeled into its holder in the airlock wall. After decades in space, the Soviets were finally learning to deal with "snakes." He looked down at the row of idiot lights below the faceplate of his helmet. All dark. No problems.

This is it then, he thought. Out we go. "Releasing science

module airlock exterior hatch." He opened the little plastic door beside the hatch, grasped the white lever between bulky thumb and forefinger, and pulled sharply down. The curved, two-meter-wide circular hatch popped out a few centimeters, pushed open by the slight pressurization of their suits' LSS outgassing. It was hinged at the bottom and now a crescent of darkness appeared around the upper rim.

Volodya looked up at the hard sliver of night and listened to the rasp of his breathing in the tiny closed space of his helmet, felt the slow thudding of his heart against his chest wall. What is this? My tenth EVA? Memories of time outside, floating above the world, were a montage in his head. Earth-orbit EVA had stunning beauty. Lunar orbit had a subtle grandeur. He pushed the thoughts away. There was business to attend to. "Are you ready, Anton?"

Serebryakov nodded in his helmet, then felt vertiginous silliness sweep through him briefly. "Uh. Ready." His voice was hoarse. He swallowed thickly and licked dry lips. "Let's go." He had been trained for lunar EVA, for a time of walking about in an airless, but still gravity-dominated desert. Of course he'd done this before, on a standard training EVA at *Mir,* then again only a few weeks ago at the space station to rehearse this task in the safer environment of heavily manned Earth-orbit. His heart was beginning to speed up and the sweat was gathering in his headband. I hate this, he thought.

Volodya turned to look at him. "Anton?"

"I'm all right. Let's get on with it."

Manarov stared at him for another long moment, inspecting his strained face through the clear visor, then turned to the hatch. Reaching out, he grasped the long hydraulic actuator lever beside the door and pulled. The hatch swung out and down, becoming an exterior platform. Brilliant light flooded in. Volodya reached up and lowered the gold sun visor over his face, then looked out.

The science module airlock faced forward from *Mechta,* so that the principal artifact he could see was *Molotochek.* Beyond the instrument-covered, green-sheathed command module, the long, cylindrical fuel tanks caught the sun in a bright, linear highlight. The vehicle, large as it was, did not dominate the view—that honor belonged to the intensely bright sun. Volodya took a deep breath to steady his nerves and pushed off, floating out through the doorway. He reached back to grasp his safety line, where it unreeled from its belt mechanism, and used friction between the nylon and his glove as a brake. He halted at the edge of the hatch/platform, and put down his right foot to anchor on a Velcro pad, teetering slowly. Far below, the bright, shadow-incised surface of Luna rolled by, huge, showing incredible detail. To his right the dim gray mare and bright highlands mottled the distant curved horizon. To his left lay the darkness of the lunar nightside. Volodya stared down from his perch at the white-gray world and felt a slight shortness of breath, not entirely induced by the lower air pressure of the spacesuit.

"I'm going up to the CMU bay, Anton. Come on out."

Staring out into endless night, Serebryakov cursed in the silence of his head. I've done this before, he thought, struggling with dismay. His mouth had gotten still drier, but. . . . He reached out and, grasping the edge of the hatchway, drew himself outside into the brilliant lunar light. The bobbing motion as he fought for a foothold made him feel slightly sick, despite the fact that he was going into his third week of microgravity, and he had to shut his eyes for a moment.

Even though so few people had died in outer space—less than a score in forty years—and only *one* man had ever been killed during an EVA, there was a compelling danger here. It was like going into combat. Anton opened his eyes and was alarmed to realize he was standing at a twenty-degree angle to the surface of the hatch. As he straightened up, he thought, I hate being in space.

Then why did you come? his inner voice asked back. Anton looked down at the surface of the Moon. It was hard to tell from this great distance, but they seemed to be flying southward across the western margin of Mare Crisium, looking toward Tranquillitatis and Fecunditatis to the south, Serenitatis far to the west. Floods of basalt had poured out of fractures in the lunar surface, and, near the terminator, it was plain to see the flow marks where later eruptions overlaid earlier ones, as well as rilles and ridges aplenty. He watched the broad scene for a minute, wishing for a good pair of binoculars. The Moon was a tough nut to crack, geologically speaking, and it had been very difficult to choose a landing site for this first, historic mission. The Apollo astronauts and *lunokhodi* had gone to relatively safe areas near the center of the Earth-facing hemisphere, but with *Mechta* in polar orbit, *Oryol* had no such limitations. After an enormous amount of bickering and argument, Vernadskii had chosen a large, double-ringed crater called Schrödinger, near the lunar South Pole. It was a fairly good location to look for the elusive lunar volatiles and contained an impressively dark haloed crater extremely suggestive of recent volcanic activity. Anton looked down again, this time without vertigo. The science calmed him, smoothing out his emotions and reminding him that he did in fact have a reason for being here. He looked up into the black sky, searching for Earth. It was there, blue and tiny, an unreal oasis in the night.

Manarov made his way up to the top of the science module, pulling himself along permanently-installed handrails. At the apex of the station, enclosed in a cage of narrow girders, were the storage racks for *Mechta*'s two Cosmonaut Maneuvering Units. The CMUs were docked in their storage racks, facing each other across the swiveling, pedestal-mounted monitoring station, actually an airtight terminal connected to the space station's main Dozhdevik computer system. He plugged the units into the terminal, signaled for general power-up, and turned to see Anton crawling over the edge of the science module into the bay. "Ready to saddle up?"

Gritting his teeth, Serebryakov said, "Right." They strapped themselves into the CMUs, fitting their backpacks into the hollow receptacle provided, plugging in the suit connectors and folding down the control-panel/armrests. When he was securely strapped in, Anton detached his safety-line reel, clipping it to a D-ring on the mounting rack.

Volodya inspected the computer display on the monitor before him carefully, then said, "Systems nominal. Disconnect." He pushed a key and the monitor connectors on the CMUs ejected the cable transmitting data to the on-board computer system. "All right. I'll undock first and go down to *Molotochek*. You can follow when I'm clear by twenty meters."

"Understood."

Volodya touched a control with his hand. The clamps that held the CMU in place released their grip, letting him float free, scant millimeters from the docking rack. Another touch and cold gas jetted from a nozzle, thrusting him gently upward. A third touch and he was halted, hovering five meters above the space station. He looked around. Green space station. Green spaceship. Wing after wing of black and gold solar panels. Black sky, white Moon. In the distance, a tiny blue and white Earth. There were, of course, no stars, what with all the glare.

He made an exasperated sound and turned to the task at hand. Too much of this woolgathering was dangerous. Especially if someone noticed.

Bronstein sat in front of *Mechta*'s computer console and waited. Finally TANK PURGE COMPLETED appeared at the prompt on the systems display. He typed in the next command on his list, checking the condition of the big storage batteries mounted in a ring around the proximal periphery of the station's engineering support module. There was a clank and he turned to see Zarkov clambering like a monkey along the "upper" wall.

The man righted himself and slipped a bare foot into a floor hold. "This makes eighteen straight hours of work for you, Slava. If you don't trust the automatic sequencer, at least let me take over. You don't want to be fatigued while we're down there. That's when the real mission begins."

Bronstein turned from the waist and met Zarkov's eyes. Was the man taunting him? Being the first Soviet to stand on the Moon might mean a lot to some, but it was, after all, merely filling thirty-year-old American footprints. "I am not so stupid as to distrust a computer, Yuri. The *Mir*-class systems designs are flawless. But if I am going to be at my post anyway, I may as well perform a function."

"They should be mating the lander with *Serpachek* even as we speak," said Zarkov. "And in four days they'll be here. Think of it, Miroslav Ilyich, two LTVs mated with *Mechta*. We'll be over two hundred and fifty meters long. A quarter of a kilometer." Zarkov withdrew his foot and began a lazy backward tumble, culminating with a steadying heel against the auxiliary solar array internal baseplate. He gave another push and caught at the rim of the docking module hatch mounted above the consoles like a blind window. "I have to get some stuff out of *Molotochek*. Anything you want?"

Miroslav started to reply, but was interrupted by the

faint ding of the encoded TTY console. He motioned to
Zarkov, who nodded and somersaulted onto the other
bench. He typed in his response code. On the screen of the
far-left monitor, lines of large amber caps began to scroll.

```
GLAVKOSMOS MISSION 01-M-14A
21 OCTOBER 2001 / 12:42:09 MST
CREW OF MOLOTOCHEK LTV / MECHTA LOL

RED BETA

ORYOL/SERPACHEK BOOST CANCELLED.
LUNAR LANDING CANCELLED.
MOLOTOCHEK RECALLED EFFECTIVE IMMEDIATE.
BRONSTEIN MANAROV CHISHAK LTV/LOL RECALLED.
ZARKOV ARTYUKHIN SEREBRYAKOV LLV(I) RECALLED.
LOL MODE SIX-YA POWERED STORAGE.
CODE BLUE OMEGA GAMMA.
NEXT MESSAGE 14:00:00 MST.
```

Zarkov gasped, "What the hell?"

Bronstein said nothing, but read the message one more
time. It was true. The fucking mission had been scrubbed.
And of course there was no explanation. He typed "Blue
Omega Gamma" into his computer and it translated as
"LTV communications encoded TTY only. Station communications on subject encoded TTY only. Maintain routine for station communications." Standard procedure for a
Bureaucratic-style cover-up. "Send a reply confirming re-
ceipt of TTY."

"Nothing else, Miroslav Ilyich? No questions?"

"They will tell us what we need to know."

As the message was being sent, Bronstein pulled himself
from the bench and floated free. He pushed along the axis
of his center of gravity and went to the window, catching
and steadying himself with its thick frame. The Moon
seemed small and far away after he had gotten used to
seeing it through video. He could see Manarov and Serebryakov, fully suited, wrestling with the cumbersome radiotelescope, trying to mount it in the secondary science
platform. He would wait until they finished before calling
them in.

His sinuses ached from the dryness of the air. Suddenly,
he realized he was on the verge of tears, but he successfully
fought them back. He took a deep breath. Somehow, he
had failed.

*    *    *

Chishak and Artyukhin had the seismic recorder partially disassembled and drifting above the utility table. As the man worked, Chishak found his attention wandering. In the glare of the work lamp he could see nothing out of the large porthole over the table. Presumably the tiny Earth lurked somewhere beyond its view. He couldn't explain how the remoteness of the beautiful blue and white planet affected his perception of himself and reality. Aside from the predictable motion sickness at first, there had been no adaptation problems.

"Could you hold it down?"

Yes, inattention caused mistakes. His hands tended to float up in front of his face if he didn't pay attention. "Sorry," he said. Much that they did was similar to factory work, though perhaps at a more leisurely pace. He was often relegated to acting as a kind of sentient clamp for one of the others, yet it was something he had desired.

It had occurred to him even as a child that man was destined to move beyond the petty confines of Earth; but he had been blinded by the need everywhere around him, and had used the fact of his "voluntary" entry into the armed services to study the myriad medical problems that plagued earthbound men. Ah, but he was so naive in those days! Thinking that the triumph of Marxism-Leninism was simply a matter of time, and that even Comrade Brezhnev's regressive posture was a holding pattern to let things settle out, to fine tune a society already the best in the world. It had taken the disaster at Chernobyl, when he was brought in to help treat the exiles from Pripat, to show him the error of his ways. The Revolution was not over—only through continued struggle would the USSR become what it claimed it already was.

The seed of doubt sowed in his breast by the nuclear meltdown was not so easily eradicated. Marxism came to seem a parody of itself, a laughable invention made simply to justify the cravings of a few men. His new wife had been very patient with him, sacrificing her needs to allow him to find his own course. He went back to school to study surgery, and his obsession brought him through the courses with flying colors. As the Soviet Union was torn by change during the late eighties and throughout the nineties, he noted everything with interest, but felt his mission far above the petty fray. It had not been difficult to transfer to the small hospital at Kapustin Yar Cosmodrome and, from there, the steps to becoming a cosmonaut himself had been small, easily taken ones.

Artyukhin looked up with satisfaction. "Perfect responses. Let's close it up and pack it."

He was almost through when Zarkov appeared in the airlock. He looked upset. "We'll all be joining you as soon as we get Volodya and Tonya in. Something big has happened. The lunar landing has been cancelled. Lyova, we've all been recalled to Earth."

Chishak's stomach muscles tightened. Was this their Chernobyl?

Grasping the CMU controls firmly, Volodya slowly slid along a diagonal geodesic toward the truss structure between *Molotochek*'s command module and flare shelter. Because the shelter was several meters wider than the habitat, it made a broad shelf to which a variety of storage bins had been affixed. He eased up to the cargo hold in question and stopped, waiting for Serebryakov to join him.

When they were in position, he reached out and turned the latch. The doors were spring-mounted and swung open silently, revealing the radiotelescope module they'd brought with them. Right now it was folded into a compact but massive cylinder, held shut by bands of strapping metal. When those were sliced by shears from the CMU's tool kit, the thing would open automatically, assuming its functional shape. Volodya looked at Anton. "You run the manipulator arm. I'll do the manual labor."

"Okay." As he slid back along the length of *Molotochek*'s command module, heading toward one side of the space station's five-ported docking module, Serebryakov wondered if the man knew the extent of his fear. *I wish I knew him better. We've been training together for a year, yet he seems—cold. It was an odd kind of coldness, too. Not like Bronstein's rigid self-control, just *remoteness*. You sometimes got the feeling that Manarov just didn't care much about people. Is he sending me off to the relative safety of a control panel because he knows I'm afraid or because he's selfish and simply wants to play with the machines himself?*

He parked himself before the manipulator-arm control

panel, then folded out two hard-attachment arms and clamped himself into place. The manipulator module, one of two, was docked to the starboard axial docking ring, halfway between the science and engineering modules. It was basically a thick canister of hydraulic machinery with an exterior control panel. A second set of controls protruded through the docking port, so the thing could be operated from inside the station. The manipulator itself was a long, segmented arm with a TV camera and grasping mechanism at its distal end. Not too different from the Canadian arm of the American space shuttles, it was essentially a space-going crane. Anton powered up the module and watched as a systems check scrolled across the monitor screen. When finished, it displayed the view from the arm's color camera. "All systems nominal. Are we ready to go?"

"Ready."

He extended the arm slowly, being careful to unfold it away from the space station structure. Even though there was little danger of puncturing anything with this weak mechanism, he might still damage a fragile solar panel or, worse still, ruin the arm itself. Even the smallest article became infinitely valuable when it had to be shipped all the way from the Earth to the Moon. A hundred-million-dollar blunder would get him cashiered. And I *want* to be here, he reminded himself, but shivered nonetheless. Finally, he swung the arm in until it was poised above the cargo hold.

Volodya held his hand out in front of the camera lens and said, "Ease it in until the camera touches my hand." Anton did so. "Okay, hold it." He folded the telescope's attach point out until it lay opposite the arm grasping mechanism. "Forward ten centimeters, then latch."

Squinting at the dim TV screen, Anton slid the arm gently forward until it was in position, then put his hand in the crane's controller and slowly closed the "fingers." The pressure sensor lights came on and a group of figures appeared in one corner of the monitor. Satisfied, he punched the lock button, securing the manipulator in place. "Done. You can release it now."

Volodya leaned into the storage bin and uncoupled the four clamps that held the radiotelescope in place. "Ready." Anton slowly pulled the thing out of its bay and began lifting it toward the far end of the science module, about as far as the manipulator arm could reach. If *Mechta* got any bigger, they'd have to add more manipulators. Volodya followed it up in his CMU and carefully guided him to the correct position. "Okay. Lock the arm in place and come on up." Anton sent the command that froze the hydraulic "muscles," detached himself from the control panel and backed his CMU away, heading upward. As he watched the surface of the science module slide by a few meters away, he marveled at how quickly he was getting used to being out here. During the period that he'd been concentrating on the task, his heart rate had gone down to near normal and the sweat on his face had begun to dry.

Using tools from their CMU kits, mostly torqueless socket wrenches, the two men quickly secured the radiotelescope by its clamps to the top of the CMU-bay girder cage, then detached the manipulator arm by pressing its quick-release latch. It let go of the telescope but otherwise remained in position.

"Good enough. Get out of the way, now." Anton backed off, retreating into the relative safety of the cage. Volodya pulled the cutting tool from his kit, opening and closing the blades experimentally. He carefully extended it upward at arm's length and slid it under the retaining band.

The metal parted suddenly, the band snapping open with a violence so sudden that Anton imagined he could hear a loud crack. It flew away into space, disappearing instantly, and the radiotelescope opened like a silver flower.

"What a sight!" Volodya shouted. "I thought it was going to hit me!"

Anton marveled. Cold? Maybe so, but not about everything.

Bronstein's voice suddenly crackled in their earphones, sounding odd, rather strained. "Good work. You'd better come inside, now. Something has come up."

Volodya looked about. "Something has come up? What are you talking about?"

"Come inside right away."

Volodya said, "We'd better fold up the arm first, though." He looked up regretfully at the radiotelescope, running the scene of its opening through his head once again, savoring the magic of it. Shit, he thought, I really *like* it out here!

And Anton, spooked by the odd quality of Bronstein's voice, felt ice in his chest, a different quality of fear. He looked down past the manipulator arm to where a jumble of shadow-limned craters glided effortlessly by, and began to remember.

Tonya looked out of the train window but could only see reflections of the other passengers lit by the feeble coach-lights. He settled back onto his mother's lap and felt a moment of reassurance, which was shattered by the car's passage over a particularly bad stretch of track. He tried to sit up straight the way she had told him to, and succeeded in quelling his fear of all this.

The car was a world of its own, self-contained, and he could forget that they were moving headlong through the Russian predawn. A hot breeze smelling of kerosene and onions passed across his face and then, mysteriously, was gone. He caught a whiff of the sour smell that seemed to bond him to his mother. The other passengers were a blur of baldness and dark clothing and rustling newspapers. As far as he could tell he was the only child aboard.

At five, a person feels very old. Babushka and he were old friends, and he had not had a reason to suspect that their close relationship was nearing its end. But he was ready for this new venture, mostly. School was what children his age did.

It was light enough outside so that the stately motion of the apartment buildings could be seen through the dark reflection of his fur cap. He had never been outside this early before, and he suspected that it would be quite beautiful.

"Mama, where are we now?" he asked.

"We're almost there, Tonyushka. This is Moskva."

The train did seem to be slowing down, and the people were folding their papers up and putting them away. They passed bright lights that made a little bit of the world garishly visible, concrete and patches of snow broken by brown grass.

Suddenly they were up, and there was a noise like a penny whistle as he was pushed forward into the rough weave of someone's overcoat. He got hold of his mother's hand and was reassured by the tightness of her grip. The crowd was moving slowly down the aisle, and he was in almost total darkness surrounded by the behemoth legs and buttocks.

After a quick passage across a frigid space, they came into a huge room, yellow and brightly lit from enormous, crystalline chandeliers. What a room! The floor was made of some marvelous translucent stuff with ripples like when you put cocoa into milk. There were great pillars that were big enough to easily hide behind. The icons of Lenin and Marx were also enormous and seemed to be made of tiny bits of glass. They came to a waterfall of steps and suddenly were riding down between two ramps taller than he was. This was an escalator! What a wonderful thing!

Tonya almost fell headlong as they were catapulted from the bottom step. "Be careful, my darling!" said his mother. Then they climbed into another train, smaller than the first and better lit. An old man with a funny gray mustache got out of his seat and gestured for them to sit. They sat and the train jostled to a start.

"Tonya, we're almost to the school. You have been a very good boy so far, but you know I have to go to work."

Tonya heard something in his mother's voice that he couldn't identify, and it made him afraid again. "Why can't I go with you?"

"You just can't. There is a nice woman at the school named Braun who will watch after you. You know your father and I want only the best for you. You know all the birds and they will be very impressed with how smart you are. But you have a whole lot more to learn. There will be a lot of nice little boys and girls just like you to play with."

He had heard all this before. But why was his mother so tense if it would be as nice as she said?

"Baba has told you all about Mr. Lenin, and what a wonderful person he was, Tonya."

"Yes. How we wouldn't have enough to eat or a good place to live if it hadn't been for him." He had a picture in his mind of a dark, thin Father Frost with a big bag of stuff, constantly handing it out to people in a long, long line. He was somehow mixed up with God and Jesus and Mary and all that. Babushka hadn't been very clear about where these people were and why he had never seen them.

"You will learn a lot about him at school, Tonya, and I want you to remember what they tell you about him."

Why wouldn't he? "Sure," he said. "I remember what everybody tells me."

"You're a good boy, Tonyushka."

The school wasn't far from the Metro station. It was dawn and there was a pretty, greenish sky. He saw a trolley. His hat kept sliding down and tickling his neck. The whole block smelled like chicken soup. "We're here," said his mother.

Immediately, he was crying. He looked up at the series of big stone steps leading to the door and let go, caterwauling with all his might. His mother grabbed him by the hand and started to drag him up the steps, one at a time. "It's no use crying," she said. "You're going to school whether you like it or not."

It was kind of funny but sometimes, when he was crying, he felt really good. Now fear and sleepiness and happiness fought in his mind like little snakes. Abruptly, he was ready to see what the school would be like.

Inside, it smelled like the museum, and they went down a long hallway. He always liked the way his mother's shoes made a loud, echoing click-click-click in places like this.

Mrs. Braun was shorter than his mother, rounded like Babushka, and had striking red hair. She looked down at him with a nice smile. "Have you been crying, Anton?" she asked.

"No."

She smiled at his mother. "I think you have made the right decision. Although this school is not directly state-sanctioned, we have fine teachers dedicated to helping the precocious child develop fully. Besides our exemplary introduction to the concepts of Soviet life, we offer accelerated courses in mathematics based on the concepts of Lazarov and Kopeiskii. But you know all this or you wouldn't be here."

"We'd like Anton to have a head start. He's a very smart boy and should get special treatment."

Tonya had found a glass paperweight on a table and was hefting it, hardly listening to the adult conversation.

"As a matter of fact, I will be his teacher. If you would like to tour a classroom with me . . ."

His mother glanced at her watch. "No, I have to get going. I'm late already." She came over to Tonya and lifted him up, planting a long kiss on his cheek. "I have to go now, Tonyushka. Be a good boy and do what Mrs. Braun says."

"Yes, Mama." When his mother had gone, the clicking

of her steps silenced, Mrs. Braun took him by the hand and said, "Let's go meet your new friends."

The other children, five of them, couldn't easily be distinguished from one another. One was a girl, but they were all pale, blond, and dressed in the same sort of wool clothing. "This is Sofya, Grishka, Seryozha, Pasha, and Valya. Students, this is our new boy, Tonya Serebryakov. His mother says that he knows the names of all of our common birds. We will put him to the test when we go on our next trip to the park."

There was more, but Tonya was already bored. He was offended by the fact that he already knew a Grishka in the apartment and he didn't want to know another. He supposed he would try to learn as he had promised, but he would do it grudgingly. Babushka was a better teacher than this woman, and he could learn more without having to wait for the others. At least he would enjoy the train ride every day. And he could play with his old friends on the weekends. He supposed that this was what was expected of him as a big boy, and would go along with it, at least for the time being.

Hermann Oberg, director of the European Space Agency, was a tall, heavily built man grown paunchy in late middle age. At fifty-five, his dark brown hair was graying at the temples and a substantial stomach bowed open the spaces between his vest buttons. He didn't think 110 kilograms was too much for a man 190 centimeters tall but, in truth, he was getting old and fat. His moon face had a cleft chin and he wore big, square, black-framed bifocals that gave him a somewhat comical air, but he could speak six languages well and knew more about more than almost anyone else in the world.

Just now he was slumped down in a big leather chair, double chin covering the knot of his loosened tie, big, pudgy hands clasped over his abdomen. He was staring at the glossy brochures spread out on his polished teak desk, deep in murky thought. Like any man given to talking to himself, he started in without preamble. "This damned conference! Why the hell are we holding it aboard *Freedom*?" And at considerable expense, too!

The idea of holding a conference on space industrialization *in* space had been poorly received in some quarters.

No. *Many* quarters. There were a number of rather pissed-off scientists out there now, grumbling about the experimenters and experiments bumped from scheduled flights. "Of course, we can't add additional flights. That'd make the conference cost a billion marks!"

What the hell. I *never* thought I'd get a second chance to go up. "One damned trip in a *Hermes* when I was named director; just a hop up in the jumpseat to service our polar platform. Shit." He remembered how the Earth had looked to him from five hundred kilometers up, just as they made rendezvous over the Antarctic. The glare of the ice, fully lit up by southern summer, had been astonishing. And the color of the Indian Ocean! What was it Hitler had said? Yes, on the occasion of the first V-2 launch, he said, *"Es war doch gewaltig!"* Too true.

"Bastard had the soul of a poet." A German soul, though, creak-creak-creak, like a robot butterfly. "After all, anyone who loved dogs and blondes couldn't have been all bad." Better watch that sort of talk. Even after fifty-six years . . . The intercom chirred and he absentmindedly popped the talk bar with one hand. *"Ja?"* The thing jabbered at him incomprehensibly. *"Verdamm . . ."* His German soul clanked back into the shadows and a feathery Frenchman took its place. "Yes, what is it?"

"Director, this is Jules Marchand." He was the ESA publicity coordinator. "Sorry to disturb you, but we've just gotten some information I thought you'd want to know about."

"So?"

"TASS reports the Soviets have just scrubbed their first lunar landing, scheduled for later this week. The wire service says the transport *Molotochek* will be undocking from space station *Mechta* and heading for Earth-orbit in a matter of hours."

Interesting. "Did the report say what had gone wrong?"

"No. Speculation here is the LLV(I)-style lander, which was due to depart for the Moon tomorrow morning, has developed some major problem and will have to be brought back down."

"Mmh. Too bad. Well, keep me posted." The intercom clicked off. Oberg leaned forward in his chair until his elbows rested on the desk and stared into the bright space scenes on the brochures. Really, too bad. He'd been looking forward to a new lunar landing for many months, ever since the Russians put a manned station in lunar polar orbit. How long has it been? "Christ! Twenty-nine years!" How old was I then? The imagery came, unbidden. He'd been standing on the grass at the press site beside Mosquito Inlet on a deceptively comfortable December night, waiting, binoculars in hand. It was dark out, but clear, and he'd been a twenty-five-year-old reporter, working for *Die Zeit,* covering mankind's *last* trip to the Moon.

It came. First, the light. There had been floodlights pointing at the Saturn V stack, a German-designed American rocket tall as a thirty-six-story building. There was a billow of red, turning yellow as the flames steadied, rushing out the blast deflector troughs, building into huge pools of smoke, all brilliantly flickering as the fire turned white. Seven seconds. Suddenly the hold-down arms let go and the great thing staggered off the ground and into the night sky. The moment it came off the pad, the surface of the inland waterway lit up as well, bright white, a mirror into hell. Or heaven.

Then there was the sound, long delayed by its three-mile traverse. It was too *large* to be a roar. It crackled like a burning bush, but the individual pops were too far apart. Much too far. And too hard. Three decades later the memory brought tears to his eyes. *Apollo 17* climbed slowly into the night sky, tipping over toward the east, groaning away toward orbit, three Americans going to the Moon for the last time. . . .

God damn them. They beat us in war and took away our engineers as booty. Dawdled around for fifteen years, then used that talent when the Russians scared them . . . for a one-shot publicity stunt. So. A half-century of space exploration thrown away because some madmen destroyed Germany and then some cowboys held a rodeo with what was left. I could be sitting on Mars now instead of in Brussels.

Ah. The hell with it. Maybe in ten years I'll have my own deep space program to manage. And the Russians will probably make that landing in six months, whenever they fix whatever problem they're having. In the meantime, I get a free trip to space. His eyes gleamed at the thought.

Volodya sat quietly in the right-hand seat of *Molotochek* before the flight engineer's control panel, watching events transpire on the two monitors stacked before him. In the upper monitor, he could see the Moon turning below. They were cruising over farside now, heading northward toward the counterterrestrial point and trans-Earth injection. It was, however, night, and he couldn't see the features he knew were below. In any case, the rugged backside of the Moon was rather nondescript.

On the lower monitor, systems information from the various parts of *Molotochek* kept scrolling slowly by. Fuel cell temperature and pressure. Engine compartment environmental data. Status of the cryogenic propellants in the main tanks. Ullage requirements. Solar flare water tank. . . . He noted that the temperature in the fluid was up a little bit and increased the speed on the little pump that kept the water circulating through a radiator vane. Electronics. Hydraulics. Life support . . . The damned thing was working just fine.

"TEI burn minus eight minutes," said Bronstein.

"Understood." The ship was intended to be flown by two men, equal partners in executing the complex sequence of tasks necessary. For all practical purposes, the others were just passengers. Behind them, in the second row of seats, were Zarkov and Artyukhin, somber and quiet, keenly feeling the disappointment of those who have lost their place in the history books forever. Further back, up against the propulsion control room rear bulkhead, sat Chishak, essentially unchanged by the news, and Serebryakov, waiting, holding off his discomfort, knowing that his chance would come again, unless things had really screwed up.

The Dozhdevik console to Manarov's right beeped, calling his attention to revised astrogational data. He inspected it, then reached out and pressed the enter key, acknowledging its acceptability. The Dozhdevik fed the data to the semi-independent control panel CPU, which initiated an automatic countdown.

"TEI minus five minutes."

"Understood."

While preparing for the burn, during the hours since they'd undocked from *Mechta,* Volodya had listened half-heartedly to the bickering and bitter speculation among the other four, who didn't have much to do now. Idiots. Why bother with all this upsetting nonsense, when they'd be home in three days and know the truth with considerable precision?

"TEI minus three minutes."

"Understood."

He turned to his right and began tapping rapidly on the Dozhdevik console, spinning the trackball as he accessed various pop-up menus. Soon all the different launch and control systems were on their own and the screen had divided into a grid of little blocks, each displaying sequential data out of a vertical stack. On the main monitors, the upper half still showed them the Moon, while the lower half, having abandoned its role as a computer monitor, now showed a view from the main engine compartment. They would record the burn for posterity. Just in case.

"TEI minus two minutes."

"Understood."

It was a bit of a mystery, though. There was no telling why Glavkosmos hadn't been willing to tell them what was wrong, even over the secure TTY channel. No matter what . . . the Americans had been here thirty years ago. No one was going to upbraid them if this landing were delayed another six months, even a year! Chishak had come up with the amazing speculation that the landing might have been called off for political reasons, that the manned lunar program was being canceled at its eleventh hour!

"TEI minus sixty seconds."

"Understood."

Volodya reached out and put his hand on the number-two backup ignition switch, noting that Bronstein did the same on his side of the console. If the computer failed to start TEI, the commander would initiate the burn. If he failed, or his button didn't work, the flight engineer would initiate the burn. If he failed, or his button didn't work . . . They stayed here.

"TEI minus thirty."

"Understood."

The Soviets were lucky. Between *Molotochek* and *Mechta,* they could survive in lunar orbit for more than a year. *Serpachek* could be up to get them in only a few weeks, days if it were fueled. It was hard to think of what it might have been like for those Americans. The failure of one nonredundent engine meant certain death. . . .

"Minus ten."

"All systems nominal."

"Five . . . four . . . three . . . two . . . one . . ."

"Commence ignition sequence."

At the aft end of the ship, small pressure-fed rockets lit up in their sockets, creating an inertial analog of gravity, pushing liquid hydrogen and oxygen down the drain. Fuel lines filled. Hydrogen peroxide boiled merrily, steam pushing the vanes of powerful turbines. The pumps sucked at the fuel, hypergolic igniters squirted their mix into the combustion chambers of the two main engines. "Main engine start, plus two nominal."

The lower monitor screen washed out in a blaze of light. On the surface of the moon below a faint glow could be seen, wan and white. A gentle acceleration appeared at their backs and slowly began to build. "Chamber pressure stabilized." If it blew up now, no one would ever know what happened. They were alone, on the far side of the Moon.

Watching the monitors over his shoulder, Anton Serebryakov thought, Going *home*! With nothing to show for it. What a fucking tragedy!

# CHAPTER 2
# November 3, 2001

Sara-Lena Skryabina, called Iskra by her friends because of her last name, regarded herself as someone above the fray of politics. She was primarily a receptionist and data-entry clerk at the Vernadskii Institute's Laboratory of Planetary Exploration. Since many of these scientists came from IKI, she had become a low-level liaison between the two groups. Active in Komsomol since her college days, she thought of it as a social organization—a way to keep tabs on what was going down. Since she earned a little extra by passing information on to the CIA, she needed to be well informed.

Iskra was small-boned and delicate, her face a perfect oval framed by dark parentheses of lissome hair. She had had to develop the strange technique of shifting her right hand back and forth to compensate for the fact that her hands were not big enough to accommodate the bulky new computer keyboards.

Her eyes opened wider whenever anything entered the lab with the round, red INTERNAL USE ONLY seal. Security was ridiculously lax. She could always get a peek long enough to earn a few precious dollars. Now, with the lab operating at a fever pitch on the Sinuhe thing, she was accumulating secrets so fast she could barely remember them all. She typed madly, using the word processor's macro function to tie into her coded phrases. Although the machine was archaic by Western standards, using a chip more than twenty years obsolete, it performed quite adequately for her purposes, either as a secretary or a spy. The woman hit the combination of keys to save the document, to all appearances a report by Pantaleeva at IKI on the results of her experiment aboard the Venara-based *Merkurii 1,* and the external three-and-a-half-inch drive's light came on. It whirred for a moment and then stopped, and she ejected the disk. She slid it into her shirt pocket and pushed back from the desk. Pintsuk and Akhmatov were having a friendly discussion by the watercooler. She made herself go over and talk to them before making her getaway.

"Good afternoon, Sara-Lena Alekseevna," said Pintsuk affably. He seemed to be straining to locate her, but, after all, he was nearsighted and she was only four feet eleven.

Akhmatov, with whom she had talked only a few times, also was able to find something to smile about, although she'd heard him ranting and raving like a madman only a few days before. "Would you like some water, Comrade Skryabina?"

"No thank you, Fyodor Karlovich. I'm just on my way to lunch. Would either of you gentlemen care to join me?"

They shook their heads in unison. "Oh, by the way, Sara-Lena, Anton will be back working with us during the next few months. Since Glavkosmos has no intention of sending anyone over here, I'd appreciate it if you would act as his secretary while he's here."

What could she say? "Of course." She was edging toward the cloakroom. "I'll prepare a little 'welcome home' celebration if you'd like."

Akhmatov pursed his poochy lips. "Good idea, comrade. He's still debriefing at the cosmodrome, of course. I'll let you know when he'll be in."

It was brisk but sunny as Sara-Lena made her way through the wooded cemetery of Donskoi Monastery, and fall had made an orange, yellow, and green melange of the world. She went straight to the massive brick Novii Cathedral, which now housed a museum of architecture. Sunlight glinted gold from the small windows of the forward onion-minaret, and hundreds of new-fallen leaves covered the stairway. Inside, in the main hall, there was a newly installed coin-operated phone. She dropped the two-kopeck piece into the round slot and dialed the Metro's lost property office. After two rings, a woman answered. "Lost and found."

Iskra spoke into the receiver. "I lost a brooch today on the Circle line, I think. It was shaped like a dolphin."

There was a long pause, long enough to speed up her heart. "I see," said the woman, and then there was another long pause. The phone clicked on the desk as she put it down, and again as she picked it up. "Yes. Your brooch was found and turned in at Kurskaya Station."

"Thank you, I will come right in and pick it up." She hung the phone up. Whenever Sara-Lena needed to talk to Harris, she would make a call like this. Like the American pranksters of the sixties, the CIA had totally infiltrated the Moskva telephone network. Although the full workings of the system were unknown to her, she had been told that, from a building not far from the American Embassy, any call, local or long distance, could be intercepted and re-routed through any other phone. It was all done by a computer the size of a television set, automatically. Calls from this pay phone were routinely monitored for just this sort of call. The "lost" item revealed her identity and the urgent nature of the information, and the station it was turned in told her where the meeting would take place. If she had wanted to meet Harris tomorrow she would have said she lost the brooch yesterday, and so on. Since she was a "lunchtime" operative, the meeting would be scheduled for twelve-thirty. Previous meetings had taken place at "Elektrozavodskaya," an island in one of Gorkii Park's small lakes. "Kurskaya" was 23 Gertsena Street, a location unknown to her.

It turned out to be a small cafe named Ogareva not far from the Kremlin. Sara-Lena was seated at a table near the window, where she ordered tea and looked at the menu. Expensive! Well, she thought, he'll pick up the tab. She ordered the mixed grill platter. She watched the crowds intermingling on the broad sidewalks. Jonathan Harris came out of nowhere, crossed the street, and came inside. Looking like a harried Muscovite in search of a lunch, he hailed the waiter and ordered a glass of beer and *katlety popazharski,* the specialty of the house. He looked at Sara-Lena and smiled. "Sorry I'm late. Pressing matters at the embassy. How have you been?"

Iskra, as always, was swept away by the handsome spy— she lost her breath and had trouble speaking. "F—Fine. I've got something for you."

Harris smiled. "That's what I heard. Important stuff?"

"I don't know. Could be. You know they canceled the Moon mission?"

"Sure. You're giving a lot of coverage on the television. Seemed like the first fifteen minutes on *Vremya* last night was speculation about it. You know something about it?"

The waiter approached with her dish of organs, and put it on the table. They watched silently as he stalked off. "I do. The details are on the diskette I'm handing you under the table." Pause. "They're going to be sent to an asteroid instead. More than that. They're going to use nuclear weapons to send it into Earth-orbit."

Harris whistled softly. "That's important all right. Are you sure that's the whole truth? Could they be planning something military?"

Iskra shrugged, a motion barely visible under her shawl of hair. "We've been assigned to develop the scientific packages for the mission, that's all."

Harris, having taken the disk, looked around. "Gotta go. You'll find a thousand dollars in your locker tomorrow. Don't spend it all in one place." He stood and started to leave, then turned back. "If the *katlety* ever comes, tell the waiter I had to get back to my office. *Adios, muchacha.*"

She cut slowly at a kidney and thought, a thousand dollars! That's at least fifty pairs of jeans!

Volodya Manarov awoke into the dim morning light. For a long time he stared in puzzlement at the dirty white ceiling above him, letting his eyes wander along the crack that traversed the room, dividing the plaster into two unequal segments. A hell of a thing, letting cosmonauts live like this. The problem was, these buildings had been here, outside Moscow, for forty years. They were getting old. By Russian standards they were, indeed, ancient.

Retreating a little farther under the down comforter, he snuggled closer to Shutka's side, savoring her warmth and the slow motion of her regular breathing. Not a nightmare after all. Just back in my bed, with my plump and toasty wife, here in gay little Starry Town, with all the other heroes.

The trip back had been as unpleasant an experience as he could remember ever having. Trapped in the close confines of a travel-trailer-sized spaceship for three days with five very unhappy men, he'd tried to tune them out with little success. Bronstein was silent, manning his console, watching the monitor, rebuffing most attempts at conversation. Zarkov and Artyukhin were positively morose, deprived almost certainly of their only opportunity to make the first Soviet landing on the Moon. When a second attempt was made, there would be other hands guiding *Oryol*. And Chishak seemed to be an unending babble of angry, futile speculation. Occasionally he thought about throttling the bastard.

Serebryakov. Volodya was beginning to worry about him. It was obvious that he was a little frightened by the experience of being in space, but he controlled it well. Look at the way he'd performed, setting up the radiotelescope. You had to have certain resources to conquer a fear that made you sweat. All the way back, he'd stared out the little galley window, watching the Moon recede. It was understandable, but of all of them, Anton stood the best chance of being reassigned to the next mission. He was one of three flight-qualified planetary scientists in the entire Soviet Union. And the other two were relative newcomers to the program.

He rolled to one side and curled about his wife, feeling the change in body presence that signaled her awakening. He nuzzled against the side of her face, feeling the softness of her feathery hair. She turned toward him, blue eyes under dark brows, still hazy with sleep. "So."

He grinned down at the rounded contours of her soft face. "Glad to have me back?"

She pushed closer, putting her arms around his chest and squeezing, rubbing her face against the side of his neck. She ran a hand down the length of his spine and trailed off across one buttock, stopping there, holding on. "Glad to be back?"

He nodded.

She pulled back, looking seriously into his face. "Are you? This must be a hard thing for you to take."

He shook his head. "Not for me, Shutka." He laughed, a single, quick snort of mirth. "I wasn't going to the Moon this year anyway. The others . . ."

"How is Anton?"

Volodya shrugged. "I can't tell. He doesn't really talk to me."

"Strange . . ." She looked away, into herself for a moment. "That's not how I imagine it should be on these long space voyages. This . . . closing out . . . almost seems un-Russian. You should be talking, like friends around a warm samovar."

"Well . . . we're not proletariat, or intellectuals, for that matter."

"I thought technicians were always intellectuals."

"So did I, 'til I met a few. We're a strange breed, Shutka. In between, almost classless."

She snuggled against him again, pressing the front of her body flat against his, pulling him closer with her hands behind his hips. "Well. I'm glad to have you back, anyway, even if you're not an intellectual."

He pushed her a little bit away and ran his hand down the front of her body, between her breasts and across the doughy flesh of her abdomen. She'd been thin and firm fifteen years and more ago, during their long courtship, but babies and a Russian diet were taking their toll. Still . . . He supposed he didn't mind. A middle-aged man's wife wasn't expected to look like a porno star and, regardless, it wasn't what was important about the two of them. The softness was easy to lie upon. . . .

As Hermann Oberg was being helped into his ejection seat aboard the *Hermes* vehicle, the pilot turned and looked over his shoulder, glowering down at the passenger. "Welcome aboard, Director." Bruno Monsaingeon was dark-haired and swarthy, with a permanent beard shadow. He was muscular and young, one of Europe's most experienced spacionauts. He had been the first test pilot to fly *Hermes* and to this day commanded four of ESA's twelve annual manned flights. In five years, he'd piled up an impressive twenty-four hundred hours in space. It didn't compare with some of the senior Russians, who often exceeded fifteen thousand hours before leaving flight status for administrative posts, but it was a pretty good record. The pilot, of course, was aware of the passenger on his manifest, but the two had known each other for some time. He gestured to the small man in the copilot's chair. "Giovanni Mancini."

Oberg nodded to the man. "Good morning, Dr. Mancini."

"*Buon giorno.*" The man was typical of ESA "second-seaters." He was a first-rate engineer who had come to the spacionaut corps already equipped with a jet pilot's rating from the Italian air force. He could have made several multiples of his annual ESA salary in private industry, but wanted to fly in space. . . . And he had to be able to fly the ship in the event something happened to Monsaingeon. *Hermes* had been crippled by ESA's post-*Challenger* panic. The six-man orbiter had been converted to a three-man transport with very limited cargo capacity. But it was *safe;* as safe as a spaceship could be. If the Ariane 5 booster exploded on or near the pad, three ejection seats would blast the crew free. If it failed at altitude, an extractor rocket would pull the orbiter free for a controlled reentry and landing. A pity it made the ship useless. It was almost, but not quite, as bad as the Japanese HOPE spaceplane, which was, incredibly, unmanned.

As the technicians sealed the hatch, shutting out a last sultry breath of tropical air, and the gantry rolled back, Oberg looked between the shoulders of the crewmen and up into a clear, brilliant equatorial sky. It was a pain, traveling to South America for a flight, and he sometimes wished they could launch from France or Spain, but that was out of the question, unless you wanted to emulate the Israelis and head westward, into an energy-expensive retrograde orbit. It would become even stranger next year, when the second Ariane 5 launchpad at Cape York became operational. Even aboard an SST, Australia was a long trip from Europe. It was sort of like traveling between major cities. You made a long, tedious drive to the airport, hopped quickly across the continent, then made another long, tedious drive to your destination.

Monsaingeon looked back at him again. "All set for your second jump up?"

"I can't tell you how much I've been looking forward to this, Bruno. I envy you."

The pilot nodded. "I've been through this twenty times and the excitement never fades. I wish I could go farther, though. Maybe you can get me on a flight to the Moon?"

"I wish I could go myself. I'll see what I can do for you. If I don't piss off too many politicians, I'll head ESA for another ten years. Don't hold your breath, though. Budgets are tight, as usual."

"As usual." Monsaingeon stared out into the cloudless sky, occasionally looking downward toward the horizon.

From his forward seat he could see the ocean. "Tell me, Director. When you were a boy, did you ever think you'd get into space? This must be like a dream to you."

Oberg laughed sharply. "Like a dream? You don't know." He shook his head slowly. "Bruno, during my first two years at university, the Americans made ten *Gemini* flights. Leonov made the world's first EVA, Komarov died, and the crew of *Apollo 1* burned up. By the time I was twenty-two years old, men were walking on the Moon."

"So? This is ancient history."

"That's my point. Bruno, the movie *2001* came out when I was nineteen. I *believed* in what it had to say. When I was young I assumed I'd *retire* on the Moon. I hoped to see Mars before I died. Look how it's all turned out. A colossal waste!"

The pilot grunted, then his attention shifted away as he listened to his headset. "Time to go." He settled back in his couch and looked at the control panel briefly, then reached out and grasped the joystick. "Put your hands in your lap, Director, not on the armrests."

Oberg assumed the required position and listened as machinery came to life. Far away, he thought he could hear the whining of fuel pumps as first-stage fuel and oxidizers flowed through the plumbing toward the combustion chambers. Maybe it was just a hint of vibration in his chair. Maybe imagination.

There was a dull thump as the sustainer-core engines came on, followed by a soft waterfall sound, slowly growing into a muted roar. The rocket, firmly clamped to the pad, began to sway slowly as the thrust of the engines built up and evened out. There came a series of almost inaudible thumps as various power and telemetry plugs jumped from their sockets. The sway damped down and . . .

There was a tremendous, pulsing bang as the four solid-fuel strap-on boosters lit off in near simultaneity. The hold-down clamps let go as a unit and Oberg, grinning suddenly, compressed into his seat as the vehicle jumped into the sky, already under fairly high acceleration. Clouds rose outside, visible through the windows, fire and shadow playing in the folds of smoke, and he remembered, once again, something he'd been told by a retired American shuttle astronaut: "When those solids light, you know you're going someplace."

His inner ears spun as the stack went through its roll program and tipped away to the east. The horizon appeared in the overhead docking windows and the Earth was already far away. They passed over the ships of the offshore recovery team and headed out to sea. Going someplace . . .

"Ninety seconds," said the pilot. He reached out and put his hand on the manual staging switch, keeping an eye meanwhile on the mission clock. Bruno had been commander of Mission 16, when the solids had achieved *Brennschluss,* then stubbornly clung to the sustainer. Quick action had gotten the team into orbit that day.

Abruptly, the acceleration, which had slowly built up to a hard six-g, dropped off to almost nothing.

"Three, two, one . . ." There was a crack of livid fire out the windows and the acceleration came back up, quickly reaching two-g. "Staging complete. Chase camera reports four ballutes deployed. Go for trans-Atlantic abort." Outside, the sky was turning dark.

It was like a dream, after all. Hermann Oberg remembered all the bitter days of his youth, watching as the Americans strode off into history on the achievements of German science. Despite his acknowledgement of German guilt, of all the terrible things his father's generation had done, he resented that stolen glory. As a teenager he liked to dream of an alternate universe, where Goering and Speer had seized power in 1938; a world where Germans ruled commerce, where German satellites flew by 1950 and the iron cross was planted on the Moon in 1962.

The horizon curved, the sky turned black, and the *Ariane 5* climbed steadily on a pillar of pale fire. The first stage dropped away, then the second, and suddenly they were in orbit, sailing across the coast of Kenya and on above the Indian Ocean. "Welcome to outer space, Director."

Hermann Oberg smiled, and thought, Better late than never.

Volodya strode across the walkway-dissected quad, drinking in the size of the world and its openness. Brisk November air soaked through his cloth jacket and awakened the surface of his skin like shaving lotion. What a pleasure this is. . . .

He always felt this way, right after a mission. It wasn't

that this . . . *nature* . . . was better than being in space, just different. The starry night outside a spacesuit, seen from the perspective of lunar night, was as grand, true enough, but it was, in some ways, almost an abstraction. Here, the grass, beginning to turn brown and dotted with colored leaves from the woods in the distance, grabbed you.

The main cafeteria was on a level below the ground floor of Babakin Hall. He took the stairs three at a time, hurrying without necessity. Unzipping his jacket, he stepped into the large room and surveyed its contents. Several of the cosmonauts looked up at him and smiled. Anton Serebryakov, of all people, motioned Volodya to join him. What does he want now? thought Manarov. Despite his reservations, Volodya nodded to the man and went to get his bacon, eggs, juice, and cereal with milk. American-style breakfasts were a particular favorite of his, picked up during his first stay at an astronautical conference in Chicago, and freshly squeezed orange juice, which was prohibitively expensive even on his generous salary, was by some miracle available to the kitchens here in Starry Town.

Wonderful city, Chicago. Clean. It could almost be Russian. Or what a Russian city would like to be.

Manarov sat in a vacant seat opposite Serebryakov. Anton was shoveling spoonfuls of kasha into his mouth, and didn't take any notice for a moment. When he finally did look up, Volodya smiled and tilted his head forward crisply. "How are things in the bachelor dorms?" he asked.

Anton grinned and sat back in his chair. "Fine. Anyplace is all right as long as you stay stuck to the floor. Not that I'm criticizing microgravity, mind you."

Manarov cut off a section of scrambled egg with his fork and put it in his mouth. He chewed with pleasure, though the eggs were overcooked. He stared past the man's shoulder at the large poster of Mars on the far wall.

"Have you heard anything?"

"Sorry, Tonya. I've had enough useless speculation and disturbed talk. I can wait to find out what's going on." He took a sip of his sweet, limpid juice.

"Sure. Okay. Before you came in Khabrov was holding forth on how the space effort was ruined. Another *Fobos,* he called it. But he's a fool, if you don't mind my saying so. I won't burden you with any of that, Vladimir Alekseevich. It's just that, when I called Pereverzev, my former boss at

Vernadskii, he seemed surprised that I didn't know what was going on. He was intimating that we're on the verge of something unprecedented. A major change in space policy, Volodya. For the better. He wouldn't say any more over a public phone; I didn't press him."

Manarov crunched brittle, smoky bacon fat. "Who else knows about this?"

"Who've I told? I talked to Artyukhin in the common room last night. I told him."

"I wouldn't mention this to anyone else. You might get your boss in trouble."

"This isn't the thirties, Volodya—or even the seventies. I—"

"Don't treat me like an idiot. I know much more about security here. For example, did you know that . . ."

"What? Do I know what?"

"Nothing." Volodya struggled to keep down his anger. He had almost revealed that Georgii Khabrov would never fly . . . because he was not really a cosmonaut. . . . Manarov had noticed how poorly the man did in several fitness exercises; he had kept his eye out and discovered, sure enough, that the weasel kept a secret notebook filled with unreadable code. It wasn't supposed to happen anymore, but it did. No doubt Khabrov's grandstanding was part of the act. Manarov sucked at his teeth and thought about sixteen years of dealing with the bureaucratic fools who still, more often than not, controlled how things happened. And who got to go to space. His anger subsided very slowly, like the pressure in a punctured tire. He looked at Serebryakov, back in his own world, spooning up the last dregs of syrupy buckwheat.

Manarov noted that the steamy inside heat was getting him damp. Here in the basement, the humidity stayed high summer and winter. He looked around at the cosmonauts still there, mostly talking in small groups, waiting for nine o'clock to roll around. The authoritarian clock on the wall said 0834. Dead time. "Do you want to go for a walk?"

Anton looked up, surprised. "Sure."

"Just over to the woods."

"Why not?"

Low, featureless clouds had come from nowhere to fill the sky. The sun peeked out occasionally; it seemed colder. They walked quickly.

"You know, Volodya, I still don't know why you wanted to become a cosmonaut."

"Isn't it obvious?"

Anton slowed for a moment, observing the other. "No. I've heard you say all that quasi-religious crap about space. Do you really believe that man can thrive in such an alien environment? Look around you. Feel the good, cold air of Mother Russia in your lungs. Can we leave this behind forever?"

Volodya quickened his pace, letting the other man catch up as he could. "Do you have so little faith in the adaptability of man? We can, and will, go into space. If we don't, what will be left of mankind won't even have the pure air you so ennoble to subsist on."

They were almost to the woods. Most of the trees were leafless already, but an old oak in the foreground still was covered in brown-orange. Tonya stopped and looked at his watch. Twenty-five minutes left. "Can I tell you something?" he asked. "In confidence?"

Manarov stopped and turned to face the planetologist. Uh-oh, he thought. What's coming now? "Sure," he said.

Serebryakov stared at something in the sky. He shook his head slowly. "I don't know if I'm really cut out for this, Volodya. I've managed to keep going so far, but although I'm getting somewhat used to it, it's very difficult for me. Sometimes I feel like I'm skating on thin ice."

"I'm not certain that I'm the one you should be talking to, Tonya. Semyonov's the one, if you want to resign."

Serebryakov raised a hand and violently clenched it. "No, Volodya. Hear me out."

A chill wind sprang up from the east. The oak shuddered violently, making a sound like the corns in a peppermill, but did not give up any leaves. "I just want to know . . . where do you get the courage? No, that's not it either. I—"

"Please. I'm not the one to say all this to. We should be getting back."

Anton turned and started to walk away slowly.

Manarov watched him go, his face a mask. Where do I get the courage? If I knew, my fortune would be made. I don't look so far inside myself. I know what the intellectuals fear most: a man is a hollow shell, without substance, a temporary thing. He put his hands in his pockets and began walking back toward the buildings.

Staring at the supple, colorful screen of his Daewoo SupeRemote terminal, Lyle Marlowe sighed and thought, "Dull. Very dull." He'd been flipping through the selection of news stories that were available for the night's show, but could find nothing worthy of being a precommercial tag. Fucking miserable. Starving Indonesians. Brazilian civil war refugees rioting in their Guyanan camps. Soviet cosmonauts retreating from the Moon with "technical difficulties." Shit, all of it.

That last might have been promising if they'd run into real trouble, maybe an in-flight casualty. . . . He could just see the headlines: "Soviet Space Heroes Defeated by Balky Nut. Brave Crew Unable to Duplicate 33-year-old American Stunt! Gorbachev Depressed! Eats Another Cookie!" Marlowe smiled thinly. Maybe I better go with the refugees after all. Milk something out of the Jonestown connection.

The DSR chirred softly, the file server break-in signal. "Yes."

The synthesizer's light baritone said, "You have a call on line six. It is coded Informed Source eighty-six."

Marlowe sat a little straighter. Eighty-six was a deep-code, identity unknown, and represented one of his best CIA covert bean-spillers. "Access."

"Hello, Lyle." The voice was, as always, flattened out by some kind of high-tech scrambler so you couldn't even tell if it was male or female.

"Hello, Max. What can I do for you?" Informants were usually full of shit, but this one had sprung some good leaks in the past.

"I have to speak quickly. This isn't a secure location."

Marlowe smirked and said, "Go ahead, Max." These guys probably had wet dreams about being "spies" in an age when intelligence was gathered and processed by machinery.

"Lyle, there's some real crap going on. You know the Soviet Union canceled its lunar landing?"

"I read the papers, Max. Get to the point."

"The point is the reason why. They need to use *Molotochek* for something else."

"Don't they have a second moonship?"

"They need *Serpachek* as a backup vehicle. The Russkis

are always real careful. Now we need to be, too. Listen: The Russians are planning to send a crew of four cosmonauts to visit the near-Earth asteroid Sinuhe when it swings through this neighborhood next spring."

"So? Is that better than a trip to the Moon?" This was cold shit. News, but hardly worth leaking from the CIA. "Does this get better or are you guys busy playing with yourselves again?"

"Asshole. Do your homework. *Molotochek* will be carrying six five-kiloton high-kinetic nuclear devices. What we call Swedish Maulers. They intend to divert Sinuhe into Earth-orbit with them."

Marlowe felt a slight tickle of excitement. Perhaps there was a lead story here after all. "Doesn't that violate a few treaties?"

"Maybe not. It may be that when we had the Test Ban Treaty revised in ninety-six to accommodate Star Wars, we shot our collective toes off. I have to go now, Lyle. Do your fucking homework. This is important."

The synthesizer said, "Disconnect."

Marlowe sat back in his chair, wondering where to begin. Finally, he paged down to the *Molotochek* story and stared at the faces of the six Russian cosmonauts, then popped up a picture of their spaceship. "Well." He touched the phone node on his screen and said, "Get me Schlossberg."

In an office in Langley, Virginia, James E. Russell, Jr., deaccessed his phone and then carefully disencoded the scrambler system. "Dipshit," he muttered. The story would probably make the news in such a garbled fashion as to be completely useless. Look at the way that silly bastard muffed the Tanaka assassination! Here the Japs were getting ready to abrogate their demilitarization compact and rewrite the MacArthur constitution. We kill the squinty-eyed little bastard and these cretins turn him into a saint!

Russell was a perfect Reed Richards clone; square face, smooth and handsome; brown hair graying at the temples. As he reached out to pop the almost-invisible screen surface of his Compaq MightyDesk III, he sighed with exasperation. Serve us right if the Russians drop that thing on Manhattan. Maybe a good thing, too. Kill Marlowe and Schlossberg both. "See if you can get me an appointment with the President. And put in a call to Bensonhurst while you're at it."

Moe Schlossberg folded his hands over an enormous paunch and looked across the surface of his desk at Marlowe. The desk was made of wood and he was probably the last working-level CTN executive to live without full-scale electronics. The only sign of *fin de siècle* splendor here was a flat-screen gas-crystal monitor hanging on one wall. When not working, it displayed a slow-motion animation of the Dali thing. The picture kept time as it dripped.

"OK, Lyle. So the CIA says the Russians are bringing this hunk of rock back from outer space. Does that mean anything in the context of known American paranoias?"

"They're using nukes, Moe. That makes it pretty hot stuff."

That got a nod. "Point one. Nukes in space. That makes it a political story. But not a very good one. We know the Air Force has nuclear-powered X-ray lasers aboard *Eisenhower,* even if we haven't used the story yet. What else?"

"They're lying about it?"

"What else is new? No, the public won't buy into this. It's just a normal tech-story. Minute twenty-five stuff."

"The CIA guy seemed convinced it was important."

Schlossberg stirred in his chair trying to find a more comfortable position. Old and fat, he thought. What the hell. "Okay, let me think. So the bastards send a crew out to an asteroid. Blast it back to Earth orbit with nukes. And . . . fuck. Then what?"

"Hold May Day there?"

"Right. Well, let's see what we've got on the damned thing." He reached into his desk and, picking up the small remote terminal, canceled the decor and called up the file scanner. "Let's see everything we ever did about asteroid Sinuhe." He clicked a few buttons and the picture came to grainy life:

The face of a much younger Lyle Marlowe dominated the wall:

"For our final segment tonight we have a story from the world of science. Astronomers from Mount Palomar Observatory today disclosed the discovery of a new asteroid whose orbit brings it unusually close to the earth. . . .

"The asteroid, as yet unnamed, will swing by the Earth,

making a perilously close approach to our world in the spring of 2002, a mere eight years from now. . . ."

The scene of the asteroid whipping through a starry sky, making a whooshing sound as it passed low above the New York skyline, was surprisingly effective.

As Schlossberg pointed to the freeze-frame icon on the remote, Marlowe said, "Shit. I don't remember doing that!"

The other man glanced at the date stamp. "Interesting. It's from your first show." He leaned back in his chair, rubbing both hands slowly across his stomach and, finally, smiled. "Y'know, I think we have a story. . . ."

Sinuhe looked very pretty and very dangerous looming above New York, and eight years had brought great improvements in computer simulation graphics.


"I don't fucking believe it." Dallas Milam's froggy voice preceded him through the office door. The bronzed, trim Californian appeared in the opening, waving a palm-sized pocket TV. John Dalgleish, British, pale, and hunkering down into his out-of-condition body, looked up and waved him into the chair opposite his desk. "Belief, Dal, is not a matter of coition."

Milam was a planetary scientist, project manager for CRAF, and Dalgleish was, at least nominally, his superior at JPL. Since the *Galileo* malfunction, more and more responsibility had fallen into the diminishingly small lap of the Briton. "Yeah. So you say. I don't suppose you've been watching CTN."

"For all my faults, I tend to work at my desk, not watch the little crystals."

"Well, I leave it on, in the corner of the screen—you know, keeps me company. Anyway, John, *you're* not going to believe it either. Those lovable Russkis have done it again. This time it's something really big. A manned mission to a Triple-A!"

Dalgleish sat back, and felt the rolls of fat on his chest and stomach come apart stickily. "But they canceled the lunar landing because of some kind of glitch—why would they go ahead and . . . oho! Our sources have let us down again. But this was on—CTN? Are you sure it's accurate?"

"Well, it's that Marlowe dude, so anything is possible. There was even something garbled at the end about nuclear weapons in space and a repeat of that Icarus garbage all over again. If I didn't know better I'd guess they were trying to say that the cosmonauts will be shooting the fucker at us."

Dalgleish's voice-integration light came on and there was a soft ticking noise. He pawed through the hard copy littering his desk and finally found the old-fashioned handset under a photo-montage of Neptune's extraordinary moon, Triton. "Yes?" Milam watched the man's jowly face go through about six rapid changes of expression. "Thanks," he said, and put down the phone. "That was somebody who knows somebody who knows somebody. CTN almost got it right for a change. The Russian Lunar Transfer Vehicle is being refurbished. They *are* going to use nuclear weapons to divert 5007 Sinuhe into Earth-orbit."

"Christ, John. Can they do that?" Milam ran through a series of calculations in his head. "I guess they can. . . ."

"This makes our little efforts look pretty puny," said Dalgleish, shaking his head. *"CRAF"*'s observations of Hamburga were okay, as good as they could be with a *Mariner* Mark Two, and at least we know that there's an excellent chance these asteroids are actually analogs to the meteorites their spectra match."

"Thanks a lot, John. You know, you never will make a good administrator. You've gone and hurt my feelings. We have a fucking great mission at Kopf, everything works right, and now we didn't do enough at Hamburga. Get your shit straight, man. The asteroids have always had low priority."

There had been so little enthusiasm for the Main Belt Grand Tour idea that Dalgleish had to fight tooth and claw to get start-up funding. For years they'd been tagging asteroid flybys onto missions, almost as afterthoughts, and the results were tantalizing but elusive. "Yes, I know. It's just a damn shame."

"We've done what we can within the budgetary constraint. Hell, if it isn't blind, well get a close flyby of 388 Charybdis out of CRAF in 2007. What more can we—fuck, John!—the Italians! This really puts them up shit creek. *Piazzi II* is well on its way to Sinuhe. What a waste!"

Dalgleish nodded. "I thought of that. Too bad we can't get our experiment back."

The other man smiled bitterly. His white teeth flashed in

an unlikely way. "I guess it looks bad for the Main Belt tour, unless there's another Sputnik reaction. But I think it's more likely that Congress will write off asteroids, like the Soviets did the Moon back in the seventies. Anything we did would look like sparrow shit compared to this."

"My rule of thumb for this job has been: No matter what happens, we get our budget cut tighter. When *Galileo* ended up a no-show, that may have been the beginning of the end."

"Those bastards make us sling the poor machine from here to eternity and then blame us when it isn't working. Most of the components were teenagers by the time they were turned on."

John Dalgleish knew the whole story by heart, but still he winced. "My daughter Janet was born a week after *Challenger,* you know. She was almost nine when *Galileo* broke down. She's almost sixteen now. And it doesn't get any better . . . just worse. Our technology gets more and more sophisticated, but we seem to get dumber and dumber. Sometimes I think that the future lies with the Soviets. They don't seem to be tied into the processes that are pulling us down."

"Hey," laughed Milam. "Don't say things like that! We really will lose our funding."

Standing in the dim hallway outside the office of the chief designer of spacecraft, Volodya turned and looked at his three companions. "I guess we'll know shortly." He turned and pushed open the door. "Good morning, Anna Ilyaevna."

The chief designer's thin, elderly secretary looked ghastly. Her waxen skin seemed even paler than usual. Tense worry lines had taken the place of the usual wrinkles. "Good! You're here! Go on in! Hurry!"

Taken aback, Volodya said, "Are you all right, comrade? You seem ill."

"Go in!"

This grows odder with each passing second. He exchanged a glance with Bronstein, who seemed equally nonplussed, then turned and pushed open the door to Semyonov's office. Inside, the desk had been pushed back a little and additional chairs had been set up. Chief Designer Semyonov was perched on the corner of his desk, weary-

looking but expressionless. Volodya looked over the face of
the men standing next to him and felt an odd prickling in
the back of his neck. The Big Four were out in force. In
addition to Semyonov, here was IKI chief Galeev, his own
boss; Glavkosmos administrator Dunaev; and General Ponomarev, head of the Strategic Rocket Forces. And . . .

The little fat man seated in the plush leather chair behind
the desk brushed at his few remaining hairs, running a
hand along the dark birthmark, and beamed at them.
"Good morning, comrades! I trust you are well rested?"

Bronstein snapped to attention and said, "Good morning, Comrade General Secretary!"

Gorbachev smiled and said, "Why don't you all be
seated." He waved at a row of folding chairs lined up along
the opposite wall. The cosmonauts stumbled toward the
chairs and sat down. "Well. We've brought you here this
morning to tell you why the lunar landing mission of
*Molotochek* was canceled. I will give you a general over-
view, then each of these gentlemen will explain some phase
of what is proposed." The general secretary slouched down
a little bit in Semyonov's chair. "Despite rumors you may
have heard, the lunar landing wasn't canceled because of
problems with LLV(I) *Oryol.* As you may have noticed
when you docked with the *Mir* complex, it is even now
mated to LTV *Serpachek* and could be dispatched to the
Moon on a moment's notice. The rumor that the mission
was canceled for political reasons is also untrue. The plain
truth of the matter is that we have found something better
to do with our precious space resources. Something that is
extremely time sensitive."

He motioned to the head of IKI, who stepped before
them. "Our scientists have calculated that a near-Earth asteroid named 5007 Sinuhe, in orbit along the ecliptic between Venus and Earth, is positioned so that it will make
two close encounters with our world. One approach will be
in the late spring of next year. The next will be slightly
earlier in 2003. After the second encounter, its orbit will be
perturbed so that no further close approaches will take
place. The first encounter will put it at approximately one
million kilometers from Earth. We are unable to calculate
accurately the second encounter at this time, but it will be
somewhat closer. Sinuhe seems to be a nickel-iron body and
may be a source of elements that will be needed for the

development of the spacefaring civilization so eloquently espoused by the comrade general secretary."

He stepped back to the desk and his place was taken by the Glavkosmos administrator. "As some of you may know, having worked in the appropriate field," he nodded then to Manarov, "the Energiya booster was developed during the 1980s with the eventual aim in mind of constructing solar-power satellites with which to supply the energy needs of the Soviet Union. We would like to begin doing that, but we find that our Space Industrialization Project is crippled because we have, thus far, been unable to discover sufficient mineral resources on the Moon. If we have to get them from Mars, or even farther away, the project is doomed and, with it, humanity itself. Now, it seems, the resources may be closer to hand. If we can get them, the future may fall into our hands, after all."

Beside him Volodya heard Serebryakov mutter the word, "Interesting."

Chief Designer Semyonov stood up from his perch on his desk corner. "I'll keep this brief," he said, smiling faintly. "We've done the calculations carefully. As you know, a fully fueled LTV is capable, just barely, of making a round trip between *Mir* and the Martian moon Phobos. In fact, that is what we planned to do during the first available launch window after 2010. That being the case, we find that *Molotochek* will be capable of making a round-trip to this object Sinuhe next spring. It will, in fact, be able to do so while carrying a substantial cargo."

Volodya's heart leaped in his chest as a vision of this mission sprang full-blown into his mind. "Are you saying," he demanded suddenly, "that we're going on a flight to this asteroid?"

Semyonov smiled. "I thought you might like that. Yes. Training will begin today, for a May launch. The mission is estimated to last about four months."

Anton raised his hand and spoke up, his voice very faint. "This is all . . . wonderful, but . . . these resources. . . . Asteroids do not stay in one place. After the second encounter the asteroid will recede out of reach. How do you plan to get them back?" His eyes were wide and he seemed quite pale.

Semyonov said, "Well. We're coming to that. Comrade General?"

General Ponomarev came to stand before them, falling into the parade rest position so characteristic of him. "As the chief designer noted, *Molotochek* will, on this mission, find itself with considerable excess cargo capacity. In addition to the usual scientific instruments, with which to assess the asteroid on your arrival, your cargo will be a radiation-hardened industrial computer from the Kama River Truck Works, a great deal of cabling, both stress-hardened mono-filament and the information carrying kind, and six high-kinetic five-kiloton tactical nuclear weapons. It has been calculated that with this equipment you will be able to divert object Sinuhe into a stable Earth-orbit."

Stunned, Volodya turned to look at Anton, but the man's eyes were shut and his skin seemed to have taken on a bluish tinge. He turned to face the front of the room again. "Six, Comrade General. An interesting number."

Ponomarev rubbed his jaw, feeling a faint, whiskery scrape. "Six." He ticked them off on the fingers of his right hand. "One to redirect the asteroid. One reserved for a possible course correction. One for braking into an ellipti-cal Earth-orbit. One to circularize said orbit." He held up his little finger, then his left hand, thumb extended, fingers clenched. "Two for backup. Just in case."

Bronstein sat forward suddenly and said, "Why are we the ones chosen to go? We've just come off a mission and it is our backups' turn."

Gorbachev himself smiled thinly at that. "You were cho-sen for the first lunar landing because of your abilities and you are the most appropriate choice for this mission as well. We do not want to jeopardize our chances of success merely because of protocol. You have the necessary mix of skills and you are already accustomed to life aboard *Molotochek.*" He laughed and said, "It only seems fair that you be allowed a crack at this one. If, that is, you want it."

He looked them over carefully, one by one, then nodded, satisfied, and said. "I thought so." He glanced at the four administrators. "Let us do it, then."

Secretary of State Arthur Barnwell was ushered into the Blue Room, and he took his seat gingerly, looking around, appalled. The new furnishings were very odd indeed. The indefatigable Mrs. Wren had imposed by fiat a strange sort of post-Yuppie nonfunctionalism on the utilitarian meeting room design. From its pale pastel walls and thin cotton draperies to the spare and uncomfortable vintage Danish Modern furniture, it made him want to give an antique Bostonian sniff of disdain. He wrapped his big hands around the formed plywood arms and squeezed. He'd hated the crap as a young man when his wife filled up their house with it in 1960. But now? And *here*? For some reason they hadn't changed the rug, which clashed terribly. There was, he supposed, something in President Wren's makeup that made him gravitate to trashy symbolism; probably the same thing that made him utter a seemingly inexhaustible string of woolly malapropisms. A sudden burst of Pleistocene imagery, graphically detailed, filled his mind, twisting his lips with a controlled smirk. Barnwell reached up and scratched his stiff, dark-gray hair, listening to it rustle and wondering why these things still went through his head. You'd think by the age of seventy . . . In any case, dealing with these Bozos every day was probably driving him crazy. The thought of the President of the United States with miniature mammoths dancing on his tongue didn't seem too farfetched just now. Though he was a child of wealth, L. Aloysius Wren was, somehow, the perfect product of the common culture of the fifties and sixties. And remarkably goofy, besides. At least he had come out of his bunker for once, probably at his wife's insistence.

With the formal start of the meeting still several minutes away, Defense Secretary Romain Bensonhurst entered the room and sat in the next chair, propping his shiny cordovan wing tips on the thin wooden surface of the coffee table. Barnwell wanted to wince at the man, whose Pacific Northwest persona seemed to grow increasingly vulgar with each passing day, but he ignored the urge. "Morning, Ben. What the hell are we going to tell him, now?"

Bensonhurst grinned, his grotesquely even false teeth seeming to take on blue highlights from the circular fluorescent fixture overhead. "Hey, Art. Don't know. It better be closer to the truth than that TV bullshit, though. What's State's version going to be?"

"Well . . ." Barnwell shrugged. "What's the *real* truth? I don't guess we know." He paused, trying to pull things together, and noticed that, as always, his Boston accent thickened with the effort of dissembling. "I don't *think* the Russians mean to do anything other than what they said.

In the past ten years there have been any number of articles in the Soviet scientific press about the idea of using asteroid resources to bootstrap their space industrial base. . . ."

"Come *on,* Art. Save the horseshit for Aloysius! I know better, and so does an old dog like you. How old were you in 1959, something like thirty?"

"Twenty-eight."

"Close enough. I was only nineteen, but I remember how scared I was after reading *Alas, Babylon.* We had 'em by the nuts then and didn't even know it! Now the tables are turned."

Barnwell made a steeple of long, bony fingers before his flat, sharp-featured face and wondered just what drove assholes like this. "What's your point, Ben? The Cold War's been over for a long time."

"I don't think so, Art. What do you suppose will happen when that rock impacts Kansas at a hundred and fifty thousand miles an hour? What do you suppose the Russians will say? *Oops? Butterfingers?*"

Jesus Christ. Barnwell felt nausea scald the pit of his stomach. This was still a goddamned *game* after all. State didn't have a turf it needed to defend. Its responsibilities were so clear cut that its budget was dictated by external circumstances. Defense, on the other hand, had to justify its expenditures. They'd fallen a long way, since the glory days of the fifties and eighties. Bush had slowly bled the military machine down to a manageable size, then Wren, for no reason other than inertia, had continued the process throughout his first term. DOD's budget was, at best, no more than two-thirds what it had been a decade earlier in real dollars. Better than a fifth of that sum went to support *Eisenhower* and SDI, so the rest of the military infrastructure was subdued to say the least.

"You tell 'im, Benny!" General Daniel J. Nelson, USAF, Chairman of the Joint Chiefs of Staff, former head of the Strategic Air Command, later tapped to lead the active deployment phase of the Strategic Defense Initiative Office, trim, blond, crew-cut, looked splendid in undress blues, four stars in a row on each collar tab. "I was twenty in 1959. I was two years along at Colorado Springs and I haven't forgotten. Pat Frank had us win that war by a cunt hair. Bullshit. A thousand B-52s and eight thousand gravity bombs against sixty cryogenically fueled ICBMs? We

would've smeared 'em off the face of the earth! Curtis Le-
May was right."

Barnwell sighed. "Maybe he was, Dan. But our predecessors made those mistakes forty years ago. This is now." He
looked around the room and saw that most of the others
had arrived. In addition to himself, Bensonhurst and General Nelson, Harveson from NASA and the CIA's Jimmy
Russell had taken chairs. As Nelson sat down, Vice-President Thomas R. McDermott entered the room, looking
considerably older than his sixty-three years. Barnwell was
glad to see him, counting him as the meeting's only other
pragmatist.

"Morning, boys." McDermott smiled tiredly. "I'm here
in my capacity as chief of the National Space Council." He
sat down, ignoring Russell's audible snicker.

DA-d'd'da-da-DAA.

DA-d'd'da-da-DAA.

Tinny, chip-generated music played through the half-
century old PA system as the door opened, framing
President L. Aloysius Wren. Barnwell winced again. The
fucking idiot couldn't seem to go through a goddamned
doorway without hearing a few bars of "Hail to the Chief."
Maybe he just didn't *believe* he was President of the United
States, and needed constant reassurance. As he entered the
room his heel scuffed the edge of the dark-blue carpet,
causing one corner to flip over. The tan backing was
speckled with black mildew.

"Good morning, gentlemen." At fifty-seven, Wren still
had his vapid good looks, his sandy hair retaining its color
as pale hair often does, but jowls were beginning to form
along the line of his jaw, bringing with them the first hints
of an ugly old man to come. "I assume you all watched
Marlowe on CTN last night."

"Good graphics," snarled Brad Harveson, obviously in
an ill humor.

Wren's eyes were like silver-blue pools in the fluorescent
light. "Good point, Brad." He smiled distantly, enhancing
an already robotic affect. "Suppose you give us your view of
what this means."

The NASA chief sat forward eagerly. "Mr. President, it
means only that the Russians are serious about their space
objectives, and are prepared to take enterprising and daring
steps to achieve them. Their manned space technology,

though inferior to ours, has been developed to such an extent that it allows them easy access to translunar space. In my opinion, bringing back Sinuhe is just a stunt, and I can't say whether they'll pull it off successfully or not. But the *idea* is a sound one! As a portable 'mine' for their solar-power satellite project, an object like Sinuhe would make an invaluable source of raw materials. We don't see this step as anything more than another sputnik, a technological breakthrough, perhaps, but not a threat."

Barnwell, waiting for an opportunity to break in, suddenly interjected, "I agree, Mr. President. We at State see the last five years as a period of retrenchment in the Soviet Union. With the Communist party losing control of many of its domestic responsibilities, they do not care to give away anything further. Yet General Secretary Gorbachev is a firm believer in disarmament. The military budget continues to be slashed, and the most practical, forward-looking alternative is their manned space program. They are literally looking for things to do with the money to keep it out of the hands of the generals."

"Hogwash," murmured Nelson, thinking, Where in the *world* did we find this radical?

"Not at all! Ten years of treaties have brought us to a significant watershed, where it may finally be possible to break the back of the nuclear genie released during the postwar period. Keep in mind that—"

"Okay, Brad. Thank you, Art." Still smiling, Wren turned his glittering gaze on Bensonhurst. "What does Defense think of all this?"

"Defense thinks it's all bullshit. Oh, I don't dispute the need for space resource utilization. We're doing a pilot study on a lunar mining project for the global SDI project right now, but I don't think that's what the Russians are up to. They just don't have the technology to park an asteroid in low Earth-orbit with any precision. Nuclear explosive propulsion is untested; given the indications from our intelligence network, we think that—"

"That's not right, Ben!" said McDermott. "Studies have shown—"

"Damn it, Tom, you'll forgive me, but your futuristic SpaceAmerica studies are the biggest crock of shit I have ever seen in my life. We're talking about hard, cold facts here; not your head-up-the-ass 'studies.' The Russians are not motivated by little-boy wonder; they want to catch us with our pants down and drive the old motherfucker home. I think our pal "Gorby" is going to drop that cocksucker dead center on America!"

Wren seemed paler than ever, prissified by the crude language. "What evidence do we have that they might be considering such a thing?"

Russell stood up, breaking form, trying to make his point forcefully. He seemed distracted. "Mr. President, there is considerable evidence." He paused, then rushed ahead with, "Our calculations show that a high-velocity impact from object Sinuhe on the North American mainland would be equivalent to exploding a thermonuclear device of just over nine hundred thousand megatons . . ."

"Oh my God," said President Wren.

". . . rendering a large portion of the continent uninhabitable, Mr. President, very possibly beginning forty or more years of nuclear winter. I don't have to explain to you that the superpower peace we have maintained for the last fifty years has lasted *only* because of equality of weaponry on both sides. Something like this. . . ." He shrugged, and sat back down.

Nelson chopped a hand into his palm. "Mr. President, you have two choices. Either you act, or you don't act. If you don't act, the country will be in the gravest peril. It is no good trying to make up fancy theories about the Russkis' motivations. It doesn't matter what their motivations are."

Arthur Barnwell placed a dry, rough-skinned palm over his eyes, blotting out the scene before him, replaying scenes from *Dr. Strangelove* in his head. I know where this is leading, he thought in bewildered despair. Shit. I *know* where this is leading!

Anton walked the halls of the building, nervous energy barely released by his quick, long strides. Actual *in situ* meteor work, something totally unexpected. If he had been asked, he would have guessed that such a field trip wasn't likely for fifty years, maybe a hundred. But would his chances to go be lost? He shouldn't have tried to be frank with Manarov; hadn't he learned from the past? Especially when he himself was unsure of what was happening within the slow, percolating processes of his brain, it was terribly unwise to try to share the process with someone else.

It wasn't that Manarov was such a bad guy. Except for a sense that he was exceptionally dogmatic in his pursuit of space, Tonya actually liked him, most of the time. It seemed that if the man regarded Tonya's weakness as something that could jeopardize his own future in space, he would take whatever steps necessary to remove him from the equation. *I've known him for* years, *yet I still don't know him!*

It's clear there's something inside me that's not suited to space. During his first mission, as part of his preparation for the lunar landing, he'd gone up as a mission specialist on *Buran*. The fear during the launch had only accentuated the disorientation and nausea of weightlessness. He had vomited endlessly, and, hours later, when everyone else was asleep, he'd had what seemed to him like a little nervous breakdown. Eventually he was able to sleep. When he awoke the episode was just a bad dream, and he'd handled his job well enough.

He turned a corner and went into the gym. Volodya was running in place, a small dumbbell in each hand. He had taken off his shirt and was already coated with a glistening varnish of sweat. A few other cosmonauts were running on the track, adding a squeaking thud-thud-thud in the background. Tonya dropped into a crouch and wrapped his hands around a thirty-kilo barbell, slightly revolted by the rich, musty smell of old perspiration that saturated the air. He hoisted the weight up, catching it on upturned palms, and then stood.

"You should learn the right technique if you're going to do that," said Manarov turning to face him. "Still thinking about quitting?"

Serebryakov frowned, lifting the barbell over his head, then letting it fall behind his neck, to his shoulders. "I wanted to talk to you about that. Forget what I said before, will you?"

"You didn't say much, if I remember right."

"No. I'm sure you got the impression that I was getting cold feet. I can't say I especially enjoy being in space, but I can tolerate it. I just want . . ."

"I won't say anything. You are a competent scientist, the only cosmonaut so far trained specifically in planetology.

You specialized in meteoritics at Vernadskii, and that study is extremely relevant here. I would guess that your expertise is very important to the completion of this mission; and I wouldn't want to lose that." He frowned himself, looking Anton up and down. "I've seen that you can control yourself. The question is, how far can you extend that facility?"

"What do you mean?"

"If the going gets tough, will you trust us to assess the situation and follow our orders to the letter?"

"Of course," he said, without thinking.

Volodya felt like throwing one of the dumbbells on the man's foot. Scientists, it seemed, had a special naïveté all their own. "The mission itself may be a gambit in some larger strategy. I don't think Mikhail Sergeevich was being entirely honest with us."

"I'm afraid I don't follow you. It's clear that they have decided to take a new perspective—"

"You haven't thought out all the possible ramifications. What about the military potential of this asteroid?"

Anton gaped. "Certainly it could be a destructive weapon, and, placed precisely, would cause a large amount of damage. But not too much more than the largest nuclear warheads; nothing like a disabling preemptive strike. The outcome of the following war would be . . . unthinkable."

"Oh?" said Volodya. "Pull your head out of your ass, Tonya, for just a minute. *Nothing* is ever 'unthinkable.' What about the threat that this poses? It would be something they couldn't stop, no matter how effective their SDI was."

"Well, it's possible, but . . . Are you questioning my loyalty now? Whether I would carry out a plan designed to bring the United States to its knees? That seems a bit extreme."

Manarov sighed with exasperation, put down his weights and stood motionless, relaxed. "Our hand may be forced, regardless of our intentions. We're not the only players in this game. . . . You should think about such scenarios before you decide." Darkened, bronze-colored hair, wet with perspiration, hung down over his forehead like a copper guillotine blade.

"I do not push the buttons that make these things go."

"And how do you feel about *being* a button, my friend?

What will it *mean* to you? Be certain that your science will not be polluted by fear, or misplaced good intentions."

Tonya came out of the VDNKh Metro station into rich, sweet sunshine. It was late May, but the winter had held its iron grip on Moskva like a true bureaucrat, deferring any real changes until the last possible moment, afraid to take responsibility for anything new. Finally Old Man Winter had been purged. At fourteen, Anton was well aware of the intolerable stupidity of the USSR. How could he not be? His school was a perfect microcosm of Soviet society. Perhaps this was on purpose, to prepare Soviet youth for the pulverizing realities of life in the "real world."

It was a Sunday and there was nothing to do. He really had very few friends in the world, and perhaps it was just as well. He was changing too fast for anyone to understand him. The endless soccer practice and competition that had filled his days in the summer and fall of 1979 would be no more. The uncouth louts that he had called friends were bastards. He could see that now. They would as soon cut off your legs and leave you in a snowbank if it provided enough of a laugh. And the irony of it was that these same boys stood tallest in class and mouthed the principles of Marxism-Leninism with the most conviction.

And he had discovered masturbation. The world had pivoted irrevocably in that single long moment when the rubbing had brought forth a cascade of swelling pleasure that culminated in wet, spasming bliss. Nothing was the same from then on. He had heard about sex and how babies came about; he even knew that something called "come" was supposed to come out of your dick like piss. But he had never known how to produce this stuff, and had wondered if he was masculine enough. Anyway, the world had suddenly become a much more complex, if more bearable, place. He knew that this was something that could not be talked about to anyone, a secret of staggering proportions that clustered together with the fact of his nonbelief in Communism.

He walked across Peace Square, enjoying the mild breezes that ruffled his hair and seemed to sooth his soap-dessicated skin. He had come to the Exhibit of Economic Achievements because the huge, permanent fair was so big that there always seemed to be a nook that he had never seen, with some delightful architectural concoction or a monstrous statue of some different type of laborer. It was also a place that offered a degree of freedom from the prying eyes of the populace. If he got really bored he could try out his English or Japanese on likely-looking tourists.

He paused before the grand upthrust of the three-hundred-foot monument to Soviet space achievement. It was, indeed, spectacular—one of the few statues to succeed in its goal. It was golden and showed a tiny spaceship, streamlined and nothing like the real *Salyut*s and *Soyuze*s that circled overhead, at the apex of curve of smooth metal fire. He had had the theory that all this space stuff was just the Soviet Union beating its meat, shooting off into space. Other than that he couldn't imagine the slightest use for it all. Space was, after all, *space*—with nothing in it.

The men who appeared on TV, the cosmonauts, seemed, for all their hearty good humor, to be a surly lot, probably his erstwhile soccer teammates grown up and made heroes. He had heard that they didn't control their ships and were just guinea pigs sent up to test how long people could live in weightlessness.

Tonya felt a sudden thirst, and went up to the kvass vendor by the gate. He gave the man a five-kopeck piece and took the cloudy, greasy glass filled with the yellowish liquid that reminded everyone of urine. There was enough alcohol in the stuff to make him dizzy, if he could manage to find four or five vendors in a row and buy a glass from each of them. Right now the weather was so good he didn't particularly want to distract himself from it. He drained the glass in one giant gulp and handed it back to the vendor. It was ghastly stuff, but he liked it.

Inside, he meandered among the clustering artifacts representing some obscure, bureaucratic notion of art. There was a small park some distance away where he could sit on the crown of a little hill surrounded almost entirely by young lime trees. It was a perfect place to sit without being seen and, for some reason, the birds liked it as much as he did. Tonya still liked to watch birds, and now, when the migrators were starting to return from their winter nesting grounds in Africa, he could occasionally catch sight of some rare interloper that didn't belong in Moskva at all. He turned right at the Armenian Pavilion and headed in that direction.

From around a bend in the path there came a strange, rhythmic booming, a repeating assembly of bass notes that reminded Tonya of heavy machinery—perhaps it was some new outdoor exhibition of a metal puncher or crimper. As he got closer the noises were accompanied by a fluttering, hissing cymbal clatter, and then, just beyond some bushes, a living, pulsing whine almost like a human soprano's scream but finer, abstracted from life to a more perfect plane. It intertwined with the now somewhat more modulated bass notes to create an overwhelming, mechanical music the like of which Tonya never could have imagined. Of course he had heard the odd Beatles tune, and, once he had pieced it all together, this music was not so different from Western rock he had heard before. But it was loud! And there wasn't a singer to get in the way of the hypnotic, full-spectrum intermingling of the thudding bass and screaming guitar. He came around a bush and saw five young people, three boys and two girls, just about his age. One of the boys was carrying a cassette player as large as a satchel, and it was from this that the music emanated.

"Hey," Anton yelled above the noise, "what *is* that?"

The boy with the cassette player, who was wearing a leather jacket and had his hair pomaded up into a crest, looked pityingly at Anton and then sneered. "Get lost, fuckhead," he said.

"No!" screamed Anton. "Hey! I like it!"

The boy and his companions looked at Anton with a little more sympathy now. "Grahnd Foonk Relrod," he said. "The red album."

Anton nodded sagely, although he didn't have the slightest idea what it was the other had said. A red record, perhaps? Communist? If this was Communism it wasn't like any he had experienced before.

"Where did you get it? Can I get a copy?" He knew it wouldn't sound anything like this on the tiny portable cassette recorder his father had brought back from his trip to Finland, but it might still sound good.

The others ignored him and listened to the music, wriggling occasionally and shaking their fists. The cassette came to an end in a baroque, retrograde-sounding anticlimax that went on and on. When it was over the boy popped a switch on the top of the box and looked again at Anton.

"If you can get me a cassette, I can make you a copy."

Anton smiled, trying to ingratiate himself with this strange-looking person. "Sure. I've got a cassette. Where do you live?"

The boy waved vaguely in the direction of the Old City. "I'm at the Tsentralnaya on Gorkii; just go up to the desk and ask for Max. He'll know you mean me."

They left Tonya standing there without a backward glance. He watched as the group bopped across a newly green lawn toward the Golden Ear Restaurant. They were now playing something similar, though now a screeching human voice accompanied the mechanical sounds, diluting them and making them less compelling. It was like adding a vocalist to a string quartet—a jarring, completely unnecessary addition. The music receded back into booming as they dwindled.

It was now just beginning to dawn on Anton. How did people like them exist? How could they get away with their outlandish dress and ridiculous hairstyle? Didn't someone punish them? Wouldn't they be arrested and sent away to the Gulag? He knew it was 1980, and things were not like the old days his mother described to him in such great detail. But he had supposed that he had to toe the line or suffer terrible consequences.

Apparently, he had been wrong.

Space station *Freedom,* Hermann Oberg concluded, was a decidedly uncomfortable place to be. As he hauled himself through the gaping hatch of a connecting node, scraping his belly against a sharp edge, he wondered for the thousandth time what genius had designed these universal pressure doors. They pivoted in the middle, unlike any door used since the dawn of humanity, and attached to some kind of bizarre rackmount. Somehow, the doors could be tipped through the doorway and reversed, holding pressure from one direction or the other, but not both. He squeezed his bulk past the door mechanism, growling at the thing under his breath. Doubtless, this was the work of some multinational committee, all salaries and no brain. No matter what angle you approached from, the door itself was *always* in the way! From somewhere, far away, a little voice spoke up, defending the door's designer: They weren't thinking about *fat* astronauts. . . .

Somehow he made his way through the node and into

the wardroom. It was, it seemed, his turn to eat. At least, that was what his schedule said. *Freedom* was meant to house twenty-four men, including twelve engineering crew and an equal number of researchers. The sixteen delegates to the first international space conference to be held *in* space would have burdened the station beyond reason. There had been a year of squabbles over this, while the thing was being planned. The technical crew could not be reduced, of course, but the researchers . . . There were some very angry scientists sitting on their hands now. Having long grown used to their territoriality, Oberg was tempted to be amused, but mankind was supposed to be in space to *do* something, not fart around and have arguments that would be at home in any urban sewer. It was, he supposed, junketing gone mad.

The kitchen/dining module of *Freedom* had been intended to serve six people at a time. It contained a table, three microwave ovens, and a "refrigerated food storage module" that amounted to a cold chest of drawers. The table was set slightly off center in the compartment, which was fairly commodious, and sat below a large porthole, from which the diners got a spectacular view of Earth. The dinner hour could turn into a mini-conclave all its own, since the heads of the various national space agencies had been scheduled to eat together. Right now the room was empty, save for one lone diner. Oberg floated over, guiding himself by touching various surfaces along the way, pulling himself into a chair and buckling the seatbelt. "Dr. Harveson."

"Herr Oberg."

Bradford K. Harveson, III, looked distinctly ill at ease. After many undistinguished years as a professor of mathematics at Cornell, he had been appointed to the directorship of NASA following the 1996 election of L. Aloysius Wren to the American presidency. He'd spent the last five years blandly defending the status quo ante and NASA continued to build whatever it had money to build. The new project startup for the *Herschel* Uranus orbiter was the crowning achievement of his administration. It would be for his successor, under a new president, to get it built and launched.

"How are you doing, Brad?" Oberg supposed he might be suffering from a little motion sickness, but this was

Harveson's third orbital junket and he seemed to adapt to weightlessness faster than most astronauts. Perhaps it was the in-over-my-head effect.

Harveson shrugged. "Enjoying being here, I guess. I like space. Sometimes I wish I'd applied to be an astronaut after I finished graduate school in the late seventies. I probably would've made it."

"Why didn't you?"

"I figured some of them would get blown to bits. And some of them did."

"So?" He said the German word, with its cargo of tonality and altered meaning. "You came up here in an antique STS-A class shuttle that's far more dangerous than it was twenty years ago. What changed your mind?"

Harveson smiled. "Being blown to bits seems a lot less appalling at age fifty-two than it did when I was twenty-five."

Oberg felt faint surprise. Perhaps there were unsuspected depths here. A bit of movement in the hatchway caught his eye. He looked up, then called out, "Professor Schnurr!"

At ninety-one, Günther Schnurr was by far the oldest man ever to travel in space and, to many, he was a harbinger of things to come. Tall, frail, spindly, with a shock of crisp white hair and bright little mulberry eyes, he was becoming increasingly famous as the personification of the space age. In a sense, he was History. Born in Bremerhaven in 1911, he'd been with the *VfR* in Berlin, then with Von Braun at Peenemunde. He'd come over with the "hundred Germans" after the war and worked on Redstone and Saturn. At his retirement from NASA in 1976, he'd said an unpleasant truth: "We gave you a twenty-year technological lead on the rest of the world. Too bad you poured it down the toilet." His coworkers of the time pointed to *Viking* and called him an ingrate. He pointed to the last *Saturn V*, lying on its side in the grass and laughed. *"Viking.* Idiots. You could be there in person."

His bitter retirement lasted for a decade, living in Titusville and watching the shuttles take off, then a lifetime of low-level metal toxicity caught up with him and his mind disappeared down the black hole of Alzheimer's disease. He was institutionalized the week *Challenger* fell into the sea. His family got him in as one of the first people to be treated by a near-magical whole-system chelating and blood washout, and he came back from nowhere at all. Those who'd known him before could not say if he was the same man, but one thing they all agreed on: He had never been brighter, or more energetic.

Schnurr's face lit up. "Ah, my little friend Hermann!" His German had a very peculiar sounding accent, the permanent mark of his having lived for a half century in the southeastern United States. He was the organizer and chairman of this conference, an outgrowth of his new career coordinating the various joint projects of NASA, ESA, and assorted Japanese, Chinese, and Soviet space agencies. He pulled himself into a nearby chair and said, "This space travel is wonderful. I feel as though I could live forever up here."

Oberg nodded, thinking of the old science fiction stories about orbiting cardiac hospitals and multi-century lifespans, but Harveson said, "Maybe not. If you stay up more than ninety days, your immune system starts to go."

"Perhaps, but that hasn't stopped the Soviets."

"Speaking of whom . . ."

Oberg looked up at the doorway. "Good morning, Fyodor Karlovich," he said, speaking Russian.

Academician Akhmatov looked very pale and tense, with new lines about his eyes that aged him considerably. Oberg supposed it had to do with the recall of the lunar landing mission, whose sole stated purpose was to put an IKI/Vernadskii scientist on the Moon. Now, the Russian winced. "Friend Oberg, the quality of your Russian continues to mystify me. Perhaps we could use your far more sonorous English at this time."

Though taken aback, Oberg laughed. "It's merely lack of practice. I get to speak German, French, and English every day. My Russian is kept up mostly by watching the international broadcast of *Vremya*." He watched as the man bounced clumsily over to his seat, then said, "You seem ill, Fyodor Karlovich. Is anything amiss?"

Akhmatov shook his head. "Nothing. Perhaps a touch of motion sickness."

"But you were all right yesterday."

"These things have their own way of progressing. It was a little cold in the taxi last night. I think being docked to the station interferes with its temperature regulation scheme." He looked about the little room. "Good morning to you all." The others nodded.

Oberg leaned forward and said, "How is the recalled lunar mission doing?"

Akhmatov looked at him expressionlessly for a moment, eyes heavy-lidded. "As you must know from the news media, the cosmonauts, though disappointed, are happy to be reunited with their families on Earth."

Oberg sat back in his chair. "We are all naturally curious about the problems you encountered, Academician," he said coolly, "and fifteen years of *glasnost* have colored our expectations."

The Russian stared out the window at Earth for a long moment, squinting to make out the contours of southern Africa, then he rubbed a hand over his forehead, massaging one temple slowly. "Sorry." He turned to look Oberg in the eye. "You too have a responsible position, Hermann Oberg. How can I chastise subordinates who leak information to the press prematurely, if I am not careful myself about what I say?"

"I . . . see." And what was this about? He looked over at Harveson, but the American seemed oblivious to the interplay, continuing to gaze dreamily out into space. "Perhaps we should order breakfast now." There was a clank as one of the station's young crewmen came through the hatch, throwing it open wider in his haste.

"Dr. Harveson!"

The man returned to the room with a start. "What is it, Bill?"

"We just pulled in the regular direct news feed off the EaStar Six comsat. Today's CTN editorial says the Russians recalled that moonship so they could load it up with nuclear weapons and head out to the asteroid belt!"

"What?" Harveson looked completely baffled. "That's absurd!" He turned to look at the Russian. "Academician, do you know anything about this?"

Akhmatov sighed gustily, looking vastly relieved. Oberg watched with interest as the years peeled away and color returned to the man's cheeks. "Well," he said, "now the leak has happened and my responsibility is at an end." He turned to face them all, almost smiling. "Colleagues, let me tell you about the correct status of Project Sinuhe. I think you will find this interesting. . . ."

• • •

Gorbachev stood on a small podium before the assembled Congress of Peoples' Deputies, looking at the quarrelsome, angry-looking mob that had elected Yeltsin. He smiled benignly, just as he had when he was president, and keyed for the text of his speech on the built-in display. He hadn't wanted to reveal the mission quite this early, but there it was. . . .

"My friends, the Soviet Union is still committed to a full-scale expansion into the inner solar system at the earliest feasible time. Unlike the rest of the world, we understand that mankind must expand into outer space, to gain a permanent foothold in the heavens, during the first half of the twenty-first century, if he is to survive as a species. Put simply, if we do not establish a spacefaring civilization at this point in history, it seems unlikely that the impoverished and desperate people who follow us will be able to do so. If we go on, confined in a finite world, then a little while down the road, in a mere generation or two, resources will begin to fail and the global economy will falter, then fall into an unrecoverable decline. In a matter of a century or two, mankind will either be extinct or reduced to Paleolithic savagery. I myself am inclined to believe the former is our more likely fate."

He paused, letting the imagery sink in. Several members in the rear gallery seemed to be having trouble staying awake. "We understand that the principal direction of the Soviet space program is aimed at erecting a permanent, self-sustaining outpost on the planet Mars. A first expedition is planned for some time after 2010, once all the necessary equipment has been proved out in Earth-orbit and on the moon. We have made great strides toward our goal; but, as you all must know by now, our first real step was halted, our lunar landing recalled.

"We will go to the Moon and go to Mars, indeed, before this century is out, Soviet men and women will penetrate to the far reaches of the solar system, setting up habitats and industries, insuring, for the first time in history, that no single disaster or political misfortune will destroy humanity before its infancy is complete. We will settle planetary space, and then we will head for the stars. . . ."

Gorbachev felt his head spinning. His words sounded so strange, like science fiction. Yet the facts were well established, and the chain of logic held. With only a little bit of exaggeration—a little bit of theatricality thrown in for effect—science fiction had become political truth. It was, after all, the twenty-first century. "Before we can make these bold strides, we must erect the infrastructure of the spacefaring civilization that will dominate the years to come. We must erect industries in space itself, so that future transport systems between Earth and space will carry nothing but people, to end the wasteful habit of transporting Earth's precious resources away into the sky! We must have factories in space. And before we can have them, we must have resources in space, raw materials from which this new civilization can fabricate its needs.

"There is nothing near Earth except the Moon, which, as you may know, is poor in many necessary materials. It is of some use, but not perfect. Mars is better, but far away in time and space. Even so, we planned to have the first expedition set up fuel-processing plants on Phobos and Deimos, so Martian explorers would not have to carry their every need all the long way from home.

"No. We must have resources in space, but near enough to Earth that the workers and their initial machinery can get to them in a reasonable span of time. Now, the Soviet Union finds itself with the opportunity to make a great step forward. We believe we have found the fulcrum with which to lever ourselves into the future. . . ."

They were brought into a small auditorium, normally used as a classroom for technical cosmonaut training. The four members of the prime crew, and their backups, pudgy Zaitsyev, the Estonian Saarmula, the phlegmatic Siberian doctor Gaurai, and Zhoresyov, a gaunt geochemist newly recruited to the ranks. They sat across the front row of desks, and Bronstein and Saarmula pulled out stenographer's pads in which to take notes.

A middle-aged, nondescript man came out on the platform in front of them and bowed slightly. "Some of you may not know me, I don't know," he said. "My name is Roman Grigoriyevich Tolstoi. I am presently head of the Glavkosmos Unmanned Flight Directorate. I am a member of the Academy of Sciences and I have been chosen to brief you on the specifics of the profile for the upcoming mission.

"As you well may know, men have never left the immediate gravitational sway of the Earth-Moon system before. The Moon, considered at the outer limits of our manned program thus far, is a stone's throw away compared with the asteroid Sinuhe. However, the delta-V necessary for rendezvous with this body is remarkably small. The reason for this is that Sinuhe is in an orbit very similar to that of the Earth, meaning that we needn't accelerate much to catch up with it.

"The journey will take approximately four weeks. Since Sinuhe's orbit lies entirely within that of the Earth, you will be launched while the Earth is ahead of the asteroid. By following an ellipse that goes outside the Earth's orbit, you will fall behind, to your own aphelion, then cross the Earth's orbit again just as Sinuhe reaches *its* aphelion. After a two-week stay at the asteroid, we will be taking a shortcut back to the Earth, cutting sharply across its orbit in a rather elongated ellipse in order to reach the Earth in about twelve more weeks. The total mission time will be one hundred and twenty-six days, well within calculated safety limits."

Tolstoi pulled out a large technical blueprint of the modified *Molotochek* command module, and tacked it up with some difficulty on the corkboard at the rear of the dais. "As you can see, there will only be minor modifications. We will be adding a full complement of exercise machinery.

"At the asteroid, you will plant a docking module and dock with it. You will conduct a thorough study of the body, including seismic, magnetic, gravitational, and geologic profiles. We will be providing you with highly accurate instruments for these endeavors. When you have fully characterized Sinuhe, you will install the steering charges, after which you will return to Earth."

Now Serebryakov signaled and was motioned to speak. "If, for some reason, I deem it necessary to study the asteroid in greater detail, will there be any slack available in the schedule?"

"That depends. If you ask early enough, we may be able to delay your return by a day or two."

"And what if Sinuhe turns out to be, as some reputable scientists have suggested, just a flying pile of loose rubble barely held together by its own gravity?"

"Comrade Serebryakov, you probably know considerably more about this subject than I do. I am with Glavkosmos, not Vernadskii or IKI, and am primarily an engineer. Should Sinuhe have no tensile strength, it is unlikely that we will be able to change its orbit with the degree of certainty necessary. In that case, we would in all likelihood scrub the asteroid orbital maneuver. How likely do you think this gloomy scenario is?"

"Not very. It is, however, still a possibility."

Tolstoi smiled condescendingly. "This is merely part one of the mission. When the asteroid is at perihelion, some months later, the nuclear charge will be detonated by remote control, directing it to a trans-Earth trajectory.

"Early in 2003, *Molotochek* will be launched again, this time to intercept Sinuhe shortly before Earth-orbit insertion. Because we need to rendezvous with the asteroid behind the Earth in its orbit, it will be necessary to loop outward a long way to drop back to where Sinuhe is. This voyage will take seventy-five days, by which time the asteroid will be ten days from the Earth.

"Now, what we know about 5007 Sinuhe. I had some notes here, but probably Comrade Serebryakov can tell us more than I have, since this sort of thing is his specialty. Comrade Serebryakov?"

Christ! On the spot. But it was true. He had so much information filed away on this subject that he could make a three-hour speech without consulting a Casio. He stood and cleared his throat. "Direct observations of asteroids were conducted by the ill-fated *Galileo* spacecraft en route to Jupiter, *CRAF,* and the Italian *Piazzi I.* We only have a detailed picture of three of them, Gaspra, Hamburga, and, the Near-Earther Orpheus. The first two are both much larger than the 0.3 km. in diameter Sinuhe, and thus the observations are by no means applicable. 3361 Orpheus, on the other hand, is only twice as big, but is of a completely different composition. On the basis of these few observations and some Earth-based science, it is possible to come to a few tentative conclusions about Sinuhe.

"We have made detailed spectrographic studies of the body and have concluded that it is most likely metallic, composed of nickel and iron. Radar bounced off the surface by the Japanese shows it to be relatively smooth in the point one to one centimeter range and relatively rough in the meter to ten meters range. As Comrade Tolstoi said, the rotational period is about ten hours. Neither of these figures is unusual for near-Earth asteroids, and it has been concluded that Sinuhe is mostly lacking in regolith and has the normal cratering expected in a body of this type."

Tolstoi nodded. "Picture a potato-shaped object with holes punched in it by random encounters with other bits of space debris. Now make it pure metal. This picture is probably similar to what we will find at Sinuhe. I must emphasize the 'probably,' however. You may find something totally unexpected."

Georges-Yves Krivine, Socialist President of the Republic of France, was an exceptionally ugly man. He was gaunt, with big, spidery hands, and stood a skeletal 191 centimeters tall. He had an undershot jaw, crooked yellow teeth, and an enormous saber nose. His head, once a garden of curly black hair, was now almost bald. Scars from a teenage automobile accident still ran here and there, cutting athwart the wrinkles. Only forty-two years old, he looked like a disfigured Charles de Gaulle clone gone horribly to seed. He relaxed now in a soft red armchair, right leg tightly crossed over the left, staring levelly out across the room, head tipped slightly down for effect. At his side sat Alain Vidal de Muroc, handsome and regal-looking at the age of thirty-nine. They were, it was said, both the architects and product of a revolution that had swept France over the past decade, blowing the postwar chaff aside and bringing the nation back to its rightful place of world leadership.

Seated across from them in a somewhat smaller chair, U.S. Ambassador Morley Pohick was patently cadaverous. Neither of the men, leading a country dominated by young men, could understand why the United States, with a reasonably young man at its own helm, would send an eighty-seven-year-old ambassador to the capital of Europe's most powerful and important state.

Krivine folded his arms and frowned. "I'll ask you again, Monsieur Pohick. Does President Wren intend any overt action to block present Soviet plans in space?"

The old man shrugged helplessly. "I cannot say, Monsieur Krivine." His voice was high-pitched and reedy, but his French, polished at the Sorbonne in the late thirties, was flawless.

Krivine glanced at Vidal, then said, "Cannot or will not?"

"I have had no instructions from my government." He paused, then lifted his head to return the President's level stare. "And I will tell you this: I do not understand what all the excitement is about. This business of asteroids strikes me as . . . inconsequential. Other than the matter of orbiting battle stations, I don't think President Wren cares how much money the Russians waste on space exploration."

Krivine sat back in his chair, contemptuous of this antiquated worldview. "Doubtless," he murmured, "that is so. Well, Monsieur Pohick, I thank you for your time and trouble. Please convey my respects to your President."

The ambassador arose stiffly, pushing off the floor with a long, thin mahogany cane, bowed with notable difficulty, and retired. When he was gone, Krivine turned to his defense minister with a wry smile. "Still they ignore us."

"Maybe so, Georges. Wren was a young man during the Vietnam era, draft age, I think. Perhaps he remembers the political trouble with France that led to our withdrawal from NATO. He may even hold us responsible for America's decline."

"There is that. I was just a child at the time and barely recall these matters. The student riots that led De Gaulle to resign seemed much more significant."

The intercom chirped quietly and a secretary announced, "Monsieur Oberg is here."

Vidal stretched in his chair, then rubbed at the dense stubble on his square chin. "Shall I go, now?"

"I think not. This is also your department. We will, in the end, have to formulate a national policy about this sort of thing."

Hermann Oberg came through the door, towering over them, seeming to fill a significant portion of the room. He bowed clumsily. "Monsieur le President. Monsieur le Minêtre."

"Please be seated."

He dropped into the chair recently vacated by Ambassador Pohick and relaxed, the sides of his paunch flowing onto its arms. "I have a presentation of sorts. If you'd like me to begin?"

"Perhaps not," said Krivine, folding his arms once more, redonning his trademark frown.

"Questions?" Oberg was disconcerted. He found it difficult enough to talk in this flowery political French instead of the almost argotlike dialect of his engineers. In any verbal fencing with a French president adept in *carte-et-sixte* he would be at a considerable disadvantage. He could feel his German persona, the most politically sophisticated of the lot, clamoring to take control, but that would be a, well, faux pas.

"Not exactly. Monsieur Oberg, as you know, France provides more than half of all the funding for ESA. Germany contributes a quarter, Italy another fifteen percent, and all the rest of EEC less than ten . . ."

Oberg pushed down a little surge of temper, feeling the heat rise toward his face, then recede. It simply would not do to be short with him just now. "Yes, Monsieur le Président. That is why all our projects have French names. And why more than half of all the work is assigned to French industrial concerns."

Krivine smiled. "Please. I am not trying to entice you to a nationalistic outburst, Monsieur Oberg. Please forgive me if I spoke in an impolitic fashion. The point is this: France provides this funding, *far* more than required by ESA regulations, because she believes that the future of humanity, ourselves as a nation, and Europe as a whole, lies out in the solar system. Monsieur Vidal and I merely want to know two things." He held up a thumb, "Is the Soviet Union going to get its money's worth out of the Sinuhe venture and," then an index finger, "Is the retrieval of this asteroid going to pose, as the Americans seem to think, a significant danger to the planet Earth?"

Oberg let his breath sigh out explosively, puffing up his cheeks. Well, he marveled, there is that. This new generation of Frenchmen, taking power in the early 1990s, had changed the game considerably. Focusing on the growing industrial might of a frequently somnolent nation, they'd poured money into ESA, bringing the *Hermes* shuttle on line two years ahead of schedule, and had beefed up their support for *Freedom* as the Americans had faded, making it a truly international space station, 40 percent owned by ESA, compared to America's 50 percent and Japan's 10 percent. Now, with Germany funding the *Sänger* spaceplane in order to get the work for its companies, there was *talk* that France might be interested in funding an expedition to the Moon. It was worth dreaming about. If *Sänger* could fly by 2010, three years ahead of schedule, and the French work began *now* . . .

"Monsieur Oberg?"

He started slightly. "I have the answers you require, Monsieur le President." He slouched down further in the chair and gazed at the two men. "As to the question of your thumb, it seems simple enough. *Galileo, Piazzi,* and CRAF gave us a fair idea about compositions and structures. The resources are there. Whether they can be brought back or not is unknown. The Soviet cosmonauts will doubtless have an answer for us by next spring."

"What sort of an answer?"

His Frog persona made him shrug, irritating the seething Kraut within. "If Sinuhe has too much regolith, the bomb project will be impossible. If the core body is too fractured, it will fragment when the first steering charge is exploded. If neither is true, the asteroid will come to Earth."

"And if it does?"

"Well." He turned to look directly at Alain Vidal de Muroc. "There is then the matter of your finger. I have telephoned Director Galeev and I think, from his reassurances, that the American fears are groundless. Deliberately dropping an asteroid on the United States would only provoke a retaliatory strike by the surviving American forces. Their submarine fleet alone could easily obliterate life on Earth. On the other hand, there is always the possibility of a genuine accident."

Vidal sat forward in his chair. "Accident."

Oberg sighed again. "If the core of Sinuhe is solid enough to withstand even a small nuclear explosion, it will be strong enough to take up an orbit well within the Roche limit. It seems likely that this object will be most useful to Soviet plans if placed in a two-thousand-kilometer orbit."

"That will require . . . straight shooting."

"Straight shooting?" Oberg laughed. "Yes it will."

Georges-Yves Krivine frowned his famous frown and his scars turned livid. "The cowboys were famous for their fine marksmanship. Do you suppose the same was true for Cossacks?"

.    .    .

Vladimir Alekseevich Manarov walked slowly down a rutted country path, feet compressing the crispy surface of the frozen mud, making a tiny squeak with every step. The snow was late this year. Soon, this path, one of his favorites since his first long stay at Zvyozdnii Gorodok, would be buried under half a meter or more of snow, and he would wax up his skies for the gasping, sweaty pleasures of true cross-country mobility. He remembered the *really* deep snows in Arkhangelsk as a reference, and Moskovskii Oblast's winters were mild by comparison.

He paused and stretched, breathing the air. This part of the woods was dominated by thin, straight birches, their gray-white trunks stretching off into the distance with a near-mathematical precision. Without the path it was very easy to get lost here. What an embarrassment for a man who had almost been to the Moon twice. He smiled and started walking again. Almost. Twice. Well, there was that. He patted his jacket pockets, feeling the crumbly Estonian chocolate bar he'd brought along for company, then the American Boy Scout compass his grandfather had given him thirty years before. The old man claimed to have gotten it as a gift from an American GI in Berlin, during that brief period of camaraderie before Stalin began to erect his nation barrier, clamping down in Eastern Europe. He supposed the story might even be true, though one had to bear in mind the exaggerations of old men. He *had* been in the army, though there was no evidence other than the compass to put him in the front lines during the final assault on the *Führerbunker*.

As the gray November sky overhead began to darken, Volodya pulled the candy from his pocket, and stripping off its silver foil wrapper, began to bite and chew. Estonian chocolate was far better than the Russian stuff, but still nothing to talk about. It lacked the creaminess of the American product and wasn't even to be mentioned in the same breath with the German candy he'd gotten from ESA crews. It would be night soon and time to head back. He pulled the compass out of his pocket, picked his direction, and then set off into the woods, ice-rimed leaves crackling underfoot.

Almost to the Moon twice. How about that? At first he'd thought it might be a record, until someone had brought up the sad case of the American Lovell. The man's assignment to the glorious first lunar orbital mission meant he would have no chance at the first landing, but did mean an opportunity to go on a subsequent mission. And so it had come to pass: assigned to the third lunar landing, he'd seen an exploding fuel cell deprive him of his only chance to go to the Moon. *Apollo* had been canceled less than three years later. I wonder how he felt about that?

Well, Volodya, you have to face this sooner or later. Why not now? You are going to be flight engineer on the first expedition to leave the Earth-Moon system. Where we're headed, the Earth will be tiny, barely noticeable in the scheme of things. You'll see it from a totally different perspective. This is something new, not a repetition of some old American stunt. How do you feel?

He couldn't tell. Objectively, it affected his chances at being the first man to set foot on Mars, lowering them ever so slightly. Or possibly raising them, one never quite knew.

Suddenly, he popped out of the woods onto the shoulder of the road he knew would be there. It was getting dark now, the temperature dropping. A brisk wind, not noticeable in the forest, was blowing leaves high into the dim twilight, making it seem even colder than it was. Pulling his collar up about his neck, he put his head down and began walking back toward the compound. This far out, he had at least an hour's trek ahead of him. He wished he had brought another candy bar.

Why don't I care more about this? Have my feelings frozen from all the hard work I had to do to get me to this place? Again, he couldn't tell. Was I always this way?

Maybe the close association with Chishak and Serebryakov was beginning to bother him. Bronstein and the others . . . they were just cosmonauts. These two . . . He understood that the doctors and scientific researchers, educated under dramatically different protocols from engineers, were a little bit different. . . . They seemed unprepared, unable to cope with the hardest parts of long-duration spaceflight, and, in a sense, proud of their weaknesses, wanting space to adapt to *them*. Like children. He had taken an immediate dislike to Chishak, but that wasn't so unusual . . . his cheap, dogmatic behavior and air of

superiority was positively old-fashioned. And Serebryakov . . .

He thought about their brief talk that morning, cut short
at his uncomfortable insistence. He hoped now the little
shit would keep his doubts to himself, not jeopardize the
mission. He stopped suddenly and stood up straight, feeling
the cold air curl around the abruptly exposed skin of his
neck, making him shiver. *How do I really feel about it? I
take these walks every night when I have the time, when I
could be home reading or playing with my kids and watching TV or fucking my wife. Why am I out here freezing in
the dark?*

It seemed like an appallingly good question. He tilted his
head back and stared into the night sky.

The clouds were clearing away now, reduced to blotches
of darkness. All over the heavens the cold, untwinkling
winter stars were appearing, peeking out through the tar-
nished silver sky. Above the trees ahead a tilted Orion was
half-shrouded by the broken clouds, each of its major stars
alternately winking out, then on again. Betelgeuse, an almost colored point of light, burned sentimentally in its appointed spot. Volodya shoved his hands in his pockets
again and resumed walking, this time keeping his face
aimed upward. *What am I doing with my life, and why?
Why don't I have an answer?*

It came to him then, more or less of its own accord: *I do
believe in the things I've been saying, after all!* Not a revelation of any significance, just, *It isn't all a sham to get me on
Mars and put my name in the history books alongside
Gagarin and Armstrong. I kept telling myself that, so I'd
be willing to make all the right political moves. And, somehow, I keep forgetting the truth.*

He had a sudden memory of himself in lunar orbit, his
first EVA away from Earth. *That powerful pulse of happiness . . .*

And again, his first EVA in Earth-orbit, clinging to the
hull of a shrunken *Mir* in 1991. Another pulse of happiness . . . and mirth. *How frightened the Canadian In-
terkosmos guest cosmonaut had been!*

He counted on his fingers, silently ticking off his voyages
into space, nine in all. Every one of them had that same
little surge of delight, concealed somewhere in the mission,
buried in his head, awaiting eventual rediscovery.

Perhaps my little Russian soul *isn't* frozen. . . .

We belong up there, and I most of all.

Troubled by a surge of unwanted memories, Volodya put his head down in the darkness and lengthened his stride, hurrying home to light and warmth and humanity.

This is the last of it, he thought. Where I go now, I go alone, with no strength but my past. . . .

# CHAPTER 3

## *April 30, 2002*

On the Danish island called Sjaelland, near the town of Helsingør, two men walked along the ramparts of Kronborg Slot. One was pudgy and old; the other paunchy, taller, and, relatively, young. They both had round faces, but one was jolly and condescending, the other furrowed and earnest. The air was cool and salty, clear enough to easily make out details on the Swedish shore eight kilometers away. Below, in the fortress's interior, the retinue of one of the men waited patiently.

It had not been easy for Hermann Oberg to catch up with General Secretary Gorbachev. The man's whirlwind publicity tour through the capitals of Europe had once again reassured the fickle populace that Russia was not the rending bear of old but a pussycat, friendly, playful, and easily domesticated. Now, with the news of *Molotochek*'s mission alarming the right-wingers, he was, as always, in the proper place to dispel Europe's fears. He had spoken before the British Parliament two days earlier, an unprecedented violation of tradition promoted by the Labor PM, Betty Bork MacKay; he outlined in broad terms the plans for Sinuhe and magnanimously offered limited mining rights to the asteroid to any spacefaring nation. Why the USSR had not announced its plans until the news had been leaked he did not say.

"But, General Secretary," Oberg's grating Russian cut the wind like a buzzsaw. "You simply cannot go ahead with the plan!"

Gorbachev stopped and looked south past Helsingør, where the sun, moving towards its solstice, crowded the horizon, wondering how the man had developed such a bizarre accent. It was a German accent, mind you . . . but flat and angular, like the voice Russian actors used when they were hired to dub in the voice of John Wayne for a movie. He smiled. "Come, come, Herr Oberg. I cannot believe that someone like you, committed to the eventual conquest of the extraterrestrial, would be opposed to a plan of such a nature. It is not only a beautiful idea, as the torso of a woman is beautiful, it is simplicity itself. Mankind will have made a genuine leap, not the paltry step the Americans made so long ago. Do you really hate and fear the Soviet Union so much that you would let your emotions blind you to real accomplishment?"

Oberg looked hard into the self-satisfied face. A Cheshire cat, smiling and smiling until it was impossible to say what other features had been there. But the irony of it all struck him, too. That *he* would be standing here arguing against a project that he wouldn't have even dreamed possible for fifty years to come. Perhaps he was wrong to do so. But the dangers were so great! He had firmly believed that the continual neck-and-neck competition between the USA and USSR was the only thing that maintained the balance of power. This was the exact kind of destabilizing influence that would ruin the slow progress toward the peaceful, spacefaring world that he wanted so badly. There was no telling how the USA would react.

"But the Americans—"

"I needn't tell you that Reagan, Bush, and now Wren have made it clear that space is open to anything and everything. We see no reason to feel squeamish about stepping on their toes. After all, *Eisenhower* is almost half-completed— and we have complained about their SDI until we are blue in the face, to no avail."

"But they won't let you get away with it. They have—"

"Nonsense, Herr Oberg. I doubt if they could stop us if they wanted to. What will they use, their 'Space Tug?' Until this asteroid is actually in Earth-orbit, it will be traveling in a trajectory that is well beyond the capabilities of their hardware."

"You don't seem to understand, General Secretary. I have known for many years that the American space program is flawed. We all know it. Virtually every NATO nation has come out against the completion of Project Overlord. There are forces at work in their government that are not subject to the ordinary give-and-take of reasoned discourse. Remember, they are basically an ignorant and backward people, cut off by choice from the flow of European civilization. Most of them are unable to locate their own country on a globe. Their media may whip the whole thing up past the point where even their leaders can't control the response."

"Ignorant and backward . . . and the USSR, presumably, no longer fits that description also?"

Oberg blanched. It was not a good time for Western European chauvinism. "Not at all, General Secretary. All I'm saying is that you should do it all more gradually, give everyone time to adapt. Future shock is a real force in the world, right now. There are—"

"You need say no more, sir." A strange illumination seemed to shine in Gorbachev's face. "What is a man, if his chief good and market of his time be but to sleep and feed? We have cause and will and strength and means to do't. And do it we shall."

Gorbachev smiled his winning smile and held out a hand for a handshake. The interview was over.

Anton was approaching the intersection with the Outer Ring Road, and signs bearing large arrows directed him in various directions. He directed his Russian-built Citroen sedan into the right lane, towards the off ramp, gently depressing the brake to slow down to fifty kilometers per hour. These Western-style cloverleafs were a relatively new addition to the Russian road system, and, for some reason, were the least well maintained. He shot onto the roughest section of highway since Bykovo, trying to slow down further in anticipation of the obstacle course to come. A poorly fitted joint in the concrete volleyed the car cruelly. By the time his speed had dropped to fifteen he was shaken to the bone. For some reason, he had expected them to have fixed the road; it was, after all, past spring thaw.

Traffic along the Ring Road was light. At one-thirty in the afternoon, there was not much traffic anywhere. Although the number of automobiles in the Soviet Union had quintupled in the last fifteen years, most belonged to enthusiastic workers who used them solely for commuting. At five, this stretch of highway would be bumper-to-bumper. He increased his speed to ninety, edging over into the left lane. Here the road was as smooth as the inside of a spacesuit, and the Citroen purred along compellingly.

Anton was gaining rapidly on a small blue car in his lane, and he swung over to the right to avoid it. Damn thing couldn't be going more than sixty, he thought. Suddenly the familiar outline of the car fell into place. It was an old Zastava 45, identical with the first automobile he'd ever owned. Yugoslavian made, it was roomy for a subcompact, and handled well, especially in the snow. It had given him years of relatively trouble-free travel. He smiled to himself. How easily one got used to a higher level of comfort and performance. He had thought himself the king of the highway putting along in his little old Yugo; now he couldn't imagine putting up with the inconvenience of the thing.

And he had almost missed the turnoff onto Entuziastov, lost again in his oblivious thoughts. He rotated the steering wheel, vowing to concentrate on driving.

Moskva was once again emerging from its winter pall-cocoon. Trees of the most enchanting shades of spring-green, somewhat in advance of their country cousins because of the city's heat-sink, filled the parks and borders along the road. The looming high rises, stretching off toward the west like ill-placed dominoes, seemed almost a respectable place to live. Anton turned onto a small side street and into the large, mostly full parking lot, finding a place to park not far from the entrance to the Zheleznodorozhaya apartment building where Darya Grazhdanina lived. It was appropriate to name the building after the train workers, since it was located in the V formed by two grimy railroads.

Anton never called in advance, somehow liking to pretend that these sessions were "spontaneous." Darya was, as usual for this time of day, home. As she ushered him into her small but attractively furnished apartment, Anton noted that her computer was on, and the thin column of text that was undoubtedly her latest poem was displayed on its monitor. "Tonya," she said, "it's so good to see you again." He took a seat on the fashionable paisley divan across from the sliding glass door to the balcony, and the woman perched on an overstuffed armchair nearby.

Darya and he had known each other a long time, yet he was continually surprised by her changes of appearance.

Now her hair was in its natural, black color, loosely hung in smooth cascades that fell over her shoulders and down her back. The width of her face was exaggerated by the center-parted canopy of hair that hung back over her ears in swags. Her widespread, man-in-the-moon eyes and flat, high cheekbones were not the stuff of fashion models, yet, somehow, they only emphasized the beauty and vitality of her look. She smiled demurely, her eyes flashing. "Can I get you some tea?"

Anton fidgeted slightly, rubbing his hand on the tasseled edge of the armcover. "Sure. Do you have any jam?" He looked up again. Coming here was never easy.

She disappeared into the tiny kitchen, hidden by long strands of plastic baubles, and reappeared in a moment with a glass mug filled with dark-brown liquid and a hint of red at the bottom. She placed the tea on the table in front of him and went back to her place on the chair. "How have you been?"

Anton relaxed slightly, leaning back into the plush upholstery and uncrossing his legs. "All right, I suppose, Darya. I'm back for a final briefing and to pick up a portable computer that I'm supposed to use on the mission. Hot stuff direct from Hong Kong. Top secret, of course."

She laughed. "Of course."

"Aside from that my life is in its usual mess. No girls, no fun. Just work and the company of three cold thugs. I'm half convinced I'll go insane during the months in space. How's Zhenya?"

"Fine. Still working on that promised novel. At the rate he's going he'll never get out of the Writers' Union bureaucracy and become a real writer."

"I did see his piece in *Novii Mir* though. Pretty good stuff."

"My *Vkys vo rtu* is finally out. Do you want a copy?"

"Sure, Darya. I always like your work. I'll take it up with me; I've got a kilo or so to spare. Maybe if I read some real poetry to those Philistines, they'll loosen up a bit. What are you working on now?"

"Nothing much. The space thing. Early spring always brings me down. But you know that as well as anybody."

He smiled. "I suppose I do. Our relationship *is* getting pretty old. What is it now, five, almost six years?"

"I haven't seen much of you since you became a goody-

goody cosmonaut, though, Tonya. I am beginning to get jealous."

"Starry Town is a long way off. And the Moon is even further. I've been very busy, my dear. I dream about you virtually every night, though."

"That's good to hear. Shall we dispense with the rest of the conversation?"

He finished the tea, letting the fruity sugars bathe his teeth and tongue. "Not yet. I like talking first."

"Of course."

"After such a long time it's hard for me to get my mind focused on sex. There's an initial barrier I have to tear down, brick by brick."

"You're just shy, Tonya; nothing wrong with that. You should let your mind unfocus; this is not a task. You have nothing to do except enjoy yourself. There are no responsibilities."

"I know that. Read me your latest poem."

She laughed. "I can recite it to you.

> Big yellow tears in the night sky tell
> Me that the essential substance has died.
> Strange and silent screams lash the night.
> The torque on the world has run down and
> Will soon dispel gravity's mystique.

"That's all so far."

"Sounds like a poem for cosmonauts all right. Is there any hope coming at the end?"

"Certainly, my silver one. A poem is not publishable if it doesn't come right in the final stanza."

"Okay. I think I'm ready now."

She came over and joined him on the divan, swiping back a sagging strand of hair, smiling like a cat. Wordless, she caressed his cheek, her fingers catching on the rough nap of his beard-shadow. He looked into her eyes' cool depths, then away. She kissed him under the ear and took a firm hold on the tight muscles at the back of his neck, squeezing and rubbing away tension that Tonya had not realized was there. Tingles of pleasure spread across his scalp, and he closed his eyes.

Suddenly, she was undoing his belt. He let his head sink back on to the back of the couch, briefly noticing the geology-like texture of the white ceiling. Darya unbuttoned his fly and spread back the flaps of his pants. He felt the weight of her head on his lap, then the tickling sensation of his underwear being peeled back. She ran her fingers under the mass of his genitals, pulling them gently away from his body. He sighed with pleasure, yet the erection had still not come. It always took a long time.

A warm breath on him preceded the sensation of being engulfed by hot, wet flab that tensed slightly as it went, pulling back slowly, away from him. He was getting hard now, feeling the familiar sensations. In some ways this initial contact was the only advantage this kind of sex had over masturbation—although after some gentle questioning Darya had developed a technique that produced an entirely different kind of orgasm from just whacking off. But of course the entire situation produced a different frame of mind that could just as well have been responsible for the different sensations.

It was ironic that his sexual life had come to this. He had decided to sacrifice everything for success and knowledge, and, indeed, he now had nothing. Without the imminent mission to the asteroid and the path already set for him by the general secretary, he would be stalled in impotent inertia, without a life at all, really. Darya was as close to him as anyone; she acted the part of friend, at least. He wondered uncontrollably what Carla was doing at this moment, and he had a vision of her face looking down at him, loose brown hair cascading around her slim face like a sloppy fringe. And then *that* look.

The ripping surges of pleasure reached deep into his torso, and the motions of the woman's head grew slower, dying off into stillness. Sweat beaded on his forehead, and his back began to itch. Instead of the peaceful relaxation that should have come, Anton felt a quick sense of foreboding that didn't go away. The skin around his shoulder blades began to crawl.

"I won't come back from this, Daryushka."

She looked up at him curiously, swallowing thickly.

"Something is going to happen out there. Something bad."

"You're just nervous, Tonya. Things'll work out all right. Don't strain your mind worrying about what you have no control over."

His eyes strayed back to the ceiling, and he studied it, looking for something. "You are right, of course. I just feel so wretched sometimes."

She righted herself, and caressed him again. "We all feel that way, Serebryusha, only some of us know that it means nothing to feel bad. Only good feelings are true."

"If it were only so simple," he said, genuinely wishing that it was.

Southern Kazakhstan, a little to the northeast of the Aral Sea, roughly midway between the towns of Baikonur and Tyuratam, is flatter than Kansas. It is, in fact, an analog of Barsoom, being Earth's newest dead sea-bottom. Along with the ever-shrinking Caspian, Lake Balkhash, and such temporary bodies as Lake Tengiz, site of the Soviet Union's only manned splashdown, the Aral Sea, now little more than a stretch of mud flats, is a remnant of the great Sarmatian Sea, which existed until historical times. In Odysseus' day, a bold seaman could have taken his ship up into the Euxine Sea, through the broad, shallow straits north of Colchis, land of the Golden Fleece, into an unknown ocean that, only in later times, had a name. And beyond that? In those days it was drying fast, but the waters still reached to the mountainous west coast of China, to the now desert Taklamakan basin and the valley of the Tarim Darya. There is no evidence that anyone made such a voyage, but the legends persist.

Baikonur Cosmodrome covers several hundred square kilometers of salt desert, slightly closer to Tyuratam than to its namesake. A political move to rename it S. P. Korolyov Space Center, in place of a small bit of Cold War indirection, never quite mustered enough support; but then tradition recovered Cape Canaveral's name as well. Founded on work begun in 1947, it was here that the *Semyorka* launchpads, platforms suspended above deep pits, were built during the 1950s and 1960s. It was from here that the first ICBMs headed for Siberia and the Pacific, from here that *Sputnik, Luna, Vostok,* and *Venara* had risen into space, each trailing a quincunx of fire. Though Old Mark Seven was still flying after forty-five years, the focus of Baikonur had slowly shifted, first to the Proton launch complexes of the seventies and eighties, then to the tall rotating service towers of the powerful Energiya and its winged manned stage, the reusable *kosmicheskii korabl.*

Though ten heavy-lift vehicles were in various stages of preparation in the cavernous new horizontal assembly buildings to the southwest, today only space shuttle *Raduga,* christened "Rainbow" after the Norse highway to heaven, stood on the pad, mounted to its fat, blunt Energiya booster. In an effort to increase safety, a solid-fuel extractor rocket had been built into the shuttle's tailcone, and that one item had saved a crew during the only flight abort in fourteen years, when one of the liquid-fuel booster engine assemblies had failed in a 1997 ascent. The efficiency of the engines had increased a little and, by and large, the system worked.

With the various service towers rotated back, *Raduga* stood wreathed in white vapor, outlined against the brilliant blue sky of a Central Asian spring. A brisk but acceptable wind was blowing, carrying the mist away in great curling sheets, and the day threatened to be warm. The swarming technicians were gone now, and an expectant hush settled over the pad. Although there were no obvious indications of activity, the launch was less than two minutes away.

Inside the *Raduga* orbiter, ten men waited with the usual mixture of fear, boredom, and elation. Manarov and Bronstein, spacesuited as for all Soviet launches, lay on their backs, feet up, strapped into the two rear seats on the flight deck. Bronstein was staring wordlessly, straight ahead, between the shoulders of Sultanov, the pilot, and Rukavishnikov, the flight engineer, where a featureless sky beckoned. Manarov had his head tilted back to see through the big docking windows behind him. In the windowless lower equipment bay, Chishak and Serebryakov occupied the rearmost seats. Above them, four more men, technicians headed for a crew rotation on space station *Mir,* were strapped into the remaining seats.

Volodya's headset was abuzz with the chatter of an imminent launch. Though he had never been a member of a shuttle flight crew, the words were all familiar. This was his tenth ascent into Earth-orbit, his eighth aboard a space shuttle, and it was all down to a routine. This was, in fact, the fiftieth launch of a Soviet shuttle, the seventh reflight of *Raduga.*

The countdown swept past the minute mark, flight crew and ground controllers discussing the status of fuel lines and pump assemblies. Unlike the American's abbreviated argot, Russian space technicians used an elaborate and precise language full of complex polysyllabic terms. It was difficult to learn, but once learned, highly useful.

With thirty seconds to go before launch, things began to happen. There was a series of clunks as various plugs began to drop from their sockets on the hull of *Raduga*. The escape platform detached itself and began to swing away. It was this object which had aborted the first launch of *Buran,* so long ago. The enormous mass of the platform had to get itself out of the way in a very few seconds. This time, it worked, and now the men were truly alone. If anything went wrong between now and launch-plus-thirty seconds, when velocity had built to the point where the extractor rocket could work, there was no hope of survival. An explosion on the pad would scatter them across the landscape. An engine failure during the period of vertical ascent would drop them back to the ground in a nonaerodynamic pirouette.

Volodya watched the platform go and smiled. We've been lucky so far. The thought of sudden and violent death didn't bother him. Much. Spacefarers everywhere still wondered about the ones who'd died. Komarov's thirty seconds after his parachute failed, strapped into a capsule, roman-candling onto the steppe. Patsaev, Dobrovolsky, and Volkov reaching out hopelessly for a valve handle as their air whistled away into space. The *Challenger* crew's two long minutes as they arced down to the sea, breathing their emergency air and knowing full well it was all over.

The countdown reached zero. There were four quick pulses as the hydrogen-burning sustainer core engines lit, a small vibration, and yellow-white light began to peer through the windows, reflected off a cloud that began spreading out onto the desert. The pulses continued, smaller, in a subtle, complex pattern, as the sixteen kerosene-fueled engines of the strap-on boosters were touched off. The light reddened, then swiftly regained its brightness as dark smoke mingled with the steam clouds. The vibration steadied and died down. Suddenly, the hold-down clamps released their grip on the rocket and they were on their way.

As always with a liquid-fuel rocket, the initial acceleration was gentle indeed. The ship rose slowly at first, its twenty engines struggling to keep it upright, taking more than twelve seconds to clear the enormous discharge-arrester towers, then the pressure began to build. The climb was straight up at first, pulling away from the Earth, burning prodigious quantities of fuel. Thirty seconds into the flight, at an altitude of some five kilometers, *Raduga* and Energiya began to tip toward the northeast, rolling to place the shuttle orbiter underneath. Volodya felt a certain tension in him begin to release. From this point on, if anything went wrong there was at least a slim chance of survival. The extractor rocket could break them away from an exploding Energiya. It would take expert piloting indeed to get the orbiter down safely if that happened but, in theory at least, it could be done.

He craned his neck forward in the space helmet, tipping his head to one side to look out the window, seeking a more natural perspective. First Lake Tengiz passed underneath, then Lake Seletyteniz, just before they crossed the Siberian border, passing between Omsk and Novosibirsk. The ground below was green-gray-brown, saying farewell to winter, and the sky outside was beginning to darken.

Sultanov called out staging and lightning flashed outside, the brilliant plumes of solid-fuel rockets briefly enveloping the stack. This was another crucial point, hard to engineer. Because Energiya had four strap-on boosters arrayed symmetrically around the sustainer core, that meant they had to leave in two units, first the ventral pair, then the dorsal. The second pair to go had to be propelled away from the ship very carefully, as they were quite close to the wings of the orbiter. The maneuver was accomplished both by aiming the solid-fuel rockets carefully and by gimballing the engines of the sustainer to produce movement in the opposite direction. The boosters swung away gracefully, one-two, one-two, and were gone. Soon their nose cones would break away and they would begin parachuting toward a recovery zone north of Tomsk, between the Ket and Chulym rivers. Each would be ruined by its impact with the hard ground, but all the pieces would survive, engines to be rebuilt and reused, hardware refurbished, hull recycled as scrap.

The flight continued, acceleration dropping for a while to

almost nothing. The low mountains of East Siberia came under them, flattened by distance and marked with clouds. Volodya looked hard for landmarks but could see little. That big river had to be the Lena, of course, which meant those had to be the Verkhoyansk Mountains, but nothing looked familiar. The pilot called staging again and there was a slight jolt as the orbiter broke free.

They rolled almost at once, belly to the Earth, and watched as the Energiya sustainer core, a huge, featureless white cylinder, receded slowly into a black sky. Suddenly, eight small solid-fuel braking rockets fired, sparkling reddish-yellow around the nose, and it began to fall away. This was crucial to the economy of space flight. The vehicle would reenter over the Magadan region, hopefully falling on land. Explosives would blast the engine compartment free for a relatively gentle parachute descent. The hull, light now and empty, would tumble to the ground on its own.

The pilot rolled them back into a dorsal-down attitude and lit off the orbital maneuvering system engines. Without this long burn, *Raduga* would have to land somewhere in the central Pacific. Theoretically, they could come down in Chile, after a long glide, but politics and recovery convenience virtually dictated an emergency landing at Hawaii. Otherwise it would have meant ditching in the water, somewhere near the Equatorial Recovery Fleet.

Volodya watched the Kommandorskii Islands recede out of his view, his last sight of *Rodina* for more than an hour, then they were over the featureless Ocean Sea. He watched the dark water and cloud sweep by below, waiting for islands and the beauty of the Andes, and felt that certain pulse of happiness sweep through his nerves once again.

Outside, over a black Earth, greenly floodlit against a starry sky, *Mir* floated less than five hundred meters away. In some ways it was the same station begun in 1986, even though no original components remained in place, but in other ways it was vastly different. It was based on the same notion, made up of those same *Salyut*-like modules, but now there were twelve of them hooked together, two basestations tail-to-tail, a docking ball at either end, sprouting five exchangeable science and engineering modules apiece. Between the modules, each one sized to fit the capacious bay of a *kosmicheskii korabl,* stretched endless sheets and trees of black and gold solar-power cells. The whole thing added up to what the Americans and Europeans called a "keel," living space for twenty-four permanent crew and another twelve short-term visitors. When the second keel was added in 2004 there would be room for forty-eight men and the same twelve visitors. This was the maximum dimension allowed for in a *kosmodom.* If any further expansion was required, Glavkosmos would have to go to the spinning wheel of a *kosmograd,* now scheduled for construction no sooner than 2017.

Bronstein eased up to where Volodya crouched in the overhead bay and floated beside him, gently bumping against his side every now and again, staring out at the space station, which, from this angle, looked a little bit like an old clipper ship. It was a distinctly Russian design, functional, all simple components, completely unstreamlined. That was the bad thing about the shuttles. As with supersonic aircraft, you had to look sharp to know if a design was American or Russian, European, or even Japanese. Sometimes he envied Manarov, who'd managed two flights aboard the old *Soyuz* ships before the shuttle fleet grew large enough to take over completely. He nudged the man. "About five minutes?"

Manarov looked at his watch. "More or less." He stared again at the station, then said, "Not an elegant design."

Seasoned enough to avoid shrugging, Bronstein, slightly offended, said, "It works. What more do you want?" Suddenly, beyond *Mir,* in the night below, somewhere in the South Atlantic, lightning bloomed. From this distance, it was a small, almost insignificant thing, but beautiful. A section of the dark clouds burst into a brilliant, blue-violet glow that sharpened, then faded. It propagated in all directions, followed by a swift succession of lesser blasts, mostly a fiery red-orange. His gaze returned to the space station. Someone passed in front of one of the small portholes, blocking the light.

Manarov said, "It's like an automobile engine. The design has evolved over time, making utilitarian changes to serve new purposes, kludged into unnecessary complexity." He glanced at Bronstein. "Have you ever looked at *Eisenhower* through the station's mapping scope?"

Still staring out at the night, waiting for the first pearl of light in the northeast, the other man shook his head.

"A disk, twelve spokes, and the beginnings of a rim. It'll look like a wagon wheel when they're finished. Then they rotate it for artificial gravity. A thousand times more sophisticated than these metal cans."

Bronstein nodded. "I suppose our own *kosmograd* won't look much different, when the time comes."

"Look. The dawn."

The thing was preceded by a ripple of colors as light began to spill over the Earth's limb. A subtle stratospheric rainbow led the way, light refracted ahead of the sun, growing into a spreading crescent that outlined the edge of the world. Volodya watched the light grow swiftly, the scene changing in fractions of a second, and supposed that nowhere else would such a sight be possible. On airless worlds like the Moon, the terminator was a sharp demarcation, dark on one side, light on the other. On Mars, perhaps . . . but Mars's tenuous atmosphere was full of fine dust, forward scattering its dawn in monochrome hues. The sun was a sudden bead on the horizon, a brilliant hole in the sky, blinding even through these ultraviolet-opaque windows. The stars had washed out, leaving the sky a featureless black void. Crisp sunlight flooded over *Mir*, etching its details in stark relief, abruptly covering it in floodlit shadows. Blue-white-brown flowed over the horizon, swept under them, and the day was begun, the sun rising with dispatch, arcing down the sky in a southbound azimuthal curve.

In their headsets, Commander Sultanov said, "Prepare for docking. Three minutes please." Manarov and Bronstein floated back to their respective seats and strapped in as regulations dictated.

Head tipped back, Sultanov gripped his two controllers and stared at *Mir* through the *vzor* optical orientation device etched into the main docking window. The flight engineer kept his gaze fixed on his instruments, especially the bright letters on his CRT screen, which gave real-time status figures on the ship's orbital/attitude maneuvering system. After fifty flights, it just wouldn't do to relax and have an accident with the pride of Soviet industry.

The pilot moved his hands ever so slightly and the ship's thrusters grunted like distant drums. *Raduga* began creeping toward its goal, accelerating to a closure rate that was no more than two meters per second. Volodya nodded approvingly. A little more than four minutes to contact.

"A little overpressure in number six fuel cell." Sultanov reached out and typed something on the alphanumeric console to his right. *Mir* grew swiftly in the window until it was no more than fifty meters away, seeming to rush toward them at ramming speed. The pilot muttered to himself, tweaked his controls, the thrusters echoed his mutter and velocity was halved. When the station was a mere ten meters away, he cut the speed again, this time to a bare hundred centimeters per second, a very slow crawl indeed. This was the most difficult part of the mission, for the shuttle's docking adaptor, just like its American counterpart, was located within the cargo bay, the pilot following a line that ended nowhere near his eyes.

"One meter," said the flight engineer.

The pilot took his eyes off the window, lowering his chin until he could look at his own big CRT. The color camera located within the docking apparatus showed him a good view of the station's incoming portal, a flower of metal and wires. Shadows grew suddenly, then there was a crumpling sound, transmitted through structural members, and *Raduga* lurched with a gentle impact.

"Contact," said the flight engineer. He reached forward and began throwing switches.

"Positive capture," he said, and "Soft dock." He reached out and twiddled some other controls. The ship moved again, ever so gently, as servomechanisms reeled them in. From somewhere there came a definite, authoritative clank. "Hard dock achieved."

Manarov and Bronstein exhaled together, then Bronstein said, "Good work, Vanya. Very smooth."

Sultanov pulled off his headset. "Thank you, colleague."

Volodya Manarov opened his eyes into darkness. In the distance something whispered, a dim, steady vibration, reassuring, like the heartbeat of a trustworthy machine. Behind it, something groaned, the ghost of machines past.

No where, no when, he thought, his mind still hazy and peculiar. I had a dream. What was it about? He wriggled his arms up out of the sleeping bag and stretched, hands brushing against the corrugated ceiling of the chamber. I can't remember. He blinked his eyes hard, feeling the slight gumminess that blood-filled sinuses brought, and looked for signs of light. It was coming back. He unzipped the cocoon and floated free in the little room. It was pleasant to wake up in microgravity.

The dream had been a strange one. He shut his eyes and concentrated. He'd been in a buoyant blue space filled with water and light. Floating free, with cool, fresh currents lazing across his skin. There were no fish and no clouds. The water had been clear, like one of the cold, spring-fed lakes he'd seen in the Far East, in the Kirghiz Republic, but in the distance was . . . blackness. Down and around all was darkness, as if he were on a deep-sea dive to some oceanic abyss. You could look up as well and the view was the same, and little particulate matter was suspended in the water. But there was light, quite intense, coming from some well-defined source, like a floodlight, or perhaps two. Still, no matter how he turned himself, the light stayed out of view behind his back.

Very odd. *Probably I was dreaming about the neutral buoyancy tank EVA simulator and somehow lost all the detail.* He shrugged and started putting the dream out of his mind, but the mere fact of its memory nagged at him. *I like having dreams, but not when they are mysterious. This one felt freighted with obscure meaning, the sort of thing you take to a fortune teller. At least it wasn't a nightmare, like the time I dreamed I was aboard an exploding shuttle.* That had been hard, tumbling end over end in a vibrating coffin while the pilots made their laconic comments over the radio. "Cabin structure disarticulated . . . pressure failure imminent . . . loss of flight vehicle probability one point zero . . ." He'd awakened in a shaking cold sweat on the morning of his first shuttle flight, cursing the vehicle's lack of a launch escape system. Say what you like about the antiquated *Soyuz*, it had been safe. One crew had even survived an on-the-pad explosion.

Light suddenly illuminated the outside of his eyelids. His eyes popped open into a tiny room filled with material things, every wall less than an arm's length away. As *Mir* orbited the earth, it slowly turned, and now the shadows had swept away from his covered porthole. He could see a rim of bright light around the edge of the cover, dimly lighting his bed chamber. He reached up, folded back the thin metal plate, and looked out.

He was looking straight down on the world from a thousand kilometers up. Because the station was docked to a fully fueled *Molotochek,* its length more than doubled, it was oriented along the gravity gradient by tidal force. Even though *Raduga* was still docked to the port on the other end of *Mir,* mass was concentrated in the fuel tanks of the now interplanetary ship. Interplanetary . . . He savored the word for a moment, then backed away from it. Too soon.

It was broad daylight down there and they were passing over the United States, heading southeast across the western desert. He squinted at the bright ground. It was hard to tell from this high up, but they seemed to be over Utah. That was definitely the Great Salt Lake, America's Aral Sea, and those were the Rockies, brown, some snowcapped, a little east of their immediate ground track. Absolutely cloudless. Perhaps they stood directly above the Roan Mountains. He'd seen photographs of the red sandstone desert and marveled at how much it looked like Mars. Astronauts sometimes trained there and said that, at dawn, the sky was even the right shade of pink.

And will I ever go to Mars? It seemed more probable now. After decades of excessive caution, Soviet cosmonauts were finally headed out from the Earth. If it seemed wonderful to be going to the Moon at last, this . . . venture . . . was impossibly grand. I am going into interplanetary space. And I know what it means. If this succeeds, and a subsequent lunar landing succeeds, we will have done everything necessary to land on Mars. We will have all the equipment. And all the training. And all the testing. And I could be on Mars for my fiftieth birthday.

He slowly pulled on a pair of shorts, then snapped shut the porthole, numbed by thought. He opened the door to his cubicle and slipped out into a dim, cool corridor, headed for the tiny zero-g shower stall in the lower part of the module. Out here the whisper of the station's environmental control system was louder, air running through conduits to all the spaces filled with men. And the groaning of the docking modules as they shifted orientation ever so slightly was louder as well, the price they paid for a station that could be rebuilt in major components.

Time to start the day. Mars was in the future. Right now there was a hard vacuum waiting for him.

Miroslav Bronstein sat in *Mir*'s mess-hall module, legs tucked under the leg restraints of a tiny, stoollike bench, thinking about his name. Silly when you considered it that way. Servant of the space station? Odd that the station commander should bring that up, even as a joke. He shook his head and took up another spoonful of sticky rice pudding from the cup. It was excessively sweet, following a fashion that seemed to be sweeping the country of late.

"Good morning, Slava."

He looked up to see Manarov floating by the table, holding on with one hand. The man was too handsome by far in his green and gold flight suit, hair combed down damp from a fresh shower. "Volodya," he said, ignoring the disliked nickname.

Manarov wrapped his legs around a stool and sat down, clipping his breakfast tray to its table well with a practiced movement, and began uncapping the various dishes. Scrambled eggs, reddish sausage stuck to little plastic prongs, applesauce, a squeeze bottle of tomato juice. . . . "Well, today and tomorrow and that's it."

Bronstein nodded, saying nothing.

"Don't you have any thoughts on the matter?" Manarov filled his mouth with sticky-looking eggs, beginning to chew with his tongue.

I hate it when people try to dig feelings out of me, thought Bronstein, looking into pale-blue eyes that he felt suited his own coloration much better. Blond hair and brown eyes. Odd. And Manarov's coppery hair probably would look good with brown eyes, instead of washed-out, rather unfathomable blue. I'd like to have eyes that say nothing. "I've said about everything that needs to be said. What do you want to hear again, that I feel honored?"

Manarov seemed amused for a moment. He swallowed a bite of sausage and swilled a bit of juice. "Just once, I'd like to hear you say you're a little scared."

"Maybe you should talk to Tonya and Lyova."

Manarov regarded him levelly through narrowed eyes. "The four of us have been in one another's company for months now. Don't you think I know a little bit about what's going on inside that flat head?"

Maybe not. Bronstein smiled at the thought. "I once watched an interview with an old German soldier who was one of the early paratroopers, among the brigade that dropped on Crete with heavy-weapon loads and smallish parachutes. He said, 'When the time comes, you either jump out the door or fill your pants.' I'd like to be that articulate, but I'm not. Sorry."

Manarov's narrow grin accentuated the fact that his teeth were better than those of the average Russian. *I can't tell him only a German would* say *something like that!* "You are that articulate, Miroslav. You just don't know it."

Bronstein nodded. "Perhaps." *He probably thinks he's letting me escape. Best to leave it at that.* He watched Manarov scrape up the last of his breakfast with interest. *You'd think he wouldn't put that lead in his belly right before their final practice EVA. He might as well be an Englishman. It wouldn't make learning to handle the masses of the bombs any easier.*

The big airlock hatch of the engineering module was located on its end. During normal operations, it was oriented toward the sun, which meant it pointed toward the Earth only at night. Now, with the station heeled over, the horizon bisected the opening. Volodya Manarov floated in the open doorway and looked out. The world lay spread out below him, dull-blue and hazy, without detail, for this region was heavily overcast, the clouds a frosting in lumpy swirls of white. The horizon was sharply curved, but a little disappointing now. From farther out it had a crisp sharpness, the blue, brown, and white circle having such an overwhelming sense of *planetness* that this scene lacked. You just couldn't see all of it from this close.

In the distance, more than a kilometer away, he could see *Serpachek, Molotochek*'s twin, floating against a sable backdrop; at this remove it looked like a tiny hatchet with a very long, thick handle. It had been left in storage mode, its partially fueled tanks being used to top off *Molotochek* at suitable intervals. Docked to the command module, the *Oryol* lander was just a small, inverted cone, whose shading barely hinted at the components from which it had been cobbled. He turned his eyes to the Earth once more, still feeling that sense of inadequacy. *It ought to be prettier.*

*Odd that I look at it that way. With all the things I've*

seen, and all the things I'm going to see, I should still fully
appreciate this beauty. A vision of the future swept over
him. I'll walk on Sinuhe, and then on the Moon. The view
from Phobos, which will look like Sinuhe, I suppose, will
be stupendous. Red Mars rolling below, high clouds on *its*
horizon, will be waiting for me. I'll walk the red permafrost
at least once before I die. . . .

That brought an incongruous sense of longing. There
was budget enough in the world to accelerate the space
programs of the developed nations a hundredfold. Too bad.
I could stand looking up at Saturn. . . . Foolishness! I
have been born at just the right time in history, in just the
right place, to be given more than I had any right to expect. . . . But the longing wouldn't go away. A man's
dreams are tenacious.

His earphones crackled softly. Bronstein, monitoring the
EVA from the control room, said, "Are you going out or
what?"

Manarov smiled. "Just filling my pants, comrade."

He shoved hard against the hatch frame and went walking on the sky.

Some hours later, Anton floated free from one of *Mir*'s
veloergometers, riding silently on a long, windy fart. He
looked at his watch: 4:09:38. Time, he supposed, to crack
open the mysterious portable computer he had been given
and check out its operation. This was a product of the
capitalist experiment in China, and, when he had been
given a thirty-minute demonstration back at Vernadskii, he
had wondered what it *didn't* do.

Anton made his way down into the docking module,
thence into *Mir-East.* Here he began pulling himself along,
moving from handhold to handhold, greeting the men he
passed. Through the sealable hatch into *Mir-West,* and on
to the storage compartment next to his "bedroom." He
pulled out the beige and gray case and took it over to a
small utility table, anchoring it on the Velcro crosshatch.
The rubbly-textured plastic box was about thirty centimeters by fifty by four, and had a Chinese ideograph logo that
looked like a sheaf of wheat and the word *Kobei* written in
roman characters. Anton scratched his chin, feeling a slight
rasp, the first sandpaper of a new day's growth, and sup-

posed that the resemblance to the Japanese city name was coincidental.

He pushed the small recessed button on the front and the thing popped open like an overstuffed suitcase, revealing the full-size LCD-cap Cyrillic keyboard and a rectangular well that held a column of iridescent three-centimeter optical disks, for all the world like a stack of large, thin coins. He folded back the top and beheld the display, slate-black without illumination, and clicked it in place.

As he did so, a bright, colorful title screen winked on, showing extremely high-resolution images of Mao Zedong and V. I. Lenin against a dynamic backdrop of an efficient-looking electronics assembly line in which clean-room procedures were being maintained. Along the bottom of the screen the wheat symbol and KOBEI ELECTRONICS COOPERATIVE, GUANGZHOU, PEOPLE'S REPUBLIC OF CHINA appeared in shimmering, almost 3-D red brushstrokes. He watched for a moment as the people worked, wondering how much memory had been wasted on this image and how long it would be before it started to repeat.

Anton was not a computer novice, and, in fact, had had a pretty advanced American graphics machine on his desk during most of his career. But he instinctively knew that the petty math-sci, word-processing and CAD/CAM applications he had performed were nothing compared to the capabilities of this machine. It was, in fact, not even a computer in the sense that he had come to expect, and was marketed as a Digital Entertainment Unit; the perfect fusion of the computer with the myriad forms of digital information storage that had been developed in the last years of the nineties. It played music, it showed movies, and, more important, it contained the programs to manipulate these sources in extremely powerful ways. Its operating system, called OASIS, developed in primitive form at Toshiba, was made up of tens of thousands of independent modules, or objects, that could be called up separately or in combinations to process digital information in a way similar to the computer languages of earlier days, but in ways profoundly more intuitive and natural.

Anton, growing weary of watching the endlessly varied activities of the masked Oriental workers, pressed a key labeled WAKE and immediately the scene disappeared, to be replaced by a complex of small 3-D boxes containing the names of individual objects, full-color icons, and brief descriptions of what each one did. He looked down at the keyboard and noticed that the individual letters on each key had been replaced by corresponding object names. What magic this all was!

He scarcely knew how to begin testing the unit. He supposed that he should by all rights choose the TUTORIAL key, but he wasn't prepared to spend the time necessary to learn the whole system yet. Instead, he spontaneously stabbed the VIDEO key. The screen went blank, then a still image showing a dark, British-looking man with a large, bladelike nose and heavy, square chin appeared. Uncharacteristically for such an imposing figure, it winked at him, then turned slightly and smiled charismatically. "Welcome to Kobei's demonstration Video-library framework," it said in perfect, idiomatic Russian, tainted by what seemed to be a slight speech impediment. "I'm Cary Grant, and, should you need any help, please just ask me."

Anton knew the machine could also accept voice input, but he was still surprised. To think that this machine was already on sale in the United States, admittedly at a higher price than most could afford. And the price would come down. . . . Impulsively, he said, "What do I do next?"

Cary flashed him a friendly, slightly enigmatic look. "That depends. . . . What did you say your name was?"

"Anton Antonovich Serebryakov."

"Well, Anton, that depends on what you want to do. To view a motion picture from the enclosed library, simply choose a title from the list by touching it and I'll do the rest."

An alphabetical list of classic movies, most of them, Anton noted, too old to be covered by a copyright, appeared on the screen superimposed over the suave countenance. Anton reached out and touched a point on the screen at random. A light appeared beneath the stack of disks, traveled to a point near the bottom, and stopped. The disk dropped down through a small slot that had opened for it and disappeared.

Suddenly the screen lit up with the credits, in Russian, of what Anton recognized as *Grazhdanin Kane,* and simultaneously the keyboard metamorphosed into a list of possible options:

SOUND UP::SOUND DOWN::ZOOM IN::ZOOM OUT
LEFT::RIGHT::COLOR AUTO::COLOR CHOICE
RUSSIAN::ENGLISH::JAPANESE::CHINESE::FRENCH
GERMAN::FRENCH::SPANISH::INDONESIAN

The famous childhood montage was beginning, and, as an experiment, he hit the COLOR AUTO key. Instantaneously the scene was transmuted into beautiful, natural color. He could easily make out the red and gold logo on the ancient sled, and the stark beauty of the winter scene leapt out at him.

"Holy shit! Is that the new computer?" It was Manarov, who had floated silently in through the open hatch. He bounced across the little anteroom and floated behind Anton, staring at the colorized movie unrolling on the screen. "Stinks in here."

Anton turned to grin up at him a little self-consciously, found himself imitating the facial expression of the Cary Grant program and wondered if that sort of thing were contagious. It might explain the noticeable artifice of American mannerisms.

Manarov watched the movie with a transparent sort of lust on his face. "I've heard about these things. They say you can do just about anything with them. Even manipulate the contents of a movie interactively."

For some reason, Anton felt a little twinge of disappointment. Volodya's knowing ways were a little bit irritating. . . . But what did I expect? The government has been buying military and industrial computers from the West for twenty years, ever since the Kama River Truck Plant deal. He sighed, then nodded. "That's what I hear. I was surprised when they handed this thing over. I'm supposed to use it to store and analyze my planetological data, but the surplus capacity is ridiculous."

"Where'd your people get it?"

"That's the stupidest part of all. My boss found this one, on sale in used condition, in a consumer electronics store in Beijing, for three thousand dollars, U.S. He was part of a delegation to the space science conference they held last year. Our people pooled their funds to buy it."

They were silent for a few minutes, watching the red

shadows of the movie in flux, then Manarov said, "You know, the absorption of Hong Kong has been a great stroke of luck for our Chinese comrades. If we didn't have a forty-year head start, we'd be needing Chinese passports to land on Mars. . . ."

# CHAPTER 4
## *May 4, 2002*

The tension was a palpable thing, like a thin layer of putty that coated everything in *Molotochek*'s propulsion control room. Serebryakov gripped the sides of his acceleration cot, transfixed by a sense of here-we-go-again. Strapped standing to the wall like this was a little like being before a firing squad. He looked forward through the room. The CM-PCR looked strange with the LLV flight crew missing. Where Zarkov and Artyukhin had ridden last fall were the crucial machines of extended spaceflight. To the left of the midline a lightweight veloergometer was bolted. Below the instrumented handlebars, the plastic flywheel was painted black, as though some space psychologist had decided that would give it emotional weight, but that had been subverted by the ground assembly team, who had used gaily colored pedals from a children's bicycle, complete with red and white reflector panels. Tonya smiled, remembering a bicycle he'd had thirty years before. Good. Now we can safely ride at night. . . . Too bad they hadn't put streamers on the handgrips.

To the right of the midline was something new to Soviet space exercise equipment, a machine that promised to break the back of the zero-g adaptation process. The *soloshnur* weight-lifting device was a substitute for all manner of inane mechanisms that the doctors had introduced over the years. It was exactly like a gymnasium exercise machine such as bodybuilders used, the weights and pulleys replaced by huge rubber bands. Because it perfectly imitated gravity, an hour a day in the thing overcame most of the effects of microgravity on the bones and circulatory system. On the other hand, an hour on this thing was agony. . . .

Buckled into a lightweight pressure suit, the kind used for shuttle ascents, Bronstein let his hand rest lightly on the engine-start master switch, listening to Mission Control's preignition chatter, listening to his heart thud. Interplanetary injection. My God! They hadn't gone halfway with their terminology, had they? Trans-Lunar injection; Trans-Earth injection. Nothing so unusual there. The Americans had done it all before, under far more dangerous circumstances, no "go where no man has gone before. . . ." Interplanetary injection was the phrase the flight controllers had been saving for the moment of their dreams, that first launch outward bound for Mars. I suppose this is the same thing, no different from a trip to Phobos. . . .

But it wasn't the same. Over the last six months, the excitement of the mission controllers and flight planners had been a frightful thing. At last, they were being allowed to do something new, something not covered in fantastically boring detail in the last three interagency five-year plans. Their eyes *glittered* when they talked about it.

"Coming up on ten seconds."

"Acknowledged." He glanced over at Manarov, who, though not suited, wore a headset and would have heard the warning. The man looked up briefly and nodded, his eyes bland, then turned to watch the data that was marching across his two CRT screens. Third time for him. Does it really become something you can grow blasé about? Probably not. He looked back at his own control panel, where green lights were blooming.

"Ten seconds."

He tensed, looking up at his own TV screens which, as always, showed Earth and engines. A trip to the Moon started this way. But this was no trip to the Moon.

"Five seconds."

The drumming of his heart accelerated, making him feel short of breath. Can I really be this frightened? No. Excitement does the same thing. Fight or flight . . . adrenaline . . . my God!

"Zero."

"Engine start."

Thud-thud, and one CRT view was drowned in white light. On the upper screen, hanging in the distance, *Mir* was suddenly picked out in a brilliant glow, *Serpachek* a tiny stick in the background. While they were gone, technicians would be preparing it as a rescue vehicle.

Bronstein took his hand off the master switch and put it on the CM-jettison abort lever. Out of the corner of his eye he could see Manarov doing the same thing.

Rescue? The pressure was building against his back now, rising to its full three-g value. A faint vibration was becoming perceptible. Disaster would leave them in an elliptical solar orbit, it was true, but one with exactly the same year as the earth. The mission had been carefully designed that way. Maximum separation would never exceed twenty million kilometers. In a year's time, short on consumables, they would come around again, and need picking up.

The ship's structure was beginning to whine as acceleration stress built up in various connectors. The thing was, after all, a collection of loose parts, held together by rivets and bolts. The vibration was growing in amplitude and shrinking in frequency, becoming two distinct motions. As the fuel was consumed, the tensile strength of the monocoque hull/tank was lessening. The engines would compress the ship, then the springiness of the metal would expand it again. At the same time, the engines would fight each other, making minute adjustments to keep *Molotochek* on heading. The result was a simultaneous pogoing and two-axis sway. Things in the room were starting to jiggle.

Rescue? It was hard to picture spending a full year drifting slowly around the sun with these three, trapped in a tiny two-room cocoon with almost nothing to do but hash over old regrets. The command structure would degenerate quickly, making the others insolent and lazy. And if they lost all sense of authority, who knew what would happen. In that kind of situation, people became careless. When the *Molotochek* came around again, the rescue mission might find only corpses.

"Coming up on shutdown."

Had it been two minutes already? The pogoing had reached the point where his back was rocking hard against the chair and his head was bouncing in the helmet. He glanced over at Manarov, whose mouth was hanging open, his head nodding rapidly.

"Ten seconds."

In the background, he heard Chishak mutter, "Damn it,

I'll never get used to this," and Serebryakov's stuttering reply, "If you have to puke, use a bag." It was true, he didn't like these men.

"Zero."

"Engine stop."

Bang. Hiss. The white light in the lower CRT faded to a red glow.

In the creaking silence, he heard Manarov say, "My God! We're really on our way!"

Obscurely, Bronstein found the man's amazement comforting.

It took about ten minutes for them to go through the safing checklists with Mission Control, shut down the powered flight subsystems and unbuckle from their acceleration stations. Tonya felt unreasonable anxiety as he ratcheted the locking lever and undid the pressure hatch that sealed them off from the ship's living quarters. Theoretically, if one section was holed, they could retreat to the other and prepare to effect repairs. There was a simplified control panel in the solar-flare shelter/escape capsule and the spare EVA suit stored in the aft egress tunnel, which could double as an emergency airlock.

At last, the door popped loose from its seal with a sigh and swung forward into the propulsion control room. He latched it to its fitting on the overhead and floated through into the next room. I don't know why I'm in a hurry, he thought. It won't look any different this time. But still . . .

The room was as they had left it, cleaned up a little, but that was all. To his right, facing aft, was the galley module, with its storage cabinets, refrigerator, and microwave oven. They kept a four-week supply of food here; the rest was stored in exterior bays, meaning there would have to be at least six EVAs during the mission for that purpose alone. Going over the mission in his head, he marveled at the growth in confidence this implied.

To his left were the entry hatches of the three closet-sized sleeping compartments. On a lunar mission, the six cosmonauts were expected to rotate their living arrangements, sleeping in shifts. For this flight each would have a permanent bedroom. As flight engineer, Manarov would inhabit the flare shelter, whose alarms would wake him in an emergency.

The middle of the room was dominated by the dining

room table, their all-purpose workstation. There was the *Ubornaya* personal hygiene module, up against the cabinet-covered aft wall, which was itself pierced by the round pressure hatch of the aft egress tunnel. Beyond that lay the escape capsule/flare shelter, embedded in its toroidal water tank.

Set in the bulkhead above the table was *Molotochek*'s only porthole, a sixty-centimeter disk of ultraviolet-opaque glass that looked out over the portside-trailing solar-panel augmentation wing. It was to this point that he bent his trajectory.

Outside, the bright Earth was still huge, but shrunken fantastically from its *Mir* aspect. The reddish-tan Sahara was flattened against the arc of its edge, a splotch of brown among the swirling white and blue. As he watched, the rim's curvature grew steeper. He grabbed a handhold and pulled himself forward, pressing his face to the glass. Now he could see the whole fat crescent. Up near the top of the right horn, lost in foreshortened cloud, was Moskva. A long, long way away. In ten minutes they'd already come almost ten thousand kilometers. His gaze shifted to the direction in which the craft was traveling. There, all was night, the stars washed to obscurity by glare. Hot bile began to boil in his stomach.

"You'll have to wipe off those nose prints, Tonya," said a voice in his ear. He turned to look at Manarov's flat grin.

"It's worth looking at." Saying it that way made him feel almost defensive.

Volodya nodded. "Someday I hope to have an opportunity to make an EVA at this altitude. What a sight that ought to be!"

Feeling a little offended, Tonya said, "Someday there'll be Intourist hotels up here. Maybe when you retire you can be a guide and spend your days showing the beautiful view to Mongolian tourists."

Manarov's smile faded. "Your American friends more likely."

Serebryakov turned back to the window, hoping to end the conversation, but Manarov spoke on. "This isn't a good way to start a long mission, Tonya. I understand your misgivings about what you consider an ill-conceived adventure. But it's too late for that. Maybe it's time for us to trust our technology. You know, the very *worst* that can happen is we become posthumous culture-heroes."

Tonya turned to stare at him again, anger flickering in and out, but he suppressed the urge to make the obvious retort. I suppose, he thought, that he feels I should be comforted by the thought of resting beside Gagarin in the Kremlin wall. . . . He felt a prickle of ghostly fingers on his neck. Except I won't be there. Disaster means never coming back. Shaking his head slowly, he said, "I'm just nervous." Manarov nodded and went away.

The congressional committee meeting room was already a bustle of noise and activity as Hermann Oberg pushed his way through the gathering crowd of onlookers toward the front row of tables from which he would testify, clutching his briefcase in one hand and a thick portfolio of notes under the opposite arm. Most of the spectators were members of the press corps, though in the back of the room two noisy contingents, one from a prospace group and the other from some antitechnological environmentalist lobby, were heckling each other.

There was a muffled thump and a curse as his briefcase grazed the side of someone's head. As Oberg turned to apologize, movement caught his eye. One of the greens, a large fat man with a tangled beard and ponytail, had a spindly, crew-cut young space cadet by the collar and was shaking him angrily. Cooler heads from both sides were attempting to pry them apart.

Oberg resumed his progress, shaking his head wearily. People like that were undoubtedly *why* America spent so much time getting nowhere. These days, he understood, the prospace groups were insisting to those few who would listen that the United States should divert its entire defense budget to the space program, preferably to their pet project, the thirty-five-year-old Enzmann Starship design. It was a sharp turnaround from a decade before, when the bulk of these people had favored SDI, despite the fact that it was raping the real program of space exploration. Now, they wanted to kill *Eisenhower,* when SDI was the only creditable space program America had on the books.

A shout from the rear captured his attention once more. Since the scuffle had continued, Capitol police were arresting the demonstrators and ejecting them from the hearing room. Bah. For their part, the environmentalists were insisting on a rollback of industrial technology to pre-twentieth-century levels, ignoring the inevitable consequences. Their catchphrase was, "Nature will find its own balance." *Schwachsinnigers!* As if the metastable ecological condition had a mind of its own. Worse still, you couldn't get them to come out and admit that their plan meant immediate starvation for billions of people.

He reached his seat at last and sank down with a cavernous sigh. Either I'm really getting old now, or this useless jaunt is beating me down. It had to be the latter, he knew. He'd always been fat and wheezy, even in his younger days, when one hard punch had flattened a drunken American Marine in that Munich beerhall. The memory came back like a video clip to be treasured. The look on the man's comrades' faces had been worth the grinding pain of a broken metacarpal bone. Afterward, before they could react, he'd turned to the lone black Marine in the gang, and said, "Him calling me a Nazi prick is like me calling you a nigger." He'd turned on his heel and fled then, telling them at the hospital clinic he'd stumbled after too much beer and fallen in the gutter. The inevitable lecture on the dangers of drunkenness, "What if you'd fallen in front of a bus?" had been easy to endure.

By now the senators were seated, the gavel rapped, and the audience rustle gradually wound down, breaking apart into individual coughs and words amid gathering pools of silence. The chairman, Ruth Petellat, Democrat of Wisconsin, was an enormous woman, full of butterfat, he supposed, her stringy brown hair drawn up into a badly made bun. "Good morning, Director Oberg."

"Madame Chairman." He opened his portfolio and withdrew his printouts of statistics on *Molotochek,* Sinuhe, and the Soviet manned space program, placing them in three careful piles for ready access.

"Well, the committee and I want to thank you for being here today. We've already heard considerable testimony from our own experts, as well as speeches by various technical attachés from the Russian embassy staff. Perhaps it's time we heard a little from a presumably impartial third party."

Oberg smiled, wondering if this hideous woman found him attractively plump. In fact, she probably looked on him as an obese old pig. "Thank you for the expression of confidence, Senator Petellat. I'll try to keep my answers as brief and to the point as I can manage."

"That would be appreciated. I'll open the questioning with one of my own: Mr. Oberg, do you believe this Soviet space adventure to be wise?"

Well. That was a promising start, giving him a good opening like that. . . . "Madam Chairman, I have two conflicting views on this matter. . . ."

From somewhere among the panel of politicians, someone muttered, "It figures," getting a small titter from the audience of reporters.

Oberg frowned and went on. "On the one hand, I think it is very unwise. In a world filled to overflowing with all manner of unregulated nuclear weapons, it is politically dangerous to make a unilateral move that can be seen as threatening by any one party. I think the press stories of the past few months have illustrated that." He reached into his portfolio and pulled out that morning's *New York Times,* holding it up so the TV cameras could pick up the headlines, then pulled out a second issue, from July 21, 1969, and held them side by side. "As you can see, H-BOMB ROCKET LAUNCHED is set in somewhat larger type than MEN WALK ON MOON. And it isn't often we see bright red headlines on this sort of newspaper." Behind him, an angry voice said, "Asshole!"

The senator banged her gavel. "While we appreciate your loyalty to your employer, Mr. Klimm, please save your comments for tomorrow's Op-Ed page. Continue, Mr. Oberg."

"Thank you, Madam Chairman. I think the gentlemen of the press make my point for me quite effectively on this issue. Where knowledge is scarce, informed decision making can be difficult."

"Yet you said you had two conflicting views on the matter."

"True. When considered as the opening move in a program of space industrialization, bringing back an asteroid to serve as an off-Earth resource base is wise indeed. If they succeed, our Russian friends may buy themselves an insurmountable lead in the drive to capture the high ground of the future."

Another senator, Lloyd Bennett Buntingberger, Republican of Idaho, said, "Even with America's already vast technological lead?"

Oberg's smile returned and broadened. They were, it seemed, playing right into his hands. "Well, now. Let us look at that. It is true you have a fine aerospace plane, while everyone else uses primitive old rocket ships. And it's equally true that *Eisenhower* is more sophisticated than anything anyone else has even on the drawing board. However, the truth of the matter is it's what you *do* that counts, not what you *could* do. Look at it this way: At the height of Project Apollo, in, say, 1970, you could have brought back an asteroid, or gone to Mars, pretty much done whatever you pleased. But you didn't. You did nothing.

"History is full of similar examples. In the fifteenth century, China was politically unified and technologically more than two centuries ahead of Europe. So why didn't they discover us, instead of the other way around? Because they *didn't*. And that's why Western civilization dominates the world of today."

Clyde Boll, Democrat of Georgia, leaned forward, lacing blunt-fingered hands together. "That's real interesting, Mr. Oberg, but it don't answer none of our questions."

"I'm sorry you feel that way, Mr. Senator. Perhaps if you'd care to ask me another question?"

"I surely would, mister. We have it on good authority the Russians intend to drop that rock dead center on this country. . . ."

Of all the idiotic . . . "Senator Boll, don't you find that notion just a little bit ridiculous?"

"I do not. Our intelligence people say that thing will hit with an explosive force of something near a *million* megatons of TNT!"

Oberg sat back in his chair, filled with contempt. "Senator, the real figure is around nine thousand megatons, not a million."

"Nine thousand megatons!? And you don't find that horrifying? Mr. Oberg, we're talking close to a half-million Hiroshimas here!" The senator's face was reddening nicely now.

"It doesn't work that way, Senator. The explosive force would equal something like two dozen thermonuclear warheads such as you mount on your largest missiles." Oberg leaned back, lacing his hands across his stomach and pushing back, lifting the front legs of his chair off the floor. This was, he supposed, another part of the reason for America's marvelous record of failure. The ignorant leading the stupid . . . He leaned forward again, letting the chair legs clunk on the floor, and began to rustle through his notes. "Explosions are, like all other spherical phenomena, subject to the inverse-square law. When you throw in things like atmospheric compression, you find, for example, that a ten-megaton hydrogen bomb is only ten times more destructive than a ten-kiloton atomic bomb, rather than the thousand times you might expect."

Boll slapped his hand on the table top. "You can't convince *me* this thing won't wipe out America when it comes!"

"I cannot force you to understand, Senator, but that does not alter the truth. If Sinuhe were to land on, um, Atlanta, making a five-mile crater in the process, it is true your state would be seriously damaged and many would die. People as far away as New York might notice that something interesting had occurred. But destroy America? You'd have to use an asteroid as *large* as Georgia to accomplish that." Oops. These yokels invited hyperbole. An asteroid the size of the District of Columbia would do the trick, but not one the size of a large football stadium.

Petellat rapped her gavel and said dryly, "I don't think this is achieving anything. Mr. Oberg, what do you estimate is the chance a Soviet miscalculation will hit the Earth, any part of the Earth, with this object?"

"Very small, Madam Chairman. My feeling is the steering charges will be too inaccurate to get it into Earth-orbit. After the first explosion, I think Sinuhe will never be seen again." Tell them that. Make them feel better. "If it *does* hit the Earth, it has twice the chance of hitting the USSR than the USA."

"And what if it lands in the ocean?" demanded Senator Buntingberger.

"Then," said Hermann Oberg, "we will have several months of bad weather." Recalling a speech by Dwight Eisenhower to the predecessors of these same men, he considered speaking a stream of nonsense words, knowing it would leave them just as well informed. Quite suddenly, he smiled.

·      ·      ·

Fifty-three hours later the lunar globe had opened out into a pale golden brown world, sweeping only ten kilometers below. Under full sunlight, the surface was smooth-looking, almost sanded, swirled and peppered with white. The craters were subdued, only circles or patches of brightness. An unruly brown and white sea, perhaps, frozen for millennia. Manarov floated before the porthole, face almost pressed to the heavy glass. From this perspective, the Moon was astonishingly different. Compared to the view from *Mechta*'s high orbit . . . what can I say? It looks . . . *real* now! This was the closest any Soviet had come to the lunar surface. After following an S-shaped curve past the leading edge of the Moon, *Molotochek* was making a gravity-boosted phasing maneuver into solar orbit, following an ellipse that would bounce them above and behind the Earth, then, after a small midcourse correction, sunward to rendezvous with the asteroid. Sinuhe was, at this point, less than twenty-six days away.

He felt obscurely surprised at himself. Real? A funny way to put it. But that was the way it felt. From six hundred kilometers, the Moon was a distant place, flat, like a painting. True, it was more worldlike than the bright yellow circle that hung in the sky over Russia, but . . . this. Upon closer inspection, the roughness of the surface was more apparent, and the quick progress of the spacecraft allowed for a parallactic sense of the third dimension. This was the farside, after all, saturated with craters large and small. Anton had told him they would pass directly over the rim of a large, degraded basin named after Sergei Korolyov, a legacy of the first *Luna* photographs.

And still the world drew closer. Volodya marveled at the color of it, from this distance. Men who'd walked there compared the surface dirt to finely ground charcoal. Where did this magnificent goldness come from?

They were down below a kilometer now, and the details rushed by almost too quickly to note. Now the surface was very three dimensional, humping and dipping precipitously, marching in rapid succession. A vast ringwall sailed beneath, its summit so close he felt he could reach out and touch it. Was that Korolyov? Once, on a whim, he'd hung over the tailgate of a truck he was riding on and looked forward along the undercarriage. The way the bumpy dirt road had rushed by, only inches from his head, seemed a bit like this.

The world was pulling away, slowing down. To his right he could see that the markings were already beginning to look tilted away from him. *Molotochek* was being accelerated by the Moon, slung toward its new orbit. In a matter of minutes, the close approach was over, and now the surface of the Moon was receding swiftly, the horizon curving sharply in on itself, becoming remote again. The markings shrank and flattened, becoming an interlocking maze of overlapping crater walls as the ship dropped toward planetary space. So. *We have a real first, at last.* Behind them, the Earth popped into view over the moon's limb, fantastically tiny, shrinking still. *How long?* It had been thirty-seven years since the Soviet Union's last meaningful "first," Aleksei Leonov's brief EVA in the spring of 1965.

*What a crass way for me to be thinking!* But it was the way he really felt. In less than a century, the Soviet Union had gone from the wreckage of a tired medieval society to sending the first expedition across interplanetary space. *Molotochek* would make people forget *Apollo 11,* as they had earlier been disposed to forget *Vostok 1. Or am I merely thinking that I am responsible for this glory?* Sometimes, it was hard to remember you were merely the symbolic representative of all the millions of people who'd worked for this day, sort of a people's deputy in space. Well. Whether the plan to bring the asteroid home worked or not, the flight would demonstrate that the technology for the Mars flight was ready. And when the third flight vehicle, *Zvyozdochka,* was ready, perhaps that expedition to Phobos could depart.

He looked back at the Earth. It was shrinking more slowly now, his senses victimized by the inverse-square law. At first, climbing away from low Earth-orbit, it had visibly dwindled. But the distance had to double to cut the diameter of the world in half. And that half was part of an ever-tinier object.

*How am I going to feel when it's gone?* The Moon was shrinking now, in the same fast way Earth had two days before. *Just like we were heading home. . . . But they weren't. Is this how Borman, Lovell, and Anders felt, heading out to the Moon in 1968?* Probably not. Americans were notoriously cold people. You wouldn't expect them to feel anything but triumph at being first.

And is that the way I seem? Not to Bronstein. He thinks I am too "psychological," as it is. Maybe to Tonya, who spends his time fretting about nonsense. He tried to construct an external view of himself. What would others see? The efficient engineer, wrapped up in his work. The ice-blooded spaceman, whose pulse rate stayed down even during launch. That was cold enough. Did anyone see the family man, frolicking with his little girls? Or the devoted husband, who loved his plump little wife? Probably not. The "Moon Pilots," as the socialist press liked to call them, were public figures who struggled to keep their private lives hidden. You had to be stern, but friendly. Valiant, but human. There was nothing worse than being a boring old cosmonaut when you had to sit through an hour on Shatalov's TV show.

Me? Boring? Never! And yet you had to ponder these things. It had been an effort to keep himself human for Shutka, for Galina and Tamara, who needed a playful father. Two decades of hard work had brought him to the dining room porthole of *Molotochek,* watching the rest of the human race fly away into black space. Two decades of fifteen-hour workdays. It's a wonder they know who I am.

On the studio's big HD monitor, the lead-in played as Lyle Marlowe made final revisions to the evening's stories:

The establishing long shot came in as a jump-cut from the postcommercial tag. It was an extreme long shot across the hard desert of southern Kazakhstan, shot without initial telephoto from the viewing stand six miles away, of the Energiya launch complex. Even from this distance, the structures were visibly large and you could see plumes of vapor rising from the single loaded pad. When *Raduga*'s engines lit, first white, then red and smoky, the cameraman did a three-second zoom-in, bringing the spaceship to full-frame close-up as it climbed past the tower. The raw footage had been shaky, of course, but the studio computer made it into a rock-steady vertical pan. The tower structure and hazy background sky appeared to do a nicely animated downward roll.

With the ship established as a motionless fiery icon, the soft trumpets of the program's theme song played while the character generator laid in the titles in brilliant blue and silver popcorn graphics. The VO announcer said, "The CTN Evening News, with Lyle Marlowe in New York!"

The title graphics did a twinkle-fade while the scene of *Raduga* going up dissolved to *Molotochek* hanging against the backdrop of the bright Earth, a sliver of dark sky visible in the upper frame. This sequence had been taken by a Soviet technical camera crew aboard *Mir* and pirated off the *Molniya* network signal. It had been subjected to considerable enhancement.

Marlowe's head and shoulders faded in as a 3-D super in front of the scene. "Good evening. Tonight's top story remains the extraordinary interplanetary voyage of the Soviet spaceship *Molotochek*." Behind him, the ship's engines flared palely and the scene dissolved to a shrinking Earth globe, enhanced from old *Apollo* footage. His lips were tight, his face made slightly pale by the computer, and his voice was subtly filtered into a gravity that perfectly suited a news report of considerable weight.

"Today the 'Little Hammer,' as it's called, and its four veteran cosmonauts, armed with an array of deadly thermonuclear weapons, rounded the Moon, outward bound on their four-week journey to the asteroid Sinuhe." The scene dissolved to a video montaged from various sources and animated to reality, the lovely blue Earth sinking from view over the horizon of a dead gray Moon.

Marlowe sat at his desk and watched the show on the monitor. Because of its largely composite nature, tonight's show was taped and heavily edited from a great deal of source material. On the screen, the space backdrop wiped to a studio scene shot much earlier in the day, the computer dropping his image exactly where it had sat during the taping, dissolving his two selves seamlessly. He seemed to flow into the background, gradually losing much of the 3-D effect, which, in this context, would have seemed unnatural to viewers accustomed to fifty years of flat studio scenes.

"Tonight we have joining us Professor Bennett Bargainax, space historian from the University of North Carolina. Good evening, Professor."

The screen cut to a close-up of a thin, bald man dressed in a rather rumpled dark suit against a plain, slightly textured blue backdrop, probably the best they could do in a

Raleigh TV station crippled by competition from the various cable and satellite networks. He smiled, showing somewhat rabbity teeth, and said, "Good evening, Lyle." He'd been coached on how to talk back to a friendly TV anchor.

"Professor, what would happen if this asteroid were to hit the Earth? What if it fell on, say, Raleigh?"

Bargainax closed his lips over his teeth, trying to look serious but seeming to have a hard time. He was probably overexcited about being on national TV, overacting. "Well, quite a bit, actually. I calculate the impact will release energy equivalent to nine thousand three hundred and sixty megatons of TNT."

"Previous reports stated the figure as being closer to a million megatons."

"An exaggeration. Nine thousand is the correct figure."

"What does that mean?"

"Well, Lyle, the impact would dig a crater twenty miles across by about five miles deep. It would cover a circle sixty miles in diameter with ejecta, something like twenty-eight hundred square miles, and would blow more than a hundred cubic miles of pulverized rock into the stratosphere. That's more than enough to start the nuclear winter people were talking about back in the eighties."

"Can you explain it in more human terms?"

The man seemed stumped for a moment. "Well. Let's see. Nine thousand three hundred and sixty megatons . . . that's something like five hundred and fifty thousand times the force of the Hiroshima bomb. Um . . . Given the Hiroshima casualty figure . . . um . . . that's enough power to kill . . . um . . . something like a hundred billion people!" He stopped short, looking thunderstruck. "Why . . . that's enough to kill everybody in the world! Enough to kill everybody in the world fifteen times over!" His delighted smile was appalling.

The scene cut to a satisfied looking Marlowe. "Thank you, Professor. In other news . . ."

At his desk, Marlowe smiled. No point in showing the useless footage that followed. They'd had a lot of trouble getting Bargainax to stop laughing. It had gone on until some kind of asthma attack had been triggered, the skinny little shit wheezing and coughing until someone found him an epinephrine inhaler. His explanation had been hard to follow. Something about understanding, *now,* where these silly ideas came from. . . .

Feelings he thought totally banished were creeping up on Tonya, and it was only the end of the second day out. I . . . can't seem to concentrate. He'd spent long moments staring slantwise out the large porthole to catch a glimpse of home as *Molotochek* was swung around during attitude control thruster testing. Manarov and Bronstein were continually bobbing about, engaged in heady cosmotechnical tasks, talking only to each other. Chishak spent the day calibrating his torture chamber. Now that they were truly on their way, Lev and he would have some worthwhile things to do, but not nearly enough to keep them constantly occupied.

The Sinuhe mission did not carry the usual unrelated scientific packages that haunted the days and nights of orbital flights. The instruments they had taken to measure the characteristics of the interplanetary medium were largely automatic. The Kobei DEU machine had disks that contained the core data from the space science of the last forty years, including the parameters of Gaspra from *Galileo* and Orpheus from *Piazzi.* If he was conscientious, he would be working with that data. But, at this moment, he just didn't have the heart for it.

Everyone was asleep now. It was well past midnight, Moskva time, and Anton had stayed up later than he should. If he were to get totally out of synch with the day/night ritual here, there would be hell to pay. A kind of buzz was running through him, a tiny, electric apprehension that overwhelmed the pleasant languorousness that put him to sleep. His mind was racing, thinking thoughts of no particular importance or meaning.

There were memories that did nothing but irritate him. His last meeting with Darya, saying goodbye to his mother once again. And further back; memories of America, and Carla. He found himself wondering why he was the way he was, vowing to be better, stronger. That gave rise to a powerful picture of himself from outside, sitting there, and of the utter uselessness of his thoughts, just tiny chemical reactions somewhere inside that head. His regrets and memories were circular, anyway; no matter how many times he had the same thoughts they folded back on themselves, ultimately amounting to nothing.

Now he was really depressed. His perspective was going, and with it the very existence of a reality other than the suffering he was feeling at this moment. He fingered the keyboard, stared hard out of the porthole, saw nothing. The unpleasant electricity was coursing through his neck and shoulders, blotting out everything but a need for succor.

One thing had helped him out of these funks before: alcohol. That at least allowed him to sleep. The idea came home to roost. There was vodka among the stores. Gorbachev had eventually relented from his hard stand on alcohol. Now, as in seagoing vessels of old, there was a supply of surcease for the weary Russian cosmonaut. Tonya found the ring-bound sheaf of *Molotochek*'s specifications and, with very steady hands, found the reference to VODKA RATION: STORAGE CABINET 144. He quickly located the locker with the incised numbers and pulled the door open. Inside was a full five-liter keg with an extractor spigot.

Going over to the kitchen module, he came back with a "glass," really a slender plastic pouch with a special attach-node, and hooked it to the extractor apparatus and began to squeeze the pumpbulb. After two empty squeezes the bulb began to do its job; the pouch filled with the clear, colorless liquid. When it was full, he slid it off its node, carried it to his mouth, and sucked a portion of the cool, burning liquid into his mouth.

This was more like it. His brain began to quiet even before the drug could have reached it. A placebo effect, of sorts. He had never imbibed in microgravity before; he knew that it was going to be fun. He emptied the first pouch and drew another, then let himself float backwards toward the ceiling, taking small sips of the stuff. How could he let himself be so stupid? Why did he torment himself, when the world offered enough pain without his cooperation?

Yet . . . even as he was congratulating himself on his solution, a different part of him was nagging, pointing out that the liquor never really helped him permanently. But all I need here *is* a temporary solution. I only have to hold out until we get back to Earth.

Another gulp and the nagging was silenced. Yet another

part of his psyche asked, Okay, now you're feeling all right. Shouldn't we get on with the work at hand? But what can I do?

He remembered what Manarov had said about using the Kobei to help with navigation. It seemed like a reasonable place to start. He wanted to get along with these people; why not do something to propitiate them? He propelled himself back toward the table, spinning like a fish, unable to distinguish between the dizziness that he knew alcohol could bring and the normal disorientation of space. The DEU was still open, and he went to the Object Library screen and activated the linker object. The Linker Choice screen, a similar display of possible objects and options, appeared. Tonya chose the I/O module, the signal analysis module, and the foreign code disassembler. Linker asked: "Input signal from foreign machine through RS-486 port and analyze and disassemble code?"

Anton typed in assent.

"Do you know the CPU type?"

"Motorola 68988-3."

"Ready to initiate connection."

He pulled the machine from its table linkage and kicked himself through the hatch into the propulsion control room. Catching hold of the veloergometer's handlebar, he pushed off again, managing a perfect flight between the two command chairs to the vast bank of switches, lights, and readouts covering the large panel that filled almost half the room's front end. The flight engineer's main panel, on the right, had a female DB-9 plug that Anton knew was connected to the correct system. He pulled the male connector cable from the back of the DEU and, propping a foot against a chair, wiggled the plugs together until he could feel they were snugly mated.

Now came the tough part. Anton had been given a perfunctory course in ship navigation, enough to know how to get the thing's attention and access the beginning menus. But downloading the internal operating system, while important for on-the-fly debugging, was not something that he would find on the main menus, that was for sure. He activated the Dozhdevik, pointing with the trackball at the most likely menu: UTILITIES. There was a little icon he didn't recognize next to the blank menu-box that next appeared, and, not knowing what else to do, he clicked on it. Once. Twice.

The machine began to emit a low, sinusoidal whine. Damn it! What's that supposed to mean?

Suddenly Anton felt a strong hand pulling him back away from the panel. He spun around and down, his feet coming up where his head had been as he tumbled back into the middle reaches of the room.

It was Manarov. "What in the hell do you think you're doing? You stupid little bastard, you . . ." Face twisted, he grabbed Serebryakov by the collar while simultaneously anchoring one of his feet under a floor strap, and pulled him close.

Anton looked at the man muzzily. He obviously didn't understand. "No . . . I just—"

Something seemed to flash in Manarov's face. "God damn it, Anton. That's vodka I smell." He seemed to be physically holding himself back from some violent action. A moment passed in which Serebryakov pulled himself down into the same frame with the other, certain Manarov would soon understand.

"Explain yourself. Now."

Anton smiled; a mistake. "I was going to download the—"

"Asshole. Drunken asshole." He slapped Anton hard across the face, making them both sway in the air.

"You were the one—"

"Look, Anton Antonovich." Manarov's voice became quiet. "I don't know what you thought you were doing. I don't really care. But I will tell you this. If I catch you doing anything from now on that will jeopardize this mission in the slightest way, I will kill you myself. Anything. Now unplug this damned thing from my computer and go to bed. You understand me?"

Anton started to mumble something, then thought better of it. "Yes," he said. "I'm . . . uh . . . sorry." There. The word was out. He looked for forgiveness in Manarov's face but found none.

They must have sat for hours in the foreign-looking, open-meshwork chairs, nursing their tea and sucking on the lemon wedges. Washed and pomaded, dressed in jeans, sneakers, and a bright yellow T-shirt that said "Cheerios" on his chest and "Eat 'em Up" behind, Tonya traded silly stories about classmates with Zhenya. The sun slid along the horizon, going north instead of down. Finally a waiter came over to them and asked if they wanted anything else. Anton peeled a five-ruble note from his smallish wad and handed it to the man. Now that he had a twin-bay Toshiba *shumyashchik,* courtesy of Maxim's black market connections, he had begun to accumulate a small fortune in rubles. "Here, take this," he said in English. The waiter looked at the bill with disdain, but walked away cramming it into his vest pocket.

"Tonya!" Zhenya said, "that's a lot of money! What if you don't have enough for a girl?"

"I've got plenty, you idiot," Tonya said, smiling. "Our chums at school are already queuing up for a copy of *Goodbye.*"

"I just hope they don't find out that the stuff you're selling is ten years old. You can only pass Cream and Grand Funk cassettes for so long before they want the real thing—BeeGees, Chicago, the stuff that they play on RFE."

"That's chicken shit compared to what we like, and they know it. Just wait until we get that Led Zeppelin tape to copy. 'Skveeze my lemon, honey . . .' They'll pay five rubles or more."

"I'll believe that when I see it."

"How much do you think they'll be?"

"A whore? I have no idea, Tonya. Could be as much as a hundred."

"Shit, Zhenya, Olga Trofimovna, our beloved classmate, would do it for a hundred. I'd guess more like fifty."

"But they do it professionally, and they must do it pretty good."

"Yeah, maybe you're right. I don't know."

"I guess we'll find out."

The sun was gone under the Church of Nikolai v Chamovnikach when they left the restaurant. The sky was a delicate pastel shade of pink, dotted with lemony mackerel patches here and there. In the small copses at the heart of Gorkii Park, it was the sooty sort of near-darkness that twilight often brings in August. The two of them, hearts beating fast from anticipation and fear, made their way like explorers penetrating a new land.

Not far from the river, on a wide tree-lined promenade that led to the Zelyonii Teatr, they saw a likely pair. Two youngish girls dressed in jeans and T-shirts and, incongruously, high heels, dawdling and laughing together as if they had nowhere to go. They both were wearing too much makeup, of the new "natural" kind, and it was this finally that convinced Anton and Yevgenii that these two were "right."

Zhenya went up first, followed, a little sheepishly, by Tonya, looking up at the dark trees and the vague impression of lacy color that came down from the twilight above.

"Hi," said Zhenya, cheerily.

"Hi," said the one on the left, a slightly chubby blonde with a snub nose. Silence, and then a breeze off the river.

Anton wasn't about to let these two slip through their fingers. "We're looking for someone," he said.

"Oh?" said the one on the right, a darker, thinner girl. "And what does that have to do with us?"

"My name's Tonya and this is Zhenya," he said, in a rush.

"That's interesting," said the blonde.

"We're looking for—" he began, but was interrupted by Yevgenii.

"We were wondering if you girls are whores," he said.

There, thought Tonya, he's done it now. But at least it was the direct method.

"Us? Little old us? Whores?" the dark girl said it with just the right spin. They were! What a relief! Tonya could feel his prick getting uncomfortably trapped as it rose against the tight denim. He pulled out his folded bills and waved them around. "We've got the money," he said.

The blonde looked suddenly uninterested. "No dollars?" she said. "Go home and get some dollars, instead, little boy. We're—" The dark girl poked her and shook her head.

"Not tonight, Manya. I feel a bit horny this evening. I think we could make an exception to our rule and put out for these fine lads—in the spirit of solidarity with the workers of the RSFSR. You are workers, aren't you, boys?"

"Sure," said Tonya.

"How much do you have?" asked the blonde.

"How much do you want?" asked Zhenya.

"That depends. Not so very much. Two hundred apiece."

Zhenya swallowed hard, but Tonya waved his wad again. "Sure, no problem." He handed half of the money to his friend, and said, "Let's go!"

"Hey," said the dark girl. "We've got some modesty. I know a place where we won't be disturbed, over by Hospital Number one, but Manya likes it in the woods."

They split up, Tonya and the unnamed girl going toward Leninskii Prospekt and Zhenya and Manya heading for the river. When they had traversed the kilometer or so to the edge of the park, Tonya stopped suddenly and said, "Give me a kiss."

The girl was amused. "We whores don't kiss, silly. We don't want to get the flu."

Tonya twisted up his face quizzically, but only said, "Yeah, right."

They came to the cracked concrete yard separating one of the hospital buildings from its heating-ventilation outbuilding. The fans in the structure were going full force, making a hushed roaring sound that seemed to screen them in. She led him by the hand to a small alleyway between two outbuildings and stopped. She looked deep into his eyes and said, "The money, please."

"Not until after," said Tonya.

"As you like," she said. Tonya was fully erect now, and he started to unbuckle his belt, not really knowing what sort of protocol prevailed in a strange undertaking such as this. Immediately she was against him, a fragrant perfume drowning out the uglier smells coming from the hospital. He put his arms around her.

Suddenly, there was a jolt and an intense, swelling pain in his crotch. She had kneed him, hard. "Wha—" he cried, falling backward, almost paralyzed, onto the concrete. The girl was standing above him, brandishing a long, sharplooking jackknife. It must have taken up all of her tiny handbag. "The money," she said.

Anton felt fear welling up in him, pushing aside the dull ballooning ache of his balls. She could just knife him and be done with it! He fumbled in his pocket and pulled out his money, rushing and dropping some of it. She reached down and took it, all 115 rubles of it. She put it in her bag, smiling.

"Stand up," she said, wiggling the sharp point of her knife. He did so.

"To remember me by," she said, moving closer. There was a rush of pain in his foot. She was stepping on his big toe with the dangerous point of her high heel! White-hot agony engulfed his foot. He tried to pull it away but this caused the pain to grow even worse. He cried out and began to bawl.

Finally, she let up. She was gone before he fully realized that she had stopped. He fell to his buttocks and ripped off his sneaker, expecting to find a ragged stump where his toe had been, but there wasn't even much blood. The toe was rapidly becoming numb. He figured the worst it could be was broken.

After a half-hour or so, he managed to limp out of the alleyway and back to the park. There was no hope of finding Zhenya. Tonya guessed that he had been robbed too. What a development! Tonya couldn't stop crying. He felt mortified.

It was completely dark, and, he knew, it must be getting close to midnight. The last train for Mytishchi left at one o'clock. He searched his pockets for coins and only came up with four one-kopek pieces. He could manage the train, but he'd have to walk back to Yaroslavl Station, five kilometers or more. He had no choice. His parents didn't mind his getting home late on a summer night like this, but they would kill him if he didn't come home until morning. He put his sock and sneaker back on and, staggering mightily, started to walk.

Miroslav Bronstein sat at his station on the left side of *Molotochek*'s main control panel and thought about his wife. Good old Irina. *I take to missing her at the oddest times. . . .* As he stared at the dimly lit airlock interior showing on his lower CRT screen, his eyes went blind, displaying instead the prolonged view of her he'd had during their last night before he'd had to leave for Baikonur. They were in their bedroom, the ceiling lights ablaze, he kneeling up, she more or less flat on her back, with two pillows beneath her hips. The awkward position made a little crease across her pale, muscular abdomen and the constant rocking motion imparted to her shoulders was wrinkling the stiff cotton sheet, already damp with her sweat. She squeezed her red-haired mons with both hands and smiled up at him, rubbing her clitoris in time with his slow thrusts. "Slava?"

He shook his head. Time for reality. "Yes, Volodya." Curiously, the habitual Russian nicknames were becoming easier for him to bear.

"We're about ready to decompress now."

"I'll put it on the second monitor." He tapped controls and threw data arrays on the upper screen. Life support for the three men in the airlock, plus systems for the lock itself.

The instruments on this side of the console were mainly concerned with the direct operations involved in flying the spacecraft. Other instruments, for the detailed monitoring of the ship's systems, were at the flight engineer's station, to the right of the center panel. This seemed to him to be the best arrangement, but there was some duplication. The flight engineer had the minimum controls necessary to actually fly the ship, though he would rapidly be swamped with conflicting things to do. If he had a heart attack, Manarov could take over from him in midmaneuver for a quick and dirty safing operation. Similarly, it was a good idea for him to have some idea of what was happening in the bowels of his ship as he flew it.

On a panel bolted to the ceiling above his head was an array of idiot lights. Once upon a time, during the days of the early *Salyuts,* that had been the principal engineering display for Soviet cosmonauts. It was thought that was all they needed, that ground controllers would do the rest. But the failure of an idiot light had killed the *Soyuz 11* crew. In any case, times had changed. Now that panel was merely a backup to the real systems displays Manarov and his computers monitored. The panel was at the moment a sea of blue light surrounding one brilliant orange lamp, the indicator for the starboard solar panel, saying, "something is wrong," nothing more.

On his upper CRT he'd called up a general engineering display, a histogram of all the ship's systems. Most of it had the normal badly-made-fence look, the systems operating in their nominal range, within a few percentage points of each other. Total electrical power was down around fifty percent, however, and the solar panel's socket gear indicated a general failure.

It was, he supposed, a marginal disaster. For purposes of life support, the ship was slightly overpowered. Even considering the experiment load, unusual in a vehicle intended solely as a transport, they would probably suffer no more than a ten percent shortfall. They should be able to complete the mission; in fact, they had no choice, given the realities of celestial dynamics, but it would be a dangerous strain on their battery systems. Dangerous. He didn't like to think about it, just now. Danger was the stock in trade of the explorer. Still . . . Miroslav Bronstein folded his arms and listened to the airlock chatter.

Anton floated behind Volodya in the crowded space of the airlock, heart thudding as usual. The sweat beaded heavily on his upper lip and it was hard to keep from breathing in gasps. *You'd think I'd get used to this. . . . I never get used to anything. How the hell does a thing like this get past the flight psychologists?* He had a sudden flash, remembering Carla's merriment at his nervousness in Houston's monstrous traffic. Twice, twice he stalled the damned car, panic braking without his foot on the clutch! *This felt like that.*

Manarov's voice crackled in his earphones. "Okay, Lyova. Decompression."

"Decompression." Chishak, seated at the airlock's internal control panel, sounded equally nervous, with, perhaps, a bit of a quaver roughening his voice. He really had no way to know how dangerous the failure was.

A sudden hiss penetrated the thick Plexiglas of Serebryakov's helmet visor and faded swiftly away to nothing. The light over the outer-hatch locking lever turned from blue to amber.

*Shit. Here we go again.* He steadied himself against the overhead with one hand, bobbing in the semidarkness as Manarov cranked the lock lever. The door disengaged from its lugs, popping open slightly, moving silently downward. Anton, looking over Volodya's shoulder with eyes already dark-adapted from the red light of the airlock, was startled to see a disk of bright stars. "My God!" he whispered.

Manarov's sigh was like rushing water in the suit radio. "Yes. I've been waiting for this." He patted his umbilical reel, then pushed off into the starry night. Serebryakov, suddenly unwilling to be left behind, followed.

Perched before the controls, his booted feet securely locked in safety straps, Chishak watched wide-eyed as they disappeared into nothingness. Manarov's voice-activated microphone came on, staticky. "Did you say something, Lyova?"

Chishak wondered briefly if he had. "No, comrade. Merely a little heavy breathing."

"Stop thinking about space-pussy and this urge to breathe will go away."

The remark made Chishak angry, but he said nothing. Why bother? Doubtless the Chernobyl divers and doomed helicopter pilots had made similar flippant commentary as the gamma rays ionized their cell chemistry. It was part of the bourgeois camaraderie.

Outside, in the spark-stippled darkness, Manarov floated slowly down the narrowing channel of the ship's umbra and stared at the sky. The northern constellations, familiar since childhood, could scarcely be picked out in the profusion of stars, and the southern ones, taught to him in cosmonaut school, fared little better. The ecliptic was decorated with ghostly *Gegenschein,* far brighter than it had seemed even from the darkness of a lunar farside orbital night. He thumbed the umbilical reel's drag brake and coasted gently to a stop. The sight of the sky was becoming strangely dizzying. He blinked hard and tried to stop his perspectives from shifting. Sometimes the hard, untwinkling stars seemed like pinholes in a black fabric just out of reach, other times . . . If I fall toward the distant points of light, far far below, I fall for a hundred billion years. . . .

He tugged gently on the umbilical and turned to face *Molotochek.* It was a vast, odd-shaped black hole engulfed by the night sky, the airlock door a small red opening near one end. Serebryakov was a tiny, vaguely humanoid figure silhouetted in a disk of wan light. He considered the man, who grew slightly in size as he floated away from the ship. What about him, now? Probably pissing his pants with terror and wishing for a drink. Maybe it was a mistake not to expose his shortcomings. That business with the liquor ration could have been fatal. But . . . it's over now; there was other business at hand. "Lyova."

Chishak stirred in the airlock. "Yes."

"Turn on the external floods, please." The universe suddenly filled with white light from a dozen sources and the stars washed away. *Molotochek* sprang into existence, a long green cylinder covered with functional excrescences.

Serebryakov was only an arm's length away now and his sun visor was up, his pale, sweat-beaded face plainly visible. "So. What do you think, Tonya?"

Serebryakov's first impulse was to shrug inside his spacesuit, but he smiled instead and said, "Leaving the lights off was a good idea. And we're far enough out that the whole inner solar system can hide under our hull."

"Glad you appreciated it. All right. Let's get to work."

They reeled themselves back to the ship and then made their way along the external handrail network to the base of the starboard solar panel. The L-shaped black and gold array was cocked at an odd angle, its servomechanism having somehow failed, probably because the same event that had cut off the power feed had also cut off outgoing instructions from the ship's computer. They surveyed the motionless thing for a while, looking for obvious signs of damage, seeing nothing. "Hmh. Probably just a chip failure."

Serebryakov nodded. The necessity of using home-designed circuitry on these things raised their failure rate, especially for silicon hardware exposed to prolonged vacuum. Japanese machinery now had a reliability rating in the four-nines vicinity. "I'll go get the tools and replacement module." He started back up toward the nose.

"Lyova. Anton is coming back to get the replacement logic box. He'll also need the type-six tool kit and a set of lanyards."

"I'll have them at the hatch."

Serebryakov returned shortly with the equipment, bobbing along the hull like one of those enormous parade balloons so popular in New York and Tokyo, and they set to work. The tool kit had its own high-grade storage battery and, when opened, sprouted a collection of devices that were coupled to the main box by their own extensible cords. In addition to being power umbilicals, the wires kept things from floating off. Anton carefully clamped the kit to a nearby handrail, then Volodya began undoing the solar panel's baseplate with a torqueless socket wrench, carefully snatching the nuts up before they could escape and stowing them in a pocket on his suit's sleeve. When the task was done the wing floated gently away, connected to the ship by two lanyards.

"Let's see now." Volodya tipped the panel away and stared up into the base. "Those sons of bitches. Star-head screw fasteners. I guess we weren't supposed to have to take this apart during a mission."

Tonya wordlessly handed him the appropriate hand tool. I guess not, he thought, smiling at the other man's exasperation. Now that he'd been out here for a few minutes the terror was, as usual, beginning to recede. Even with the floodlights on, the velvet backdrop seemed unreasonably beautiful. He looked away from the work site and began scanning the heavens. The brighter stars were still visible, and one lemony little jewel caught his eye. Hmm. Probably Saturn. If you stared hard enough, you could imagine the presence of a tiny disk. Let's see. What else can I spot?

Volodya pushed the head of the screwdriver into the socket, holding the solar panel's baseplate rim with his other hand. What was it the American engineer had told him on that tour of Kennedy Space Center? *Righty tighty, lefty loosey.* I wonder if you could make a rhyme like that in Russian? Probably not. He locked his feet around a handrail and began to apply pressure, knowing it would come off only with great difficulty. Damn it. He started to shift his grip, taking better hold of the screwdriver, and . . .

*WHAACK!*

The hard vibration came up his arms and entered his body, leaving through the top of his head, leaving behind a chaos of reeling senses. Volodya felt himself unfold into a starfish shape and the world was going end over end, *Molotochek* rushing past his eyes, slowly getting smaller.

Tonya's voice shouted, "My God! Volodya! What was that? What happened!?"

What indeed? He thumbed the drag brake on his umbilical reel, then set the little electrical motor to drag him back in. The dull-green ship was spinning round and round before his eyes. . . . He gagged and set his teeth against rising vomit, swallowed heavily, forcing it back into his stomach. The ship came up quickly and he grabbed at the spinning handrails. One of them clanked against his faceplate and then he was still, pressed against the hull, shoulders wrenched, breath coming in short, uneven gasps. Dear, sweet . . . Why didn't my life flash before my eyes?

And Bronstein's voice rasped loud in his earphones. ". . . attention, for God's sake, Volodya! Check your suit integrity! I've lost telemetry on you."

He tried hard to focus, but his head was still spinning. "I . . ."

Anton's voice cut him off. "I see the problem. The life-support signal connector's come unplugged from his umbilical reel. I think I can . . . there. It's back in."

Bronstein sounded relieved. "All right. It's back. Volodya?"

Rolling onto his back, Manarov looked into the depths of black space. The solar panel was a tiny, flat elbow, brilliantly lit up by sunlight, slowly getting smaller. "Shit. Anton. The CMUs. We've got to go get it."

Serebryakov suddenly felt enormously sick. "Go get it. But . . . we *can't.* I mean . . ."

"We *have* to have it! We can limp along with one, but—"

"Volodya," said Bronstein, "how are you going to solve the celestial mechanics problems of this, uh, rendezvous? Have you thought about . . ."

"Sla-*va.* Think about it, comrade pilot. We're in solar orbit. The distances over which we can treat it as a simple three-dimensional vector are very large." He turned to Serebryakov. "We've got to get moving on this."

"I . . . yes. We have to do it, then." Compressing his lips, trying not to think, absolutely not to *think* about what they were about to do, Anton headed for the CMU bay.

Out of nowhere came Chishak's voice. "What the hell *happened*?"

By the time they rigged out the CMUs and went scooting away from the ship, the runaway solar panel was a glowing flake, three kilometers from *Molotochek* by radar. The maneuvering units would allow them to leave the vicinity of the ship in relative safety, but still, it seemed a death-defying thing to do; it would be at least four kilometers out by the time they caught up. No one had ever taken a CMU that far.

Lyova watched them go, shrinking into the oppressive night, dwindling until they were nearly gone. "Good luck," he finally said, much too late to sound anything but desperate.

Once away from the ship, they could see the earth and its moon, tiny dots against a black backdrop, one bright blue, the other a duller gray-white. Serebryakov stared at them until they set behind the edge of his helmet. It was . . .

hard to believe they'd come so far from home. "What do you suppose *did* happen?"

Manarov floated silently inside his suit, listening to the rustle of his breathing and the faint whine of the life-support system behind his back, watching the solar panel slowly grow before them. It didn't seem to be getting any closer, just bigger, and it was tumbling very slowly, perhaps one revolution every two minutes, with just a hint of a second-axis spin. Fortunate thing, that. Most of the angular momentum ended up in me. "I don't know, Tonya. We'll have to look at the evidence."

"You don't suppose . . ."

"Probably, but . . . look, we're less than sixty seconds out. Let's just wait and see."

The thing grew swiftly before them now, becoming a bright black-and-gold wall, blotting out the stars, reflecting distorted images of the tiny Earth, Moon and sun. They braked to a stop with a complex thumping of their cold-gas OAMS thrusters.

"Well, now. Judging from what happened, it must have been on the proximal end of the wing."

"Maybe not," said Serebryakov. "It took a lot of energy to break the lanyards. Perhaps leverage from an impact on the distal end . . ."

"Using me as a fulcrum? Look, we've got a counter-clockwise tumble here, and I was holding the ventral side of the panel stem." Odd, how the nautical point of view sufficed to give them an absolute frame of reference, even here. "That's how I wound up with most of the spin. If this thing was tumbling at sixty rpm we'd never get it back."

"As you say," muttered Serebryakov. "I'm not used to thinking about things this way."

"Doesn't matter. We'll soon know. You take the distal end and I'll take the proximal. Let's get it started back."

They went to their appointed places and began clipping themselves to carabiners welded to the edges of the panel, maintenance attach points. Suddenly Manarov hissed through his teeth.

"What is it, Volodya?" Anton thought he knew.

"Double craters, back to back, about eight centimeters in diameter, connected at their bases by a common three-centimeter hole. It looks like we were shot by an explosive bullet!"

Anton was silent, finishing the job of attaching himself securely to the wing, wondering what it would have been like if the object had gone through one of them. An unpleasant death, most likely . . . That old Disney movie, with the astronaut's faceplate brilliantly lighting up from within, then going dark, filming over with blood . . . He shivered. "You suppose there are any more of these 'bullets' around here? We're not that far from the inner sun-Earth libration center."

"Uh." Manarov clipped home his last attachment. "I guess so. But our velocity relative to any particles gathered there would be very low. That thing has to have been in a cometary orbit."

"Just a stray, then. Bad luck."

"Shit. Let's get this goddamned thing back home. We can have our nervous breakdowns later, over tea and cookies. . . ."

They were back around the shiny new table, drinking from microwave-heated vials of honeyed tea, feeling safe despite the limited protection *Molotochek*'s hull would afford from passing meteoroids. "Christ, Tonya," said Manarov. "What are the odds that we'd encounter something like that?"

Anton considered, twirling the hot cylinder back and forth between his hands. "Very small. Vanishingly small. But I've been thinking about something. There's a meteor shower in early May called the Eta Aquarid shower. It's supposedly associated with periodic comet Halley. I made just a few preliminary calculations, but it looks perfectly plausible that we were hit by a piece of Halley. That would certainly explain the momentum. But still, particles that large, even in a meteor swarm, are extremely rare. Running into one is more than bad luck."

"That's what I was thinking."

"It's sort of ironic. I was reading up on the discovery of Sinuhe; and it turns out that the principal goal of the study was to quantify how much debris there is in the region surrounding the Earth. Of course something as small as our friendly visitor wouldn't have been caught."

"Well, as they say, we have used up our bad luck and have nothing left but good fortune. Although it could have been so much worse."

"During one of the EVAs I would like to try to take a sample from the puncture. Maybe I could pin down where it actually came from."

"Sure thing."

There was a pause for about twenty heartbeats.

"About last night," Manarov began, turning a palm upward as if he were introducing a cabaret act, "I apologize for losing my temper."

Anton looked down at the table. "No. It was my fault. Though I do not fit the profile of alcoholic well, I am unusually susceptible to the effects of strong drink. The temptation is sometimes overwhelming. I must admit to you, Volodya, that last night I almost lost it. The Russian Soul effect, I guess. They call it clinical depression nowadays. With me it is rare, but when it comes it is overpowering. Liquor fixes it up quick, though; and it doesn't seem to come back, at least not right away."

Manarov was leaning back, frowning slightly, as though he were about to make some kind of damning judgment. "I suppose we all have our biochemical quirks," he said slowly. "Do me a favor, will you, Tonya? If you feel depressed again, let me know. Trust me, if you can."

Trust him? He supposed that, by admitting his weakness, he had already opened a kind of communication with the man, but it seemed a one-way street. Tonya might tolerate the man and even enjoy his company; but he would not trust him. "I'll try," he said, looking into the shiny blue eyes for some sign of weakness.

"Good," said Manarov, looking at his watch. "Well, it appears as though I've got some time to kill." He smiled engagingly. "Nothing new. From now on the principal activity will be coping with boredom. Are you having a good time with your Digital Entertainment Unit?"

Now it was Anton's turn to smile. "Yes. It's really not very difficult. You want me to get it?"

Manarov nodded, and the planetologist detached himself from his seat and pirouetted across the room to his sleeping compartment. As he brought the computer back he noted Chishak and Bronstein through the hatch, engaged in some sort of arcane experiment. The commander was floating outstretched while Lyova attached wires to strange, metallic cuffs on his arms and legs. Tonya shuddered. Was this how they would spend the rest of the trip, being guinea pigs for a slightly mad scientist? He turned away and velcroed the computer to the center of the table.

Taking his seat once more, he cracked open the machine and turned it on. "How about chess?" he asked. "The Kobei programmers packed an inordinate amount onto its ROM, including a sample chess algorithm to demonstrate the use of the task-learning object."

Volodya watched the opening screens as the other man navigated to the chess module. "Can we play each other?"

Serebryakov stole a quick glance at the flight engineer. Did he want to reestablish some kind of superiority by beating him? "Of course. Let me just do this. . . ." An elaborate, black and red board appeared on the screen, and Anton folded it down until it was parallel with the keyboard, flat against the table. He touched an icon along the left side of the board and amazingly detailed, three-dimensional human-figure pieces appeared on their appropriate squares. Slightly foreshortened to mimic a player's viewing angle, the pieces seemed to actually stand above the board unless one looked carefully. Another touch and the pieces transmuted into the appearance of good old lathe-turned wood, much easier to play with. "The luck of the draw— you're white. Just touch the piece you want to move and the square you want to move it to."

Manarov moved in a precise, learned manner and almost won in the opening, but slowly, almost imperceptibly, Serebryakov's strange, intuitive play was gaining him an advantage in pieces. At the end, Anton almost had him, but he made a stupid mistake that cost him the game. Each sat back from the board with greater respect for the abilities of the other. "It's almost time for the daily checklist," Volodya said, enjoying the victory and feeling more tolerant of the planetologist's foibles than ever. "That was a good game."

Anton nodded. "Yeah. I haven't played for a while; it's not good to get rusty."

Manarov eyed him with something like amusement. "No," he said. "I guess not."

# CHAPTER 5
## *June 1, 2002*

Hermann Oberg rested his vested, jacketed paunch on the podium, which was a little low for him, and stared calmly out across the sea of diplomats that was the UN General Assembly. The varicolored men rustled with Brownian motion, bouncing off one another now and again, meeting with glad cries or hostile looks. The polyglot sound of their many voices was as the surf.

The men were, as always, slow in getting to their seats. The third-worlders wandered around a good deal, conducting most of their business on the fly, buttonholing the industrialized West and the Asian littoral for financial assistance, trying to cadge free military supplies from all and sundry. *Plus ça change* . . . In recent years, their success at these tasks had been remarkably poor. Oberg felt a slight twinge of anger at this unwanted emergence of his French persona, but, with resignation, it was necessary. These were diplomats, after all, and he would be giving his speech in French tonight.

Gripping the edges of the podium with broad hands, he rested his weight forward, hearing the wood creak. What a pitiful mess, he thought, carrying the global parliamentary hopes of a leadership sixty years gone. It was the anti-Axis allies who'd first styled their combined armies the "forces of the United Nations," even before this body came into being. But this pathetic mess . . . Somehow he didn't imagine this ugly crew followed the notions of the great French parliamentarian Robert and his authoritative tome, *Les Rules d'Ordure.* The thought made him smirk. These folk probably didn't even know about Hoyle. Hm. *"Sieg hoyle?"* he muttered.

Secretary General Carnera, just mounting the rostrum, gave him an extremely odd look, but Oberg, lost in time, failed to notice it. He was imagining himself standing before an outdoor amphitheater, filled with thousands of black-clad, torch-wielding young men. Iron Christians. The crowd was chanting something, *Horst Wessel Lied,* perhaps. . . . Oberg prepared to fill his lungs and bark like a dog.

The secretary general held out his hand and said, *"Guten Abend,* Hermann."

Oberg looked down on him, silent for a moment, then slid back through a two-dimensional slot to this lower reality and took the proffered hand in his own. *"Buenas noches,* Primo."

"It's good to see you again. I look forward to your remarks." He gazed out across the chamber. "They seem to be coming to order at last." The secretary general was a large man, with big, flat hands, the nails deformed and spatulate, with a heavy, bony jaw. In youth he had been athletic and powerfully muscled, but old age was stripping him to the bone. He stooped over the podium, rapping for attention, then went through a perfunctory introduction of Oberg.

Hermann Oberg stepped up to the podium and stared hard at the audience of diplomats. Shit. This is a waste of my time. These little bastards aren't going to listen. And even if they do listen, they're not going to understand. Well, it was mercifully short, in any case.

"Esteemed Secretary General, members of the Security Council, honored Ambassadors . . ."

His lips were writhing and sounds were coming out, appropriate phonemes for the appropriate interpreters, men's heads cocking, their attention shifting to their earphones, right or left according to handedness, but it had ceased to carry meaning even for him. Memorized, the head-tape of a canned speech continued to roll, driving muscles, pushing air.

*I come here tonight with an appeal to sanity.*

*There is no danger.*

*True, the Soviets have carried thermonuclear weapons into solar space, but their purpose is a noble one. There is no danger.*

*This is a true example of swords into plowshares. With the retrieval of asteroid Sinuhe, we begin to harvest the bounty of the sky for all mankind. There is no danger!*

*If the Soviet planners have miscalculated, the first explosion will rupture the asteroid, or send it on a path away from the Earth. We may never see it again. Truly, there is no danger. . . .*

*And if we succeed in this noble venture, the rewards will be manifold, for the road to a prosperous future will be opened for all. . . .*

Less than seven hours before rendezvous, Manarov sat in his flight engineer's seat, staring at the lower CRT screen. Aten-asteroid Sinuhe was a murky, elongated crescent, almost featureless, set among a sprinkling of stars. It was a very low resolution image despite the excellent optics, only about twenty-five picture elements across, and blown up like this, the pixels showed as individual dots. Not much detail there, perhaps the hint of a large depression near the left edge. Yet he was *seeing* it; until now it had only been a point of light in the eyepieces of the largest telescopes. Mysterious still, it awaited them. He watched it for a long time, spellbound. The angular momentum was . . . low, too slow to see. The crater did not move relative to its surroundings; but of course he shouldn't have expected movement. He did a rough calculation and estimated that this crescent only represented about a quarter of the surface if it was reasonably regular. Since they were approaching from the nightside, the crescent shape was caused by lighting angle, not shape.

He turned away suddenly.

Lara, Larisa, little Shutka from the past.

Is that what brings me awake now? Only five weeks since that last sweaty night. Well. Missing her is nothing new.

He shifted in his chair, bumping against the loosely fastened lap belt, buoyant, or so it seemed. The air rustled around his head, driven by a dozen little fans, and the ship's structure ticked distantly. A month in steady sunlight was baking the thermal blankets, the heat leaking in on one side, the other growing cold. Strange they hadn't thought of that. Once out of Earth-orbit, there was no night, and this was a hell of a lot further out than the friendly neighborhood moon. Discussions were underway, even now. After the encounter, on the long voyage home, they'd probably opt for the American solution: rotisserie mode. Shut down the three-axis stabilization system and put the ship in a slow spin. It would work, though there would be inconveniences. And it would play merry hell with the active heat-exchange system that kept their cryogenic fuels from . . . expanding.

He looked back at the asteroid. Sinuhe, son of Senmut. Physician. Explorer. Hypothetical novelist. Surely it isn't this little piece of nothing that caused my unease? Some politician had been quoted in the liberalized Socialist press as referring to it as a "space Zil." Pity the bastard couldn't be here now. Even without scale, you could see it was in fact quite a substantial little hill, something of a space soccer stadium. No, that isn't it. I'm thrilled to be here. This is my little place in the annals of achievement, if nothing else.

He put his feet up on the control panel, pushing himself back into the chair, using his leg muscles to simulate gravity, then cupped his hands behind his neck and pushed. Better, but not much. Nerves? No. Yes. Maybe. He unstrapped and floated back to a position between the two exercise machines and wondered, what is it that I want? Gravity, or rapid movement?

Gravity. So be it. He put two fifty-kilogram weight straps on the rear pivot arms, then slipped into the *soloshnur* device, straddling the bench, feet on the rubber footpads, shoulders under the floating bar. Push. Oof. Like standing up again after a few days in bed. Down. Push. Oof. Down. The sweat started out on his brow and began to grow little coalescing spheres in his armpits. Push. Oof. Down. Push . . .

His nervousness began to sink out of the world as blood coursed into his brain, laden with muscle-demanded oxygen. The fire of burning glycogen heated his soul.

It's not the rock.

Or space.

Or my stupid feelings about the life of career decisions.

Larisa.

Lara.

Little Shutka from the past.

Memory was an anodyne, and welcome.

He climbed the stairs from the Vladimirskaya Metro station slowly. The crisp fall weather was giving way to winter, and the sunlight was already slanting precipitously from a low, washed-out sun. If the leaves had still been on the trees, Kuznechnii would be in dim twilight. As it was, the watery light was barely strong enough to cast a shadow. Summer was so short. Already ice was beginning to crisp the margins of the river, and night was coming before suppertime. Summer might be the time of white nights, but this was the season of gray days. At the top of the stairway, Volodya stopped and sniffed the air, redolent with the smell of burning leaves. *Still, it's a good time of year. And I love this street.* He began to walk briskly down the sidewalk, noticing for the hundredth time the bunting and posters draped over the house where Dostoevskii had spent his last years. *Died a hundred years ago. Well, I never did like his canting spiritualism.*

He stopped in front of the baroque portico of the institute's library, and studied the weathered red doors. *Working on a Saturday again—when was I supposed to have some time to enjoy himself?* Even his mother was beginning to worry about how hard he worked. But he still hadn't mastered the grinding difficulty of tensor calculus. And, sooner or later, he would have to start gathering material for his thesis. *I* have *to understand it. . . .*

Spontaneously, he turned and began to walk down the street toward Ligovskii. *There isn't enough time for everything; but, just this once, I will let it go. I'm still young, after all.*

*Yet, for all the work, 1981 hadn't been a bad year. I've gotten laid twice. . . .* His lips twisted slightly as he watched his feet scuff along the cement. *Not* bad, *three times in eighteen months! Still . . .* more stories were coming back from Afghanistan. Some soldiers had been there for two years now, and rumors were coming back with rotated troops. The Mujaheddin were . . . elusive. Things were steadily getting worse. No end in sight. Babrak Karmal. The extensive use of Central Asian troops was lessening; more and more trustworthy Russian soldiers were being cast into the fray. When you talked to foreigners, they kept saying "Vietnam" and "Why can't you see what's going on?" All you could say in return was, "Why didn't you?" Which sounded pretty weak.

Still, it wasn't *all* like that. The news from space was heady indeed. The steady drumbeat of crews to the *Salyuts* went on and on, building up a knowledge base that would one day see men on the planets. . . . Best of all, foreign activity was picking up. The *Voyager* pictures from Saturn had been spectacular, sparking rumors that the long-awaited *Yupiter* probe would be funded. The American *kosmicheskii korabl,* called *Columbia,* had flown at last. . . . The sight of it touching down on that dusty lake bed might light a fire under someone. . . .

He stopped and stretched, shrugging his heavy backpack full of engineering texts into a more comfortable position, looking around. *What do I know about this corner? Something . . . That's it. The old coffee shop I went to once with Pisovskii.*

He went down the little flight of stairs to the basement level, pushed open a warped, black wooden door, and stepped into a dim, papirossa-smoky room. *It was unchanged?* Not quite. The place seemed, incredibly, even dingier than the last time he'd come in. The posters on the walls were shabbier, the walls themselves implausibly scabrous. *Surely this sort of place was unlicensed. . . .* And of course it wasn't so. Taverns of all sorts, even ones intended for rebellious teenagers, could get a license from the city government and party apparatus. Money, even rubles for a place like this, changed hands, or perhaps the bribe was paid off in bartered service. *A dive like this was probably bought with a blow job.* He walked over to the bar and bought a bottle of cheap Lithuanian beer, a beverage definitely *not* on the establishment's license, then went over and sat down in a dark corner booth.

*What the hell am I doing here?* In fact, there was something else about the place that was noticeably different. The clientele was younger. The girls were in that first bloom of young womanhood. The boys, on the other hand, looked like spindly, blotch-faced children. *I wonder why those girls have anything to do with them?* It was a bit startling to see a steamily attractive girl let a little boy grope under her skirt. . . . Volodya smiled. *That's why I never came back. I was too old for the joint two years ago.* The clientele was the same age it had always been, of course.

There was a chirruping of voices from the next booth, the girls there no longer whispering. One of the girls stood up, bidding her friends farewell, and headed for the door, buttoning up a long cloth coat. Volodya watched her and when the door opened, letting in sunlight, got a good look. She was beautiful, tall, thinnish, but with large breasts, obviously encased in a solid sort of bra. Wood for the fire. Her face was square and handsome under chestnut hair, with bright blue eyes, features absolutely regular, the overall effect rather German-looking. Here on the Baltic that was neither implausible nor uncommon. Varangian-descended Russians with the "ripe wheat" hair of north-central Europe were widespread.

The door closed. Volodya suddenly pushed his bottle of bitter beer aside, rose to his feet, strode across the room shouldering his satchel, and followed her out the door. She was already many meters on her way, walking swiftly to the north, head down, hands in pockets, long hair streaming around her shoulders. He walked rapidly after her, steadfastly closing the gap between them.

"Hello?" It was meant to be a hail, but it came out as a weak question, infirm, almost quavering. She heard anyway and stopped, turning puzzled, pale eyes on him. He supposed he wasn't a very threatening figure.

Now what do I say?

Uh . . .

She grinned a rather crooked little smile, showing even white teeth. "So. I saw you looking at me. . . ." Her voice was a smooth, midrange soprano.

Volodya felt a touch of panic. Come *on*! You've got to say *something*! "Yes, I . . . My name is Volodya Manarov." There. That was a definite move. Volodya. No Vladimir Alekseevich. He held out his hand.

She took her hand out of her pocket and, when she touched him, her fingers seemed fantastically warm. It didn't make any difference that they'd just come out of a cozy pocket while his knobby knuckles had been dangling foolishly in the cold autumn air. They were just . . . *warm*. Her smile evened out as she said, "They call me Shutka."

"They call you Joke?"

She laughed then, a high peal, distinct syllables of amusement that bore little resemblance to a girlish giggle. "I'm afraid so."

Uh . . .

"Why?" Brilliant question, asshole.

"Well," she turned slightly and glanced sidelong up the

street, rocking back on one heel and straightening the other leg so her short black boot protruded from under the hem of her dark-brown coat, then turned back to face him. "I *suppose* I could tell you it's because of my *fantastic* sense of humor, but . . . When I was eight and first studying English, I looked up the word I thought sounded most like my name. It translated as *Shutka*. My father thought it was *very* funny. . . ."

Uh . . .

She grinned again and shook her head, cascades of brown hair, ever so slightly wavy, spilling around the fur collar of her coat. "My name is Larisa Petrovna Kondratyeva." She looked at him expectantly. "Lara."

Uh . . .

"The word I looked up was 'lark.' " She grimaced with frustration.

Uh . . . hah! "You mean like the bird?"

*"Stupid!"* One of her small fists thumped off his chest. "Like jumping around and having *fun!*"

He shook his head and smiled. "I guess Shutka's a pretty good nickname for a girl to have. . . ."

She put her hands on her hips then and gave him a candid, penetrating look. His breath caught in his lungs. "Hmh. How old are you?"

Uh-oh. "I'm twenty. I'm a student at the engineering institute."

She took a step back and her eyes brightened considerably. "Twenty. Well. I'm in tenth class. I'll . . . ah . . . be sixteen in a few weeks."

Merciful heaven!

And she said, "Come on. I'll let you walk me home."

And, somewhere along the way, after trading aspirations and stories of family life, as the shadows grew so long that they bled together, she put her hand in his pocket and laced her thin fingers among his own.

Sitting in an archaic press booth above the UN General Assembly floor, Moe Schlossberg could see himself reflected in the nearly floor-to-ceiling glass. It was an odd sight, one that did not match the image of himself that lived in his head. Slouched in the chair, arms, as always, across paunch, long, relatively skinny legs stretched out, he was funny looking. His legs were big, but the rest of him seemed collapsed, his shoulders sagging, his smallish chest seeming to sink into a swollen midsection. He had almost no neck and a small, square head, hair cut unstylishly short for the year 2002. He sighed. *I look like a fat midget standing on giant legs. And my face!* It was double-chinned and jowly. . . . *Shit. I look like Broderick Crawford did on* Highway Patrol. He could remember, dimly, watching the program during his early days in America, when his English had been weak. *How old was I then? Eight?* A skinny German kid brought from München against his will and thrown unprepared into the second grade.

*How the fuck did I get so old looking? Christ. I'm only fifty-three!* It probably had something to do with the image in his head. The Moe Schlossberg that lived there was a lordly fat man, sleek and powerful, big-headed, a bit like the vast detective of, what? *Can't remember.* The oddity was he was still young and strong inside, despite his ungainly appearance. The 250-pound Moe Schlossberg who drank alone in various New York bars could still kick the shit out of a much younger man. *The problem is I stand much taller than I sit, and it draws in assholes and bullies. So admit it, you enjoy the look on their faces when the little toad on the barstool suddenly turns into a towering dinosaur.* Fat, old, whatever, six feet two and that much weight will put a strapping young jogger on his back. He had begun to walk where he could in Manhattan, even go out of his way on occasion. It was ten blocks from his apartment on East 51st to CTN Rockefeller Center, and he walked that as often as he could, maybe two or three days a week. The UN building was practically around the corner, and he had walked here. Marlowe's plastic look had practically crumbled when he'd suggested that they cover this personally.

Down on the floor, Hermann Oberg had finished his speech, pleading uselessly for sanity on all sides and the final business of a long day was begun. Schlossberg smiled. This was a Security Council vote. Under the rules as amended in the late nineties, it *could* have some teeth. The permanent members, superpowers all, had gotten fed up with the old post-Korea status quo and made a *few* changes. UN police actions were possible again, and the power to do anything about it had been stripped from the third-world voting block. . . .

Time. He sat forward and listened as the resolution was read. Long-winded blather, of course. Gently condemn the government of the USSR for carrying thermonuclear weapons into planetary space. Backhanded slap at all spacefaring nations for putting nuclear materials of all kinds into orbit. Gently condemn USSR for endangering welfare of all peoples of Earth. Softly demand that USSR abort mission and return spaceship *Molotochek* to Earth for unloading of deadly cargo.

All members but one, permanent and temporary alike, vote aye.

Ambassador Yuri A. Rafikov, towering gray eminence, stands up by himself. "The people of the Union of Soviet Socialist Republics choose to exercise their veto." Sits down.

Okay. It's over then. Time for a late-breaking news story. He swung his chair around to face Lyle Marlowe. Shit. Look at that. In repose, the man's face looked completely artificial. Smooth, shaved, no beard shadow, glittering, blinkless eyes. J. Fred Muggs haircut. Talking chimpheads on the news. He looks like a robot, waiting for divine animation. Power to ROM to boot-track to command processor upload . . . "Well. What do you think?"

Marlowe came to life suddenly. "Bland. Very bland. I don't know how we can slant it into an interesting piece. Maybe use Oberg's speech, followed by Rafikov's veto, with appropriate anti-Soviet commentary?"

Schlossberg's moist lips quirked slightly. Asshole. You're not supposed to *say* we slant news stories! Still . . . "We've got to do something with it. This is dull shit. These diplomats could put the world to sleep with an announcement that World War Three was in the offing." He sighed. Sighed? Been doing a lot of that lately. And I'm *at least* five years from a good retirement. "Tell you what. Do it your way, more or less. Use Oberg as the voice of sanity, you know, noble European appeal to reason, then use that hysterical thing from Ambassador Banana"—How could these African diplomats stand to run around with names like Banana and Bongo?—"to show the third-world slant, then use the Rafikov thing, just the one line to show Russian coldness, their indifference to world opinion."

"Should I show Ambassador Burden-Hale's speech?"

Another gusty sigh moved papers on the little desk between them. "No. If we used that, we couldn't use the Banana thing. Too much duplication. Keep the American slant out of it entirely. No sense letting the hoi polloi know how close we are to being third-world dipshits." Somewhere, not very far away, a little editorial voice was saying. It's just *hoi polloi,* "the people," *hoi* means "the."

And when the CTN trumpet theme announced a special report, several minutes later, *hoi polloi,* one supposed, heard merely the truth.

Sinuhe! Anton took a deep breath and let it out slowly. The approach had brought them across the sunward face of the asteroid and the view was almost two-thirds phase. A distinctly irregular shape, from this angle not unlike an oblong, bumpy gourd; neutral gray in color and riddled with arcuate ridges and shallow depressions like rotten spots. He ticked off the small list of things determined from Earth-based observation. Rotation rate about ten hours, rough on decimeter scales but probably lacking a regolith, a clear Class M spectrum. He downloaded a new picture; already substantially larger. Smaller punctures were becoming visible near the terminator, a pepper-and-salt effect of shadow and light. It *was* rough, rippled with weathered-looking ridges and fractures. Enough detail to make it seem enormous, even at this range. He had to remind himself that it was just a little chunk of rock, more closely related to the nickel-iron meteorites they had picked up in Antarctica than the real worlds of the solar system.

"Well, my friend, what do you think?"

Briefly amused to find himself perched upside down on the "ceiling" of the control room, Anton looked over his head at Miroslav Ilyich in his commander's chair. The position had been necessary because of the unhappily short cabling that came with the DEU. *Molotochek's* video system only could be accessed from the main data bus in the control panel; and for the delicate rendezvous neither Manarov nor Bronstein could relinquish their chairs. "It's magnificent," he said, and meant it.

"It seems pretty much as we expected," said Manarov, making a small adjustment on his board. "A broken piece of debris, cratered and pitted."

Serebryakov shook his head. "Ever since we saw Phobos we've had a pretty good idea what these things look like.

Orpheus looks much like this, but is large enough to hold a bit of its regolith and is quite a bit darker. The surface is almost totally shaped by large and small impacts, a process that can be mathematically simulated with ease. But we still don't have the least notion of what they're like *inside*."

Volodya turned back to his CRT, accepting the changing relationship with Tonya now that they were here. This was the planetologist's domain, *his* area of expertise, and he would be remiss if he didn't give the man his due. "As you say. Do you see anything unexpected?"

Anton studied the image on the screen. "Well . . . Where to begin? It's a very uneven surface. I suppose I should have guessed it would be like this from the radar. I was still picturing a miniature Phobos, something with a regolith, I suppose. Of course we won't be able to get around in the traditional manner anyway, so the shape shouldn't be too much of a problem. But it's amazing how little regolith there is: the asteroid seems almost completely stripped, although I'll need to see higher res pictures to be certain."

Bronstein was repeatedly running a hand over his hair, and Anton suddenly realized he was trying to keep the small bald spot on the crown of his head hidden. He didn't know whether this made the commander seem more human or not. It was rather strange. Abruptly, the man looked up at him and smiled. "It's ours, comrades. We made it."

Anton was knocked off guard by this sudden manifestation of good humor. "Congratulations, Miroslav Ilyich, I—"

He turned to Manarov. "Volodya, the ship's performance has been completely up to snuff. Nine hundred and thirty-two kilometers to go at a relative velocity of sixty-five kilometers per second. Right on target, with nominal fuel consumption."

Manarov stiffened slightly at this effusive outburst. He smiled slightly. "It had help, Slava. Anton's portable came in very handy in analyzing the inertial residuals. I was able to compensate for a slight deficit in the main engines."

Bronstein gave him a sudden, astonished stare, then his face darkened. "I thought I said that the Dozhdevik would be used exclusively for mission computations."

Volodya shrugged. "Everything was verified by the on-board system, at least to the extent that it was capable of."

"Damn it, Manarov, we *talked* about this! Now I find you've deliberately countermanded the decision," Bronstein said.

Anton, still unsure of what was going on, said, "The DEU has a far superior math capabil—"

"Enough, Comrade Serebryakov; I'm talking to Vladimir Alekseevich. Tell me, how do you plan to justify your actions?"

Volodya was examining the readouts on his CRT, as if oblivious to what was going on, and then, after a long moment, turned to face the man. "This is neither the time nor place to have this dialogue. The final burn is only six minutes away, and it cannot be botched. If you wish, you can make an accusation of insubordination when we return; flight computations are within my purview, and I chose to perform them with the best available equipment. Take a look around you, Comrade Commander, and notice our surroundings." He turned back to the monitor as if nothing had happened, and said, "Five minutes, thirty seconds."

Bronstein reddened, but said nothing. After a while he turned and placed his hands on his control panel. "Very well. On my mark, five minutes. Mark."

Volodya glanced up. "Anton, get Lev and assume your acceleration positions. This'll be a good strong burn."

When they were corseted into their vertical cots, Bronstein, now apparently back to normal, turned back and said, "All strapped in? Two minutes."

Chishak, who had overheard the commotion of a few minutes earlier, nodded, and said, "Nothing like a good fight to clear the old dialectic, eh?"

Bronstein turned away without a word.

*Molotochek* had been turned around at their leisure some days earlier, so it was correctly positioned for this final maneuver. Anton watched the two engineers work, happily interfaced with their instruments. He could make out Sinuhe, now almost filling the video monitor's screen.

"Ten seconds at my mark. Mark." Bronstein's voice was completely flat.

"Ready."

Serebryakov felt a moment of panic followed almost immediately by a meaningless flood of relief. Some dreams were like this. Which would be worse, if the rockets exploded or failed to light?

"Five."

He closed his eyes and listened to the silence, waiting for it to end. Watching a digital clock change was quick compared to this.

"Zero."

"Engine start."

Thaaar . . . ka-thud. The ship's main engines, which had been inactive for weeks, seemed to fart before igniting properly. The can inverted and Anton found himself on his back looking up. He opened his eyes and looked over at Chishak. The man seemed more uncomfortable this time, for some reason.

"It'll be over soon," Anton said.

Lev nodded and tried to smile. "That's what I tell my patients before surgery. You won't feel a thing."

Again the deep thrumming was accompanied by all sorts of tiny, scary noises as *Molotochek* reacted to the stress. Anton remembered as a child trying to sleep with his head on his mother's lap in the back of the little Moskvich that his father's friend Yuri owned. The car had bounced and jolted across the puddles and potholes on the road to Yuri's dacha. This was a lot like that.

Finally it was over. The engines shut off and the acceleration suddenly disappeared. Anton, driven by an astonishingly powerful curiosity, undid the straps as quickly as he could and projected himself forward. Only a small section of Sinuhe was visible on the screen, a pockmarked, crack-scribbled surface without order or reason. He whistled.

Volodya had been double-checking his numbers. "Nominal performance. Point three kilometers distance. Sinuhe solar orbit matched to within point oh-four meters per second."

"Are you ready to start mapping?" Anton asked.

Volodya changed over to the wide-angle camera, and a half-Sinuhe appeared. "We have to get rid of as much of that residual velocity as we can first. Why don't you get the DEU?"

He thought he saw Bronstein flinch, but when the man looked at him he was smiling again. "We are at the mercy of our planetologist now, I suppose. So be it. Yes, Anton Antonovich, get your magical machine."

•     •     •

From a little more than a tenth of a kilometer away, Aten-asteroid 5007 Sinuhe filled almost a third of the sky. Volodya hung in space, gripped in the embrace of his Cosmonaut Maneuvering Unit, snug in the whispering stillness of a spacesuit, and stared. It was a mountain in the heavens, from this perspective a little more than 300 meters wide, perhaps 400 meters tall, hanging in the black void, by radar altimeter 107 meters from his face. A neutral, slightly yellowish gray; not like metal.

Despite a comfortable suit temperature of twenty-one degrees Celsius, he felt a cold wind stirring against his spine, raising gooseflesh along his arms, tensing the erectile flexors of his nape hair. By God. Look at it! An enormous, perpendicular mass, going up, up. And below, a sheer cliff, dropping into the abyssal night. He looked beyond his feet, dangling into the celestial south, pointing roughly at Carina, keel of mighty Argo Navis, and tried to drink in every particle of this experience. A new world. Is *this* how it feels? He tried to breathe slowly and evenly, focusing his awareness on the vast universe before his senses, ignoring the sped-up flutter of his heart. So . . . Here. I. Am.

And Sinuhe hung there waiting, indifferent to his presence. Right now it was oriented with its broad end toward the sun, with a ragged terminator hardly distinguishable from a real edge far down near the bottom. And of course there were craters, by the dozen, by the hundred, diminishing in size until they disappeared into the graininess of the surface. If you remained motionless and just stared, stared fixedly at a single point on the edge of day, you could see the rock move, but slowly. Here, a half-meter-wide crater would move its own width, from sun into shadow, in less than a minute; but at this distance, a meter was a flyspeck.

His earphones crackled. "It's beautiful, isn't it?"

Volodya nodded to himself. "Yes, Anton. There's no denying this is as good a definition of beauty as I've ever seen. My feelings overwhelm themselves."

Serebryakov felt an odd mixture of surprise and regret. What is it about him? With every turn of the wheel he reveals some new and engagingly human facet, but always something I don't like.

Volodya put his hand on the two controller toggles and rolled his CMU, adding a transverse vector to point his feet

at *Molotochek,* suddenly demolishing the very real sense of
up and down supplied by the asteroid. The aft of the spacecraft, puny by comparison, pointed into the dark and starry
sky, where the tiny, blue-white disc of Earth glowed eerily,
more than six million kilometers away. Odd. Right now I
don't want to go back. He was facing Anton now. Five
meters made the spacesuited man a featureless white ho-
munculus, stuck fast on the surface of his square CMU
box. "Time to go."

"Yes." Anton began his own roll and jetted toward the
external storage bins at the aft end of the command module, where it joined the toroidal water tank/flare shelter.
Time to go, he thought, wonderingly. Another long moment in history. Who am I, to be here? No one, and it
doesn't matter. Attend to the task at hand.

Silent now, they floated to the bin and opened it, pulling
out the folded mass of the hastily designed Sinuhe docking
truss. No gravity here, no bulbous, spider-legged lander.
The two men gripped it hard and gently jetted backward,
hauling it free. On Earth it had weighed in at an immovable
280 kilograms. Here, it weighed nothing, but . . . Mass.
That was the thing.

It took a lot of CMU gas to get the mechanism positioned motionless by the nose of *Molotochek,* but finally
they were ready, clipped to the thing's attach points, as
rigid a connection as was possible with this equipment.
"Slava?"

"Ready, Volodya. I've got all six forward cameras running. Two each tracking you and Anton, another two fixed
on the asteroid in wide-angle mode. We're recording everything aboard ship and transmitting to Earth."

"Yes. I . . . guess this is it. Ready, Anton?"

"Ready."

"Then, I'll count down from five. On my mark, thirty
seconds at full thrust. All right. Five. Four. Three. Two.
One. Mark." Their thumbs pressed the thruster switches on
the right controller arm and the CMUs pushed against
their backs, the hiss of the jets faintly audible, sound transmitted through the structure of the suits. The cables at the
attach points went rigid. "Five. Ten. Fifteen. Twenty.
Twenty-five. Thirty. Mark." Thumbs let go.

"Jesus," said Anton.

The mountain was growing.

The earphones crackled and Bronstein said, "Telemetry says you have a perfect burn. No spin detectable."

Volodya felt himself smile through the tension that deadened his face. "Good enough." And Sinuhe, bright and dark, slowly swallowed the sky, a mountain turning into a world. They were headed for a big flat spot centered on the visible face of the asteroid, about twenty meters from the terminator, not far from two overlapping five-meter craters that made a pretty good infinity sign.

The world before them swelled rapidly, flattening out as they fell into its space. Anton had a few freezing moments to know they might die if they failed to brake properly, then Volodya's affectless voice said, "On my mark, thirty seconds of full reverse thrust. Five. Four. Three. Two. One. Mark." And by fives the count went on. Hiss. They fell forward against the front liner of their suits, thumbs pressing on the left-hand controller toggle. Hiss.

The count went to thirty and they came to rest.

And the mountain became a world.

They unclipped from the landing truss and floated free above the hard, battered surface. A great, mad, pummeled chaos stretched in all directions, crater-saturated, like some kind of friable target after many days of shooting practice. Sinuhe's gravity was reeling them in, but so slowly. Volodya's voice said, "Go ahead, Anton. It's yours. Touch it."

Serebryakov felt one more bolt of surprise tear through him. "I . . . I . . . No. You."

Chishak's voice said, "Someone had better do it."

"Give me your hand then." They gripped gloves and reached out, touching the surface simultaneously, a collective motion. Little wisps of yellowish dust rose around their fingers, but there was clearly little or no regolith here.

"Well," said Anton. "What do we say? There was nothing planned." An omission? Where was the state-supplied script?

Volodya laughed, feeling the tension drain away. "Why bother? This isn't Mars, after all, or even the Moon. Come to think of it, Russian doesn't *have* an indefinite article for us to mislay!"

Anton laughed then in his turn. "True. And for now, this is our little world. Perhaps we'd better find that contingency sample. . . ."

They set about their respective jobs, working together in a harmony of common cause, floating above bright-yellow ground, pulling themselves along by its irregularities, taking out hammers, breaking off hard little chunks, photographing their points of origin, stowing them away.

And in due course the Sinuhe docking truss dropped to the ground of their new world of its own accord, bubble-light in gravity too small for them to feel.

Spacesuited again, Bronstein sat in the command chair before the left-hand control console and watched a slightly magnified view of the blocky, CMUed figures of Manarov and Serebryakov bob around on the surface of Sinuhe, a hundred metres away, completing the process of setting up the docking truss. It had been a long, agonizing task in the uselessly tiny gravity of Sinuhe. Using an explosive, reactionless gun, they had driven a dozen pitons into the surface, each silent firing sending a jet of bright gas dissipating into space, preventing the gun from flying away on its own solar orbit. Now, firmly wired down, they were using a large hand dogger to drive eight huge screws through loops in the truss frame and down into the metal "bedrock" of the asteroid. Their heavy gasps and grunts of exertion were activating the suit microphones, making an odd, intermittent cacophony. Rasp. Silence. Oof. They had to stop frequently for, despite the powerful LSS air conditioners, their helmets kept fogging up. Angry curses had long since given way to wheezing.

Finally. "That's it," gasped Manarov. "The platform's as stable as it's going to get."

"Understand," said Bronstein. "It'll be good enough." He waited while the two men unhooked themselves from the piton network and backed away to a safe distance. Safe? Hah. If I wreck the ship, we're dead men. It was cold comfort to know the thought hadn't crossed the others' minds. Well, maybe Volodya's.

He put his hands on the two joysticks and said, "All right. Arm the secondary OAMS thrusters, Lyova."

Chishak reset a pair of circuit breakers, then typed the appropriate command sequence into the Dozhdevik computer console. Lights changed color. "Ready."

Bronstein made himself breathe slowly, evenly, feeling a pilotlike gravity steal over him, that calm that reaches through the gauzy curtain of death. The right-hand controller was for pitch, yaw, and roll, the left for X-, Y-, and Z-translation. It was this latter that he now eased forward. A ring of thrusters around the aft skirt of *Molotochek* began to putt at steady intervals. Chug . . . Chug . . . Chug . . . He eased the stick forward a bit more. Chugchugchug. Back to zero. Silence. And Sinuhe began to swell in the upper CRT screen.

The camera feeding the lower CRT, set for narrow angle, had been commanded to hold focus on the docking truss, giving a view mimicking what Bronstein would have seen had he been sitting on the nose of the ship, his eye in the middle of *Molotochek*'s androgynous docking ring. A reticle had been superimposed on the screen. The asteroid grew until it filled both screens and the two spacewalkers were out of sight. Bronstein pulled back on the left controller. Chug. Chug. Chug. The rate of closure shrank to a very low value and the docking truss was a large object on the screen. So. He rotated the left controller, Y-translation, and made the two rings concentric, then rotated the right, rolling the ship into full three-axis alignment with the truss. Yes. The truss grew ever so slowly. At the last moment he twitched the left controller backward. Chuff. Clunk. His head bobbed slightly in his helmet. Soft dock achieved. He reached forward and flipped a switch. Servomotors in the nose reeled the ship into hard dock and locked it down.

Bronstein smiled and opened his helmet visor. "Disarm all OAMS systems. The Hammer has landed."

Chishak flipped a series of circuit breakers and watched as the corresponding lights changed color, thinking, A new world! And I am here! He hadn't expected to feel this way, but now that they'd arrived, he felt a sudden anxiety to go outside, to plant his boot, however lightly, on the surface of Sinuhe. Say what you like, Lev Mikhailovich Chishak would go down in the history books as well. The mounting excitement made him feel a little lightheaded, the effect, he knew, of accelerated pulse, rising blood pressure, and a hormonal flush.

Anselmo Bustamonte stepped into the darkened interior of the satellite control room and carefully closed the door behind him. He was a tall, lanky Neapolitan with a shiny mane of black hair and an indefinable air of sad caution. He was still feeling the bite of the cold humidity that had plunged Milan into a dense, drizzling fog, and for a moment regretted the decision to place the lab in the industrial North. Even June wasn't safe from these cold spells. He pulled off his thin trench coat and tried to brush some of the water off, then hung it up.

The impressive array of HDSS CRTs on the wall were all functional now, as *Piazzi II* approached its destination. On the largest of the screens was a real-time image from the spacecraft's narrow-angle video CCD, which showed a tiny pinpoint of light only a few pixels across in its center. Even on Aeritalia's low budget, the camera system aboard *Piazzi II* was a genuine marvel, many times more sophisticated than the imaging systems of similar spacecraft designed in the early nineties. And since Sinuhe was only a few tenths of an AU away, the high-gain antenna on the main bus could transmit at a truly amazing baud rate, enough to provide "live" video, twelve two thousand by two thousand images per second. It was a miracle of engineering, and would have thrust Italy into a central position within the newly reformulated ESA virtually overnight. Certainly the country's prestige within the EEC would have been strengthened as well, reclaiming the technological lead she had lost during the late Renaissance.

Except for one simple, damnable problem. . . . The Russians had gotten there first, and with a manned mission at that. *Piazzi II* would be a mere footnote to the voyage of *Molotochek.*

Of course, they would go on with it, farce that it might be. If the craft performed well, it would impress the engineers, if no one else. There might even be a *Piazzi III,* since the backup parts were all tested and functional, if they could find another near-Earther close enough in delta-V.

A few dedicated technicians manned the necessary stations, and Bustamonte went over to each in turn, asked questions about status and upcoming events, praised them as a good manager should, and became more and more depressed. The computer uplink supervisor, an old friend from his University of Rome days, had been pitiful, talking of the new programming that was to allow for the presence of the Russian spaceship. As he put his coat on for the short trip across the campus to his office, Bustamonte was mumbling to himself, savagely.

He damned Russia for its successes, damned the EEC and ESA for their weakness. He damned that Kraut bastard Oberg. He clearly remembered the stir that *Sputnik* had caused, even though he was barely five at the time, because his father had read to him from *Corriere della Serra* in such a commanding tone. It was probably the Russians that had gotten him interested in all this to begin with. The USSR changed, Italy changed, but certain things remained the same. The Italian destiny had been thwarted again.

He had been a dedicated Mason all his life, a result of having an atheist for a father, and voted, more often than not, for the most left-leaning of the candidates, favoring the kind of Socialism that a relatively poor country like Italy needed to clean up the ignorance and inefficiency. When the USSR had, finally, seemed to work out the bugs in their style of Communism, eschewing the bully-boy attitude that had characterized their relationship with the rest of Europe and becoming a sort of paradigm for integrating limited democracy with a powerful, centralized system of government, he had even joined the party, but had let his membership lapse when he saw how far the Italian Communists were from learning any lessons.

Russia was a role model for other countries. Plain evidence that a country could learn and change. Why, then, was it that Italy, politically at least, remained chaotic, impotent? Was it religion, that old bugaboo of his father's? Was that what was wrong with America, too? Or was it too much freedom?

He sliced through the gathering mists, vowing to join the party again, and this time he would seriously work toward a political change in the country.

Miroslav Bronstein flexed his body slightly against the stiff CMU brace and felt the slippery internal fabric of the EVA suit. He pulled down the sun visor over his field of view, considerably darkening the already dim silhouette of *Molotochek*. Damn, why did he feel so uneasy leaving the ship in Lyova's control? The thing was powered down, and there was nothing he could do to endanger it. Maybe it wasn't Chishak at all. Bronstein was reluctant to let the thing go, unwilling to change from ship's commander to spacewalker. He pushed the feeling aside, knowing that he was subject to a kind of mental inertia at times like this, an unjustifiable love of the status quo.

Seventy hours of practice made flying the Cosmonaut Maneuvering Unit almost second nature, and it took only a moment to orient himself and start toward the others. Just in his frame of vision, his inky shadow contorted itself across the uneven surface, giving him a sense of the asteroid's topography that the numbers coming from the radar only hinted at. He kept his feet pointed toward the asteroid, but otherwise his old space sense kept him from thinking in terms of up and down. This was a rendezvous target, although a huge one, and not a planet.

Manarov was close enough now to make out the red flag rectangle on his sleeve. "Welcome aboard, Slava. We've found a fresh crater over here. You've got to see it."

From this vantage point, only a hundred meters or so away from the spacecraft, the asteroid appeared very different. Above the gentle hillock that had been the horizon, a jagged, more irregular promontory could be seen, looking almost like another asteroid moving in tandem with Sinuhe. And, as he moved toward the terminator, the dazzling, cheesy surface had changed into an intensely irregular wilderness, shotgun-sprayed and shattered with black. Volodya motioned to him, over this way, over this way, and he modulated his course slightly to intersect that of the navigator.

The three of them came together and stopped about five meters above the asteroid. "So," said Serebryakov, "do you want the full tour? There's an amazing amount to see; much more than I'd expected."

Bronstein shrugged inside his suit. "Start with the simple things, Anton. Tell me what I have to know."

"Very well. We go down to the surface here. Don't worry about the gravity, it takes about a minute of waiting before you are accelerated enough to matter."

The man's tone of voice made him uncomfortable. "I have considerable experience with this kind of situation." But do you? We'll see. Abruptly, the others changed their orientation, bringing the CMUs into a horizontal attitude, and floated toward the surface. Only a second behind, Bronstein followed.

From the new perspective, the rock wall loomed and the starry darkness at the edges no longer looked like a sky.

Bronstein saw it immediately: a bright, whitish-gray puncture, circular, very new looking. As they came closer it was clearly metallic looking.

"This crater," said Tonya lightly, "must be less than a century old." There was no sign of the micrometeoroid and solar wind effects that had degraded the rest of the surface. The metal was melted and scoured to a respectable shine. "A high-velocity particle, like the one that nearly stole our solar panel, but with a larger mass. If you look closely, you can even see signs of a Widmanstätten pattern in the smoothest parts."

Bronstein grunted, impressed. "Okay," he said. "Next on the agenda."

"We've accomplished all the objectives of this first EVA, Miroslav Ilyich," said Serebryakov. "We have our contingency sample, I have made my initial assessment of the asteroid's composition and history. With your permission, I would like to circumnavigate Sinuhe along the terminator and take a few samples."

"No. The schedule calls for only preliminary observations in the vicinity of the touchpoint."

Volodya cleared his throat. "Come on, Slava. That was obviously an overly conservative checklist. We *were* tired after installing the truss, but we've had a long enough rest. This isn't like a lunar excursion—the CMUs do all the work."

Damn it all! Manarov was developing into a real shit. "All right," he said. "But no samples until EVA number two. Just take a look around, follow your buddy system rules, and be back in half an hour."

"Where will you be?" Serebryakov sounded genuinely curious.

"I'll be waiting for you, here."

Tonya looked down from a height of about thirty meters. As he had suspected from the mapping photography, this end of the asteroid was distinctly different from the rest. Increasingly, the surface had taken on a shattered appearance with a roughly grainy texture. Although the color and albedo of these broken patches was about the same as the surrounding material, it was easy to deduce that these were areas of silicate inclusion, an extremely important clue to the early history of Sinuhe. Among other things, they would provide a means of direct isotopic dating of the asteroid.

Volodya appeared over the nearby sun-washed limb and jetted in his direction. "Nothing over there," he said, "at least that I could see. The large crack ends after about sixty meters. What have you found out?"

"It's very interesting, Volodya, *very* interesting. Sinuhe is going to tell us a lot about where it came from. As I told you, the best bet for its origin was as a small pocket of liquid metal in a parent body too small to form a full-fledged metallic core. We call them raisins, like in raisin bread. At this end, it looks like we have some of the surrounding material, and a fairly large transition zone. From all the hundreds of meteorites that have been found on Earth, it was never possible to piece together the whole picture of how these metallic pockets were integrated into the surrounding rock. Look at that area over there, with the intersecting fractures. If my guess is right that's pure silicate achondrite; and if it is we'll be able to characterize Sinuhe's parent very accurately."

"So. That's excellent, Tonya. You should have your work cut out for you."

Anton smiled to himself. "Yes, indeed. I just wish Miroslav had let us take samples."

"He's right. There will be plenty of time for that. Now you should just . . . enjoy yourself."

He laughed. "Right."

In a kind of controlled way, Anton did just that. He took a long moment to just look around, not in an analytical way, but just to get a sense of *really* being here. Amazingly, the fear that had been hiding just below the surface of his mind just sort of fizzled away and vanished. Suddenly the enormity of the thing rushed in, showing him his insignificant but not so bleak place in the whole. And the rolling turmoil that gently sagged to a low, bumpy horizon gained, for the first time, an absolute sense of reality, of existence. He looked at the little Earth-jewel far away and laughed.

"I wouldn't mind dying right now," he said, to no one in particular. "Volodyushka, this is the moment I've lived for."

Lyle Marlowe leaned back in the antique leather upholstery and examined the digitally enhanced image in his monitor. This was a coup of sorts, for CTN. Wren had become almost a recluse since the launch of the Russian spaceship, and a face-to-face "no-holds-barred" interview would score top ratings if for no other reason than the novelty of seeing the President once again. In fact, Marlowe had been strongly encouraged to stick close to the asteroid topic, undoubtedly because Wren had a policy statement he wanted to orate upon. He glanced at the monitor again; forty seconds to air time. He smiled uncomfortably, and watched the creature do the same. It would not be the first time that the President had been late.

John-John Fingol, the dwarflike White House chief of staff, came out of the electronics room with a panicky look on his face. "Uh, if you could, Mr. Marlowe, we'd greatly appreciate it if you would stretch out your intro a bit. We'll dub in Wren for the opening. It looks like he'll be here in a minute or two."

Marlowe nodded, looking professionally irritated. This was nothing new; such trickery was extremely commonplace in the electronic newsroom. He had interviewed an empty chair once for a full thirty minutes. But it made it more difficult to get into the proper frame of mind. An invisible bead of sweat popped onto his upper lip.

"Thirty seconds." Lyle plucked the little radio earpiece from his collar and inserted it deep into his right ear canal. "Good afternoon, Mr. Marlowe," said the fragile voice of Dina Clefton, his researcher, from the van outside. "We're all ready here. Ten seconds to air. We have the Wren image ready to go in the chair beside you. Five. Go."

Marlowe straightened his posture and looked deep into the central CCD. "Good afternoon. I am here with the President today for a special exclusive CTN one-on-one interview." He looked at the empty chair and smiled. "Good afternoon, Mr. President."

Wren's voice said, " 'Afternoon, Lyle. I am glad to be able to welcome you to the White House again."

Dina said, "The President is smiling warmly, nodding his head in acknowledgement."

"Thank you, sir. As you know, there are many developing events in the world at large today. The Indonesian crisis. Starvation in Africa. The continuing drought in the Midwest. The Russian mission to Sinuhe. The American public wants to know how you are responding to these multiple crises. They want to know—"

A clutter of hurried footsteps and President Wren appeared, flushed and out of breath, at the door. "—how increasing expenditures on projects such as the *Eisenhower* space station at the expense of social programs—" His makeup man straightened his suit and patted his face here and there with pancake. Fingol planted a hand on his shoulder from behind and inserted the presidential prompter earphone into his ear. "—helps this nation face the problems of the third millennium." Damn. Marlowe hadn't wanted to take such a argumentative tone. But it wasn't his fault. Just reading the news was interpreted by many as outright hostility to the administration.

Wren leaped into the empty chair, took a deep breath, and signaled his controller. Lyle assumed that that meant the real interview could begin.

"Uh . . . Yes, Lyle. It's good of you to state the problems of the world so succinctly. As my predecessor once said, you can't make an omelet without breaking a few eggs. Only through strength can the United States continue the almost sixty years of world peace that have been such a blessing to us all. I might remind you that more than a dozen nations now have nuclear weapons and that most if not all of them are working on the space technology required to launch them at the United States. *Eisenhower,* when it is finished, will provide the strength necessary to continue the peace."

Marlowe groaned inwardly. Wasn't his earpiece working? It was tough to conduct an interview when the responses were this disjointed and unresponsive. Another day pulling political teeth. "I see. Well, let's try to deal with these concerns one at a time, shall we?"

"Certainly, Lyle. Shoot."

"NASA telemetry indicates that the Russian space probe *Molotochek* has reached its target asteroid successfully. Sources I have talked to indicate that it now seems likely that the nuclear charges will be planted and the asteroid will be launched at Earth on schedule. Since your statements denouncing the project last year, we have heard relatively little from your administration. Could you bring me up to date?"

Wren smiled boyishly. Even in person he projected a certain charming naïveté. Years of careful practice had paid off. "Certainly, Lyle. It is imperative that all Americans understand what my position is regarding the asteroid." Pause. Marlowe counted six. This was like working through an interpreter. Finally Wren spoke. "During the last seven months, we have been working to dissuade Mr. Gorbachev from his mad scheme. All our diplomatic initiatives have been rebuffed. The time has come for action and not words. Back when I was a teenager I was keenly interested in America's relationship with the rest of the world, and so I took particular note of what we now call the Cuban Missile Crisis. As many of our audience will know, the United States was confronted by a similar mad plan concocted by Mr. Khrushchev and his advisors. They wantonly put missiles only ninety miles from the American mainland, and President Kennedy quite rightly forced them to remove them. For a time, it seemed to the average American as if there might be a war; a ghastly, nuclear war between the two superpowers. But Jack Kennedy was not daunted by these unsophisticated fears and went ahead to actually prevent a potential nuclear holocaust through a policy of great strength. So much for history . . ." He paused again, two, three, four. "Today, although much has changed in the internal structure of the Soviet Union, we see a great many parallels between the Cuban Missile Crisis and the situation we now face."

"You are no Jack Kennedy, however," said Dina into his ear. Damn the woman! Marlowe's façade almost crumbled.

"I will not equivocate about this, Lyle. The United States is prepared to take whatever steps necessary to prevent the emplacement of this Sword of Damocles ninety miles over our heads."

Lyle nodded and projected seriousness. "Could you be more specific about that, Mr. President?"

Wren smiled patiently. Two, three. "We have discussed a number of possible responses. Of course you know, Lyle, that in any situation like this in which surprise is a necessary, often the crucial, part of an action, it would be extremely unwise to speculate at any length . . . uh . . . about it. I can assure you that certain steps are being taken even as we speak. Should Mr. Gorbachev not turn aside, we will continue to take those steps. That is all I can say at this time."

"All right, Mr. President. Now I'd like to ask you about something a little closer to home. . . ."

Two weeks, Volodya thought, to characterize a whole world, then lead it to destruction. What was it about the concept of "world"? Something compelling . . . As he contemplated his dinner tray, he realized the mission planners had made a little mistake. Though Sinuhe's tiny gravity was not enough to impact on their month-old microgravity habits, it was enough to change things subtly. If they could somehow have rigged *Molotochek* for a belly landing, they would be *sitting* at the table instead of strapped to chairs, and the trays would have rested lightly on the tabletop. Now, though . . . if you left your dinner sitting loose, instead of properly velcroed down, the tray would slowly drift toward the forward bulkhead. He watched closely. Yes, the butterscotch pudding was imperceptibly creeping toward one rim of its cup. Well, the planners could hardly be blamed. *Molotochek* had never been intended to come closer than ten kilometers to any body whose gravity was greater than that of its own fuel tanks.

World. Hmh. I guess I know what it is. A world is a place to me now, like Moskva or the Arctic. Space is . . . everywhere else. Not a "place," just the region between. Interesting, the way words became inexorably wedded to subtle emotions.

Sitting across from him on the starboard side of the table, facing the porthole, Anton was ebullient. His voice crackled with excitement as he talked on and on about the asteroid, how it had met his every expectation. No, it had surpassed all of them, presenting him with undreamed-of *surprises*! Volodya smiled as he listened. A man is always humanized by his own enthusiasms.

At the forward edge of the table, Bronstein was silent, spooning up his dinner, sucking from a box of irradiated milk, but listening closely to Anton nonetheless. You couldn't tell with him. Or, not yet. Volodya watched his face, saw that it was reacting minutely but steadily to Anton's voluble discourse. No, you couldn't tell, but. . . . As each plateau of the mission was successfully achieved he seemed to unbend just a tiny bit. His happiness with the docking operation was pleasant to see. Maybe titanium would become Wood's metal, but . . . right. You couldn't tell.

Chishak, floating above the aft table edge, being pulled out of his chair by a phantasmical force, only scowled. Who would've thought that this pale and colorless space doctor, clearly frightened by nothingness, would be so desperate to go outside? Soviet space shrinks referred to this sort of thing as "the Mike Collins Effect" or "the Buzz Aldrin Effect," depending on its intensity. Even in the warmth of a collectivist team, it was painful to sit an arm's length from a spot in the history books. He was staring at his dinner as if it were some kind of manure . . . and suddenly he snapped out, "Will you shut *up*? It's hard enough to enjoy my meal dangling by my asshole from the ceiling. . . ."

Serebryakov looked at him in astonishment, a piece of black bread halfway to his open mouth.

Bronstein leaned against the back of his chair for a moment, staring hard at Chishak, then said, "Well. We don't need any of that here, comrade."

Chishak flinched slightly, perhaps, Volodya supposed, at the slight, biting emphasis on *tovarishch*.

What the hell . . . this isn't the first time something like this has happened. On the other hand, we can't be brought down early when members of the crew are no longer speaking to one another. Why do people do this? I'm *happy* to be here. And a secondary voice, from somewhere deeper inside, muttered, Of *course* you're happy to be here. *You* got to go outside, asshole.

Chishak was capping over his dinner tray now, a bitter expression on his face. "No, we don't need any of *that,* do we? Nothing but the flight plan. The Fucking Plan! You might as well be a marionette."

"Lyova," said Anton.

"Shut up." He unbuckled from his chair and floated up, snatching his tray from the tabletop with a rasp of separating fabric eyelets. He pushed himself over to the refrigerator unit and put his dinner away, then spun to look at them again. "I . . . Hell. Sorry." He pushed himself toward the door to his sleeping cubicle and disappeared.

The others sat silent for a bit, looking at each other, then resumed eating. Serebryakov seemed absorbed in the food now, perhaps running his monologue inside. His face slowly became more and more dreamy.

And why not? What is there out here, now, but us and hardware? We'll sleep and dream and tomorrow we'll go outside again. There were six planned EVAs during their two-week stay at Sinuhe, spaced at roughly forty-eight-hour intervals. Tomorrow's would be in many ways the best and most interesting, a general survey of the place, taking pictures, making a gravimetric map. It would lead to calculations so prodigious it would require extensive CPU time on Starry Town's precious Cray II. Aye, there's the rub. Where do we *put* the goddamned bombs?

His dinner forgotten, Volodya leaned back, closing his eyes, drifting slightly to the left, pulled gently by Sinuhe's tiny charms. What do I remember, and why? My parents. Sisters. Schoolmates. Friends. Those are all people. Shutka. Love. Those and other things. Things. The rockets. A whole world in the desert. Another whole world. American. Spaceships by the sea. Say what you like, I've been alive.

The *things,* the places, were distant today, pushed aside by people, faces. What *do* I remember? Shutka. Love. And *why*?

His breathing slowed, and he remembered.

It was the bright spring of 1982, during the long, dreary autumn of Brezhnev-time, when you began to realize the boys *weren't* coming home from Afghanistan anytime soon. The tides were about to turn, but no one knew it yet, halfway between two boycotted Olympic Games. Still . . . The grand polity of the Soviet Union was beginning to stir, a rustle of whispers sweeping the land. Solidarity, they said, and, Why not us?

But Mr. Evil Empire held power now in America, the weasely former CIA chief his right-hand man. And the Old Man was . . . old. Andropov and Chernenko were waiting in the wings. What then? The deluge? *Surely* the vast sea of plump, bland, smiling technocrats who ran things would just let it happen, would let things go to hell, just as they always had. Surely.

Volodya and Shutka walked hand in hand on the pedestrian walkway over the tiny Smolenka River, going over to Dekabristov Island. Of Leningrad's 380 bridges, this was

among the least inspiring: old, yellow stones, rusting iron-
work. . . . A fine, icy snow had tapped at their windows
the night before and left a centimeter-deep ice-rime that
whitened the concrete, crunching underneath their feet.
Soon, battalions of fat, broom-armed babushka-soldiers
would sweep through the district and the stuff would be
gone for the summer, when Leningrad could pretend once
again that it was a fine European, even Scandinavian, city.
Volodya could feel her hand, warm, as always, in his cold
paw, the little bones delicate beneath a thin overlay of sat-
iny skin. As they strolled, he watched the ground in front
of his feet, rolling backward into the recent past.

Just my luck, to be in love with a girl too young to
fuck. . . . But, she wasn't, not really. Tenth form was the
end of things for Russian secondary school. In a mere two
months, L. P. Kondratyeva would be what Americans
deemed a "high school graduate." Girls were known to
marry at that age, have babies. . . . Is that what I want?
The image of himself as a father was . . . what? More
than a little frightening. In any case, Shutka was entering a
teaching institute in the fall, would come out in two years
qualified to teach in the lower forms. Only experience
would give her the right to teach the upper forms, unless
she wanted to pursue a three- or four-year degree.

He looked down at her out of the corner of his eye. Her
head was thrown back, blue eyes on the sky, coat thrown
open to show a crisp white blouse, dented out by her sweet,
firm breasts. . . . God. An incredibly pretty, Western-
style girl . . . Two years . . . What will be happening in
two years? I'm out of engineering school. Shutka's out of
teaching school. Time enough. And what if it all works
out? Hard to know. Next year, our transcripts go out to
various agencies. In the fall I'll have to start preliminary
applications. . . . The Strategic Rocket Force. The
Tushino Machine Building Factory . . . The Molniya Scientific and Industrial Enterprise!

The rumors were that something big was in the offing. In
the wake of 1981 and *Columbia,* Comrade Eyebrow had
put matters into a higher gear. Now, you heard two things:
One was that a Soviet space plane was entering the airframe test-phase out at Baikonur. The other thing was just
a word: *Glavkosmos.*

Baikonur. Hmh. That, I think, is where I want to be.

And this *Glavkosmos* . . . Papa, perhaps, can find out. . . .

They turned the corner then and found themselves at Grzegorz's house. It was a narrow building, old, sandwiched between two larger structures, somehow surviving from another age, part of what gave Leningrad its special character. The street came to an end two blocks away, and beyond was the low, marshy ground where they said high rises would one day stand.

That name . . . What a hell of a way to say "Grigori!" Grzegorz Glinka was a Polish student, son of a Central Committee official. He was small and thin, very young looking, with a thready little mustache, stiff, mousy hair, and incongruously large, bony hands. He had a private townhouse and, astonishingly, a Volkswagen *zhuk*.

No wonder the fucking Polyaki have troubles like *Solidarnoshch*. . . . On the other hand, Comrade Eyebrow has a Rolls Royce to keep his Zil company. They scraped up the steps and went in without knocking. Cabbagey things were cooking in the kitchen. Probably he was making those asinine purple potatoes again.

Saturday afternoons at Grzegorz's were becoming a tradition with them. It was all very well to spend time with his parents or hers, or to wander about the city holding hands; but here they could have something resembling privacy. Other people from the engineering institute came here as well. Comrade Glinka was the only one who had *space* for a private gathering these days.

They walked into the big parlor, full of ratty furniture, and were hailed by Pyotpalch and Vanya. The two young men, one round like a pumpkin, the other very thin, were sprawled on a sagging sofa, focusing on the laughing fat girl between them. Good old Katrinka . . . He shuddered inwardly, remembering his one time with her, more than a year ago, now. What a *smell*!

I'll have to make *certain* Shutka never finds out about that one. . . . He'd been honest with her, made certain she understood he'd been with a woman or two. It seemed to be all right. She'd questioned him enough to establish that his experience was limited, then dropped the subject. And now it's a year since I've gotten laid! Okay. But these fumbling and smooching sessions are wearing me out!

"VlaDEEmir? LaREEEsa?" Grzegorz called from the

kitchen. "Welcome home! Pull up a soft spot. We'll be eating soon!"

"Hello, Shutka." That was from Grzegorz's girlfriend, Sasha Gruzinskova, a tall, angular, good-looking medical student from exotic Astrakhan. She seemed to like Shutka, and to have no use whatsoever for Volodya.

They stood talking for a minute, about nothing really, then Shutka took him by the hand and led him upstairs. He followed with resignation. This had been going on for months, and he didn't know any way to push it to the next stage without hurting her feelings. They would kiss and he would get an erection. She would rub it through his pants and let him palpate the outside of her brassiere, maybe let him stroke her behind. . . .

On the other hand, last weekend she'd let him reach up her skirt. The slight wetness coming through her panties had made him come, and *that* had been unpleasant to walk home with. A toilet-paper dabbing had been insufficient to get the sticky, smelly stuff out of his shorts. He'd had to rush to the bathroom and rinse them in cold water.

They got to the top of the stairs and went into Grzegorz's bedroom, which was more than a little comfortable compared to what they were used to, and closed the door. Shutka dropped her long coat to the floor, stretched, and turned to face him. Her expression was oddly serious, as if . . .

"What's wrong?" Is she tired of me? Have I said something? . . .

She shrugged, then, slowly, as if fighting with herself, reached into the pocket of her skirt and pulled out a little, square plastic packet.

What is? . . . He saw what it was and gasped, "Shutka!"

"Volodya, I'm . . . I'm *tired* of going home in damp undies."

He nodded slowly and, taking it from her, inspected the roman-character printing on the package. I've got to be cool about this. . . . "Interesting. An *American* condom. What do you suppose *Nyuda* could mean?"

"Do you care?"

He saw that she was still dead serious and smiled wanly. "No. Shutka . . . Are you *sure* you want to do this?"

"Do you love me?"

He nodded slowly. "I love you. I want to marry you. And I'm willing to wait."

She unbuckled her belt, unzipped her skirt and let it drop to the floor about her ankles. "I'm not. Two more years of fooling around like this and I'll probably evaporate. . . ." She started unbuttoning her blouse.

Volodya watched her get undressed for the first time and wondered about himself. *You'd think I would've been able to detect something like this coming. I must be awfully stupid. . . .*

Beautiful clothed, she was overpowering naked.

Volodya and Slava were at *Molotochek*'s exterior storage section, wrestling the massive ground probing radar instrument out of its bin. Tonya was already securing the first of the two mushroomlike receiver antennae, replaying the dock installation in miniature, about twenty meters from the touch point. He looked up and watched the others for a moment, listening to the hoarse grunts that corresponded to their motions. Radio contact, for some bizarre reason, seemed to banish the sense of isolation that he normally felt. He abruptly realized what it was that *Molotochek*'s extended fuel cylinder reminded him of: a huge fluorescent light element stretching into the sky. He smiled. "You two look like you're having fun. Do you need any help with that?"

"No," said Manarov. "We've got it. This thing is a bitch, you know? What does it mass, four hundred kilograms?"

Anton resumed drilling into the metal. "Something like that. Most of it's shielding. It's far more accurate than a seismic monitor would be."

"If you say so."

The thing *was* a problem. Even in the rarefied Sinuhe gravity, the massive instrument developed a gravitational acceleration that was difficult to counteract. It looked something like an old-time *Apollo* capsule, with a cylindrical instrument housing atop the bell-shaped pulse generator. Manarov and Bronstein finally managed to position themselves on either side of the thing, gripping a flange near its top, and, on full CMU thrust, levitated it down to a flat, relatively crater-free space far enough from the docking truss to avoid interference. "Whew," whispered

Volodya, feeling sweat on the side of his nose. "All right. That's done."

"The *lebed*'s are in about the same mass range, Volodya," said Bronstein quietly. "And they don't have a conveniently placed grip like this did. I will have to rethink how we move them around."

"We need a carrier of some sort," said Volodya. "Too bad they didn't supply us with a rocket platform."

"No one's ever worked in this kind of mini-gravity before," said Tonya. "I expect that no one bothered to do the calculations."

Volodya shook his head, but the drip was intractable. Ah well, it'll evaporate someday. "At least things stay where they're put," he observed.

When they had the device and its antennae set up, Anton went to work doing the necessary calibrations while the others returned to the ship to get the far less unwieldy gravity meter. He maneuvered himself down until he was "standing" on the surface, moved forward until the CMU arms bracketed the thing, and took hold of the flange to anchor himself in place. Sinuhe did its best to look like a planet from this orientation, and Anton didn't fight the illusion.

Ground probing radar was not a new technology; it had been used in a primitive form as early as the eighties and had virtually replaced the old thumpers for profiling sub-surface lithologies and structure. However, there were several significant difficulties introduced by the free-floating nature of the "ground" they were probing. The pulses would be severely distorted by the concave-convex nature of the surface, and much of the energy would be lost out the farside, resulting in a much lower signal-to-noise ratio than normal. The industrious workers at the Yenisei Instrument Samfab had geared up to produce this heavy-duty, more powerful GPR in record time, but the resulting machine was ten times more massive than it needed to be and considerably underengineered. Anton smiled to himself. He was slowly coming to appreciate the advantages of a directed-market economy. One-of-a-kind manufacturing was a Soviet specialty.

Volodya and Slava swooped down like flying squirrels and paused nearby, hanging against the backdrop of the sky. "All right, Tonya," said Manarov. "Is it ready?"

"Just about. Just have to start the data recorder." He flipped a toggle switch abruptly, and almost launched himself in the process. "Oops," he said. "I almost forgot. First series; fifty megahertz. And here we go. . . ." Tonya felt a click through his glove as he engaged the button, then short vibrations that must have been a kind of *bzzt*. The small oscilloscope mounted among the switches showed an extremely complex multiwave return, of course undecipherable. After two minutes, Serebryakov looked up and said, "Well, it appears to be working correctly, but we won't know until we've gotten the analysis back from Earth. I can do some preliminary work with the DEU, but even it isn't powerful enough to unscramble all this."

"Now for the fun part," said Volodya, grinning. "Sample collection."

They moved around the sunlit portion of the asteroid at a snail's pace, swimming in graceful ballistic trajectories less than a meter from the surface. When Tonya noted something of interest, they would stop, anchor, and painstakingly document the appearance of the area in both stereophotographs and verbal descriptions, then take a sample. If the find was loosely attached, this was easy. But cutting out a section of bedrock could take as long as five minutes. At regular intervals Bronstein would set up the gravitometer, set it on automatic, and move far enough away to eliminate his own bantam mass. These readings would allow them to further refine the global harmonics identified from the ship and produce an extremely accurate map of Sinuhe's mass-distribution.

Tonya looked back at the bifurcated bulge they had just traversed, wondering once again what sort of genesis could have produced such a wrinkled, cracked surface. They had been following a large, sinuous crack that Volodya had nicknamed the "Grand Groove," unsuccessfully looking for material at the bottom, and had come out into a region with a scalloped, dimpled contour, for all the world like a magnified version of the regmaglypts he had seen on terrestrial nickel-iron meteorites. But how could that be? The more he thought about it, the more it seemed that the birth of this little chunk of metal had been more complicated than he had imagined it could be. Regmaglypts suggested a high-speed passage through an atmosphere of some kind, but, even in the gas-rich early solar system, the small planetoid that had spawned Sinuhe couldn't have had such an atmosphere. Perhaps the catastrophic event that had disrupted this body had created a short-lived gas-envelope? It didn't seem likely. He shrugged. It was clear enough that there was much to be learned from this tiny near-Earther; and, if he didn't push himself too hard, his subconscious would do the job of piecing together the required new theories.

Bronstein and Manarov were looking back at him, beckoning him to hurry up. It was true, time was running out for this EVA. The jutting spur of silicate material rose behind them as he jetted in their direction. Enough of these metal samples, he thought, merrily, now we get to something *really* interesting.

Anton's fingers moved frenetically across the DEU keyboard. On the screen, a detailed, multicolor cross section of the irregular asteroid hung in indefinite blackness, showing the onionskin variations in composition blossoming in the main body, the broken spur of silicates, and the scattershot transitional zone between the two. What a fucking program! It had swallowed the data Manarov downloaded from IKI's Cray and spat out a fully graphical interpretation in under a minute!

"Volodya! Come and look at this!"

The flight engineer vaulted out of his seat and supermanned the four meters to the utility table. Tonya grabbed at him as he went by, holding onto the seat with his legs, and drew him down.

"Jesus, Tonya, that didn't take long."

"I had already explained to it the SEG-Y format that IKI would send. But it's still amazing."

"So what do you see?"

"Really, it's a remarkably homogeneous body. Apparently it has never been subjected to the kind of large impact that would disrupt it internally. You can see the layering caused by gravitational fractionation, but the DEU is emphasizing very slight differences in composition. I told you about the raisin bread theory, right? Well, what we have here is an almost undisturbed raisin. Pure nickel-iron, except for the spur."

"So much for your flying rubble pile. Goddamn it, Tonya, we *will* be able to fly it home!"

"The thing is as solid as an anvil. However, I'm not so sure about the discontinuity between metal and pallasite. It seems clear that most of the silicates were cleanly stripped off of Sinuhe during its early history. There is a slight possibility that the spur will break off under pressure."

Manarov eyeballed the image on the DEU. "That could be a problem. . . . I guess we could come up with a solution that would allow it to drop off without affecting the course."

Serebryakov nodded. "You're the flight engineer. However, I wouldn't worry about it too much. Olivine is pretty hard, and there isn't anything to suggest a crack. I doubt the relatively small quake caused by the nuke will knock it loose."

"I take it then that that's a 'go' for the rest of the mission?"

"Ummm. Yes. Sinuhe could hardly be better suited."

The hours came and went, and Anton worked on. As the first *in situ* planetary geologist, he had responsibilities far beyond those of his companions. A preliminary report of his observations had to be prepared as quickly as possible to demonstrate that real science could be done out here on the hoof, in real time. Otherwise, many would argue that there was no point sending trained scientists just to gather data. The men at JPL had called it "instant science." He had been like this at university, focused in on his task, virtually oblivious to everything else. Occasionally Bronstein or Manarov would interrupt to ask him something or find out how the analysis was going. The sun came, lancing bright golden rays through the porthole to make a bright-yellow oval that crept from the bins above the control room hatch to the floor in front of Chishak's sleeping compartment, and went. Manarov, who had been up early, retired to his escape capsule/bedroom at about six.

The DEU's word processor, customized to resemble his old "WordTsar" program at work, occupied relatively little of the machine's processing time, and Anton found that the silence of the spacecraft, interrupted by curt exchanges between the doctor and the commander, was distracting him. When he had been working on his thesis, he had used music to screen out the rest of the world, and he suddenly realized that he could play selections on the Kobei simultaneously with writing. Shit! Where had he put the headphones? Aaa, no one will care if I play it out loud. He pressed the key that returned him to the object library and selected the music object. The intro was similar to the video object's, but the "host" was the world-renowned musician Akiyo Hashimoto. There were only a limited number of actual recordings among the supplied disks, but other songs could be synthesized by the machine from an extensive library of written music. He had spent many hours on the trip out interactively manipulating these songs, but somehow they weren't the real thing. Among the firmware choices was an old favorite of his, The Moody Blues' "Days of Future Past." Certainly no one could object to that! He started it up and turned the volume up before returning to the word processor.

Another hour passed. He had finished all the initial descriptions of the asteroid and it was time to start coming up with conclusions. Yet the theory that would tie all the observations together was still not there. Instead, he felt a mysterious, almost-resolved certainty that he knew what was going on, but just couldn't put it into words. It was useless to go on until the words came. He thumbed up the volume a bit and stared at the dark Cyrillic characters on the screen.

"Goddamn it! I can't take it any more!" Lev came shooting through the hatch and caught a corner of the table. "Will you turn that crap off! I've had—"

Anton cringed back, taken completely by surprise. "Wait a min—"

"You have no right to pollute the air with that stuff. I simply will not put up with it any longer. Do you hear me?"

Anton clicked it off with a tap of a key. For some reason he wanted to explain himself to this wild-eyed stranger. "It's just music, Lyova."

"I repeat, I will not tolerate it any more. I am within my rights."

"You know, silence can be just as much of an imposition. You've had your quiet. Rights like that extend only so far."

Bronstein now appeared in the connecting hatch, looking curious and not a little amused. "What's going on here? What's the matter, Lev Mikhailovich?" At the other end of the room, Volodya stuck his head out of his bedroom, groggy and red-eyed.

Chishak looked at the man, calming down a little.
"That . . . that *music* gets on my nerves. It is bourgeois
and repetitive, performed by cretins with the skill of dancing bears, and, worst of all, encourages the most antisocial
of behavior."

Bronstein was now smiling openly. "Now, now, Lev. It's
not that bad. I'm afraid rock 'n' roll has become the sound-
track to our lives, East and West."

Chishak was reddening now, aware that he had gone too
far. "I have said what I have to say, Miroslav Ilyich. Shall
we return to the regimen?"

Bronstein grunted. "Talk about 'getting on your nerves.'
Oh, very well."

Anton reluctantly put his mind into idle and began to
look for the headphones.

With the door open, Volodya's bedroom in the flare shelter was like the bottom of a hole. He was bobbing in the
middle of a space that would have been barely large enough
to hold six men. Yet another modification of the *Soyuz* capsule originally designed as the command module of a
moonship which would have carried Pavel Belyaev and
Valerii Bykovskii to the Moon some time in 1968, it could
have been quite spacious. It was substantially bigger than
the coffin-sized "bedrooms" inhabited by the rest of the
crew. As a free-flying spacecraft, it held three men comfortably. As befitted an escape capsule, a second row of
couches had been installed.

What a fantastic ride that would be! Since signing on the
Soviet lunar program Volodya had been trying to visualize
what an emergency lunar return would be like. The return
trajectory of an LTV was always aimed at the atmosphere
under the projected path of the return ellipse. What if the
braking maneuver failed, then? Simple enough. Punch out
in the *Soyuz* capsule, experience automatic reentry. Probably ocean recovery—six men with their internal organs
oozing out their assholes.

God damn. Eighteen g's . . .

For this mission the two center couches were gone. Now
Volodya floated in the space that their absence made, sighting along a series of concentric circles that led all the way
to the front end of the spacecraft. Before him, a featureless
tunnel extended forward to a hatch two and a half meters

away. The hatch was open, letting him look further through the meter-long access bay into the living quarters. And the hatch on the other side of that was open too, so he could see the smaller circle of the hatch into the propulsion control room, another three meters on. Beyond it lay a small, dim circle, the open hatch to the airlock. The series terminated, finally, on the dark dot of the closed hatch behind the docking mechanism, a full ten meters away.

Within the dimly lit airlock, something moved. Volodya waved, and a tiny spider shape popped through the hatch. Well. The bullshit game. Volodya smiled and watched. We'll see.

Bronstein drifted slowly through the propulsion control room, straightening out briefly, like a diver, so he could thread the hatchway. Good enough. Halfway there. Hard to know how far you could go under these circumstances. Sooner or later air resistance would stop you, but ten meters was too short a distance for a measurable effect. He smiled. Bronstein was off center now. He straightened, barely clearing the access bay hatch, and collided with the port wall, ricocheting to one side.

"Shit."

Volodya laughed softly. "But pretty good, nonetheless."

Bronstein climbed through into the shelter, pushing the hatch shut behind him. "Nice place you have here."

"Palatial, yet cozy. My testicles feel privileged."

Bronstein's smile was wan. "I've thought about that. Irina and I still talk about children."

"It's not the worst thing to talk about." Bronstein's wife was a handsome, muscular middle-aged woman, in much better physical condition than Shutka, though she'd never been anything like pretty. "Think you'll ever do it?" Slava was a rarity among the cosmonauts his age in being childless. The asshole cadre liked to joke that it was because he and Irina didn't know about sex yet, it not having been a required subject in school.

"Well," he shrugged, then said, "I had myself sterilized when I was a young man. Irina knows."

"Hmh." The noncommittal sound barely covered his surprise. What the hell . . . And I've known him for fifteen years! "Why do you think about it then?"

"The usual reason." He settled onto an acceleration couch, drawing the chest strap down from its cartridge.

"My nuts still work, you know. Only the plumbing's been disconnected." He rubbed a hand over tired features. "You can get surgery in Germany to reverse these things. It's only a couple of thousand rubles."

"Think you will?"

"No."

They sat in silence for a while, staring at each other in the ruddy light of the emergency control panel, Manarov thinking, *I wonder what brought this on?*

"We're having a lot of trouble for only five weeks out."

Manarov nodded. "I've seen worse, but not this soon." *Shit. I'm going to have to say things.* He looked levelly at Bronstein, not wanting to discuss the subject any further.

"Well. You're second in command. I want to know what you think. Why is this happening?"

He shrugged. "I guess . . ." *Fuck. I have to say these things.* "Serebryakov's a dipshit. Nice guy, really, but a dipshit. Chishak's a self-centered asshole, through and through. Neither one of them's had any training in how to hold things in. They . . . can't suppress themselves like we can. Emotional bullshit. Not pilots. Not engineers." He sighed. "What can I say. They're wet inside."

"Do you think—"

"I'm not finished yet." *I guess this is as good a time as any.* "You're not doing a good job handling them. Going too much by the book. You and I, we're just . . . fancy machines. We belong out here. Anton and Lev . . . They're like the Russians in the old books. You need to treat them differently."

Bronstein looked away for a minute, his eyes reflecting the colored lights of the control panel. "I don't think I'm just a fancy machine."

"Nobody ever does."

Bronstein looked back at him. "You think I'm doing a bad job?"

"Maybe. You have to do things differently."

"Why do you think they made me commander instead of you?"

*Bad. He's not listening.* "Because I'm an engineer, not a pilot. Some people don't know the difference between a shuttle and an interplanetary ship. . . ."

"Asshole."

"Maybe so. But if you don't listen to what I'm telling you, you're going to fuck things up."

"Is that right? What do you think I should do, wipe their asses for them?"

"Is that what they need?"

"If it is, they shouldn't be out here."

"It can't be test-pilot heaven forever and ever."

"Maybe not. Tell me what's right."

Manarov sighed, forcing down the little smoke-curls of anger that threatened to ignite his temper. "Serebryakov's got a real job to do. For him, nothing. Chishak . . . Unless one of us needs emergency surgery, he's about as much good as a yeast infection under your foreskin. That's why he got so pissed off tonight."

"So?"

"Let him go outside."

"He's not properly trained."

"An EVA is an EVA. He knows how to wear a spacesuit."

"Still . . ."

"Think about what it means, Miroslav, to come all this way and then stay in this tin can. . . ."

Bronstein stared at the control panel for another little while. "Shit. I'll . . . take it under advisement." He undid his chest strap, opened the hatch, and floated away.

Manarov closed the hatch after him, then turned to inspect the control panel readings himself. Well, you said your piece. Hard words for a friend. Maybe you are just a fancy machine. He closed his eyes and thought about Shutka. Does she love a fancy machine?

Unaccountably, he remembered watching her give birth to their first daughter. She'd been so embarrassed, shitting in the delivery room like that. Hell. It'd been hard not to laugh, right through the mild horror he felt at her pain.

Why did women go through all that pain? Maybe they didn't know. . . . All right, then why did so many of them do it more than once? Because they had to. . . . And men married them, helped them make children for the same genetically deterministic reasons, even though it meant something akin to slavery, a great deal of work for so very little gain.

Human beings were, after all, just very fancy machines. And life was driven by demon ROM. . . .

So much to do.
So very few choices.
Yet, here I am, nonetheless. . . .

Lyova pulled himself through the EVA hatch and took his first direct view of the asteroid. He was still reeling from Bronstein's unexpected announcement that he would be going on the third EVA. The sun-washed hillock, cut by dazzling gold-orange reflections on his visor, was startlingly bland. Looking into a high sun made Sinuhe seem a featureless pile of dust, sizeless and obscure.

He jumped as he had been instructed, following a little arc, and positioned himself in the CMU, checking out the controls at the end of the arms. Sinuhe gently receded like a dream, and a slight spin revealed a slow panorama of the world. It filled the sky, almost as full as the treeless steppe of home, startlingly big, though he noticed that an instrument set up at the horizon was still quite close.

As he completed one spin, he saw that Manarov and Bronstein were both out, already removing cabling from the ship's capacious store. He had almost reached the top of the spaceship, and an acerbic "Don't wander too far" from Slava made him turn his attention back to the CMU. It seemed as though his last EVA back at Earth had been done by someone else, and the controls seemed alien. Okay, he thought, get ahold of yourself. This is not a game. A quick burst stopped his spin, and another started him back toward the others. It wasn't really so difficult.

"Are you having difficulty?" That was Manarov, and there was a genuine touch of concern in his voice.

"No. No problems. It takes a few seconds to adapt."

"All right, we are going to need you to help with the charges."

Right. He knew this was coming. It wasn't so strange to have a fear of radioactive substances out of proportion to their actual toxicity. He remembered watching the laughing, joking denizens of Pripat during the evacuation. One in a hundred would die unnaturally, with either the hideously metastasizing bone disease or the more subtle but equally painful leukemia. But of course these bombs emitted very little radiation, and would only produce a much more natural death—instantaneous incineration. He twisted his lips scornfully. Even today, there was so little a doctor could do.

"We'll form a sort of troika for each charge, Lyova," said Bronstein. "I'll be on the right, Volodya on the left, and Lyova, you steady it from beneath. To start we just take them down to the surface. Ready?"

Chishak tried a few precise course corrections and found that he hadn't lost the knack. He came up before the open bin, stopping precisely. Inside, barely visible, were the five tactical nuclear weapons, long, fat cylinders that looked a little like galvanized metal trash cans. "All right," said Bronstein, "positions everyone. Charge number one."

The primary explosion site was located about ninety yards "down" the asteroid, in a flat valley opposite the silicate spur. Lyova worked hard, twisting and stretching within the confines of the spacesuit, and he began to wonder why he had wanted to come out so badly. Finally, the bombs were positioned correctly, and Bronstein and Manarov began to lay the extensive cable that would connect the explosives to a solar-arrayed control node on the other side. The asteroid itself would serve to shelter this station and its relatively sophisticated computer system from the intense shock waves.

Chishak, ignored for the moment, found himself separated from the others by a little ridge. His radio still burped and chirred with interference, but he could no longer make out what the two were saying to one another. Abruptly, he thought to himself: alone. He searched the dim skies for something recognizable, then, realizing the problem, raised the sunshield and looked again. Wonder and some other emotion fought for control within him. He had managed to avoid the clichéd gee-whizzes for a long time, insulated by the ships that had brought him into space, but he could put it off no longer. There was the Earth, barely larger than a BB, but solid and round and bright blue-white. All seven billion people, reduced to something that he could cover with the tip of a pinky, a speck in the sky he could accidentally overlook. All the suffering, gone. All the death, gone. The other emotion welled up in him fiercely and he recognized it as happiness. The lump in his throat was so sentimental; corny, the Americans called it.

For a hundred years, it seemed, he had pushed everything away. In the dense press of people all around, he had fought to clear a space for himself; had defined himself as different, special, separate. But here, so far away, the pressure was suddenly relieved, *pssst,* like opening a barymetric tank. He swept his gaze over the sky, encompassing the open vault of space, still infinitely larger than his aspirations to selfhood.

Had he been trying to commit suicide, little by little, all these years? But it felt so good to live!

So this was why he had come to space. Some small part of him had wanted this, connived, inveigled, and by cunning had gotten him here for *this.* Alone. Myself. At last. The stars smiled with wild abandon.

"Oh. *There* you are," said Volodya in his ear. "I thought Slava told you not to wander."

Lyova turned to signal the man. Indeed, he had wandered far.


Later, Chishak and Bronstein made a final reconnaissance. Not that much left to do but check out the control node and make sure everything was secure. And, they had been informed, the Italian satellite was coming. They ought to record that for posterity.

The asteroid was broadside to the sun now, and they had come some seventy degrees around the short circumference, standing a dozen meters from the dark, irregular line of the creeping terminator. The tail section of *Molotochek* protruded above the horizon, cut by a sharp terminator of its own.

Bronstein, bobbing a few centimeters above the ground, bouncing off compression effects in the soles of his boots, contemplated the tiny, blue-white disk of Earth. If you looked sharply, you could pick out a tiny, wan Moon nearby, contrast-washed to near invisibility.

So, he thought, there lies humanity, concentrated onto the bull's-eye of a single target. One little disaster, a roving Juno, no more, and we'd be the temporary remnants of God's proud experiment. Four men, living out their year or so of supplies, then darkness. It was a sobering thought, and plausible enough to make a good reason for getting mankind off the Earth. I wonder if we'd have a chance, even now? There're a few women aboard *Mir,* but . . . probably not enough to make a viable gene pool. Still, we'd get a few months warning if a Juno came sailing by, thanks to the Americans. We could get a dozen shuttle loads of people and supplies into orbit. They'd survive, so long as their orbit didn't pass over the impact site. . . .

He pictured being aboard a crowded, terror-stricken space station, flying inexorably into a vast wall of incandescent debris, thrown back into space by an unimaginably huge explosion. What a thought . . . You wonder if humanity could stop such a cosmic disaster. Probably not. Not with all the hydrogen bombs on Earth.

"Look," Chishak was pointing off into the darkness, at a seemingly featureless point in the sky. Bronstein squinted at the indicated place. Was it . . . anything? No . . . yes! He could see a very dim reddish-yellow light. Flickering. Flickering. Gone. He stared at the spot where it had been, perplexed, then raised his sun visor, ducking his head back into the shadows of his helmet. There. It was coming in from the sunward side, but you could see it, a tiny moon, complexly shaped, swelling slowly. Light sparkled again, little purple lights from a dozen hypergolic thrusters, and the probe came to a halt about two hundred meters away, flying formation with the asteroid. Sunlight glinted off its black solar cell panels and you could see the glass lenses of a dozen cameras.

"Behold: *Piazzi II.*"

"Do you suppose they can see us?"

"I hope so." Amusement was a barely perceptible overtone in Bronstein's voice.

Bronstein tried to imagine the scene at mission control, back in Italy. The Western Europeans were proud of their capability in space, both collectively and as individual states, but it was . . . nothing. The slowly coalescing political entity of the EEC, with its 330 million people the richest aggregate on earth, was, even more than America, helplessly focused on the "nowism" of the capitalist ideal. Space was, at best, a pleasant diversion. Well. Let them divert *this.* He waved at the spacecraft and, to his intense pleasure, one of the cameras rotated his way, scanning this part of the surface. You could just *see* them, grim before their consoles, feeling small. And the Italian people, watching it all on their fine Japanese HDTVs. . . . Perhaps the Italian Communist party, always a strong contender, would get a little boost at the polls this fall. It'd be interesting if Fallaci won the presidency. She had the best tits in politics, a lot better than Prime Minister Betty Bork MacKay's withered old dugs. . . .

*Piazzi* edged slowly closer. When it was floating fifty meters above the ground, there was a tiny, wavering puff of gas, and something broke away. It was the "Hopper," an elfling of a lander, slowly dropping down their reference vertical, toward the man-trodden ground of Sinuhe. It took a seeming eternity for it to reach the surface, and, when it touched, it bounced high, righting itself with its gyros, taking several more bounces before coming to rest.

"Let's go." They toggled their CMU controls and began drifting toward the soccerball-sized object, all antennae and pedicles. In purpose it was not very different from the unused probes the USSR had flown on the ill-fated *Fobos 1* and *2,* in the eighties, but vastly more sophisticated in size and instrumentation. As they approached it, the probe's pedicles popped out and it hopped through a slow arc to a new location, hardly bouncing at all after a gentle landing.

They braked to a stop a couple of meters away. "I think it's . . . cute," said Bronstein.

In truth, it was. He could picture a news conference on their return. The best part of the mission? Why . . . watching that cute little *Piazzi* hop around, I suppose. Those Italians have a real way with technology. . . . It was the Gina Lolobrigida of space probes. . . . Ah, the splendid mortification of it!

Bronstein leaned closer, drifting above the surface until he was less than a meter away, floating horizontal over the probe. "You know, this is a very good design. Much better than our work. If these people had any *ambition* . . ."

Chishak felt a little nervous, watching him like that. "Miroslav. Don't you think you'd better move back?"

"Why? This thing doesn't have any rocket fuel aboard. It's just an assembly of flywheels and springs and . . ."

Like that, the *Piazzi* probe hopped. The pedicles popped out and it flew off the surface, not very fast of course, but then Bronstein's faceplate was only thirty centimeters away. Chishak heard the clank through his earphones.

"Shit!"

No! Get *away* from the fucking thing! Idiot! Bustamonte fumbled with his controls, finally got the remote communication system on-line. "Uplink command!" He was, unreasonably, shouting into the headset. "Is this Giancarlo? This is an emergency. Send a nonmaskable interrupt to the Hopper *now*! Do you understand? I don't care if we lose it or not. Remote override sequence fourteen. Now. We can't be—"

He stopped, speechless, spellbound by the crystal clear image of the cosmonaut's helmet, growing like a balloon. And inset in the mirrored curve was the Hopper itself, closer, larger. Jesus Christ in heaven! Any moment now . . .

In his ear, a pitiful, apologetic voice. "The Hopper isn't responding. The downlink signal isn't getting through." Of course. The fool was in the way. And *Piazzi IIh* would follow its own inevitable decision-tree.

A sudden motion, and the Hopper was sailing horizontally over the asteroid's surface. It had vibration sensors, and the readout on the leftmost screen showed a momentary surge in amplitude. The collision.

For a moment all hell broke loose in the control room. People were arguing, cursing. He could let them continue, or . . . "All right people. Whatever happened, it's over. Giancarlo? Let's try RCS-twelve. Everybody? Back to work. We've got a spacecraft's health to worry about."


The probe ricocheted away, gliding over the surface, bouncing every now and then, coming to a stop near the horizon.

Chishak felt a cold sweat bead out onto his face. "Jesus, Slava! I *told* you. . . ."

"I . . . hear a hissing sound." Bronstein's voice was flat, the same voice you heard from pilots as the ground rose up to kill them.

"What?" Chishak could hear the rising panic in his own voice.

"There's a hissing noise somewhere in my suit. I've got to get back to the ship."

Crick.

Chishak could see Bronstein's face through his faceplate, mouth slightly open, eyes wide, staring in horror at the little tree-shaped crack that was starting to grow from a mounting grommet along one edge of the glass. A distant voice in his head said, Interesting. There must have been a hidden flaw. The voice was calm, but it was surrounded by a sea of growing panic.

Crick.

The hissing was loud enough to hear over the radio now. Oh, shit . . . thought Chishak.

"Fuck." Bronstein twisted at his controls and began to fly away rapidly, aiming for the tail section of the ship.

He'll have to make a midcourse correction, thought Chishak. The airlock is below the horizon.

Crack-crack!

"Ohhh . . ." said Bronstein, seeming to wheeze. "It's . . ." He started to cough over the radio, then choke, a peculiar bubbling sound.

My God! What should I do?

"Slava!" That was from Manarov, aboard *Molotochek.* "Lev, what's going on out there?"

Chishak could hear himself panting. He's not going to make it! The radio was silent now, and he could see that Bronstein was well past the point where he should have made his turn. He's going to fly right past the ship! I'll have to go get him! Bronstein was starting to tumble, end over end, backwards, from the gas jet that spurted out of his helmet.

"Hold on, man! I'm coming!" His voice echoed in his helmet. Shouting would do nothing to change what the others heard. Over the radio circuit, they were all close by.

He fumbled with his controls, snapping switches this way and that. Jesus, he's going to die! The CMU's thrusters came on suddenly, and he jumped off the surface of Sinuhe. What? What? I'm going the wrong way! Somehow, he was rising vertically off the little planet, jetting into a trajectory ninety degrees away from Bronstein.

He fumbled other controls and began to spin. What's happening? I can't do it! Sinuhe appeared and disappeared cyclically before his eyes, beginning to grow smaller. "My God! My God!" he screamed, "I'm losing him!"

The sweat began to fly off his face, centripetal force imitating gravity on the inside of the glass, fogging the faceplate. He screamed again, "No! No! I'm losing *me*!"

It's true, said that remote, calm voice. You're flying off into solar orbit. This is *your* Chernobyl, Lyova. And he thought: Goodbye, sweet Natasha. And . . . Babushka . . . I'm coming. . . .

Night grew before his eyes, and he was gone.

In *Molotochek*'s control room Serebryakov listened with growing horror as Bronstein began to choke and die. "Slava . . ." he whispered, and turned to face Manarov. "Volodya? We . . ."

The other man, his face still, expressionless, shook his head slowly. "There's nothing we can do. Bronstein is . . . finished."

"But . . ." He listened to Chishak's incoherent screams, then to silence. "Lyova?" He leaned closer to the condenser microphone on the control panel. "Lyova, can you hear me?" Silence. "Volodya?" He was feeling his own surge of panic now. Dead? Two men lost? What would become of them? The mission was . . . over. They would be lucky to make it home.

Manarov floated up and away from the control panel. "We'll have to go after them. Suit up."

"Both of them?"

Dark lines seemed to be sinking into Manarov's face. "The asshole has only fainted."

"What about Slava?"

"Well. We can't leave him. You go after Chishak. I'll . . . retrieve our friend."

Serebryakov stared at Manarov's face for a long minute. What is he thinking now? What feelings are under that mask?

They drifted into the airlock, and began to prepare for their task. When the airlock door opened, Anton was, somehow, unafraid. Was this heroism?

And Volodya stepped out into night, thinking, This is a long road we follow. Where am I along the path? Somewhere . . . where feelings don't reach . . . a dead man waits my coming.

All the magic days finally arrived.

Volodya was lying on his marriage bed, naked, stretched out on top of the covers, hands beneath the back of his neck, staring at the cracked plaster ceiling of Oo-oo's little apartment. Minsky was spending the night at Grzegorz's house tonight, giving them a bit of privacy. It wasn't bad either. Oo-oo had a private bath and shower. . . . And even if he hadn't it was better than spending their wedding night behind a screen with parents and brothers and sisters tiptoeing around waiting for them to fuck.

He smirked to himself in the semidarkness. Do they really? It was hard to imagine, but there were *so* many jokes! He listened to the quiet hiss of the shower, Shutka sluicing herself clean in what would soon be the last, for them, of Leningrad's excellent water. The sound cut off, in a diminuendo of splattering sounds and musical dribbles. In another minute, she'd be out.

Do I regret not having waited? No. This is magic enough for me.

School was over, their few belongings packed, and in the morning Grzegorz would drive them out to Pulkovo Airport and the beginnings of a new life. New? No. This is the *first* life for us. He felt smooth exultation. Tomorrow! I can hardly believe it. The trip would be in two quick stages: a civilian flight to Novosibirsk, then a special military transport to the big air base at Leninsk.

They both graduated from their training programs on the same day, a bare six weeks ago, and by then he already knew where he was going. Glavkosmos was forming up, putting long new fingers into a thousand private pies. It was hiring young engineers, stealing old ones, mixing things together to produce a burst of hybrid vigor. So here I am, on my way to join the engineering support team of Energiya and the fabled *kosmicheskii korabl.* It had been an all-military project, still was in many ways, and represented Comrade Eyebrow's final great legacy.

We can almost forgive him, leaving us with this. . . .

I'm damned lucky. The first launch of the carrier rocket's been delayed just long enough for me to get in on it. Six months, no more . . . Luck had been with them both. With his position secured, it had been a relatively easy step to getting Shutka a teaching job in the Leninsk school system. These would just be the children of engineers an1 other resident staff; cosmonauts' kids went to school in Starry Town, but what the hell. . . . Luck. No other word for it.

The bathroom door opened and Shutka came out, naked and steamy from the shower, her wet hair glued to the sides of her head, plastered on her upper back. She came to the foot of the bed and stood looking down at him, frowning in obvious mock anger. "What? No erection? What kind of a useless husband is this?"

He lay still, looking up at her. Slim. Damned nice. How many times am I going to think that? As long as it takes me to believe my good fortune. Though she had a tendency to put on a bit of weight during the long winter, there was none of it now. You could see little hollows above her collar bones and the delicate tracery of pelvic blades bracketing a smooth, faintly rounded abdomen. The undersides of her pale breasts were domes, with so little sag that there was no perceptible crease. It would all change, he knew, with time, but right now she was perfect. Change? So what. When I'm a fat and jowly senior engineer, perhaps she will still love me. "Hmh. Get in bed. I'll show you useless."

She threw up her hands in triumph. "What a relief! I thought you were going to lie there and stare at my pussy all night, frozen with virginal terror!"

"What *is* this? Surely you're not going to *talk* me into a hard-on. . . ."

"Ah. A heartless bastard, I see. No sensitivity." As she spoke, she crawled up onto the bed until she was straddling his thighs. "Hmmm . . ." She lifted his flaccid penis out of its hairy nest. "What could this odd-looking thing be for?"

"Garden hose."

"Hmmm . . . Unlikely. Not much of a hose, if true. Does it stretch?" She pulled. "No. Bah. Useless . . . But . . . wait! Something's happening!" She wiggled it back and forth. "The damned thing seems to be . . . *pressurizing!*"

"To calculate the head of a pipe you merely multiply the area of a fluid cross section by the total pressure exerted."

"*Head,* you say?" She gripped the thing firmly now. "I'll have you know, sir, I'm not your trashy sort of tart!"

"Oww."

She looked down at the glans peeping from her fist. "Purple. How disgusting." She hunkered down on his thighs and licked at it. "An interesting little twitch, that."

"Little twitch?"

She released it from her fist, then ran her tongue along the underside of the shaft. "Well. That seemed to elicit a bigger and better twitch."

"Bigger."

"There seems to be an odd sort of an echo in here. Is something wrong with your speaking apparatus?"

"No, nothing wrong."

"What a relief. Let's see what happens next." She put the whole thing in her mouth, slid her face slowly in until her nose was buried in pubic hair, then slid back, leaving a lot of moisture behind. Volodya grunted and reached down to grab her by the ears. "Interesting," she said. "The subject is speaking in tongues now. I'll have to write a journal article in the morning. . . ."

He growled and, grabbing her by the shoulders, pulled her up onto his chest, then wrestled her around until she was underneath him.

"Well," she said, "the subject seems to exhibit some unusual aggression. Perhaps my article should focus on . . ."

He forced her legs apart with his knees and pushed hard with his hips until his wet penis suddenly disappeared into her cunt.

"Oooo . . ." she said.

"Interesting," he said. "Speaking in tongues is contagious."

The three of them were there in the cramped airlock, surrounded by the giant bodies of their cast-off suits, breathing hoarsely in the dim light of the three small portholes. They looked at each other, wondering vaguely why things had gone so wrong. No one spoke for what seemed like an hour.

Tonya was numb, unable to tell if he felt anything about the death of this authoritarian, changeable man. He could still see the ghastly, blood-smeared, bloated face inside the cracked faceplate. They had brought him back, crammed him into the cargo hold, closed him into the darkness. . . . Damn, damn, damn, damn. Fear surged up in him, the antithesis of his happiness, eating, gorging down his little soul. He straightened up. No. I will not let it have me. The stiff, slick spacesuit undergarment constricted his legs, biting into the small of his back unbearably. The moment, dim and unignorable, pressed against him and, if he paid very close attention, the prickling fear would subside. He tried to regulate his breathing, thought about Darya, and slowly became himself once again. Life goes on, he thought; until it ends.

Finally Volodya cleared his throat. "What a goddamn dumb thing to happen. And to Slava, of all people."

"I don't know why he did it," said Lyova quaveringly.

"Damn human perversity," muttered Tonya. "It strikes when it's least expected.

"And now he's gone. Just like that." How trite the words sounded to Volodya's ear. There *should* be appropriate words for an archetypal situation like this. But there never were. Language itself was a silly, meaningless ritual. They had just one word: dead. Volodya's was a joining of two very long-lived families, and he had experienced the death of close relatives only twice. He remembered the funerals of his grandfather Sergei and favorite aunt Zhizhi with a confused mixture of fear, bitterness, and regret. No matter how many years passed, they still didn't come back.

Chishak seemed to have recovered a little bit of his normal self-possession. "It happens in a million different ways. At least he died quickly." The standard physician's balm; but Bronstein had not died so quickly that he did not feel an ample portion of the pain and terror and unimaginable fear that he had seen in a thousand faces.

Suddenly Volodya looked up. "We're in trouble."

No one asked him why. It would come. "I can't fly *Molotochek* by myself. We just might be stuck here forever."

Volodya floated in his little chamber bathed in night-sweat. All the lights were turned out except the ones on the emergency control panel. The room was clothed in an eerie rainbow, mostly blue and green, but with little scintillae of orange and red here and there. The moving melange of text and image on the tiny CRT screen made shifting shadows in the corners of his vision. And before him in the darkness floated the face of Miroslav Ilyich Bronstein, colonel in the Strategic Rocket Forces of the Union of Soviet Socialist Republics, aged forty-five years.

Remember the last time you were in here? Remember what we talked about? What about it, old comrade? Did I kill you? Did I make you relax when I talked you into letting Chishak go outside? Did I make you think space travel was *safe*? Hell. Stupidity killed you, Miroslav Ilyich. You learned a lesson, little half-breed Jew from the industrial east: Out here, stupidity is suicide. You killed yourself.

Nobody told you to put your head in the lion's mouth.
Now he's bitten you off. Goodbye, Miroslav Ilyich.

So. What now?

He undid his chest strap and bent over the control panel,
reading the numbers, then punched up the lights. What
now, indeed? He pulled out a moist towelette and wiped
himself clean, relishing the quick-dry feel of the scented
alcohol wipe. This is the last day. Time for a solution. He
pulled on his jumpsuit, opened the hatch of the flare shelter, and floated out.

The living quarters section of *Molotochek* was, as always,
brightly lit, Serebryakov and Chishak strapped to their
bench seats, legs wrapped around the chair columns, eating
breakfast. Anton looked up. "We were about to wake you."

He took a carton of premixed cold cereal and a bag of
grape juice from the refrigerator cabinet, floated over to the
table, and attached himself to a chair. Popping open the
drink, he sipped from its integral straw. A bit tart, really.
Maybe the Americans had hit upon a decent final solution,
after all. Most of them picked a selection of "Budget Gour-
mets" from the local supermarket prior to a flight. With a
freezer and a microwave, why bother with special arrangements?

He ate in silence, disposed of the remains, then turned to
Serebryakov. "You ready to start coming up with some
answers?"

Anton shrugged. Me? What answers could I have?

"How critical is the situation?" asked Chishak.

Volodya looked him over carefully. Afraid? Still blaming
himself? Doesn't matter. He has no part in this. "It's hard
to tell. The ship was intended to be operated from Mission
Control, since it has an unmanned mode. . . . On the
other hand, we're something like twenty light-seconds from
Earth. That could fuck things up."

"What, exactly, do they want to do?"

"Well, with a forty-second response factor . . . They
want to alternate telemetry and command bursts between
the Cray and the Dozhdevik on a forty-five-second cycle.
That's a full minute and a half between command sequence
corrections."

"Will it work?"

"Probably."

A little corner of Anton's mind felt amused at that.

Probably? What is "probably"? He tried to read Manarov's face but, as usual, got nothing. "There must be a sound alternative. Why can't you fly the ship?"

Volodya smiled. "Who's going to be the flight engineer? What if something goes wrong during the boost?"

"One of us . . ." Chishak began.

"Ah. One of you." The smile broadened, then faded. "There's a fatal flaw in this mission plan, you see. The way *Molotochek* was designed, for autonomous missions to places like Mars, with a six-man crew, there was a spare pilot and flight engineer aboard. Unfortunately, Zarkov and Artyukhin are sitting around in Moskva, probably glad they're not here." That was unkind. They were brave, bland cosmonauts, probably yearning to be here.

Anton felt his exasperation rise up, overwhelming the first worm tracks of anxiety. "Are you telling us there's *no* alternative? What are the odds Mission Control's plan will succeed?"

It was Volodya's turn to shrug. "If this were an American ship, or even a European one, I'd have some minimal confidence. As it is . . . Our automatic control technology, despite everything, sucks shit. Why do you think our planetary probes fail so often? Why do you think there's been no Soviet *Voyager*?"

Anton felt a cold hand in his chest. That hit home, and, suddenly, he felt the fear come swarming in. "There's got to be something . . ."

"What do you suggest? I can try to train you, Anton, but we've got less than a day. . . ."

Serebryakov slumped in his chair, thinking about Lovell, Haise, and Swigert. There is a certain . . . terror . . . here. He can tell me what I need to know in a day, but I'll never remember it, not in a crisis. I'd have to have a computer for a brain. . . .

Volodya watched the man's face change and felt an oddness form in the pit of his stomach. From somewhere, the feeling welled up: This is a genius I'm looking at, but in the wrong field. . . . "Tonya?" he said softly. "What is it?"

"Could you program a computer to do the flight engineer's job? It follows a rigid set of rules, after all. You could do the task if a computer could isolate problems requiring immediate attention. . . ."

The disappointment was remarkably intense. Machine

triage? It was a compelling idea, the way, in fact, Western technology worked, but . . . "I could do it, yes. But the Dozhdevik is wholly inadequate for the task. We'd need the Cray, which is why Mission Control . . ."

Anton smiled. "Volodya. Think. The Cray represents an American technology that is *fourteen years old*!" Would he get it?

"So?"

"Remember the night I got drunk?"

Fuck. The Chinese-made Digital Entertainment Unit was a 1024-node parallel processing array, with ten thousand times the power of their pitiful Dozhdevik machine, comparable, in fact, to a 1980s-vintage supercomputer. "Do you really think we can . . ."

"We can try. If it isn't working by tonight, we can go with Mission Control's plan."

"You two are nuts," muttered Chishak. "What if you kill us?"

"Then we're dead," said Serebryakov, marveling at his own words.

Manarov, nodded slowly. "All right. Get it out."

They put the machine on the table, securing it with Velcro tabs, then Volodya sat before it, squinting at the brightly-lit keytops. "So." He reached out and stabbed a key that said INTERRUPT.

The screen flickered and an iconic touchscreen appeared, dominated by the legend, DEU LOW-LEVEL OPERATING SYSTEM—COPYRIGHT 1997, MICROSOFT, INC. The keycaps changed to the Cyrillic alphabet.

He looked over the choices and sighed. One more level. He reached out and touched the KILL icon, a dagger-pierced heart. The screen flashed and turned dark, drive lights flickered here and there, then bright-yellow words wrote themselves into the upper left hand corner of the screen: I/O ROOT DRIVER—COPYRIGHT 1996, INTEL SYSTEMS DIVISION, INC., followed by a cryptic ">" prompt. Now the keycaps were all roman capitals.

"Well?" asked Serebryakov. He was a little stunned by the swift sequence of changes. Though he understood that there was an underlying unity in the way all computers worked, this demonstration was a little . . . horrifying.

Manarov typed the word LISP, pressed the enter key,

and watched a familiar screen come up. So. He turned to look at Anton, and said, "I think I can."

Moskva, 1989. Anton sat back from the work table and sighed. It took a full ten seconds for his eyes to focus correctly. This was getting to be too much. He was no cartographer, and Phobos was not a place made to map. Dramatic photomosaics of the tiny moon, courtesy of *Viking Orbiter 1,* covered the wall; in one, dominated by the large crater Stickney, it looked very much like a cocktail olive with the pimiento removed. Two of the first distant images from *Fobos,* showing little detail, promised even higher resolution views to come. Not to mention the data that would come back from the Hopper.

His eyes ached from looking at stereopairs, and his shoulders felt stiff and tired. Was this why he had become a planetologist? No; well, maybe. The necessary attention to meaningless detail exhausted him, drained his spirit. But, of course, a precise control network of Phobos was absolutely necessary for analysis of the spacecraft's scientific data; and that data would provide for his revitalization. The Americans had been there first, and, without the work of Duxbury and Wu there could have been no reference grid at all. He picked up NASA Reference Publication 1109, available thanks to the new accord, and riffled through the many crater-riddled images. Yes, if he concentrated, the wonder of it all would come back. Phobos, moon of Mars. Captured asteroid. Who knew what they would find? Nobody. That was the point.

Yes, it had been a difficult thing to keep the wonder in view for the last two years. He had come to the institute as part of a program initiated from outside, and so there had been resentment, amplified by his ambiguous relationship to the party. Many still treated him as if he had gotten his position immorally. The result had been months and months of shuttling from one project to another, never really getting to do any science. Now, finally, *perestroika* was beginning to shake things up. A new big boss named Akhmatov, a scientist, not a bureaucrat, had reorganized the *Fobos* effort after the loss of *Fobos 1* and placed him and Alyosha Grigorenko on the photogrammetry team.

The room was dry and warm; they had done some amazing things with these old palaces. He went to the single, large window: outside, an April snowstorm was raging, painting the old, dirty piles of ice with a fresh coat of white. He *was* tired. The winter had gone on too long; grayer and snowier than usual, and it had taken a toll on him. Damn, he thought. I wish spring would come.

In the corner of his mind he noticed a commotion somewhere down the hall, but things of that sort were common here in IKI headquarters and he didn't think about it. He strode over to where the single PC was chugging away, generating a contour map of Phobos's anti-Stickney hemi-"sphere," checked the scritching plotter, and started the next entry in the log. He could bitch, but the work was good. It kept his mind completely occupied, until he was tired enough to go back to his little shared room in the workers' dormitory.

He looked at the doorway just in time to see the emaciated Grigorenko appear, pale and distraught.

"They've lost *Fobos 2,* Tonya."

"What?" Anton stood abruptly, almost bumping the plotter. He stared into the man's bloodshot, oriental eyes for a long time, and it sunk in. "Oh, no! Not *again!*"

Alyosha smiled grimly. "I'm afraid so. They never regained contact after the fourth photo series."

"Damn. Damn. Damn!" Anton felt his whole edifice crumbling like cheese. After all the work! "God damn those assholes at Glavkosmos! I knew that design was risky; but to lose *both* of them!"

"We haven't had much luck with Mars. Though I understand the infrared instrument worked very well. We can finally contribute something to the knowledge base."

"Think about how Karamzin must feel! Now he really will be a pariah."

"It wasn't entirely his fault."

"You're absolutely right. It's the fault of Comrade Kovtunenko. He's responsible for the bollixed-up design of those spacecraft."

"There's quite a storm brewing down the hall. You should see Sagdeev. He's saying the same things as you, but louder. Says there'll be hell to pay."

"That should mean something. They say old Roald has somehow gotten in quite well with Comrade Gorbachev. Maybe he can talk some sense into them."

"What do *we* do now?"

"They'll try to reestablish contact with the spacecraft. But once the antenna pointing is lost there's maybe one chance in a thousand that they'll succeed. I don't know about you, but I'm getting out of here. To get drunk." Anton reached behind the computer and shut it off in mid-chug. He went to the small closet where they stored their office supplies and got his heavy blue parka. "Coming?"

Volodya sat in *Molotochek*'s left-hand seat before an unfamiliar control panel. Ten seconds. Well, either it would succeed or fail. The odds against them were no greater than if they'd trusted Mission Control's long-range guidance. The pilot's station was uncomfortable for him. Whereas the engineer's console was mostly instruments, with just a few emergency controls, this side of the panel was the other way around. Instead of the usual exterior views, they'd thrown the Dozhdevik screen on his upper CRT and the DEU's on the lower. Five seconds.

It had been hard to convince Mission Control of the worthiness of their plan; Ponomarev was reported to be quite angry, but they'd gotten their way at last. Serebryakov sat nervously in the right-hand seat, holding the DEU in his lap, wires trailing off, snaky, to their various connector ports. Its screen was windowed into mazy confusion, filled with icons that would flash at trouble—high-tech idiot lights—and the keycaps had been programmed to display the names of several dozen Dozhdevik macros. Theoretically, Anton could see a problem and select a proper response from his menu of buttons. Theoretically.

Four.

And the more complex problems? The DEU would display a schematic of the problem on the lower CRT. Volodya could compare its statement with the Dozhdevik's native indication on the upper CRT, then dictate a complex response to Anton. Again, theoretically.

Three.

What the fuck am I worried about? The worst that can happen is we'll be blown to bits . . . or stranded in solar orbit for a year. I wonder if they'd be able to retrieve us with *Serpachek*? That awful word. Theoretically, at least.

Two.

God. I feel sick.

One.

Uhhh . . . Deep breath.

The rockets thumped into life, transmitting power through the load-bearing structures of *Molotochek*, finally pressing their backs into the cloth webbing of the command station acceleration cots. Dozhdevik and DEU displayed numbers and symbols, icons changing color in an analog histogram display. Columns of text scrolled by unread on the upper CRT. If it ain't wrong don't leave it, said the DEU. Dozhdevik—mute, inglorious, obsolete—complied.

From his seat against the propulsion control room's rear bulkhead, Chishak watched their heads begin to bob and sway, and listened as the ship began to groan and ping. Shit. This was scary when nothing was wrong. Something began to rattle in the living quarters section, probably an improperly secured dish . . . or a welded seam about to rupture. Every once in a while, Manarov could be seen to reach forward and make some minute adjustment on the control panel. Serebryakov seemed frozen, clutching the DEU box with whitened hands.

What the hell am I afraid of? I wasn't afraid at Chernobyl, just horrified. Something had to be behind this strong, spine-twisting terror. Chernobyl was an accident in progress, men already burned, me with too much to do in too little time. This is just . . . potential. I am waiting to be disintegrated. I wonder what it would feel like. People who've been in explosions say you feel pressure, that it happens slow enough to . . . observe. I guess that's why you always hear them scream. Would this be like that? Probably even worse. The engine compartment, where any explosion would likely start, was almost a hundred meters away. We'd feel it coming. In fact, the command module would probably rupture, flinging them out into the vacuum of space, to spend long seconds dying. . . .

Just like Bronstein.

The shuddering of the engines was getting bad now, making him sweat and gasp. This seemed to be taking forever! He watched Manarov work, watched the way Serebryakov kept his eyes riveted to the DEU screen. Suddenly the planetologist jerked one hand free and held it poised, clawlike, above the glowing keyboard.

"Don't," said Manarov. "There's not enough time for the program to run."

"But . . ."

"Forget it. The anomaly won't build up to criticality in the time we have left."

Chishak found himself trying to hold his breath. They're doing a good job. . . . The fear suddenly began to subside. What is it? Yes, I guess I . . . trust them. Like the men I worked with at Chernobyl. We might all die, but . . . together.

BANG.

Rumrumrum . . .

Silence.

You could hear Manarov breathing, surprisingly hard, amid the faint creaks and pops of the hull as zero-g reestablished its sway. "Good."

Anton said, "It . . . looks like a normal engine shutdown."

Volodya leaned over and stared at the DEU's display, then up at the Dozhdevik screen. "Yes. And . . . It looks like the anomaly was from an oscillation in one of the hydrogen fuel lines. Probably one of the tiedown rings has fractured. We'll have to go out and take a look. There are spares for that sort of thing."

Anton snapped the lid on the DEU, cutting off its display. "Right. Some time in the next three months."

Volodya laughed. "Of course. There's . . . plenty of time."

And Chishak's voice, embedded in a sigh, whispered, "Well done. Thank you."

They were on their way home.

# CHAPTER 6

# *September 7, 2002*

Shuttle *Taina,* Mystery, hung against the starless night, its cargo bay doors yawning. Volodya reached up and turned down the contrast on the monitor a little so the maximum detail could be seen. The bay was empty except for the outward-pointing cylinder that would mate with *Molotochek*'s docking ring to allow passage between the two ships. In one of the observation windows located just above the docking adapter, he thought he could see a face and a waving hand. "Good to see you, *Taina,*" he said. "We've come a long way to be here with you."

"Acknowledged, *Molotochek,*" said the voice of Vasili Kryuchkov through the earphones.

Manarov typed a command into the Dozhdevik and the docking checklist appeared on the lower screen. He glanced over at the DEU, quietly plugged into Bronstein's empty station, and sighed. "Let's get this over with, shall we, Vasya?"

"Nothing easier. Here we come."

A fanning puff of propellant spurted from a reaction-control thruster at *Taina*'s nose, and the ship began to orient itself. It grew slowly to fill the monitor, until all he could see was the gaping barn doors and the circle of the docking ring. Without a pilot, *Molotochek* was essentially a passive element in this equation, and there was little to do except watch the video.

Their transfer directly to a shuttle, rather than a rendezvous with *Mir,* was a final commentary on the problems of the mission. The flight dynamics had put them into a twenty-three-degree Earth-orbit, rather than the planned fifty-one degrees, too far off course to be corrected by the ship's remaining fuel. They were being picked up now by a shuttle, with its big cross-ranging capability. *Molotochek* would have to undergo a partial refueling operation before it could get back to the space station for full refurbishment. Too bad. The two extra shuttle flights amounted to a waste of more than five hundred million rubles.

"Got you!" The heavy bang sent a shock through the ship. Volodya sensed the movement of the servomechanisms. "Hard dock."

Serebryakov appeared, dressed in the spiffy civilian jumpsuit created by an obscure branch of Glavkosmos for appearances before the press. Red with white piping, and posted with the mission insignia as well as those of Vernadskii, IKI, and Glavkosmos, it was impressive. And Anton too looked fit and healthy: Chishak's regimen had done him good. Volodya smiled. "We won't be going quite yet. I've got to do a preliminary safe of the ship."

When they opened the airlock, cool, relatively fresh air poured around them, and they breathed it in, tasting the sweet flavors of Earth for the first time in many months. The narrow corridor leading into the shuttle was crowded with bodies. Kryuchkov came through first, captain's prerogative, a dark, jowly man laughing and shaking hands. Two others followed, and the little airlock was totally filled. Goodwill and fellowship bubbled up, and it was obvious that these others were more than a little envious of their accomplishments. They retreated back to the control room, where additional crew from the shuttle joined them. It was as if they all wanted to be a part of this historic moment.

Kryuchkov shook hands with Volodya once more, striking him vigorously on the back and laughing. "I can't believe it. Our very own planetary explorers. It's a shame about Miroslav Ilyich, though."

"You should see the crowds down at the 'drome," said a young, very blond man whom Volodya thought he remembered from Starry Town. "This is the biggest day since Gagarin. We aced the Americans once again!"

Kryuchkov grimaced. "And they've let all the Western media into the landing area. CTN, Globo, BBC, everyone. It's a real circus."

"Well, I need to put on my last fresh outfit," said Volodya. "Then we'll be ready to go."

"Fine," said Kryuchkov. "We'll leave Filipchenko, Romanov, and Zaikin here to finish the work. You three deserve a change of pace."

Anton, strapped securely into a contoured flight seat in *Taina*'s middeck, looked idly at the prepress edition of *Pravda* dated September 7, 2002. Extremely large, red headlines proclaimed, COSMONAUTS RETURN TO EARTH, MISSION TO PREPARE SINUHE TOTAL SUCCESS. At the bottom right, a glowing tribute to M. I. Bronstein was enclosed in a thick black box. His own name jumped out at him from four or five places in the text, and he shook his head ruefully. For some reason he hadn't expected all the hoopla. It made him uncomfortable, reminding him of his past hatred of cosmonaut hyperbole. He was certainly not a hero of any kind.

He slid the newspaper into a large plastic pocket on the side of the seat installation and listened. There it was—the unmistakable sound of wind, tenuous atmosphere shooshing past the orbiter's body. This was it. He began to feel himself being pressed forward against the restraining harness. Inertia, but with a little gravity mixed in. He turned to Volodya in the next seat, saw the glittering, excited eyes, and felt a touch of nausea. The whispering air was growing louder, and a dull, low-bass rumble started, making the sound into a throaty white-noise roar. Already the g-force was strong enough to make raising an arm difficult, and he gave up and let his head loll back against the cushion. Reentry had been difficult for him during his two previous times, and he wondered how his microgravity-deconditioned body would react. For four months he had adapted to weighing zero, and, soon, more than a hundred kilograms would be pushing down against him.

Still, he thought, the days of parachuted descent modules dropping haphazardly into the dry Central Asian steppe were long gone. A five-g deceleration was not uncommon with the *Soyuz* landings, compared with less than two for the comfortable and safe *kosmicheskie korabli,* flying down a cushion of air to land at Yubilyei Aerodrome's long shuttle runway, just to the north of Baikonur's main technical zone. No one, to his knowledge, had suffered any ill effects from this short ride; and he guessed that he would make it all right, too.

Anton began to feel a bit faint, and a ruby miasma decorated with a thousand points of light came out of nowhere to float before him. A steady buffeting replaced the roar, and the acceleration began to tail off. The red fog dissipated quickly. He felt *Taina* banking into one of the drastic hypersonic S-turns that were necessary to slow the craft sufficiently for a landing. He took a shallow breath and let it out.

As the inertia diminished, gravity increased, and, after what seemed a long time, the former was almost entirely gone. Now *Taina* was a simple, though unpowered, airplane, flying downward toward the tiny strip of concrete a few hundred kilometers away. Anton's head was clear, but the gravity infecting his limbs felt very peculiar indeed. He sat forward as far as he could, and brought his heavy right arm up before him. Even with the long hours of exercise, it wasn't easy. He rubbed his face and let the arm fall. He smiled. Gravity was nostalgic, in a way, and it made him anticipate landfall even more.

"Christ," said Volodya, laughing a little. "We're going to make a great spectacle out there. I certainly hope they're not expecting anything strenuous from us."

Tonya tried to visualize what it would be like. After a long-duration space flight, the average cosmonaut was just able to smile and shuffle his feet as he was carried, and, even though it was very temporary, it was not thought good to display a heroic cosmonaut in this weakened condition. A moving stairway had been built to convey them from the shuttle hatch to the ground with as much dignity as possible, but the problem of what to do then was considerable. Hopefully they would have the wheeled couches ready.

Kryuchkov piloted *Taina* down over the small new service town of Mars Gorodok, making the obligatory heading-alignment circle to bring it onto the correct glide path for final descent. The shuttle's nose lifted slightly, increasing angle of attack and decreasing speed even more. A long, silent moment; then the first sandpaper thunder of contact bounced them hard in their seats. They were down; back; home. Anton relaxed completely for the first time. His premonitions had been wrong. He had not died. The danger was over.

After a minute of rough riding the shuttle rolled to a

stop; and the silence came back, this time stronger, more profound, holding a message of sanctuary.

In the new decade of the 1990s, Moskva seemed like such an extravagance. Tonya, stroking his coarse bushy goatee, looked out from the window of the new office and marveled. Just a day back from the stark, empty distances of Antarctica's Queen Maud Land, everything seemed new and unreal. Even the snow in the parks and on the roofs, bright in the artificial light, seemed like civilized snow, in league with the plans and aspirations of man.

And to return to a promotion, a new desk and window, made it seem all the more strange. In his absence Vernad-skii had been reorganized once again, and though Akhmatov was still in charge, there were many new faces in the middle bureaucracy. The *Fobos* debacle was still working its way through the Russian space program, and, though of course the scientists at the institute had nothing to do with the reasons for the failure, things were changing here as well. *Perestroika* in action. The little placard on Tonya's desk said, ASSISTANT CHIEF OF METEORITE STUDIES. Unbelievable. He wondered where Khvalinskii had gone. No one was ever dismissed, he knew, though there were fates worse than dismissal. Probably to the dreaded Geological Survey of Siberia project. Grigorenko was gone as well, and, guiltily, Tonya felt relief that this shadow-person was no longer by his side.

Things were changing so fast, all around him. He had been at Novolazarevskii for only two months, and the So-viet Union had continued to metamorphose, beyond all ex-pectation. The threats of crackdown were all bluff, and liberalization continued at an incontinent pace. Tonya was beginning to realize that Comrade Gorbachev was for real. And it was more than just cosmetic change. It was beyond the point where the clock could be turned back. He had tried to ignore politics all these years, too distrustful and cynical to even prick up his ears when the new slogans were announced. But *this*—it looked different. Nineteen ninety-one would be something.

So, it was quitting time. Ten minutes after quitting time. He had managed to spend the entire day mooning about, accomplishing nothing. Not good for a twenty-three-year-old assistant chief, but it was easy to do in this semiprivate cubicle. He turned off his brand-new Korean XT, noticing the unnatural silence, punctuated by furtive office noises, as the machine's fan ground to a halt. Most everybody was already gone. He put on his overcoat, flimsy and light compared to the monstrosity he had worn in Maud, and started through the door.

Another Alyosha, Aleksei Borisovich Yusupov, appeared out of the cometary office and hailed him. Tall and stooped, a little older than Anton, he had expressive, long-lashed eyes atop a great, parrot-beak of a nose, almost a deformity. Somehow the man was able to establish immediate rapport with everyone. He had a sly, humorous manner that somehow made his face seem normal, or at least natural. "Ho, congratulations on your promotion, Tonya," he said, coming up close. He looked around suspiciously. "Things are *really* happening, my friend. I just wanted to—" A few bundled-up scientists trundled past, and he was quiet until they were out of earshot. "—a word to the wise. All this may be temporary. There is a good chance that we are going to be combined with IKI as a cost-cutting measure. Space is not very popular these days. You remember the joke about going to Phobos for sugar? Well, *Krokodil* has taken it a step further; there's a cartoon showing *Buran* hitched up to a team of oxen, cutting wheat with its wings. And that's the popular sentiment. You should hear my uncle go on about it—waste and waste and waste and waste. Granted, he can no longer get the kippers he likes for breakfast; but, if he's typical, and I think he might be, then things are going to get pretty lean here."

Anton leaned back and regarded the man, his first impulse to shy away from this confidence. "Yeah," he said finally, nodding. "It's a hard winter, and it seems to get worse every year. I can't believe how empty the stores are. And the supper at the dorm was hardly worth showing up for. In Antarctica we feasted, compared to this."

"Mark my words, Tonya. We may not get through this winter at all."

A cold, dry wind swept through the streets, carrying tiny crystals of ice that gave the streetlights a rainbow aura. After the perpetual daylight of the Antarctic summer, the cloud-hidden February sky was dark indeed, and the precipitous building-cliffs closed him in to the point of claustrophobia. Tonya walked, hunched over against the wind, still caught in the circular reveries that had occupied his workday. As before he had left, his nights seemed empty, without purpose. He stayed at work when he could, but felt obligated to leave when there were no projects in progress.

He always seemed to find himself gravitating to Red Square and the Kremlin, and tonight was no exception. He looked up at the elaborate facade of the GUM State Universal Store, decorated with an enormous portrait of Lenin, looking deadpan down on the dark street. Anton had never noticed what large ears the man had. He turned into the entrance on a whim and pushed through into the warm interior.

From the almost deserted exterior, he suddenly found himself amidst a crushing throng of people, walking this way and that in an entirely unhurried way. Many were clearly from the provinces; big-nosed Georgians, square-faced Kalmucks, orientals. It was always like this: Even in the worst of times Moskva was much better supplied with commodities than the rest of the country. GUM was arranged much like a Western mall, but built in the baroque style popular in the nineteenth century. Hundreds of shops opened out into the three tiers of a two-hundred-meter-long gallery. Above, past the several packed bridges that spanned the central opening, a curved ceiling of dark glass arched.

Anton opened his coat and continued to walk, dodging the shoppers that happened to get in his way. The shops looked mostly bare, yet the few shopworn items that sat on the shelves were getting an inordinate workout from the consumers. Anton thought, things must be worse than I thought. What a paradox: For the first time, things are beginning to loosen up, and the results are catastrophic. Almost as if there were some law of balances being exacted.

"Tonya, yes, hey, Tonya Serebryakov!"

He turned and saw a well-dressed man waving from an overhead gangway. Something familiar—darkish, square face, coiffed brown hair, pointy nose, eager eyes. Zhenya!

He waved back. It had been a long time, at least six years, since they'd last met. Zhenya pointed to an open space near the fountain and indicated where they would meet.

They shook hands formally, and looked at one another. Zhenya was still taller than him, perhaps even more so than he'd been at sixteen. The little bit of baby fat that had softened the angles of his face was gone, and the resulting visage was severe and a little too earnest. He looked well fed and prosperous. They shook hands again, this time holding on a little longer and actually feeling the contact. Anton was genuinely grateful for this intrusion into his funk.

"How've you been, Tonya? God, it's been a long time. I never thought we'd get out of school in one piece. Well, what's your life been like these past six years? Did you go into astronomy like you wanted?"

The babble of questions was funny, so like the teenager he had known. The years peeled away like so much sunburn. "Yeah. I've been all right. I actually did get into the space program. I specialize in meteorites, you know, shooting stars."

Zhenya looked at his watch. "That's great. Look, I've got to get back to the *Medvedy i Myod* by seven. Why don't you come with me?"

The prospect appealed. Spontaneity, perhaps. "Sure. I've got nothing better to do."

"Excellent. Let's go."

*Medvedy i Myod,* the Bear and Honey, was a rather large, airy restaurant not far from the Aviamotornaya Metro station. A sign on the wall announced that it had received a license from the government to purchase supplies from independent food vendors. A musty, rotten-wood odor couldn't mask the pungent, meaty smells of Russian cookery. Zhenya led Anton past the occupied tables into a large back room, where a mixed group of loudly arguing young people congregated around an ornate, old-fashioned bar. Most acknowledged his presence with a nod, a few called out.

Zhenya, smiling broadly, nodding back, made his way up to the bar. "Tonya, what'll it be? No restrictions, here."

Anton paused. Not having eaten, he knew vodka would knock him for a loop before he had time to size up this bunch. "I'll just have a beer."

"Sure, I remember you were pretty susceptible. A beer, Slava, my usual, and a plate of pirogi." The man behind the counter, a plump ectomorph with a graying handlebar

mustache, poured the drinks and put them on the bar, then
retreated to the kitchen. When he returned, he carried a
large platter of steaming dumpling appetizers.

Tonya scooped up a hot handful of the meat pastries.
This was certainly a step above what they ate at the dorm.
He tasted one and let the garlic-onion filling spill out onto
his tongue. Perfection. His mother made a variant of this
whenever he screwed up his courage to visit, but it was not
nearly so spicy. He had, in fact, almost forgotten that food
like this, prepared specifically to cause gustatory pleasure,
existed. He took a long pull on the glass of beer, enjoying
the cool mingling of flavors. "What now?" he asked.

"It's the birthday of a woman named Darya Traktorovna, a poet. That's why I was at GUM, to get a little
something. I didn't have time to go through the usual channels. Anyway, we should be starting any minute."

Traktorovna? A nom de plume? "I didn't ask you,
Zhenya. What do you do now?"

"Oh, me? Well, I'm a writer, of sorts. At least I aspire to
be. I work at the Writers' Union. Nothing important or
impressive. Just shuffle the usual shitload of papers. Believe
me, Tonya, no one can produce paper like writers. That's
how I got to know these people. They *are* writers, published in *samizdat* at the least."

"I think that—"

"Here she is, the birthday girl. Happy birthday, Darya.
Many returns. When do you want your gift?"

The woman sidled up carrying a tumbler of what was
probably vodka. She was, at first glance, strange looking.
Strawberry blond hair piled up above a wide, sculptured
face. Exotic, large eyes that reminded him, subliminally, of
the man in the moon. A small, red mouth. "You really
shouldn't have gotten me anything, Zhe. I don't want anything from you but your . . . friendship."

"Oh, come on. This is an old high school chum, Tonya
Serebryakov. Works with the space program."

"Oh?" she smiled. "That happens to be one of my interests. Do you know any of the cosmonauts?"

Anton cringed slightly. Another cosmonaut worshiper.
"Uh . . . No. I'm with Vernadskii; the science end of
things. Meteors, that kind of thing. Shooting stars. I just
got back from Antarctica."

Zhenya looked at him strangely. "Really? What in the

world were you doing there in February? Must be awfully cold."

"No. As a matter of fact, it's summer there now. You know, the Southern Hemisphere. Fallen shooting stars accumulate in the ice, which makes it an excellent place—"

"That's fascinating, Tonya," said the poetess. "Why don't you come to my group over here and explain it." She led them over to a knot of five or seven men and women, vigorously debating some obscure point.

"No, no, no!" said a pretty girl with a skullcap of dark, curly hair, barely out of her teens. "Solzhenitsyn, the second he stepped out of *rodina,* lost all his relevance. Look at that bloated old fool Aksyonov, since he got tenure in Baltimore. His books are *shit,* plain and simple. None of them has the slightest idea what's going on here."

"How absurd!" shouted a short, bulbous man with a harelip barely hidden under a shaggy mustache. "You act as though Aleksandr Isaich renounced his humanity with his internal passport. There is much in *The Red Wheel* to command our attention. He is a—"

Darya broke in with a curt gesture of her hand and a barking laugh. "Oh, come now. It's a well-known effect. Look at Turgenev. Those who leave are doomed to failure."

"Another explanation," said a quiet voice, "is that, once the repression is gone, so is the genius. That is why we have seen nothing of merit in the wake of *glasnost.*"

Zhenya laughed inappropriately. "It's the truth. Once the pressure is off—phffft! There goes the muse."

Anton listened carefully, waiting for a subject to arise that he might feel qualified to comment upon, but none came. He drank his beer, and then two more. The birthday celebration was quaint, fun in a childish way. And the close press of people and their wild argumentation seemed to remove a weight from his mind. This was what he had been looking for, comradeship, fun.

At the end of the evening, he stepped into the cold air, refreshed. He took a deep breath, colored by the unfamiliar tang of alcohol in his sinuses, and started for the dorm with a pleasant buzz drowning out the cold.

As the big Tupolev jetliner specially commissioned to fly them to Moskva rolled to the end of Yubilyei Aerodrome's main taxiway, Volodya sat back in his seat and stared out the little window through heavy-lidded eyes. After only thirty hours of Earth-gravity, it felt almost normal again, and he could get around pretty well if he shuffled. He could feel his seat rock ever so slightly, almost *feel* the gravity pushing down on him, as the forward fuselage of the plane bounced over expansion joints in the concrete. There was a more pronounced movement, down then up, as the pilot hit the brakes and they came to a stop.

Everything seemed new, enhanced somehow by the long trip in space. The familiar scrubby dead sea bottom out the window was beautiful. Even the utility buildings and fences were beautiful. The seat was biting into his back, compressing tissue that had spent four months forgetting what pressure was.

*This has an air of unreality to it. I can't believe I'm back. . . .* The brakes let go and the plane slowly rolled forward, turning, out onto the runway. *It's been a* long *fucking time.* The jet stopped again, squatting on the concrete. The throttles went full thrust. They bounced for a moment, then the sound eased off. *All right, boys, the engines work. Roll.*

The roar built back up and this time they moved, slowly at first, then faster, accelerating. The plane thudded across tarred expansion joints, lump, lump, lump, the procession growing faster, fainter. Volodya glanced briefly at the tab settings on the wings and felt the lightness of the vessel in his skeleton. *That's enough. Rotate.* He could imagine the pilot pulling back on the yoke and, sure enough, the nose tipped back and the ground noise of the wheels vanished.

*Funny as hell if I was killed in a plane crash after all that.* Out the window the ground fell away, flattening. The plane tipped toward the northwest, continuing a steep climb. The wings sliced through a thin mist that thickened suddenly, and the ground was gone. *Funny as hell . . .*

Bronstein, in his spacesuit the whole four months of the voyage home, lashed to the hull of *Molotochek,* was, even now, in a box under the floor, headed for a hero's welcome in Moskva. Headed for the Kremlin Wall, becoming a little casket of ashes, to stand in a niche near Gagarin, Komorov, and the others. . . . *Now, spirited back to the Earth, it was finally starting to hit him. Dead. Still dead. For all that we seldom talked, we were allies in running the show. It's one thing to deal with snot-nose civilians, there's no* worldview in common. But Slava and I were much the same.

Chishak and Serebryakov, the former in a crisp, new uniform, the latter in a plaid shirt and trousers, shared the row of three seats across the aisle, talking idly. Mostly it was Chishak, reiterating how glad he would be to see his wife again. Anton said little, though he seemed amiable enough.

Probably glad to be back on the ground. Volodya leaned closer to the window, watching the hazy cloudscape roll underneath. It was unusual for these hot, dry lands to be so overcast, but it happened. It was already autumn in Starry Town now, with breezes hinting at the winter to come. The plane was scheduled to land briefly in Magnitogorsk, then head on directly for Moskva. The press had already lost interest in them, and there wasn't expected to be much of a crowd at Sheremetyevo Airport.

For some reason, Volodya's mind shied away from thinking of Shutka. *It's all a dream to me now. We'll be like strangers. . . .* It was never like that, of course, but the feeling was hard to beat down. He remembered returning from his first months-long space mission. As they lay in bed together, cooling, the sweat evaporating away into the night, she'd said, "It's like you never went away." *That was the way it would be this time . . .* and he felt a sudden fierce longing in the pit of his stomach.

He listened to the mutter of Chishak's voice, Serebryakov's occasional response, and wondered, *What does Tonya have to come back to? He must have parents, a girlfriend, something like that, but he never talks about them. I know nothing about his personal life, just that he spent longer years studying than I ever did, that his life is wrapped up in dealings with the civil list hierarchy . . . just that he has a drinking problem and somehow strives to control it.*

*And* something *has happened to all of us. For all the words that have flowed between us, some of them seem to have . . . meant something. . . . Perhaps we are growing into our roles. . . .*

*We'd better be. February is coming.*

A cold feeling flowered in his heart.

Late Friday night, May 15, 1987 . . .

Volodya stood with a little group of junior engineers on

the rubbly parking lot beside Temporary Industrial Facility No. 78, looking out across the flat plains of southern Kazakhstan, not far from where a disheartened Alexander the Great, on his way to China, gave up and turned back. A freezing drizzle fell from the black sky, turning to rainbow haze on the floodlit horizon. They were huddled together near the rusty railroad tracks, looking over a low, scrubby ridge, through an old barbed-wire fence, toward a scene of splendor.

A little more than two kilometers away, a pair of launchpads stood partially completed, fat assemblages of girders, 100-meter-tall rotating service towers, on a little rise built up to hold huge subterranean flame channels. They were surrounded by cranes of various sizes and types, still now, abandoned, and the whole was bracketed by a pair of 225-meter-high lightning protection towers. Beside them stood smaller structures bearing the artificial suns of the largest floodlight assemblies the world had ever known. But for the black sky, it might have been day.

Beyond the immense construction site, another three kilometers away, stood the lone operational Energiya launchpad, Experimental Complex No. 103. By comparison with the new construction it was an ancient thing, built in the late sixties for the failed lunar booster. The little knot of Glavkosmos engineers was as close as anyone would come to tonight's launch. Any closer and their peril would be too great. Even here, an explosion might shower them with debris. Volodya leaned against his fence post, remembering Beregovoi's words: "If it blows, get in the building; don't stand there gawking at the pretty fire!"

His lips pinched at the memory. Well. I know better than that. Still, the temptation was a surprising one. He could recall a rainy day at the engineering institute in Leningrad, standing outside under an overhang talking with a classmate. Suddenly an electrical transformer on a utility pole across the street had malfunctioned, making a loud, prolonged hum, then exploding with a bang and falling into the street. His friend had taken refuge immediately, but he had just stood there, transfixed by the beautiful ball of green fire, by the unexpected power of the event.

In any case, I'm lucky to be out here. Or not so lucky. This launch was being managed by engineers from the Molniya Scientific and Industrial Enterprise, because the

Soviet space shuttle, a military project from its inception, was their baby. Engineers from the new Glavkosmos agency would not take over until the system was declared "operational," maybe in a year or two, maybe never.

Things are beginning to change.

Maybe. Maybe not. In the past eighteen months, suspicious cracks had begun to appear in a system that had, in many respects, served him well. There were some signs the *Nomenklatura,* Comrade File Cabinet's secret civil service, might be losing its grip. But do I want them to? Good question. The *idea* of freedom is a wonderful thing, but . . . Here it is so simple. You pay your dues, do your job, kiss appropriate asses on cue, and climb up the ladder.

Gorbachev says we are failing economically, the farms are inefficient, the factories useless . . . but here I stand, looking at a rocket ship as sophisticated as anything produced by the industrialized, immeasurably wealthy West. There are . . . contradictions. The benefit of *Nomenklatura* rule was a support of the status quo and a reluctance to interfere with success. Now, that was changing. Brezhnev, who'd kept things going on the same old course for twenty years, was gone at last. These new people seemed, incredibly, to be turning loose the reins of power.

What happens if they do? What if we become like the Americans, subject to legislative approval and project-by-project funding? Will we fall down that same black hole?

A couple of cosmonauts with vaguely familiar faces came strolling up. They weren't among the ones he knew best. Igor Volk and the "Wolf Pack" team that would be flying these things in a year or two were scattered between here and Moskva, helping out at Mission Control, working with the launch crew. One of the men nodded to him. It occurred to him vaguely that this was one of the horde of Aleksandrovs that plagued the cosmonaut corps. It was silly. Even one of the Bulgarians had been named Aleksandrov. Come to think of it, the Bulgarian and at least two of the Russians had been named Aleksandr Aleksandrov . . .

"Shit! Here it comes!" muttered one of the other engineers.

Out on the launchpad, things were changing. The mobile service structure had been rolled back long ago, leaving the rocket exposed to the drizzly night. Now the long plume of white vapor climbing from the nose of the Energiya sustainer core suddenly dissipated. Expansion valves were shutting, the cryogenic fuel and oxidizer top-off operations concluded. Less than a minute to go. Volodya felt his heart beating softly at the base of his throat, and a certain shortness of breath. This was bound to be better than the *Semyorka* launches he'd seen . . .

The main sway arms holding the rocket steady began to pull back into the fixed service tower, leaving only the spindly mechanisms of electrical access arms and looping connector cables. Here and there you could see prototypes of the special machinery that would support a manned launch, escape platforms and the like, already folded well out of the way. Less than thirty seconds to go now. Bolted to the side of the rocket, sticking out strangely, was the black mass of its payload, a special wingless third stage that had been cobbled together out of a used *kosmicheskii korabl* engineering test model. It had given good service since coming here on the overburdened back of a converted Mya-4 bomber three years ago.

Suddenly, the floodlights turned wan. Orangish light flared at the base of the structure, soundless, flowing liquidly down the flame channel. Simultaneously, you could see the distant spray of the acoustic suppression system, blowing away as steam, carrying off the sound of the engines in accordance with the laws of thermodynamics. The light turned yellow, then white, and a faint waterfall sound began to build.

"God!" someone muttered, "the engines work!"

Volodya felt a thrill building inside, climbing up the bony ladder of his spine, standing the close-cropped hairs of his nape on end. They *do* work! Even now you had to think of that big crater not so many kilometers away, where the moon-rocket of 1969 had blown away its launchpad and a hundred junior engineers. . . .

Eight seconds and the sustainer core engines were at full thrust. Volodya put a hand on his chest, feeling his flesh pulse through the jacket. Is that my heart, or vibration from the rocket? Red fire blossomed around the base of the Energiya in a dense swirl of black kerosene smoke, roaring down into the flame channel, mixing with the colorless hydrogen smoke, then out onto the hard surface of the scrubby wilderness. The flame yellowed and its light flickered on the inner surface of the fat cloud that rose up now, beginning to hide the launchpad and its rumbling inhabitant.

The electrical access arms disconnected abruptly, like the opening petals of some gigantic robot flower. "There it goes!" The noise began to grow louder.

It went slowly. With its twenty engines at full thrust, the last hold-down clamps released and the soft metal retarder bolts oozed out of their sockets. Two fat balls of yellow fire blossomed as the ship lifted above the stage, pressing in on the column of almost invisible hydrogen flame in the middle. Long seconds went by as it climbed up the tower, the candle flames of the strap-on boosters licking through the girder work. Steam rose and horizontal columns of smoke boiled out across the landscape.

"Fucking shit! I can't believe it!"

Energiya cleared its tower, climbed to a preprogrammed point in the night sky, and began its roll program, tipping away toward the northeast. The engines were pointing at the spot on which they stood and the noise became very loud indeed. The wires of the fence began to sing, a faint whine, vibrating the fence post beneath his fingers.

Someone said, "The wall of the TIF is falling down!"

Volodya didn't hear it go, disregarding the spray of debris and the shouts of dismay and merriment from his companions. He listened to his shallow breath, blowing plumes into the cold night air, and watched his spaceship disappear into the orange clouds.

When it was gone, he turned away from the self-congratulating group of junior engineers to face the two space explorers, men he barely knew:

"Comrade cosmonauts . . . I am a systems engineer on the Glavkosmos wing of the shuttle project. How do you suppose I might apply for admission to the cosmonaut training program?"

The two men stared at him for a moment, then looked at each other and burst out laughing.

They were ushered along a dim underground corridor from the Kremlin's Senate Tower upstairs to a small room in the Lenin Mausoleum. There, Mikhail Gorbachev shook their hands warmly and motioned them into three carefully placed chairs against the far wall. Still only partially adapted to the strong gravity, Anton was grateful for the rest.

Gorbachev himself stood nervously, pacing a little within the confined space. These things were . . . necessary foolishness. "The ceremony will begin in just a few minutes," he said. "First, I want to extend my sincerest condolences for the loss of your comrade. Raisa and I were very solemn after we heard the news." He sighed gustily, looking down at them, clasping his hands behind his back, so the front of his suit coat spread open. "I'm sorry I couldn't attend the debriefing, but my presence was absolutely required in Vladivostok after the earthquake." He watched them nod with varying degrees of sincerity. Well . . . "Needless to say, we're all very proud of you. I will present your medals and announce your new ranks at the end of the ceremony. I understand you're scheduled to speak, Vladimir Alekseevich?"

Volodya nodded. "Yes, General Secretary. I'm to say a few words describing what we found in nontechnical terms for the many young men and women who dream of entering the cosmonaut corps one day."

Gorbachev pulled a calculator-sized computer out of his overcoat and punched a few keys, then banged it against the heel of his hand. "Hmh. Dead battery." He turned it over and looked at the Russian factory trademark stencil. "Well. As I recall, you're scheduled to speak after Comrade Yeltsin. You will find your own words displayed on the teleprompter should you need assistance."

Manarov shifted his weight on the hard chair. Buttocks took a long time to get back to normal. What am I supposed to say to that? The interview with a junior-grade Kremlin speech writer had been . . . What? Idiotic. "Thank you, Comrade General Secretary."

"I'd better warn you, though, about the act that you'll be following. It seems Comrade Yeltsin's speech will not be the simple accolade appropriate at this time. He's planning on using this occasion to launch an offensive against our space program, and the Mars project in particular. He has always been an opponent of space and an ally of the *Zelenisti*"—he said the word with distaste—"that wish to abandon technology altogether and set the clock back to our distinguished prehistory. You know how much damage they did in the late eighties and early nineties.

"So, Vladimir Alekseevich, you may be called upon to defend our current expenditures. I've taken the liberty of preparing a few opening lines for your speech so it will seem to be a natural response to Yeltsin's accusations."

Volodya sat still, looking up at the man. Not *quite* like the bad old days, but . . . No matter. Our aims are essentially the same. "You can be assured I will be sincere."

"Excuse me, General Secretary," said Lyova, "but Yeltsin himself has amassed a huge personal following. Is there any chance that he will be able to do this thing?"

"My dear Comrade Chishak, despite what you may have heard, the Communist party is still in firm control of planning the future of the USSR. While our elected assembly is necessary to maintain the ongoing *perestroika,* we will not allow the ignorant masses to stand in the way of the only hope of mankind. As long as I am . . . in charge around here, we shall not sacrifice our dedication to the enabling technologies that we have spent so much time and money building. Does that answer your question?"

Lyova grinned, unpleasant rubbery folds appearing on his long face. "Yes, I believe it does."

Timofey Yurievich Bogdashevskii was halfway through reading the anchor text of *Vremya,* 14 September 2002 edition, from his teleprompter.

"Now, friends," he was saying, "we must turn to a sad event in the news. Ceremonies were held today at the Kremlin, interring the ashes of pilot-cosmonaut Miroslav Ilyich Bronstein, colonel in the Strategic Rocket Forces of the USSR, commander of the interplanetary spaceship *Molotochek,* three times Hero of the Soviet Union, who was killed in a deep-space accident this summer during investigations of the near-Earth asteroid Sinuhe. The heroic cosmonaut was borne to his final resting place by his comrades and flight crew members. Also honoring him as pallbearers were Communist party General Secretary Gorbachev and President Yeltsin, who was recently elected chairman of the Democratic Union party." Bogdashevskii resisted a little smile at that touch. Only our second freely elected president, and already an opposition candidate holds the office. We may be no Poland, but still . . .

On the rear projection system that made up the wall behind him, a videotape of the event was being displayed.

Trudging up the path to the newly opened burial site, eight men bore a little bier on their shoulders. The front two positions were held by Gorbachev, roly-poly and elderly, and Yeltsin, roly-poly and getting there fast. The two men were quite short-looking, the poles of the bier several inches above their shoulders, just a resting place for their hands. Behind them stood Manarov and a tall, dark-haired, rather un-Russian-looking military officer. The poles rested solidly on their shoulders. In the places immediately behind the ornate little casket stood Chishak and Serebryakov, behind them two shorter men, a pair of nondescript air force officers, for "balance." They stepped slowly, to somber Russian music, rather bassoon-dominated stuff. As they drew to a stop before the opened wall niche, Gorbachev turned and began to speak. Behind him, the unknown cosmonaut could be seen to grimace.

"The crew of *Molotochek* will be returning to Sinuhe, preparatory to braking operations intended to place the asteroid in Earth-orbit, next spring. Colonel Bronstein's position on the crew will be filled by Estonian cosmonaut Sirje Saarmula"—he stumbled a little bit over the outlandish ethnic name—"who is a commander in the Red Fleet. An experienced cosmonaut, with more than eighteen hundred hours in orbit, this will be Commander Saarmula's first deep-space mission."

The scene behind him shifted as the teleprompter went on to a new page. "In other news"—thank God for continuity writers—"trading was suspended today at the Leningrad Stock Exchange when it was discovered that several floor managers have been selling futures options on the black market. Union Prosecutor Natan I. Vishinskii announced . . ."

Back in Starry Town. Back among the living. Anton stood at the rear of the small classroom and watched the sky through a metal framework of windows and the skeletal silhouettes of already bare poplars. The September sky was a deep blue, covered with a fan of converging contrails, some tapering to needle-thin points. In the nearer sky, winds aloft had smeared the clouds out into sawtooth irregularities. A daytime moon, pale and almost invisible, was the sole reminder of the vastness of space they had left behind. Warmth billowed up from the radiators under the windows, an additional barrier to the autumnal firmament. Anton reluctantly turned to see the entry of the Estonian cosmonaut who would pilot *Molotochek* during the second leg of the mission, Sirje Saarmula. Volodya and Lyova, talking quietly, came in next. Serebryakov made himself cross the room to join the conversation.

Manarov looked at him curiously as he walked up, blue eyes lit by an unreadable expression. He smiled. "Good morning, Tonya."

Anton stared at him for a moment. It seemed as though the bond that had developed between them was dissolving. Inexplicably, he felt repelled by the happiness evident in his friend's manner. "I'm alright, Volodya," he said, "I just wish we could get out of here and start our vacations."

Manarov nodded once. "Understood." He turned to gesticulate at the Estonian. "You've met Seryozha? He's a good pilot. I think you'll like working with him." The smile was fading fast, Volodya staring at him hard enough to force his gaze down.

Saarmula was a handsome man, neither thin nor stocky, who stared at one through heavy-lidded, suspicious eyes. Longish brown hair in two loose locks curled down over his high forehead. His cheekbones and square chin were clear evidence of his Estonian ancestry. Anton found himself staring at a small mole on the man's upper lip. "Glad to have you aboard," he said.

The new pilot ran his hand through the hair, which stubbornly fell right back where it had been. "Thanks. Uh . . . Here comes Roman Grigorievich."

The chief of Unmanned Spaceflight came in, followed by their backups, Gaurai, Zarkov, Zhoresyov, and a new pilot to replace Saarmula, the voluble, balding, blond Popovich.

"Well, good afternoon, gentlemen." Tolstoi looked smug enough to put wrinkles in the clear tissue of his scar. "You are, no doubt, wondering why you've been called here; and some of you are wondering whether you will ever be let go. I have been authorized to wish Comrades Manarov, Chishak, and Serebryakov a happy furlough, starting at fifteen hundred hours. But first . . . *first,* I have been delegated to remind you of your duties to yourselves and your country. You may want to sit down for this; it will take a while."

Why in the world? Tonya sat in a nearby chair and

stretched out his sore legs. What was the sense in going through all this now?

"As you are no doubt aware, the retrieval of the asteroid Sinuhe has developed into an international issue. Political forces are now at work, both inside the Soviet Union and abroad, that seek to discredit our space program and force us to cancel the mission. In that light I must caution you not to become involved in any of these controversies. There have already been a number of unfortunate incidents in which the casual remark of a cosmonaut has been distorted and used for propaganda purposes. Gentlemen, and you three, I urge you to be very careful when you speak. You are now worldwide celebrities of a sort, and the Western newsmongers will be hot on your heels."

"Should we talk to them at all?" asked Volodya. "This could be an excellent opportunity to boost the project, space flight in general. Why not take it?"

Tolstoi wagged his head, clucking softly. "Vladimir Alekseevich, you must realize that digital distortion of video/audio playback has become a common technique. The most unscrupulous splice out-of-context comments with questions that have been designed specifically to produce the desired effect. As far as I know, they are not yet fabricating interviews from scratch, though what keeps them from crossing that line I don't know. If possible, do not talk to them; simply smile and keep walking. Any more questions?

"Secondly, I wanted to tell you that *Molotochek* has undergone extensive evaluation, and is in perfect condition for another interplanetary voyage. It has been towed up to a five-hundred-kilometer orbit, and is already being cleaned and reprovisioned. So, at this moment, everything is go for phase two. All right, comrades. I guess that's all. Enjoy yourselves."

Tonya and Volodya were sitting on comfortable plastic chairs in the open-air beergarden at the Culture and Recreation Park for officers just east of Moskva's central city. A large copse of trees, mostly rid of their bright-yellow leaves, crowded up to the pavement and rustled quietly in the barely noticeable breeze. They had been fortunate to find a place like this open this late in the year, with October so near. Anton watched a small pleasure boat float slowly down the narrow, stone-walled Yauza River. The muffled cacophony of Moskva traffic was barely audible here.

Volodya relaxed and took a sip of the dark beer, imported from Denmark. *Elephant Piss,* it was called. Weird. Anton invites me down to Moskva to see the sites and, suddenly, I prefer his company to Shutka's. It's true, however, that I have already had ten days and nights inseparably welded to the woman. But Tonya—haven't I gotten enough of him yet?

"It was a good movie," he said. "Though that stuff about the bridge collapsing was a bunch of guff. They never built things that flimsy, even in those days. The tsars lacked intelligence; but they always hired good architects."

"If you say so. I'm always offended when they mangle the astronomy in a movie. It's so annoying when the Americans spend millions of dollars on one of their space epics, and then don't even get the most elementary facts straight. You'd think they could get a high school teacher to proofread the script for a hundred dollars, maybe less. Our movies are usually accurate as far as they go."

Volodya nodded. "I don't know why science fiction movies have never really caught on here. Must be some reason."

"Our illustrious space program is so good, we have no need for fiction," Anton said, smiling facetiously. "From what I understand, it is the opposite in America. They dote on the wild fantasies in their movies and literature and show no enthusiasm for the reality."

The sun was low, glinting off the Olympic swimming pool beyond the soccer field. Volodya looked at his watch. "Well, Tonya, I want to thank you for showing me the insider's Moskva. I hope you'll let me show you Leningrad some time."

"I enjoyed it, too. I haven't been back to the Arbat for many years."

"I don't suppose we'll be seeing each other again until January. I'm taking the family for an extended Black Sea vacation. They deserve it."

"Of course." Anton felt a sudden surge of loneliness. *"You* deserve it, Volodya. Maybe I'll get away, myself. But this is not really a vacation for me. There's a lot of work to do at Vernadskii; and, if I am to get full credit for my discoveries I'll need to be there."

"Well, good luck, Tonyushka." He pulled out a billfold and withdrew a few garishly colored ruble notes, pinning them under his bottle.

"Good-bye, Volodya."

Alone again, Tonya contemplated the suds in his beer and drained it down. A stiffer wind, still not especially cold, swept through the park, scattering the myriad leaves. Here he was, for some reason on the brink of tears. He tried to find the Moon, but it was nowhere to be seen; he had lost track of the phase. It was as he had feared: left to his own devices, the old directionlessness had come back, in spades. He thought about going to stay with his mother in Mytishchi for a while, but the idea was not appealing. They had gotten their mother-son act down perfectly over the years, a ritual as stilted and pointless as any in the church. She would invite her friends over to meet the famous cosmonaut, and there would be a great deal of ridiculous fuss. No, that was not a possibility. His father was now working in Trans-Altai, and the few letters they exchanged showed no emotion. He could not even consider going to stay with him.

What then? Bury himself in his work? No. He had been working without respite for months; and, though a part of him found that option attractive, it made his skin crawl. He signaled the waiter, a vodka. When it was brought he drank it down and ordered another.

And, of course, there was Darya. The furtive masturbation he had carried out aboard *Molotochek* had been very unsatisfactory; and there was a deep longing for the woman only slightly buried under his consciousness. He had large amounts of back pay in the bank, enough, perhaps, to pay for a week or two of companionship. The alcohol was starting to work its magic. The idea was very appealing—just hire her out until the money ran out. She was very particular about her privacy though, he knew. She might just laugh at him. Still, any port in a storm. One more drink would probably settle matters, so he ordered and, after paying his tab, drank. *Ah, well, what have I got to lose?*

And her apartment wasn't especially far from here. He stood, swaying slightly, and tried to gauge the distance. *Let's see. Entuziastov must be due south of here, and he could take Zolotozhskii Val Street to Ilyicha Square.* He started walking in that direction.

Anton made his way along the pleasant, wide avenue, feeling the quick cool that was enveloping the world as the sun reddened near the horizon. The alcohol was buoying him up, making everything into a dream. It wasn't difficult to find the Zheleznodorozhaya apartment complex, and he found himself retracing his usual path to the woman's rooms. He stopped and sat on the stairway just before her floor, and tried to muddle out what he would say. "Hello, Darya, how's about a two-week fling?" or "I'd like to make a proposal." A proposal! That was an idea. Get her for free; make an honest woman of the cynical poetess. Well, no, that wasn't a very promising line of attack. Ah, shit! He decided to wing it.

She opened her door just a crack, clutching a pink towel around her with one hand. Her hair was a bright, tawdry red. "Oh, Tonya. Well. Fuck, I would love to see you right now, but, as you can probably tell, I'm engaged. I saw you on TV. I can't tell you how excited I am about the asteroid and all that. Oh, well, sorry. If you can come back tomorrow, I'll be able to give you some time. But now . . . 'fraid not. See you." The door closed with a metallic click.

The world closed around him, and he saw how futile it all was. No one. Not a single goddamn person on the entire face of the earth cared whether he lived or died. Thirty-six years old. Half his life gone. What a comment on his personal worth! He turned and slowly descended the interminable stairs, not quite ready to let the tears come forth.

There was a small hard-currency bar across from the Andronikov Monastery, the kind that catered exclusively to tourists. Anton always kept a few twenty-dollar bills in the back of his wallet for emergencies, and he went in. A large bald man, obviously American and plastered, was slumped over the bar, a wad of green currency in his hand. As Anton sat at the bar he seemed to wake up, and looked over smiling loosely. *"Do-broy dee-yen, pa-zhal-sta.* Do you speak English?"

Anton said "vodka" to the attendant, then, reluctantly, turned to face the drunk. "Yes. I speak English. Do you speak Serbo-Croatian?"

The man looked taken by wild surmise. "Serbo-what? No, I don't know it."

Anton let the caustic liquid work on his gums and

tongue before he swallowed it. "I just got back from outer space."

Now he seemed to have caught on. A game. Sure. "I just had the most boring day in my life. This tourism crap is not what it's cracked up to be. I wouldn't be here, but my grandfather grew up in Moscow. Left after the Revolution."

"I see. And you are considering emigrating?"

"Emi—? No, no sir. I just want to ask one question before I go back to New Jersey. What in the hell do you folks think you're doing? All the goodwill, and now you're throwing it all to hell with this asteroid thing. I thought *my* grandchildren wouldn't have to put up with this nuclear crap any more. Now you want to start it all over again. What I want to ask you Commies is, why?"

Tonya looked into the man's careworn, pimple-scarred face. The alcoholic haze seemed to be dissipating. Did he know who he was talking to? "I have no answer for you." He slid off the stool and went to look for another bar, absorbed in memory.

America! Anton pushed the pedal to the floor and the snazzy red 1991 Toyota Celica accelerated wildly along the dusty two-lane road. After all the years of wondering and yearning, here it was, stretched out before him. It was warm and sunny for April, with high featherlike cirrus that trailed long, curved streamers of ice. Anton shook his head, ticking off the events that had culminated in this trip to the Lunar and Planetary Science Conference. Luck, and more luck. Even this dazzling car with its astounding automation was the sheerest stroke of good fortune, since Vernadskii had, in its usual cost-cutting mode, reserved the least expensive rental car for him. They had even balked at that until it had been pointed out that there was virtually no mass transit in Houston and the hotels nearest to Johnson Space Center were still miles away.

It had all started on that barren, windswept expanse of blue ice under the dark wedge of Vørterkaka Nunatak, when, after a day of looking for meteorites in the area they would most likely come to the surface, he had noticed something dark under the ice near the latrine. A little bit of digging had brought it to the surface, an umber, pitted object no larger than a fist. For a long time it was thought to be an ordinary Cl Carbonacious chondrite, and had been catalogued as such. But, when he had done a cross section, everything had been wrong, and it began to look as though VN 141 was an entirely new type of meteorite—a highly consolidated breccia that had been exposed to a high heat at virtually zero pressure. The material, where it had not been destroyed by passage through the Earth's atmosphere, seemed to have been exposed to a bath of hot gases such as might be found in the Martian preplanetary envelope, and the more he thought about it, the more likely it seemed that VN 141 could be a piece of Phobos dislodged by the giant impact that had created the crater Stickney. Its density and color index were exactly right, and this led him to write a paper on the meteorite's origin. As a result, Akhmatov himself had suggested that he be part of the expanded Russian presence at the LPSC.

So here he was, in the land of the free and the home of the brave. This morning's conferences on cratering were the least interesting to him, and so he had taken this opportunity to drive around and get to know the country. His principal reaction was that, once you got away from Houston, it wasn't all that different from rural Russia. There were many dilapidated structures that would fit in nicely among the dachas that littered the countryside around Moskva.

He reigned the car over into the parking lot of a garish, plate-glass-window-dominated building standing alone in its own nest of parking lot. The glass caught the reflection of the car as it pulled up, shiny and incredibly streamlined. Tonya was proud to step out of it, feeling just like an American, perhaps, closing the door with an offhand little slam. Stores like this *were* America, they and the fast-food restaurants that were everywhere. What a fucking luxury! He pushed open the glass door, into the already air-conditioned climate inside, and took a deep breath. Yes, antiseptic, inhuman. Just the thing. The clerk, a short, fat Hispanic woman with enormous cheeks, grimaced at him and he nodded back. Before he knew it he was in amongst the aisles of product. Product, product, and more product. Each wrapped more garishly than the next, calling out to him, buy me! buy me!

He fingered a candy bar, reading its name: ZERO. Nothing bar? Strange. He looked around again. He was alone in the store, except for the clerk. How did they stay in business without customers? The magic of American capitalism: Somehow it didn't need to make sense. Tonya stepped over to the vast, glass-doored refrigerated section, loaded with hundreds of brands of soft drinks. So, this is what I craved all those years. The reality seems strangely . . . barren.

"Can I help you find something, sir?" The clerk was bent over the counter to see him better, her starched white uniform bunching up around her shoulders.

"No. No thank you, miss." He went deeper into the store, out of her line of sight.

What was her life like? How did she live, in one of the little hovels up the road? What a difference that must be, coming from a dirty, dilapidated shack to this magnificence. He shook his head. All right, tourist. You've gawked enough. Just buy something and leave.

But what? The choice was enormous, and, he supposed, there were terrible products there, beautifully wrapped just to entice an unknowing customer such as himself. If he had a bad reaction, got sick, what would happen? Here there was no free medical care; he had it on authority that even the simplest medical procedures could run into the hundreds of dollars. Of course, Vernadskii would pay, but they'd probably dock him for the amount. Well, he wouldn't get sick. That was just an unreasonable fear.

He went back to the candy rack and pulled out a Zero bar, and went up to the cash register. "Seventy-five cents, please."

He dug into his pocket and pulled out the change he had gotten to make phone calls. Three big quarters. For a nothing. You could get a big loaf of black bread in Moskva for that much, no matter how bad times were. He paid.

"Thank you, sir."

And he was back outside, back in his car, back on the highway.

Once again he turned over the idea of defecting. This, this nebulosity, could all be his. All he had to do was throw away his career. It was certainly unlikely that he could go to work for the scientific establishment here in America. On the whole, he thought, it was probably not a good idea.

He was already heading down among the undisciplined stores and restaurants of Space Highway One. The digital clock said that it was eleven-thirty, and he wanted to be there for the poster session that followed the main presentations. He turned into the gate, showed the small badge with his name on it, and was admitted, just like that. They must have dramatically relaxed security during this period of rapprochement. It was hopelessly lax. He spun into the parking lot behind Gilruth Building, throwing gravel, and pulled into a space.

It was traditional for those who had prepared purely visual papers to mount them on bulletin boards in a small classroom on the top floor of Gilruth. After the three-hour main session, the scientists would adjourn up here to drink coffee and talk about the posters. He came in to find many people already here, bent over to read the small text on the graphs or laughing and trading anecdotes. He sighted Alyosha Yusupov and made his way over. The man was talking to a muscular, tanned blond man whose nametag said DAL MILAM, BROWN UNIVERSITY. Behind the two of them a high-resolution photomontage of the asteroid Gaspra loomed. Tonya walked up, entranced by the picture, tremendously enhanced from the real-time images he had seen. "Wow," he said. "I didn't realize that *Galileo* had obtained that level of detail."

Yusupov licked his lips. "Yes. They've got a new algorithm for adding multiple images to increase resolution. Oh, Tonya, this is Dallas Milam. He has been selected to manage the CRAF mission for JPL. That should bag us another asteroid before the end of the century."

Tonya shook hands with the man, who beamed. "Hamburga, of all the ludicrously named possibilities, but you probably know that. You're the one who found the piece of Phobos?" What a strange, rough voice the man had.

"Well, that may be a bit too emphatic. There *are* certain indications that—"

"Oh, excuse me." They turned to see a slender, beautiful, dark-haired woman with metal-rimmed glasses regarding them. Her nametag read CARLA CRONIN, U OF HAWAII. "Has a geologic map been drawn up for Gaspra yet?" She was looking especially hard at Milam, probably noting the *Galileo* team cloisonné on his lapel.

"I don't know," he croaked. "You'd probably have to talk to someone from the astrogeologic branch of the

USGS. I think I saw Donnie Rickett around here somewhere."

"You are interested in asteroids?" Yusupov, with his strong cunning, had sighted her as a potential victim.

"Well, yes and no. My primary interest is meteorology. Modeling essentially stochastic events. I was working on Martian dust storms, but it occurred to me that there might be some potential in looking at the history of the asteroid belt using some of the same techniques."

"That sounds fascinating, Miss . . . Cronin. My name is Alyosha, this is my countryman Tonya, and this is Dal. We were just talking about something similar."

Milam raised an eyebrow. "Oh, yeah, sure. We still have so little knowledge of the asteroid population on the fine scale necessary. I'm afraid such calculations will have to remain in the realm of the theoretical for the time being."

"What about the near-Earthers? I understand that there has been some attempt to catalog them."

Milam shrugged. "No, I'm afraid not, Miss. A man named Zook, who you may meet here, has been trying to get funding for such a project. But so far, no takers."

"Oh, that's too bad. Well . . ."

"Miss Cronin, it's time for lunch. We were just going to the Wendy's outside the gates. Would you care to join us?" Yusupov was smiling, but in a totally unthreatening way.

She looked at her watch. "Okay."

Alyosha started toward the door. "Tonya can drive us in his brand-new Toyota."

Dawn, from the depths of a closed-off alleyway. Tonya opened his eyes and saw an endless expanse of dim, gray brick. Cold and damp had eaten into his flesh and he was too stiff to move without pain. His mouth tasted like rotten cheese, and his lips were dry and cracked. Damn. I did it this time. He tried to peel back the consciousness to find the memories underneath. He remembered flying giddy through the night, the shop fronts spinning along a corkscrew path. Vomiting once, twice. Then finding a place to anchor, holding down to stop the nauseating dizziness, slipping into oblivion.

He stood, hurting everywhere. The glorious cosmonaut returns home! He stumbled off, hoping for a landmark.

The tears had never come.

# CHAPTER 7
# *January 30, 2003*

Moe Schlossberg sat in his vast, empty office at CTN Headquarters, New York, lost in dreams of the past. The art deco flatscreen TV on his wall showed the flapping lips and meaningless head jerks of Lyle Marlowe, voiceless, the sound canceled. In any case, he was slowly becoming deaf and blind to the output of his own long labors.

Insensate, he thought bitterly. I grow insensate. He remembered his grandfather, wizened and silent, unsmiling, toward the end. Old men do that. The soft inner voice said, You're not old yet, only fifty-three. He rubbed his big hands over a softening paunch and sighed, letting his chin sink down to a resting place on the uppermost of its many *Doppelgängers*. But fat men grow old fast. I'll be dead in a decade, or maybe a little more.

He recalled a lifetime of failed diets and felt a little fuse of anger light somewhere, far down inside, with a hiss. Even now, with all the biochemical knowledge in the world, thin men look at you with curling lips. Tired of being fat? Stop eating so much! But I eat less than you do. Fuck, you must have done *something* to get like that! The scornful implication of sin made him want to step on the little bastards . . . and sometimes he had. He watched Marlowe's face working. Little bastard.

Studio AI had placed a tiny clock in the corner of his screen, with a script memo tag beneath it. Suddenly the words "Sinuhe Segment" popped up. Time. He called forth the sound.

The buttery, shit-wouldn't-melt-in-my-mouth voice rolled up, lugubrious. ". . . for tonight's special segment we have a further update on the progress of the Soviet mission to asteroid Sinuhe. I take you now live to Mount Palomar observatory in California and CTN's science correspondent, Warren Runtibbie. Warren?"

Marlowe's image grew small, shrinking to a disappearing dot as the Palomar remote unfolded flowerlike onto the screen. The petal exteriors covered the gray-out blink of a fast video shift. "Good evening, Lyle. Tonight is, of course, the moment we've been waiting for. Sinuhe is, as we speak, making its closest approach to the sun. It is at this point, which scientists call perihelion, that the Soviets will make their attempt to shift the asteroid's orbit, so it passes between the Earth and the Moon, in position for a further maneuver that will brake it into Earth-orbit."

Marlowe flinched invisibly as his picture came back on the screen, artfully superimposed, as if he were in the room with the other man. Asshole Runtibbie seemed to be swallowing his words tonight, repeating phrases and words unmercifully. Sometimes you could almost hear the little shit stutter! He was a poor sort of performer but, unfortunately, the only one with a grasp of scientific jargon. Since the public never complained, they must either believe what he said, or tune him out. Some studies *did* show that unfamiliar words on TV were simply ignored. . . . "Interesting. Warren, since the asteroid is now millions of miles from Earth, how are we going to monitor its progress? For that matter, how are the Soviets going to detonate their bombs?"

Runtibbie grinned ingratiatingly, lank hair dropping onto his forehead. "Well, Lyle, I don't know what the Soviets have up their sleeves, but we here in America have a few scientific tricks stuck up our scientific sleeves. . . ."

Jesus. We have to *do* something about this guy. I'd better talk to Schlossberg after the show. . . .

He turned his back to the camera and gestured to two people waiting silently behind him. They stepped forward. "With me tonight are the original discoverers of our death-asteroid, Doctors Martin Hackline"—the man was a little mouse turd, defined by thick, heavy, black-rimmed spectacles—"and Jack Paar . . ."

"Georgia."

". . . excuse me, Georgia Paar." The woman, who seemed to be a little shy of forty, verged on beautiful. You could see she would have been rather plain as a teenager, maybe even a fat pig, but she had taken the course some women do, maturing well. Now, of course, she would have to get old.

"Did you hear Lyle's question, Georgia?"

The woman, who seemed dazed, nodded, her long ponytail shifting behind her neck. "I think so."

"Well, could you tell our audience just how you plan to monitor the detonation tonight?"

She smiled shyly. "Uh, well, despite its closeness to the sun, both we and the Russians will be monitoring a radio signal from the computer node on the asteroid. Unfortunately, we won't be able to *see* much from Earth; if we're lucky, we'll be able to use the optics aboard the *Piazzi II* spacecraft, which is still traveling along with Sinuhe. The imaging system . . ."

"Now, wait a second. Wasn't this *Piazzi* destroyed by its . . . encounter with Commander Bronstein?"

The woman looked dumbfounded. "No, no. The Hopper was destroyed. The main spacecraft is still quite operational."

"Let me see if I've got this straight: The European spacecraft *Piazzi* is close enough that it can take a peek at the asteroid for us and see the bomb detonate?"

"Um. That's right, Warren. Actually, they had to back it off a few thousand miles to avoid any damage to the spacecraft. . . ."

A look of desperation gripped Runtibbie's face. "Interesting. And when is this event due?"

She looked at her watch. "Let's see . . . about three minutes ago. . . ."

Warren Runtibbie blanched.

Back in the CTN studio, Lyle Marlowe shouted. "Fuck! That *asshole*!" and signaled frantically to his booth-ensconced director. The man punched up the thirty-second delay live timeout, routed in a raw voice-over module, quickly adjusted it to roughly match the astronomer's voice, and said, "Let's see . . . in about two minutes . . ." and sent it out over the broadcast with the image.

Back at Mount Palomar, Georgia Paar said, "Wait! Wait! You don't understand! There's a light-speed delay! The signal won't get here for another ninety seconds! We're *ready*!"

In the background, placing a hand over the lenses of his eyeglasses, Maarten Hakluyt began to giggle helplessly.

Far away in space and time, not far from the orbit of Venus, asteroid 5007 Sinuhe swept placidly along, rotating slowly, baking in the harsh light of the inner solar system. The mission computer, a heavily modified IBM PS/2 Model 90, ticked away its instructions.

Clock one says it's time.

Clock two says it's time.

Clock three says it's two more minutes.

Clock four says it's time.

Clock five says its thirty-seven more seconds.

Clock six says it's time.

The rules say it's the mean of the closest three out of six.

Then it must be time!

The sun sensor looked at the sun.

The Aldebaran sensor looked at Aldebaran.

The Jupiter sensor looked at Jupiter.

Nope, eleven more seconds to go.

Four . . .

Three . . .

Two . . .

One . . .

Bang.

The impulse went out to bomb one. It only took a microsecond. What happened then only took a millisecond.

Fission lit off fusion, bomb-trigger triggering bomb . . .

On the leading edge of the asteroid, a child's toy balloon swelled up in the quicktime of quantum mechanics. The ball, a blue-violet hole into another dimension, grew out of nowhere, a bright plasma of bomb debris and a little bit of asteroid. No noise, no atmospheric shock wave, no fantasy-inspiring mushroom cloud. The ball swelled and grew dim as it expanded, dissipating in a few minutes into interplanetary space, leaving behind a glowing, radioactive crater twenty meters across.

A substantial chunk of the bomb's five kilotons of kinetic energy punched into the asteroid, reflecting around inside its solid metal core, expanding some fractures, welding others shut. But much of the energy went the other way, changing the asteroid's velocity just a little bit. Just enough.

Asteroid 5007 Sinuhe was bound for Earth.

Back at CTN Headquarters, New York, Moe Schlossberg sat back in his chair, thunderstruck. Fuck-puds, he muttered. I'm surrounded by fuck-puds.

And that soft little voice attached to the base of his brain said, Sure, fatty, you *always* knew that. But listen, the asteroid thing *worked.* *Now* what do we do?

Volodya sat on the dacha's porch, looking out into the early evening darkness. The sunset was over, and lights had come on in the ragged tier of similar cottages that partially hid the slate-dark expanse of sea. Now Venus reigned in the clear, blue-black sky and the other stars were coming out quickly. Even here, he thought, the winter darkness comes early. True. And it was getting cold. In the daytime, the sun was good and warm, and you could go around in a long-sleeved shirt. But January was the closest they got to winter hereabouts, and even with the moderating influence of the sea held in by the mountains, it wasn't exactly paradise this time of year.

Girlish giggling came out of the dim, blue dusk, and two little shadows came running up the walkway. Volodya slumped down in his chair a bit, wrapping his fingers around the neck of the bottle of thick Mexican beer you could, amazingly, buy even in this remote town, and watched them run. God. They're getting big. Does that mean I'm getting old? Galina was eight now and Tamara five. They were pretty little girls, plump and healthy, with curly blond hair, Galina's beginning to darken a bit, and rosy Russian cheeks. "Better come in now," he said to them. "It gets cold here at night."

*"Daddy!"* squealed Galina, "You call this *cold?"*

Little Tama dashed across the porch, patent leather shoes clattering on the boards, and jumped into his lap, snuggling her face into the front of his flannel shirt. He nuzzled her hair, and she said, "You smell like beer." Before he could respond she wriggled away and then the two of them were gone, banging into the house, shouting to each other.

Hmh. You took the pleasure of your children as they

doled it out, unaware. I suppose I'm lucky. Some people's children are repulsive little pieces of shit. Mine are just wrapped up in being kids. . . . And I'm gone so much of the time. Well. They will grow up. And I will grow old. Somehow, sitting in the cool darkness, drinking his beer, that didn't seem like such a terrible thing.

The screen door banged again and an indistinct form came out into the night. "Volodya?"

He looked up at her. "I'll be in in a minute, Shutka. I want to breathe in a little more of this fine night air." The smell of the Black Sea was actually a little on the musty side, but . . . "Two more weeks," he said.

She slid onto his lap, a substantial weight, putting an arm around the back of his neck, caressing the short hair of his nape. "I'm . . . trying not to think about it," she said. "This is going to be very dangerous. And Slava . . ."

He hugged her, noticing that she'd put on a couple of new kilograms during their vacation. "Slava did something very stupid. I hear the government is going to have to pay the Italians for ruining their little spacecraft."

Shutka sighed her exasperation. "It's easy to do something stupid."

Volodya put his hand on her thigh and slid it up toward her trunk, stopping where he met the juncture of her legs. "I know it. I've been escaping from the consequences of my own stupidity for many years now. I keep wondering how long this lucky streak can go on."

"Sometimes I wish you'd retire. They'd let you have an administrative position."

He nodded slowly in the darkness. "They would. Yes. And I couldn't do it." He squinted up at her face. "You understand?"

She kissed him on the forehead, a dry little peck. "I always have."

But do you? he wondered. How much pain am I causing? Do my little girls miss me when I'm gone for half a year? Does my wife die a thousand deaths when she hears there's trouble in space? You talk to people and they answer, but it doesn't make any difference. They tell you what they think you need to hear, because they love you. He squeezed her thigh softly. "I'm grateful for that. It would be hard to do these things without you."

They sat in silence for a little while, holding onto each

other, then Shutka said, "Come inside now. Let's have dinner. And the girls will want to play. They love your stories
about space."

They rose and went in through the banging screen door,
holding hands, fingers interlaced.


Volodya thought, 1991. All over but the going away. I've
signed my name on a door in the Cosmonaut Hotel, kissed
the chief engineer goodbye and ridden out to the pad.
Volodya sat in the far left-hand seat of *Soyuz TM-17*,
crushed hard up against pilot-cosmonaut Sasha Krimnev,
within arm's reach of Canadian Intersoyuz-cosmonaut
George Buckminster Smiley. Too many of these bastards
taking our flights, he thought. Hard currency was a funny
thing. The seventeen million Canadian dollars his government was paying for this eight-day trip was less than a
tenth the cost of the mission—but the value of those dollars
was beyond calculation in terms of what they'd buy in the
West. The computer imports alone would more than cover
the cost of the flight.

He looked around the shadowy cabin, at the winking
idiot lights on his antiquated control panel. And the worst
of it is Shutka sitting in a grandstand a few kilometers
away, waiting for the fire. On the elevator ride up to the
capsule, they could hear the *semyorka* vehicle groaning
softly to itself, telling them about the temperature differen-
tial between the kerosene and liquid oxygen contained in its
paper-thin hull. It had been cool in the elevator, the frosty
rocket wiping out the heat of a Kazakhstan summer sun.

Even sitting here, with space helmet closed, capsule but-
toned up, he could hear little sounds, a tick of metal changing shape, the whine of distant machinery. The space
outside the capsule's porthole was dark, the aeroshroud engineering lights long having been discarded in an effort to
shave a few kilograms off the rocket's weight. Well. I guess
my childhood question has been answered: I'm afraid I'm
going to be blown to bits.

He looked up at the plumb-bob gravity indicator dangling in the center of the cabin. It was swaying slowly, an
indication that the rocket was itself swaying on the pad, its
motion not entirely damped by the big hold-down clamps
outside. The rocket, uprated fantastically since its initial

flight in 1956, was so top-heavy now it would tip over in an instant if left standing by itself.

The voice in his earphones said, "Ten seconds, boys. Bon voyage." Capcom's Ukrainian accent made the French ludicrous, like an American TV-Russian. *Bawn why-udge.*

And so the countdown went to zero. The ship's twenty engines, derivative of a 1940s design, stuttered to life, hypergolic leaders giving a nonmechanical ignition. The plumb-bob spasmed suddenly, swinging a full ten centimeters out of true, twirling wildly overhead. That would be the hold-down clamps letting go, arms folding majestically back from the launchpad. The Canadian sat forward in his seat, rising up, face pale, eyes big.

Volodya glanced at his useless panel of lights and grinned. I'm lucky to be here. We'll be going aloft on modern *zenit* boosters soon. And next year the shuttle.

Pressure began to build up on his back. The *semyorka* was staggering off the pad, clearing the tower. Not far away, Shutka would be watching it climb on a complex candle flame of power. He hoped her heart wasn't beating as fast as his own. God. I have to go to the bathroom now! But no provision was made for shitting in these suits. They'd be on board *Mir* soon enough. The oscillations began to die down and the plumb-bob began to rock back and forth mechanically, with a frequency of about two beats per second and an amplitude of about five centimeters.

Sasha said, "Smooth lift-off." He'd been up twice before over the last six years.

Volodya grunted and reached out to tap one of his dials, which didn't seem to be working. Damn. The things were all cannibalized parts anyway, the result of long decades of strange economy measures. Even parts of the *semyorka,* indestructible pump components and the like, were salvaged after they came crashing down on the desert.

The sounds of the launch were dying down now, becoming a smooth, humming rumble. It was too bad they had to ride in these things. The shuttle had been ready for two years now, but no one had gone up in it. Too expensive, they said in Moskva. Volodya felt a faint, quickly suppressed twinkle of anger. Too expensive. Hmh. This *perestroika* was a wonderful thing, but it could easily kill the space program. The shuttle *was* too expensive, if you were talking about launching satellites like the idiot Americans.

But they hadn't built it to do the same things as before. . . . No, it was now time to do bigger things, better things. We have the means to get out to the planets now. It's time we went.

What a hideous thing it would be if we fucked up the same way as the Americans! What if we build the hardware, then toss it away? It was a fear shared by most of his colleagues. The old days of stable funding were gone: it was project-by-project now, just like in the benighted West.

A shame we have to ride in these things . . . but I'm glad I'm here. Gagarin felt what I'm feeling right now, on that bright spring morning thirty years ago.

Suddenly, the Canadian said, "I feel sick," in his pitiful Russian.

Volodya looked over and sighed. The man was staring at the plumb-bob, watching it go back and forth. Goof. We'll be lucky if he doesn't puke in his helmet. "Close your eyes, comrade. You're just getting carsick."

There was a sudden jolt and the plumb-bob bounced high, swinging about the roof of the cabin.

"What was that?" The Canadian's voice betrayed no small amount of fear.

Volodya marveled at it. They'd trained with him for months! Hadn't the man paid attention? "Staging," he said. "We're almost there."

And they were. In a minute the aeroshroud would break away and a darkening sky would peer through the porthole. Volodya turned to look, waiting, suddenly short of breath. I'm . . . here, he thought. At long last, I'm here. The wait, not so very long after all, seemed worthwhile.

There was no doubt about it. Washington was the worst of all places to have a capital. John Dalgleish sat back in the sumptuous cushions of the stretch limo and surveyed the passing scene through ice-rimed, foggy glass. The last time he'd been here the place had been a goddamn sauna, and now it was colder than hell and buried under two feet of aging snow. He watched the deserted vistas of massive stonework slip by, shaking his head forlornly. Ever since his quadruple bypass operation, it had taken huge bouts of California infrared to warm decrepit bones. He'd lost forty-seven pounds in the last three months, and his flesh seemed transparent to cold. Even the steady blast of hot air from the car's heating system didn't help. Damn it all. Why in the world couldn't they move the capital to San Diego like sensible people?

And of course National had lived up to its reputation as the worst-planned, least orderly airport in the world. The snow had fallen on Monday, and they still hadn't gotten all the runways open. Two hours of circling in the opaque whiteness had done nothing to improve his temperament. He looked at his watch. 10:22. They would wait for him, he supposed.

The limo slowed down and through the distant front window he could see a gate and security booth and a few bulkily dressed guards. The gate fell open and the limo moved forward, passing over an ample speed-bump that caused it to flex disconcertingly. A steep, meticulously plowed ramp led downward to a blank white wall, and, when they had passed muster with the guards there, the wall opened to reveal a dark, concrete garage. The White House, like 10 Downing St., was infinitely larger than it appeared from outside. The parking garage was just the uppermost floor of a huge warren of offices, meeting rooms, and bunkers, many of them built in the last five years. Dalgleish remembered his surprise during his first visit here in 1998, expecting to meet the president in the famous Oval Office, to find himself taking a ride on a secret subway to God knew where.

The door opened, and Dalgleish looked up to see a familiar face. Garth Haney, one of Fingol's men, was tall, swarthy, and impeccably attired in formal morning dress. He offered a hand, which Dalgleish waved off, and watched with what seemed like humor as the scientist managed to get out.

"Good morning, Mr. Dalgleish. Sorry about the snow."

Dalgleish grunted. "It wasn't your fault. I just wish I'd brought a heavier overcoat."

Haney motioned toward the concrete-framed elevator and started to walk. "Don't worry about it. We'll get you one."

The quick descent brought back the fear of sudden death that continued to haunt him. Any sudden change made him feel strange, and the lowered gravity made him feel like he was going to come open along the huge seam in his chest. Goddamn it, that *is* a stupid fear. Scar tissue is *much* stronger than plain old skin. I've got to get my mind back on business. I've got at least a few years left, and, in that time, I can make a *real* contribution. If only I can keep from coming apart mentally.

The two of them stood side by side in the little falling cubicle. Elevator etiquette was strange: just stand still, look straight ahead. Like you don't really exist while you're in transit. Waiting for your new incarnation.

The elevator came to a stop at what the digital display called LEVEL GREEN 5, and the doors parted to reveal an enormous, thickly carpeted room with a large oak table at its far end. Most of the chairs were already filled, but a few people were still chatting in front of another table covered with pots of coffee and an assortment of pastries. New Age muzak tinkled in the background.

"Here we are, Mr. Dalgleish. The President will be here in a few moments."

Dalgleish stepped out and heard the elevator close behind him. He went over to the buffet and looked over the assortment of tasty, but, for him, inedible items. They never did have anything dietary at functions like this and, in all probability, they never would. He found a tea bag and a pot of boiling water and made himself a cuppa. The others were looking at their watches and heading for their seats. Typical. The milk was in an immovable metal dispenser. He couldn't add milk to the tea until it finished steeping, and the milk was stuck here. Americans had never really figured out the mysteries of tea. Dalgleish quickly grabbed another cup, half filled it with milk, and went over to the table carrying a cup in each hand.

Brad Harveson, Dalgleish's boss, was sitting near the end. There was an empty seat beside Harveson with a sign that said JOHN R. DALGLEISH, INTERIM DIRECTOR, JET PROPULSION LABORATORY. That's me, he thought, carefully putting down his burden. Brad turned, an artificial smile almost hidden by the nervousness in the large eyes. "John. Good to see you." They shook hands and Dalgleish lowered himself into his chair. His gaze traveled around the table parabola. Bensonhurst. Nelson. Russell. Barnwell. Christ, even Vice President McDermott.

"So. The shit's finally hit the fan, which has scattered it in our direction. But why am I here?"

Harveson smiled again, this time with a little more

sincerity. "Wren wanted you, John. Personal request. I think he's getting tired of seeing the same old faces."

"Okay, so I presume that means he doesn't want to hear the same old bullshit. I'm prepared to give him my opinion of the Sinuhe thing, if he wants to hear it."

"Say anything you want. NASA has no official position, yet. Just remember, the big boys are all here. I have my opinions too, but I'm prepared to be ignored. Sinuhe is an ill wind . . ."

"Gentlemen. The President of the United States."

Wren came out of a secret door and sat in the overlarge chair at the table's head. He carefully pushed back a lock of lacquered orange hair and beamed at them. "Top of the morning to you all," he said. "As you know, I've called this meeting to discuss all the ramifications of the Russian asteroid thing. I've talked to a number of you individually, and, I have to admit, I'm genuinely at a loss about all this. All I hear is speculations, some of them pretty wild. I needn't repeat how important it is that we make the right decision here." He slouched forward and made a steeple with his hands. "The more I think about dropping the asteroid on, say, Fort Wayne, the less I get it. Even if they cause a tidal wave that wipes out the East Coast, it won't mean that we can't counterstrike. I mean, what's the point?"

A bizarre combination of emotions appeared on Secretary of Defense Bensonhurst's face. Just for a second, pique and sodden discomfort distorted the patrician countenance: caught red-handed. "There are several scenarios being worked out by the think-tank boys, and direct attack is only the simplest. It's the potential for destruction that I've been trying to drive home. I must remind you that as long as Sinuhe is in orbit, the USSR has the ability for mass destruction within our country, whether they choose to use it or not. It is an ability that a thousand *Eisenhowers* could not remove."

"But they know we'll hit them back, right?"

"A policy of Mutual Assured Destruction is no longer acceptable. We cannot go back to such folly."

"Yeah, sure. I think I understand you. But, damn it, Ben, it's all so hypothetical. Mr. Russell, why don't we have any hard poop about this?"

Russell twisted in his chair and smiled uncomfortably,

constipated visions dancing through his head. "Ah, Mr. President, yes, well . . . back in the summer of aught-one the Russians did some pretty effective housecleaning. They neutralized more than ninety percent of our electronics; we have nothing inside the Kremlin, these days, so we've had to rely almost exclusively on our agents. Unfortunately, they haven't come up with much."

"That's because your folks are only looking for proof of malevolence," said Secretary of State Barnwell. "You can't find something if it doesn't exist."

Russell was unfazed. "We have *clear* evidence that they've been conducting detailed simulations of high-speed impacts within their scientific community. In addition, *Cosmos 4931*, launched last August, was clearly designed as a test-platform for experiments similar to our Barney Rubble concept of the mid-nineties. Which means they could be planning to use the asteroid as a source for orbital debris . . ."

Wren held up a hand. "Now wait a minute, Jim. That's the first time you've mentioned anything about debris. I remember the Rubble thing. We dumped it because it was too destructive; you couldn't control well enough where the stuff went, and you couldn't stop it once it got started. Why would the Russians be interested in such a thing?"

"Besides," muttered Dalgleish, "it's a *metal* asteroid. . . ."

"What was that?" asked Wren.

Dalgleish avoided looking at Harveson's upset face. "If Sinuhe were that fractile, the steering charges would have demolished it."

Wren looked back at the CIA chief. "Jim?"

Russell shrugged. "I assume there's a middle ground here somewhere. An asteroid just, uh, *fractile* enough." He smiled thinly. "As to your original question, just why the Russians would be interested in the Rubble concept, I must defer to General Nelson in matters of orbital warfare. Perhaps he can answer your question."

Nelson nodded, running a finger around the lip of his coffee cup. "Up to now, Mr. President, I've concentrated on the danger of a ground impact, which would be bad enough. As you know, the nuclear arsenals of the two superpowers have been cut by more than half during the last fifteen years. Whole classes of weapons have been eliminated. The Russians have been harping about SDI since it was barely more than a concept, and it is clear that they feel the completion of *Eisenhower* will be a major destabilizing force. Once our ability to destroy ballistic missiles from space is complete, they will be all but defenseless. That is what we have been striving to achieve at the negotiation table, and, to an amazing extent, we have been successful. Within the department, we have come to regard Sinuhe as a bold plan to eliminate the potential of SDI once and for all."

"B-b-but," stammered Wren, "are you saying that we forced them into this position?"

"Not at all, Mr. President. We have merely acted in our own best interests. It's foolish to think that the Russians have not been doing the same. We just won, that's all. And now they are trying to change the rules of the game; cheating, if you will."

"Come, come," said Barnwell, who had, after all, started his career as a lawyer, "this is all circumstantial evidence, mere speculation."

"And it's silly, to boot!" Brad Harveson's voice was perfect for irreverent outbursts, and he used it to maximum effect. "The whole idea is nonsensical. You don't need a Sinuhe to kill *Eisenhower*. There's enough mass there to destroy every piece of hardware in orbit."

Romain Bensonhurst paused, let a second pass, then another. "Precisely. Mr. Harveson, you have put your finger on the *exact* problem. We feel that the Russians may be planning to use Sinuhe to render low Earth-orbit unusable. They can, and will, break the asteroid into hundreds of thousands of chaotically orbiting pieces of metal that will forever prevent us from erecting the space shield foreseen by Ronald Reagan."

"What are you saying?" asked Dalgleish. "That the Russians will forsake all future uses of space in order to keep us out too? That's *very* hard to believe. . . . Even if it *were* possible . . ."

Bensonhurst stared at him for a long moment. "Mr. Dalgleish, you can believe what you like. Most Americans, victims of the wishful thinking syndrome, have ceased to take the consequences of nuclear war seriously. I can assure you, however, that even now a nuclear war would inflict a hundred times more pain and suffering on the world than it has ever known before. The Russians know more about the destruction of war than we do here in America. No matter how friendly and appeasing they appear on the surface, they will never, *never* let us gain the upper hand that *Eisenhower* represents. We expected something of this kind, but nothing quite so . . . novel."

Wren now looked totally bewildered. "But . . . I thought that *Eisenhower* was supposed to insure *peace.*"

"And it is," answered Bensonhurst regally. "That is why we must do everything in our power to make certain that it is completed."

The President let his head fall into his hands, rubbing his eyes hard. "Jesus. I had such a good time at the last summit. I was beginning to think this problem would go away. But here it is again, difficult as ever. What are we going to do?"

"Nothing," Harveson snarled. "These old boys are tilting at windmills. The peril they speak of is imaginary."

John Dalgleish took a shallow breath and looked around. No one was buying it. Fear tickled at his heart. Damn it, he thought. For my imaginary posterity. "Mr. President," he said, "you are at a pivotal moment in history. There are many in this room who stand to gain by maintaining the status quo. You do not. You can, finally and forever, stop playing this stupid game with the Russians. They no longer want to conquer the world, if they ever did. They gave away Eastern Europe, Lithuania, the Kuriles. They have consistently cut their weaponry back further and deeper than we. It's time for us to trust them for once. Cut the hatred feedback. Let them . . . uh . . ." His heart was palpitating, an irregular beat. He sat down suddenly, vertigo welling up.

"Speeches," said Bensonhurst. "These words are not new. America has not gotten where it is through weakness. Only through strength have we brought the cowardly Communists low. His words echo Chamberlain, among others. We cannot afford the noble sentiments of the philosopher, we in the trenches . . ."

The President raised his hand, frowning. "All right, Ben, all right. You've made your point. Thank you for your opinion, Mr. Dalgleish. Are you okay?"

Sitting motionless seemed to have helped. Dalgleish nodded slowly.

"Very well then. I see we are no closer to a solution. Well, General Nelson, let's suppose your theories are right, for the time being. What can we do about it?"

Nelson smiled grimly. "The approach velocity of Sinuhe will be in excess of five miles per second, which requires a great deal of power to match. A *Saturn 5* would do the trick, if we still made them. With our present fleet, our options are limited. We have the capability to send two warhead-loaded OTV's on a high-speed flyby—"

"OTV—you mean the little tugs?" Wren, proud of his familiarity with the space program he'd long championed, was regaining some of his composure.

"Yes, sir. There are a full complement of OTV stages and guidance packages in orbit. We can get a pair of refurbished twenty-four-megaton warheads into an STS-B payload bay and assemble the whole shebang on orbit. We launch them past Sinuhe at high speed and detonate the warheads at closest approach. This offers the added advantage of surprise. The Russians won't challenge a *fait accompli*. . . ."

"But . . . won't they demand an explanation for the OTV launch itself?"

Nelson shrugged. "We can say that they're just there to monitor the Earth approach."

"Sounds good," said the President. "I'd like you to follow up on that. Do whatever you have to do to get that option ready, in case I choose it."

"Very good, sir."

"In the meantime, I don't like to do nothing. Mr. Harveson, tell me what you'd recommend to keep the Russians honest."

Harveson shrugged. "I—Well, we could *actually* use an OTV to monitor the Earth insertion. And if they aim it at New York . . ."

"Yes, what then?"

"Well, we kiss New York goodbye. It would be going too fast to intercept."

"I see. I don't like that idea much, Mr. Harveson."

"No. Well, there isn't—"

"Mr. Dalgleish. Give me a chance to be the nice guy you seem to think I am. Do you have a suggestion?"

Dalgleish sat forward and the room assumed an unnatural clarity. This was it. His big moment, part two. "Send an American astronaut aboard *Molotochek*?"

Wren looked surprised. "You know, I thought of that a while back. Turns out the life-support module for the ship won't support a fifth crew member. Sorry." He turned back to the others. "Okay, Jim, get on it. I won't let you all down."

Horror grabbed Dalgleish by the nape of the neck.

There. An equation that perfectly matched the cooling profile of the Sinuhe "pluton." A step closer to visualizing the large parent asteroid from which it had come. They were calling it "The Egyptian" now, this hot, two-hundred-kilometer asteroid that had been born early in the history of the solar system, when there were plenty of short-lived radioisotopes around to heat things up.

Anton's thoughts pushed back further to the supernova that had contributed its cataclysm-made new elements to the coalescing solar nebula. He wondered whether it was this great explosion that concentrated the tenuous galactic gas sufficiently to start the gravitational collapse, as some had speculated. He shook his head, feeling the *connectedness* of it all. Causes stretched back ten billion years; great cosmic events happening unawares and leading to the tiny consciousness-apprehended effects that people called "Life."

It was so easy to look at things in an unconnected, perspectiveless way, to forget even that there had been the day before and would be another day to come, much less all this. Too much perspective was just as bad, and human dignity shrank into meaninglessness measured against the Cosmic. He seemed to bounce back and forth, with no happy middle ground.

He turned back to the Mathcad equation software and stared at the integrations on the screen. His 80486-derived clone was barely sufficient for this kind of processing, and he longed for the DEU, which he'd had to turn back in. It was probably sitting on old Akhmatov's desk gathering dust.

If one assumed that The Egyptian started out as pure chondritic material, it was possible to deduce how much heat would be produced from this source, and if there was something left over . . . He bit his lower lip. One might, *might,* be able to understand whether this early protoplanet had been heated by the intense solar wind of 4.6

billion years ago. Lying just forty-seven kilometers under the surface, Sinuhe had spent more than a million years slowly cooling and differentiating into its present form. The Egyptian's surface temperature affected just how fast its internal heat was radiated off into space; and if this rate was slower than it should be, Anton might be able to shed a little light on the principal unknown still left in the study of meteorites and their genesis.

"Are you still at it?" Tiny Iskra Skryabina appeared in front of his desk, a disapproving look on her face. "Christ, Anton, you have to take a break once in a while. It's nearly six. Time to go home." She sat on a hard chair up against the wall and flipped back a loose wave of hair with a toss of her head.

Tonya took a moment to come back to himself and his drab office floating at the edge of the snowy Moskva night. The woman was wearing a coarse-knit lavender sweater maybe five sizes too big that came all the way down to her knees. "Oh, hi, Iskra. You know how it is—I might be on to something."

She looked serious. "Anton, you're my boss. I know I shouldn't say anything. But we've all noticed how . . . lost . . . you've been since you got back from the asteroid. You wander in at nine or ten, work until you're kicked out by the custodians, hardly have anything to do with the team you're supposed to be leading."

Serebryakov smiled and tried to rub the tension out of his eyes and forehead. "I appreciate the concern. It's true that I haven't adapted well to being back. But I'm all right, I—"

"Why don't you come home with me tonight. No . . . I don't mean anything like that. I'll heat up some of my mother's cabbage rolls and we can watch TV. You know, just for a change of pace. If you like, we could talk, comrade to comrade."

It was the best offer he'd had . . . and he wondered if maybe he should take it. But Iskra was a proper little Communist, always "Mikhail Sergeevich this" and "Mikhail Sergeevich that," which tended to grate. Still . . .

"No, I don't think so. Thanks just the same. I want to polish this math a bit more, then I've got some administrative tasks to finish."

The woman stood, pulled down the sweater fastidiously,

and started gathering up trash around the printer. "All right, Anton Antonovich, if that's the way you want it." She collated the thick sheaf of bad printer runs into a neat pile and dumped it into the wastebin with a thump. "I guess I'll see you in the morning." She turned and disappeared through the dark doorway.

So, here he was, again. He rotated his chair and propped his feet up on the radiator, watching the large, streaming flakes that filled the world outside the window. It was kind of touching that Skryabina had shown some concern. She was a strange bird.

The humming computer fan covered any noise; made it seem even quieter than it really was; and the quiet magnified the grandeur of the snowfall. Anton remembered staring up into the huge snow nimbus of a streetlight, sled in hand, watching the silent downpour for what seemed like an hour. How old had he been then, nine, ten? Somehow the world had been so personal and intimate, like a show put on for his own amusement.

It wasn't that way now. The responsibilities of conducting an "adult" life burdened and mystified him. Even now, a month and a half after coming back from Sinuhe, his bags hadn't been unpacked and the dust was still thick on the surfaces he didn't use regularly. Damn it all. He had tried to restart his life, but it was increasingly clear that he didn't really have one. Only Sinuhe, a poor substitute indeed. What did the religious types say? Something like "what profit a man who gains a whole world, if he loses his soul in the process." For such a tiny world, he had lost, what? The habits that had kept him going, at least. It was too bad that the Orthodox beliefs were such a crock of shit. . . .

He'd never gone back to Darya's. He felt hurt and, stupidly, angry at her. He wondered what she must think, if she thought about him at all.

Tonya turned to the computer, tapped a key to bring back the blanked screen, and began to reimmerse. An image of himself flying beside the Grand Groove came into his head. He would be going back. . . .

Volodya and Shutka sat together on the upper platform of the VIP grandstand near Energiya Launch Complex No. 2. This widely spaced group of six pads, built in the late nineties, lay about twenty kilometers to the northwest of the three pads at Complex No. 1. Three of the pads, having seen launches earlier in the week, were blackened, crawling with refurbishment teams. *Buran,* bolted to its launch vehicle, cradled atop its horizontal rail transporter, lay in its hangar, waiting its turn.

Tanker No. 4 sat on its pad, wreathed in vapor clouds, counting down. The white rocket glittered in the bright winter sun, bulbous, bracketed by four dark strap-on boosters. The tanker stage itself was something new, these four launches its first four flights. Like previous cargo stages, it was a black mass, derivative of an early testbed model of the shuttle hull. Previous versions had been disposable. Now, in a bid for further economy, the hulls were equipped with a coating of a charrable Lucite-derivative, and the ships had stubby wings. Theoretically, with a scraping and respraying, they could be flown again.

The theory almost held up. Numbers one and three sat at the end of the shuttle recovery runway, banged up from a high-speed landing but more or less intact. Number two, of course, was a splattered mess in the desert about fifty kilometers to the west of Leninsk.

On the pad, the vapor cloud began to dissipate. Valves were closing and the countdown was finishing up. Shutka, aware of these things though she usually didn't come to launches, gripped his arm. Volodya looked down at her for a moment, at her worried frown. She seemed more nervous about this series of launches than he could fathom. More than sixty Energiyas had gone aloft over the past fifteen years, forty of them in the past five, since the inception of the manned lunar project's flight phase. This was just one more. He turned his attention back to the pad.

This was the most hectic flight rate Baikonur Cosmodrome had ever seen. The standard, for more than a generation, had been two launches a week, and Energiya launches, whether manned or not, had never exceeded one a month. That might be the source of her worry, but probably not. I'll be aloft again in two days, the length of time it takes to put a shuttle on the pad. That's cause enough.

The count reached zero. It was the familiar sequence: first the sustainer core engines lit, orange-white, then transparent, now the sixteen kerosene-fuel strap-on engines, red and smoky, then brilliant yellow-white. The ship squatted on the pad for a little while before teetering slowly into the sky, clearing the tower after an eternity. Strangely, it seemed even longer to him as a ground observer than it did when he rode the monster's back himself. The sound stuttered into their ears at last, twenty long seconds after ignition. By then the rocket was well on its way.

Volodya let his head tip back, following the vehicle's trajectory, feeling Shutka's hand grow ever tighter on his wrist. It went through its long vertical ascent, then . . . His eyes squinted at the bright sky. That's . . . odd. The roll program went through its appointed arc, then continued for another fifty degrees. The ship began to tip imperceptibly into the northwest. Volodya felt his heart start to trip-hammer in his chest. God. There's nobody aboard. It's just a hundred tons of hydrogen and liquid oxygen. . . .

A flower bloomed against the pale-blue sky, first clear white, then tinged around its base by smears of reddish-orange and black. The day brightened for a moment and he felt Shutka twitch at his side. As the cloud billowed out from its source, growing tendrils, the roaring sound of the rocket engines went on and on, for almost a minute. . . .

It came as a thump against their chests, louder than the engines, or anything else they'd ever heard from a distance. Volodya, dazed, found himself thinking, It's not as loud as some rock groups I've heard . . . on the other hand, you practically have your head in the speakers at a concert. . . .

He put an arm around Shutka and watched the debris begin to spread. Mostly they were arcing up toward the north, toward the area west of the railhead, but the rocket's ground track had been slow, most of the velocity still vectored upward. The smoke trails of the various fragments were spreading in all directions.

Shutka stared upward, silently, watching the cloud grow until it towered over them like a thunderhead. "Volodya?" Some of the trails seemed to be pointing right at them. "Is it going to fall on us?"

He shook his head slowly. "I don't think so. . . ." Out on the desert, kilometers away, the first piece whanged down in a puff of smoke. "We'd better go inside." Below them, people were already vacating the grandstand. At the foot of the stairs a soldier he didn't know was gesticulating, calling his name.

When they were inside one of the refreshment trailers, he could see other people's eyes in unusual profusion. They're all looking at me, wondering how I feel. It's too late to turn back. Sinuhe is coming. In forty-eight hours, I'll be part of the first crew to ride a post-explosion Energiya. Good. I won't have three years and more to worry about being blown to bits.

"Volodya?" It was Shutka, still clinging to him, still shaking faintly. "What happened?"

Good question . . . "An accident. Just an accident. The crews have been so hurried lately. . . ." He stared down at her pudgy face, creased with astonished fright. "There's no stopping now. Ever since *Soyuz 1* . . . We have accidents. We just call them accidents and try to do better. We just keep on track. . . ." It was the party line and, for once, he was glad of it.

There was a loud clang as something bounced off the trailer's roof.

Night had come almost immediately. For Tonya, still on Moskva time, the luminous, silvery Las Vegas twilight seemed to be especially appropriate for the odd, lover/stranger relationship between himself and the American meteorologist. From the balcony of her room, the thousands of artificial lights came on to push back the alien darkness of the desert. Four margaritas. His letters, composed with care, had shown him to be intelligent, witty, and passionate. What in the world would happen now that they were together? A song from a Cream record, "Sitting on Top of the World," was occupying that part of his mind normally in control.

*Asteroids 1993,* sponsored by the University of Arizona, had provided the perfect means to bring them together. Their joint paper, entitled "Remnant Momentum in the Asteroids and Its Implications for the Solar Nebula," was mainly Carla's work, and he was not really certain if he agreed with its conclusions, though the arcane mathematics seemed to bear them out. Well, it didn't matter; at conferences like this fully a third of the papers were not taken seriously and most were never heard from again. His own theory about the genesis of VN 141 had disappeared without a ripple.

As far as Carla was concerned, he would just have to try

and relax and let it all happen. He could see the laser-printed "I love you too, Tony, and I have decided that we were destined to meet and fall in love" in his head. Odd sentiments for a scientist; but then again she specialized in stochasm, the study of probabilities within a distribution curve. Perhaps it was a scientific insight. He smiled. Under the veneer of anxious anticipation, he was happy, as far as he could tell. It would go well.

And if he married Carla and settled in Hawaii? She had already said that she found him acceptable. But what a change that would be; to be a Russian émigré in Honolulu —no, the idea was *too* bizarre. And yet, many claimed that Hawaii was the best place to live in the world. On the island of Hawaii there were excellent observatories, and the lava fields were considered the best available analog to basaltic eruptions on the moon and planets. Well, he was getting ahead of himself.

He turned back into the hard, beige room. She had changed greatly in a year and a half. The glasses were gone, and her hair was long and straight, as was the current fashion in America, caught behind rather large ears and streaming in a shiny, cohesive black stream. Still, she was beautiful in that American hybrid way, small, thin nose, high cheekbones, strange, sexy mouth. There was no trace of ambivalence in her. How had she become a scientist?

He came into the room and collapsed on the bed, kicking off his shoes, savoring the pleasurable feelings that made everything seem so clear. "Vell," he said, slurring a little, unable to keep the Russian phonemes out of his English, "so are you ready?"

She sat back, suddenly serious. "Tony," she said, and the word sounded ominous. "Tony, I've got something to tell you. I guess I should have said something earlier, but, but, well, I didn't. It's about us."

He sat up, aghast. This was the type of preface that never boded well. "What do you mean?" he said, quietly.

"The letters got out of hand. I said some things . . . Well, there were things in those letters that were premature. Tonya, I can't commit myself to someone I know so little. It was easy to pretend, it *is* easy. But I think we've got to stop and ask ourselves, how could this really work?"

"How?" he echoed.

"Tony, I met someone a few weeks ago. A student of

mine, I'm afraid. We, well, we have something, something more than letters between us. Not that I don't like you, or even love you a little. But I have to tell you, after the conference, that's it between us. Maybe I should have waited until the conference was over, but I want us to be truthful with one another."

The room was swaying. A little part of his mind was burning like a blowtorch. *So all of it was in vain. So I have deluded myself like a foolish child. Of course she couldn't love me.* He staggered toward her, and the alcoholic effect was gone, replaced by a fiery light. His eyes burned as well, and tears started down his cheeks.

She got up, and he could see fear in her eyes. There was a quiet pause, almost calm, before he raised his hand and hit her across the face. She turned away and fell back into the chair, slumping down onto the floor. Immediately he was repentant, aghast, wondering how he could have done such a thing. The scene that had preceded the blow was already a phantasm, unreal. He dropped to his knees and placed a hand against the warm brow, brushing back strands of darkness. Her eyes were closed, but there was a fluttering behind them, as in REM sleep.

Then, the eyes opened. Withering hatred. She pushed him away firmly, stood, brushed down her skirt, and walked quickly from the room. She didn't bother to close the door.

Secretary of State Romain Bensonhurst and Air Force General Daniel J. Nelson, Chairman of the Joint Chiefs of Staff, sat together in a small room, buried beneath the Ronald Reagan Executive Office Building, waiting for President Wren.

"So what do you think, Benny? Can we sell it or not?"

Bensonhurst shrugged, slouching in his chair. "Don't know . . ." *Ugh.* He pushed his upper plate back into place with his tongue. *Have to get the damned things readjusted one of these days.* "I thought we had it sold last time, but I can't say what the odds really are. We've been doing a lot of talking, but . . ."

Nelson's gaunt face creased with mild irritation. "Getting cold feet, Benny?"

"Fuck." The false teeth came loose again at the uvular stop and he pushed it back again. *Hell. Implants, that's the* ticket. Stop being such a chickenshit. You're getting old. Surgery's coming whether you like it or not. Tooth implants are nothing. . . . "You know what we're risking, Dan. Even if they *drop* it on Kansas . . ."

"Son of a bitch. Even if they *don't* drop it on Kansas, we can't let them get away with something like this. You want another Cuba, this time in orbit?"

Bensonhurst eyed the man, wondering how much of his own propaganda he believed. "Well, no."

"Then we *have* to stop them!"

"Look, what's the *real* situation?"

It was Nelson's turn to shrug. "This morning's radar plot indicates closest approach at about eighty thousand miles."

"So if they do nothing and we do nothing, Sinuhe will never be seen again. . . ."

"Right. Don't be such an asshole. They're fueling up their ship now, ready for departure next week. You think they fired two billion rubles into orbit, *excluding* a major launch accident, just to throw us a curve ball? Dipshit. They're *going* to do it!"

Bensonhurst laid a careful cap on a simmering brew of anger that threatened to boil over. "We're talking about nuclear confrontation here, Dan."

"Fuck. If we stand by and let this happen, we're talking about a world run by the goddamned USSR! We're talking about the end of our history as a great nation!"

It made him feel uneasy, all right. They already have a leg up on us. One more push and they'll ram it home. . . . "Sure. I just don't want it to be the end of everything else as well. . . ."

The door popped open and President Wren walked in, alone. His contact lenses, they could see, were out, his eyes a pale, washed-out blue, bloodshot, tired looking. He ambled over and sat down in the room's third easy chair. "Evening, Ben. General Nelson."

The officer, suddenly on his feet, saluted briskly. "Mr. President."

Bensonhurst watched them with wry amusement. A military man respects his superior officer. "Good evening, Al." Rub it in. You have to salute him; I'm his old buddy from way back when.

Wren sat erect in his chair, hands on knees. "So, what's on tonight's agenda?"

Sitting back, folding his arms across his chest, Bensonhurst said, "Al, it's time for us to decide on the OTV thing."

"OTV thing . . . Oh, uh . . . Sinuhe, right?" He seemed pleased to be able to pluck the name from memory. "I thought we'd already decided what to do."

"We did. This is go/no-go time. The asteroid's on its way in."

Wren nodded slowly. "When is it expected to arrive?"

"Dan?"

Nelson glanced through the papers in his clipboard. "On or about May eighth of this year, at four-seventeen P.M. Eastern time. That's plus or minus twelve hours, right now, but we have high confidence in the time and date."

Wren seemed baffled for a moment. "Ten weeks? Closer than I expected . . ."

"That's it. If we're going to do the OTV mission, put a kink in their plans, we have to start the ball rolling tomorrow. We can schedule an extra shuttle launch, but *only* one. . . ." said Bensonhurst.

"I thought the 'Orient Express' was more flexible than that."

Nelson shifted in his seat and smiled. "The cargo is too heavy for a transatmospheric vehicle, Mr. President. However, we do have an STS-B stack ready for padding at Vandenberg. And the OTVs are already in orbit, waiting to be fueled up from the *Eisenhower*'s main tanks."

He nodded slowly, seeming to draw into himself, almost disappearing. "So everything is ready. . . ."

Nelson's smile broadened. "That it is, Mr. President. We've refurbished two old twenty-four-megaton gravity bombs, loaded them with fresh radioactive—"

"I don't know. I *just* don't know . . ."

O-*ho*! thought Bensonhurst.

Nelson, looking alarmed. "But I thought we'd *agreed,* Mr. President!"

That brought a look of wan agony. "But . . . a nuclear *weapon* . . . What do I *tell* people?"

Bensonhurst reached into his coat pocket and brought out a tiny PROM-pack. "Al, what I've got here is the rough draft of a speech that might take care of that. If you'd care to look it over . . ."

Not too late. Anton threw open the car door and got out in front of Darya's apartment building. A train was passing beyond the ice-rimed trees at the end of the parking lot, throwing out a loud roar and clatter, somewhat muted by the frigid, dense air. He shut the car and locked it. Fortunately, Russia had changed and it was no longer necessary to remove the wiper blades for short periods.

He stood for a second in the cold air, feeling it penetrate his coat. Yes, he was scared, and his mind automatically tried to keep him calm, generating spurious thoughts. With a Doppler diminuendo, the last of the cars disappeared behind the building and the sound trailed off into city-normal.

In the warmth of the building, he stopped again, peering up the long flight of steps. What was he doing? Fifteen hours before he had to leave for Baikonur, and he was wildly rushing to see a woman, a whore, to do what? He had called and, when she had said she was free, said something crazy like, "I've got a surprise for you." It was obviously the explosion of the Energiya tanker which had set him off. His own death could come just as suddenly, and for just the same reasons. He started up the steps, methodically, rhythmically.

She invited him in and they kissed, passionately. Her hair, still that awful shade of henna red, was short and curly, widening her face to the point of unattractiveness. "It's so good to see you, Tonya," she said. "I'm really sorry about what happened when you came before; but it was—"

"That's all right," he said, stepping over to the glass door to the balcony, which was frosted in a bizarre, scalloped pattern. "I understand that you have other things to do beside entertaining me."

"Well, I expected you to come back, Tonya. It's been almost four months."

He turned, smiling uncomfortably. "Well, here I am."

"You didn't die."

"No. But the mission is only half over. Day after tomorrow, I go back into space; back to the asteroid. You may have heard something about the explosion—"

"About the Energiya? Yes."

"It could happen again."

"So? You're a scientist, Serebryusha. You understand what probability means."

He nodded. "Yes. Darya, I came here to . . . to ask you something."

She watched him closely, but said nothing.

"I am a hero now, of sorts. My salary is quite good. Enough to buy you the things that you seem to need. You can quit your 'entertaining'; go back to being a full-time writer."

She smiled. "That's sweet, Tonya, but—"

"No. Hear me out. I am not trying to buy you or anything like that. You can do what you want. I won't try to interfere, if I do come back this time. I am proposing that we, just, well, live together. Share our lives, a little bit. I have found that I can't do it alone."

"Well," she said. "You *have* surprised me. I don't know what to say. Sit down. I have to take this in."

They sat, in stiff little chairs across an oriental rug from one another. Tonya let his head fall down into his hands, then, thinking better of it, made himself sit erect. An urge to add more reasons welled up in him. "I know that this is an impossible thing, Daryusha. Throw me out. I am just panicking. I'm weak. When I came here before, I was at the end of my tether, alone and lonely, with no one to trust. I was—"

"You know, Tonya, if you'd just called first it would have been a simple matter to arrange—"

"All right, I understand. Forget about it. From the moment I first saw you in the Bear and Honey a part of me has been . . . *with* you. But I can understand it if you—"

"Wait a minute. Things aren't so cut and dried. I am not necessarily what you think I am. Tonya, your idea appeals to me. But I have to be clear about this: you are a famous cosmonaut, with all the potential pluses and minuses that entails." She paused for a time, staring into the translucent glass/ice. Anton, amazed that he had gotten even this far, sat still, afraid to disturb what appeared to be a promising direction in her thoughts. "If the truth be known, I *am* dreadfully tired of this life. And I'm getting old; I'm thirty-two, Tonya, not the best age. I can see where it's heading; and it isn't a pleasant thought."

"I wish I knew more about you."

She smiled suddenly. "Let me tell you then: I was nineteen, fresh out of school, when I first screwed someone for money. An editor of a *samizdat* magazine called *Ruskii Idiom.* I had brought him a collection of my school poems, and he laid me on his couch. After the orphan house, I was smart enough to know better; but everything seemed so reasonable. . . . He slipped me thirty rubles and published 'Flint.' And if it hadn't been for that I wouldn't have been discovered by *Ogonyok* four months later. Since *perestroika,* it's not so easy to make a living from art. But editors are so understanding. I have been treated with respect by most of them; the money has almost been an afterthought."

Tonya, perspiring heavily at the armpits, pulled off his coat. "Yeah, I always imagined that there was more going on between us than just money. I don't know, you always seemed to go out of your way to make me feel better. And your prices were low. . . ."

She laughed, a throaty chuckle, her head thrown back a little. "I never did make a whole lot. Just enough to supplement my writing earnings. Enough to have my own apartment, my own Moskvich. Well, it's stupid to reflect on the past while the future beckons. Sure, Tonyusha, I'll be your wife if you'll have me."

Anton, nearly doing a double take, got out of the chair and took a step toward her. "That's *fantastic.* I never would have . . . Well, what do we do? I don't have much time. The Marriage Palace?"

"It's on Griboyedova, right? Sure. I should put on a dress."

Gorbachev sat grimly before his men in a little chamber deep within the Kremlin. "Well," he said, and looked at each of them in turn. There was a little smile on his lips as he thought, They'll squirm now. They were all high in the hierarchy under Brezhnev, remembered what it was like. Are they wondering if their heads will roll? Fortunately for them, the old days were out of reach. The CPSU's power did not extend to massive purges of the bureaucracy, not even the military bureaucracy. For that, a consensus was needed.

In a way it was funny to watch them. General Ponomarev sat still, glowering. You could see his anger, close enough to the surface that you didn't need a Gypsy mind reader to tell what was going on underneath. Miserable Glavkosmos bastards, you could see him thinking. Always fucking things up. Never should have let them have authority. Punishment. Punishment! Gorbachev folded his arms, wondering how close to reality his imaginings might be. Punishment! Hah.

The space twins, Dunaev and Galeev, kept looking at each other. Decades of running Glavkosmos had taken away much of the former's famous gruffness. Gorbachev's smile twisted slightly, remembering Sagdeev's denunciations. "An odious person." You had to wonder. It had been mostly over the *zek* issue, but . . . hell. Maybe old Kosmic Roald just thought the man bathed insufficiently. Galeev, now . . . He was Sagdeev's handpicked successor, with his own accumulated string of impressive failures. If I could I'd fire them all. No. No, I wouldn't. I'm used to looking at these men. I'd like to see them gathered around my deathbed. He pushed the thought away uneasily.

Chief Designer Yuri Semyonov, a stiff, gray presence, folded his arms across his chest and pushed his feet out until they rested heel-down on the carpet. He cleared his throat and looked Gorbachev in the eye, a flat and level stare. Gorbachev stared back, thinking, This one always knew what he was doing. "Comrade Semyonov. A suggestion?"

"More than that, Mikhail Sergeevich." Aha! Friendly but formal. "This accident was brought on by the fact that this project has exceeded the capacity of our Energiya launch-rate capability. Nothing more, nothing less. That, in turn, was brought on by the fact that we do not have a proper orbital fuel dump. Its construction was scheduled for the eighteen-month period preceding the first Mars launch, nearly a decade down the road."

"So. You think this was an ill-conceived venture, after all?"

Semyonov shrugged. "No, Mikhail Sergeevich. As you know, I was opposed at first, but no longer. This has been . . . an excellent idea." He paused. "Though I could wish we were better prepared to deal with . . . contingencies."

"Ah."

"In any case," interjected Dunaev, "we have to press on. Sinuhe . . ."

"The asteroid is coming, whether we meet it or not," said Galeev.

"There *is* that."

Yuri Semyonov swept his level gaze over the other men in the room. "I think we all understand that we could not turn back now, even if we wanted to. The *kosmicheskii korabl* is on the pad. The launch crews are on edge because of the explosion. They'll be careful enough. In any case, the quality control procedures are much tighter for manned launches—"

"Why is that, Comrade Chief Designer of Spaceships?"

Semyonov caught the dangerous glitter in Gorbachev's eye, took a breath, decided to ignore it. This man, after all, had been the original architect of change. "Because quality control costs money . . . Comrade General Secretary of the CPSU."

"As much as an entire Energiya launch cycle?"

"Not quite."

"Perhaps, then, when this is all over, we shall have to reassess this policy."

"In any case," interrupted Galeev, hoping to end this unpleasant exchange, "we have a meeting with the flight crews for *Molotochek* out at Starry Town in just over two hours. We'd better get going."

"I'm curious," said Gorbachev. "Which shuttle is on the pad?"

"Uh. *Buran,* Mikhail Sergeevich." Friendly again.

"Hmm. *Buran.* The oldest one, isn't it?"

"Yes, Mikhail Sergeevich. It came out of the heavy machine factory in Tuchino fifteen years ago."

Manarov sat with his back to the wall in the meeting room, legs braced so the front end of his folding metal chair came off the floor. To his left sat Sirje Saarmula, newly appointed commander of *Molotochek,* to his right good old Sasha Krimnev, senior cosmonaut pilot attached to the lunar program, now appointed commander, in place of an ailing Popovich, of the backup crew that would take out *Serpachek* and rescue them if things somehow went . . . awry.

In the context of . . . things as they were, it was an unhappy thought. Things could go very badly awry at this stage of the mission. Am I afraid I'll be blown to bits again?

Damned right. The explosion cloud of the destroyed Energiya towered in his memory. *This mission begins to seem like an act of extreme temerity. What could we have been thinking? Easy enough. Since giving up the Stalinist doctrine of military adventurism, since casting aside the burden of political dependencies, we've achieved a great deal. This didn't seem out of reach. . . .* He shrugged and let his chair legs clunk on the carpet. *Too late now. And the high and mighty were gathered before them.*

Dunaev was standing at the front of the room, motioning for silence. "Men. This is our final briefing session. Tomorrow afternoon the *Molotochek* crew will be aboard *Buran,* climbing toward orbit. Departure for Sinuhe is scheduled for five days hence, on the morning of 24 February. Refueling operations for *Serpachek* will commence on 15 March, at a . . . somewhat more leisurely pace." He leaned his buttocks against the desk behind him. "I won't try to fool you. We almost lost it on the tanker. We can't afford any more mistakes."

*We couldn't afford the first two,* thought Volodya. *Slava dead was one thing. A man turned out to be easily and cheaply replaceable. But an Energiya launch cycle was a costly thing.* They'd had to push the *Molotochek* departure back by a full forty-eight hours to get another tanker on the pad and into orbit. . . . *Well, it would be interesting to see the on-orbit refueling operation from close up.*

"As you know, we've made a slight change in our operational plan. As scheduled, *Molotochek* will proceed to Sinuhe on an ellipse outside Earth's orbit, making rendezvous with the asteroid after a seventy-five day flight, when it is some two hundred and forty hours from Earth encounter." Dunaev smiled. "We still haven't been able to explain that one to the news media. It may be hopeless. In any case, on 1 May, *Serpachek* will be placed in an elliptical high Earth-orbit, targeted for a close lunar encounter on 9 May, just after the Sinuhe-Earth rendezvous period. If something has gone badly wrong and *Molotochek* is proceeding out of cislunar space, *Serpachek* will make a gravity boost maneuver and attempt to catch up with the damaged ship. Should that be successful, both ships will proceed around the sun, the crews returning to Earth aboard the rescue vessel in approximately one year. . . ."

*That assumes a lot.* Volodya crossed his legs, staring at

nothing. It assumes that what went wrong didn't kill us, of course, a fine hope. It also assumes that the problem lies in *Molotochek*'s propulsion module, that life support is intact. A reasonable assumption. And if not? There was an American short story I read once, long ago, called, what? Ah, yes: "The Cold Equations." He shivered. I can hardly wait.

In the background, Dunaev was saying, ". . . in a way, this is our great experiment. The Sinuhe mission has tested our hardware, stressed it to limits for which it was never really designed. When the mission is over, succeed or fail, we will proceed with new plans. If we succeed, Sinuhe will be the Kosmograd base we've longed to build. And we're going to Mars on schedule, as soon as the lunar base is complete. Beyond that . . . Comrade Semyonov has shown me plans for an uprated vehicle which can operate throughout the inner solar system. Glavkosmos is drawing up plans for a base in the Main Belt asteroids, perhaps on Vesta. The limits of what we can do, with the technology we can foresee, can actually build, are quite remote. . . ."

Volodya had seen the plan for a nuclear-powered inner-system ship. It would work, though it wasn't all that could be desired. Where am I going? Mars? Yes. Vesta? Perhaps. Where do I want to go? Saturn? Too far. I shall have to be content.

I have, he thought, fallen into my dream.


Moe Schlossberg stared emotionlessly at Lyle Marlowe. Might as well get this over with. It was hard to understand where his enthusiasm was going to these days. Somehow, over the past year, things had seemed to grow . . . tasteless. I overeat because I always overate. I go to work because that's what I do with my days.

Marlowe's bland face jerked up from the script outline he was perusing with an odd look. "What?"

Oops. What is it kids say? The first sign of insanity is hair on your palms; and the second sign is looking for it? That's me. Goofy all over. "Nothing. The script, Lyle. Tell me what you think." If, that is, you *do* in fact think. . . .

Marlowe looked down at the outline again and sighed, slowly shaking his head. "I just don't know." He looked up at his boss, writing a sort of weak earnestness over his features. "Look, I know this is a complex and difficult subject, but *surely* it can be made more digestible than *this.* Maybe using the staff science writers was a bad idea. There must be *someone* around here who can make this stuff understandable to the man in the street."

Schlossberg smiled. That's why I'm asking *you,* shit-for-brains. "All right. Given that a straightforward treatment of the Russians' Sinuhe project is out of the question, what sort of presentation can we make that *will* make sense? By eliminating the technical end of things, we eliminate practically everything but pictures of rockets taking off. Interviews with scientists have turned out to be hopeless . . . not to mention those idiotic Soviet 'spokespersons.' " That brought a momentary bizarre image to mind, some kind of a human mandala.

"Well . . ." Marlowe stared at the outline again, as if he could force an idea out of the slick paper by main telekinetic force. "I don't know if you'll go for this, but . . . sensationalism."

Great. Sensationalism. "What do you mean, Lyle? This whole thing is nothing if not sensational. The problem is it's also incomprehensible."

"Right. Look, the average dork in the street is only interested in how events affect his life and immediate surroundings. You know, the fire down the street is more important than wars and terrorism and that crap. He wants to know how it'll affect his job, or maybe whether it'll keep his wife from putting out after the eleven o'clock news is over."

Schlossberg rested his forearms on his gut. "So?"

"So even if this thing works and the Russians get rich off it, the effects are too nebulous and too far down the road to matter. Since we won the Cold War, the international situation has turned too complex, too subtle. And too spread out. People are tuning us out, Moe. You know it as well as I do. If it weren't for the spread of *potential* holocausts, they'd switch right to *M\*A\*S\*H* reruns after the local news. *Potential.* That's all we have left. And we damn well have to make the best of it."

"Well, that's nice. Interesting even. What's the point?"

"What if it *fails,* Moe? The Russians don't just go broke, you know."

"Sure. Two failure modes. Most likely the asteroid goes sailing off and the Russians have wasted six billion dollars. Worst case scenario, the bastard plunks down in Kansas and Oz goes to Barsoom." I must be getting stupid in my old age. Shit. Old age sets in hard when you're young. "Okay. The military has been pushing that one, and we've been getting good mileage out of it. The script you're holding focuses on that issue, pretty much."

"Right. And it has too much technical material, too many interviews with dopey fat guys in lab coats. And it's too *early.*"

"What do you want to do then?"

"Two specials, covering the end of the world."

Fuck. "What if it's *not* the end of the world?"

*"Potential,* Moe. That's the key. Listen, we do two shows. A two-hour special the day before the encounter, 'THE END OF THE WORLD?' " He threw his arms wide, illustrating a yard-long fish, "Three-D titles, everything the graphics department can throw at them. Let's *show* them the worst-case scenario as if it were really happening!"

And fuck again. Schlossberg sat back in his chair with satisfaction spreading through him like warmth in the wintertime. *I knew* there was a reason to talk to this guy. "Hmm. Maybe a little extreme, but I see your point. What about the second show?"

"Cover the real thing live. Space hookups, feeds from all the big cities. We can rent a half-dozen supersonic jets and get under the projected ground track; station crews here and there. If it *does* plunk down in Kansas, or Iraq or something, we can be *there!*"

"And what if it *is* the end of the world?"

"So what? You can't *plan* for it. Not really. We have to assume there'll still be ratings on the day after."

Moe Schlossberg stared at Lyle Marlowe, feeling the interest stir through all of his components. This is bullshit, but it's *good* bullshit. Hell. Where is Orson Welles when we need him? Of course. Dead. Like all good fat men.

"Okay," he said. "Let's do it."

*Buran,* Blizzard, the oldest of the Russian shuttles, hung upright from the enormous Energiya sustainer core like a giant woodpecker on a small tree. First launched in 1988, it was fourteen years old, though little more than the airframe itself remained from the craft that had woozily performed an automatic reentry and landing. Even so, the shuttle *looked* old, tired and charred from its thirteen fiery descents.

Anton stepped carefully from the gantry elevator onto the cleated rubber floor of the girdered service arm, thirty-five meters above the pad. He stopped, took a deep inhalation of the frozen steppe air. At minus-fifteen degrees C, it burned dry in his nostrils, smelling of acrid kerosene. A necessary trip to the bathroom had delayed him, and the eight others who would ride *Buran* up were already aboard. An engineer named Zorin, responsible for final closeout of the gantry, suddenly appeared beside him.

"The rocket will not fail again," he said.

Serebryakov turned to him and smiled. "That's not what I was thinking."

Zorin smiled back, sympathetically. "It's natural to feel some fear. Even now, it is not a simple undertaking. And after the tanker . . ."

Anton started again toward *Buran*'s entry hatch. If this man was trying to clear him from the gantry, he was succeeding. In truth he wasn't thinking about the danger. The half-day honeymoon, spent in the newly renovated Hotel Rossiya, had turned out to be a revelation for him. From a slow beginning of stammering confessions they had built to a flow of heart-wrenching truthfulness, traded equally. They had talked of their childhoods, before they had made the decisions that formed their present courses, and found much in common. The sham that was poetess/whore and cosmonaut/planetologist had fallen away, and that small room overlooking the Kremlin and the river became the entirety of the world. She had shown an enormous amount of empathy and patience, helping him to stay erect long enough to get inside, and, with slow, gentle thrustings, he had managed to consummate the marriage to both of their satisfactions. When dawn light filtered in through the lattice curtains, he had awakened and they had done it again, this time without problem. At Domodedovo Airport they had said goodbye in a civilized, polite way, kissing only briefly. And now the whole thing seemed like a strange, delirious dream.

He was met at the hatch by another engineer, who led him into the shuttle middeck space. *Buran* and *Ptichka,* slightly smaller than the later ships, had little enough room for the additional technical crew that helped strap him in. Chishak, laughing nervously, asked, "All set?"

He shrugged, stepping gingerly across the "wall" to his seat. When he had been strapped in, back down, feet up, the engineers left, closing and pressurizing the hatch. There would still be more than an hour to launch, and the others were chatting about current soccer results, leaving Chishak and him out. It didn't matter. There would be enough time for interminable conversations in the months ahead. He began to think about the honeymoon again, and drifted into a hazy kind of almost-sleep.

Suddenly there was a sharp crack outside the hull, and Serebryakov popped awake, suddenly alert. All right, he thought. "Here we go." The ship swayed slightly as the escape platform pulled back.

All the familiar feelings came back. The fear, the apprehension. A little exhilaration muted by nausea. The crackleroar started suddenly, modulated and complex. Not being able to see was the worst part. Vibrations shook the craft and his bones resonated with the deep, serrated rumble. He looked up, over the heads of the others, at the middeck ceiling, at the closed hatchway where the pilots were in control, along with Manarov and Saarmula, real cosmonauts, allowed to sit by the flight deck windows. Chishak said something, but it was just a meaningless punctuation to the rocket noise.

Forward. Forward. The pressure against his shoulder blades built up almost imperceptibly. He felt as if he were suffocating, terribly aware of the strangeness of being in a tiny room sitting on a pillar of fire.

Seconds passed, giving way to minutes. At three g's the shaking became violent, punching him against the padding in the seat and rocking his head in a rhythmic oscillation. He closed his eyes and tried to relax. This was nothing new. From somewhere a reserve of strength kicked in, and when he opened his eyes he was calm.

And then it was over. The sustainer core dropped away and they were riding on the quiet huzzah of the OMS engines. Once again he had cheated his destiny. Life would go on. Forward, but along a strange trajectory. Back toward Sinuhe, toward an appointment with history.

# CHAPTER 8
## *February 22, 2003*

L. Aloysius Wren stood behind the podium looking nervously down at his little speech. It was a hell of a thing really, the best his writers could do with the monstrosity Bensonhurst and Nelson had cooked up. Damn you anyway, Ben! He looked up through the clear protective shield and was gratified by the way the throng of reporters seemed to be mesmerized by his colored contact lenses. Color theory was a many-splendored thing. They were starting to quiet down, looking at him expectantly. It had taken many years to civilize these ravening predators. Of course, having press conferences at such wide intervals helped. Made them realize that he could do without them, but they couldn't do without him. He fast-forwarded to the end of the speech, watching the large letters scroll across the podium-screen. Lame ending, too. What a mess.

All right. I'll just *read* the fucker. Why do they do these things to me? Nelson now, you couldn't say what he was up to. Like virtually all professional military, he was a bequest from ages past, some kind of Vietnam fighter pilot, brought into political play during the Reagan years. But I thought I could trust good old Ben. Through the barrier, he could hear Fingol shouting at the reporters to shut up in his surprisingly reedy voice, calling them to order. Wonder if he's disappointed he never got a chance to run for the presidency. Had the brains for it, more than anyone since Nixon, maybe even since Coolidge. A man for all political seasons, easily the ablest within the Republican cabal . . . if only he just didn't *look* like that!

He pressed the touchnode activating his earpiece, signaling for a reply. "Ready Mr. President." Jo-Lee Hooker's voice, confident and clear, came into his head.

President Wren looked earnestly and intelligently out across a sea of eyes, letting his lips fall slightly open to show even, white teeth that set off his smooth, brown tan; squinting, bringing out the character lines that age was slowly deepening. The text of the speech had started to roll. "Gentlemen, I'll make this brief. We're here tonight to discuss certain developments in the American space program vizaviz"—God damn them! I *said* no abbreviations!—"uh, recent activities in deep space by the Soviet Union. I refer specifically to what is now being called the Sinuhe Project."

Interest was blossoming on faces here and there in the audience, men and women who worked for space and technically oriented publications. One big round girl was holding up a cordless microphone and twiddling something on her laptop. Voice actuator. Interesting. He continued, "As you may recall, the United States government has issued a number of diplomatic objections to what we consider to be a very ill-conceived project. This attempt to return an asteroid to Earth-orbit is *very* dangerous. All reputable scientists here in the West feel that such a task is simply out of reach of our present technology; and *our* technology is at least a decade ahead of that available in the Soviet Union. *If* Project Sinuhe works, it will only work by the sheerest accident. We don't *mind* if the Soviet government chooses to waste somewhere between six and ten billion dollars on an outer space boondoggle, though we regret the additional hardship this will bring to the long-suffering Soviet people. We do most strenuously object to President Gorbachev's—"

Someone shouted "Yeltsin," from the floor.

"—President Gorbachev's willingness to cavalierly place the entire global environment at risk. In the event that Sinuhe should strike the Earth, though the immediate consequences are under debate, there can be no doubt the resulting explosion will bring on the nuclear winter that our generation has, for good reason, feared. By their actions, the Soviets come perilously close to returning the world to the Cold War terror that held us in its grip for a half century and more. We thought Stalin and Brezhnev were dead. Perhaps we were mistaken." Heady stuff, this! Wren was beginning to get into the act, enjoying his words.

"Now, the United States cannot stand by idly and let Sinuhe go where it will unchallenged. Therefore I am tonight directing that NASA and the U.S. Air Force prepare a mission to intercept the asteroid as it approaches the earth in May of this year. Two pairs of coupled Orbital Transfer Vehicles"—whatever the hell *that* meant!—"will go out to the asteroid and will monitor Soviet activities at close range. This will be an unmanned mission, of course. Data transmitted by the vehicles will alert us to any danger that develops, let us decide in advance what actions must be taken.

"We wish the Soviets every success in this endeavor, however mistaken it may be. We *cannot,* however, let it pass unexamined, unchallenged by the technological prowess of the United States of America. End of—" Oops. He looked up.

"MRPRESIDENTMRPRESIDENT!"

"Mr. Fingol will answer your questions. I have a cabinet meeting to attend." L. Aloysius Wren turned and fled into the darkness, back to his bunker and assured safety.

"Fuck!" screamed a woman from the *Ad Astra Daily* contingent. "What good is *this* going to do? *More* fucking bullshit!"

"Ladies and gentlemen, *please,*" said presidential Chief of Staff Fingol. "One at a time please. Uh . . . Yes. The portly bearded gentleman in the back row. You seem nice and polite."

The man stood, smiling wryly behind lustrous brown whiskers, "Miles Baggiagalopo, *Near Star Journal.* If I understand correctly, two two-stage OTVs are going to make a flyby of the incoming asteroid. Since the closure rate will exceed ten miles per second, that makes rendezvous impossible. How will they make any useful observations in a span than cannot be more than a few minutes?"

Fingol shrugged. "I wouldn't know. Um . . . Yes. You there next to him, the fellow with the gray hair and beer belly."

This one stood, brows crushed together into a dense scowl. "So. Wilson Martin, *Planetology Digest.* What if the Russians screw up and drop it on D.C.? What good is an OTV going to do?"

"Give us time to duck. Next question. You there, baldy . . ."

· · ·

Volodya came through the docking port into *Mir*'s aft work module, last to debark from *Buran*. The space station was exceptionally crowded, and, with the addition of the nine who'd ridden up on the shuttle, contained thirty-seven cosmonauts, the most that had ever been housed in a single space structure. The American media had made much of the previous record, held by the twelve operational and twenty-four construction astronauts aboard the unfinished *Eisenhower*. He smirked. Well, Vladimir Manarov accomplishes another first. . . .

Technicians and scientists sprouted from the walls, monitoring experiments or taking notes on the several old-fashioned portables set into the bulkhead. They greeted him cheerily, wished him luck. Some wanted to shake his hand, and he accommodated them. Stuck in low Earth-orbit, doing what was essentially drudge work, most hardly thought of themselves as cosmonauts, but they were here, in space, nonetheless. For them, it was nothing more than a career. Volodya realized that, if he hadn't been lucky, this is where he would have ended up, at the very edge of space, unable to go further. Could he have been satisfied with just a taste? No. Bitterness and frustration would have dogged him to his grave. So small is the difference between a happy life and its antithesis.

At the far end of this complex, beyond *Mir-East, Mir-West,* and the axial work module and docking port, nearly a quarter of a kilometer away, *Molotochek* waited. And beyond that, Sinuhe, and the future.

Clouds had obscured all but the highest peaks of the Sierra Nevada, but the Valley was clear, a pale emerald wash extending to the horizon. Heather April Ferguson, astronaut, put the nose of the ancient NASA T-38N down and watched the checkerboard farms and orchards around Bakersfield crawling underneath. Beautiful, after the desert erosion of Texas, Arizona, and Nevada; full of life, even from the sky. A transcontinental flight was always a revelation to her. So much of the country was bone-dry and desolate. Desertification was a word that you heard more and more on the evening news, but this part of the country was unchanged from when she'd first flown over it commuting to college in Tucson.

Not long now. Her skin tingled with anticipation. Once more into the lurch, or was it breach. Lurching into the celestial breach. Kind of poetic, that. She stretched languorously in the comfortable leatherette seat. This would certainly be different, launching over land in *Aldebaran*. The feelings would be the same, she supposed, though maybe watching the mountains passing below would give her a *real* sense of how fast they were accelerating.

Her brow crinkled up as she remembered the scene from the previous evening, with her boyfriend in Cocoa. The guy fucking acted like he owned her, and they had only been living together, what was it, four months? It really bugged her. He acted as if the secrecy code was a joke. Thought, as so many did, that the military aspects of space were part of an old, moldering military-industrial complex, irrelevant now that the Russian Bear had turned into a teddy. Now that she considered it, she realized that he was turning into a fucking hippy; he didn't take anything seriously, not even his career. Damn if she was going to be dragged down by a lost little boy four decades out of synch.

She'd argued with herself about NASA's subjugation to the Air Force before applying for her job. But . . . There was only one game in town, after all; only one way to follow her dream. An image of herself at eleven: a questing little girl who wouldn't take no for an answer, learning the planets, entranced by her first and subsequent viewings of *Star Wars,* wondering what space was *really* like. As she entered her teens, the classmates who merely thought of her as advanced began to ridicule her, throwing spitballs at her and worse, isolating her from their society. She still couldn't understand it. Even now people stared at her strangely, for no readily apparent reason.

Her accomplishments spoke for themselves. Master's in Applied Physics from the University of Arizona. One of only nine women astronauts, and the only one certified for MMU. *The* expert on OTV cleanup and repair. When people stared at her she stared right back, undaunted by their anachronistic ideas. She could afford to ignore them, as long as she could have space.

The brown hills of the Coast range were creeping over the horizon, and Vandenberg couldn't be far beyond. Imagine, she thought, saving the earth from cataclysm. Blowing up the much-ballyhooed asteroid Sinuhe. Star Wars for real. When the news is released, we'll be heroes. That could easily mean a promotion to a command position within the corps. But would that be a step toward or away from her dream? She didn't know.

Anyway . . . She plucked the switch on the console that turned on her headset and spoke into the microphone. "Vandenberg, Vandenberg. NASA 4151 requesting coordinates and landing info."

They were clustered around *Molotochek*'s porthole, bodies projecting toward the four cardinal points, heads pressed together, watching the earth sink away from them into the darkness. "God," muttered Sirje Saarmula. "I can't believe how fast it's shrinking." Their bodies were still thrilling to the stress of acceleration, reacclimating to zero-g.

Chishak nodded slowly, feeling the top of his head rubbing against someone else's. "I know. You always have to wonder if this is the last time we'll see home."

"I would," said Serebryakov, "prefer not to wonder that. I've . . . almost had enough wondering for one lifetime." *And I wonder if I'd rather be back with Daryushka, now. Is this a big mistake for me? Did I* have *a choice?* The black velvet sky seemed to pull at him, as if it wanted to suck him out into the eternal night.

Manarov tried to hold his breath, but the window was fogging up anyway. He'd always had an exceptionally moist breath, derived from the good circulation that kept his fingers and toes warm on winter nights. Shutka, whose feet could get appallingly cold, was always teasing him about that. "It'll shrink fast as long as we're nearby. Beyond lunar distance the size change is quite small. We'd have to be halfway to Venus before you'd lose the naked-eye disk."

They were all silent for a minute, watching the world go away, then Saarmula said, "I feel like a virgin." He chuckled. "How many times is this for you, Volodya? I forget."

"Uh. Four times . . ." *Four times?! Twice to the Moon, twice to Sinuhe, knock on wood. Well. That's a record, itself. Somehow the idea was unappealing, even silly. I've lost a lot of that on these missions.* A voice in his head played out the catechism. *Coming out into a vast and empty cosmos . . . I am . . . small. Look at the world* there, dropping away. It too is small. Everyone and everything, all of mankind, all of history . . . even the span of geological time shrinks away to nothing in the vastness. The universe was already old when Earth was born. It will be young yet when Earth has died. We are as nothing . . . a . . . dustmote in the heavens.

There was another long silence, then Saarmula said, "Well. And when we pass the Moon, I will be the first non-Russian in interplanetary space."

"Not quite," Chishak pulled back a little from the porthole and lifted his head. "I am from the Ukraine. Zaporozhye."

The Estonian laughed. "Oh. Well, then, the first non-Slav. That will have to do."

Volodya looked back at the earth. "First non-Russian . . . non-Slav . . ." He laughed softly. "I see no borders."

"Farewell, Daryushka . . ." whispered Serebryakov, then, "Farewell, *rodina.*"

Silence, then, "More than that," said Manarov. "Farewell, *rodimir.*" It seemed to spring up out of nowhere. *Rodimir.* The great mottled world was already a whole sphere, visible in its totality through the little round window.

"What do you mean," asked Saarmula. *"Rodimir.* That's not a word, is it?"

Manarov pressed his face to the glass. "Look at it, so small and far away. All land and sea. Our great *rodina,* motherland, blends right into it all, indistinguishable. There *are* no nations to be seen. *Rodimir,* I call it. Mother Earth." Manarov watched the world float away. I am changed by it, he thought, as so many others have been. Becoming another man, torn apart by the immensities around me, reassembled in another way. I cannot know what I will become . . . and I don't care. I . . . wouldn't trade this moment for immortality.

Silence enveloped them for a long while.

It was the mid-1990s. Volodya stood naked at the foot of his bed, looking down on Shutka. Three months isn't a very long time, he thought, but I feel shy nonetheless. And heavy too. Five days back in gravity and I'm not a heart attack victim any more . . . but my bones are made of lead.

She lay spread-eagled on the mattress, naked as well, looking up at him with shining dark eyes, distorted by her seven-months' pregnancy, but still slim and young underneath it all. "Get in bed, Volodya. I don't want to wait any longer."

"Greedy," he said, kneeling clumsily, then crawling to her side. "Impatient."

She put her hand on his shoulder and let it slide down the length of his arm. "I have a right to be. Three months, Volodya. Eleven weeks. Seventy-nine nights!"

"Seventy-eight! There was that morning before the launch. . . ."

"All right, seventy-eight then."

"Sticky in my spacesuit. Very embarrassing . . ."

She grinning, reawakening to the rapport of their relationship, and grabbed at his crotch. "And you'll be sticky in your spacesuit again tomorrow, my lad, if, that is, you can rise again in the morning."

"I seem to be rising right now."

"We'll take care of *that*."

The tension was building in him swiftly and he knew the first time would have to proceed in good order. He slid his hand across the globed expanse of her belly and down into the familiar thatch of hair. "Hmh. You seem to be very wet here."

She grinned, snorted with laughter. "It's been like that for weeks. I thought it was waiting for you but old Lizaveta tells me it's just the pregnancy. I'm greasing up for the grand opening."

He rubbed his fingers together. "Feels a little like raw egg-white. . . ."

"Don't you go clinical on me now. This is supposed to be a wonderful, spiritual moment. . . ."

"I would've thought it to be a wonderful, horny moment."

"Beast." She grabbed him by the scruff of the neck and began pushing his head downward. "Ahhh . . . my big chance, now that you've been weakened by exposure to the great nothing-at-all . . ."

He felt a little flex of panic, wondering if he'd be revolted by her condition. No. It doesn't matter. Even if it *was* disgusting, I'd never hurt her feelings. He slid his head down onto her thigh. "I can't see you any more." Hmm. At least it appeared to be odorless.

"I don't mind," she said. "I haven't seen that region in almost as long as you. See what you can discover, explorer of new worlds."

"Old worlds, too, I guess." He rubbed his face in her pubic hair, feeling it crisp and damp on his freshly shaven cheeks. Mm. I've been dreaming about this since halfway through the mission. He levered himself up a little so his chest was across her thigh. "You all right? I'm not too heavy?"

"I'll let you know," her voice was a rough whisper.

I guess my feelings about weight are colored by zero-g. Too bad I can't take her up . . . He lowered his face again and stuck out his tongue, carefully brushing aside the strands of coarse hair with his fingers. . . . By God! She tastes *sweet*! He slid his tongue downward, into the opening of her vagina, and found her full of a musty, good-tasting fluid. How strange . . . He pulled away and asked, "Have you been using something? Your cunt tastes pretty good. . . ."

She groaned softly. "No. It's just me. I don't know . . . whatever . . . please . . ."

He put his face back down into its nest of hair and began to lick around, caressing familiar structures, first up one side, then down the other; around the opening, then back up across the middle. Her clitoris was swollen into a small, stiff knob, almost like a little bubble under her skin. Her breathing quickened steadily and the wetness increased, until Volodya could feel it beginning to intrude on his nostrils. It was, he supposed, as good a way to drown as any other.

She began pushing her hips up harder against his face, rocking her pelvis to quicken the motion of his tongue, and her gasps became longer, broken by little intervals of breath holding. It was over suddenly, almost without warning. She grunted and pushed her hips up, so that, for a moment, his nose was covered up, then fell back, breath rasping in her throat.

"Oh. Volodya."

He pushed up on one elbow and peered over her distended abdomen. "So. Worth the wait?"

She grinned, face covered with sweat. "Worth the wait. Wipe off your face and come up here."

He grabbed the blankets and dried his chin, then kneeled between her legs. "All right, then. How are we going to work around this thing?"

She spread her legs wider and said, "We'll manage somehow."

STS-B(001) *Aldebaran* was already on the launchpad at Vandenberg by the time they climbed aboard. Standard order. The vehicles were mated in the Horizontal Assembly Building, the orbiter lifted and clamped to the back of the RV-3 booster assembly, then the mated vehicles picked up together and deposited in the strong arms of the Erector Transporter. The whole thing, close to five million pounds, was then dragged out to the launchpad and stood on its tail. At that point, *Aldebaran* was no more than forty-eight hours from launch. Power it up. Let the onboard AI systems check things out. Fuel it up, check it out again, stuff the people aboard, and away we go.

From the road out to the launchpad, the second-generation shuttle was a beautiful sight. Major General Arthur Pories, chief astronaut for the Department of Defense, former B-1B pilot, stared at it through the skylight of the crew bus as they drove up through a gathering California dusk. By God, you had to give those bastards at NASA credit. The TAV was a wonderful thing, true, but *this* was a rocket ship! I'm glad we get to use them.

*Aldebaran* was a fully reusable ship. The orbiter, half as large as its booster, was a tailless delta design, with little vertical stabilizers on each wingtip. It had integral tanks for its cryogenic fuel, while the payload bay was a flat canister clamped between its wings. Safe. That's what you'd call it. The five-man crew module was an ejectable cabin that could survive almost anything, could push them out of the hopeless fireball of an on-the-pad disaster, dropping them safely on the beach a few miles away.

The booster, RV-3, one of five so far built, looked a little bit like the old external tank of the original space shuttle, STS-A, and its unmanned variant, STS-C. A *little* bit. True, it was more or less cylindrical, but it had its own engines and stubby little wings and landing gear. . . . Radio control would carry it back through reentry and swing it around a long glidepath back from the central Pacific, whence most payloads headed south toward polar orbit. This flight would be a little unusual, eastward over the Nevada desert toward the space station, bringing the booster down in *Florida* of all places. NASA had screamed for a Canaveral launch, but with this cargo . . .

Nope.

Up the elevators they went to the airlock hatch in the midline, then through the tunnel to the crew cabin. The air around the ship was cold, the hull creaking as it flexed, full-scale war between the balmy air and the hydrogen within. Inside, it was toasty warm as they were strapped into their seats by the pad crew. Times were changing all right. No more white room, no more spacesuits. Just guys in coveralls to help you lie down . . .

Pories thought wistfully about the old days he'd never known. See it in the Smithsonian . . . *Apollo 11* with a dummy inside . . . you looked, but you couldn't believe it. How the *fuck* could three guys live in that thing for two weeks? When they were strapped in, their shoulders *touched*!

They popped him in the left-hand seat, then remote pilot Eigenveidt in the right, then April Ferguson in the middle. The two-man flight crew, above them in the nose, had been in here for an hour already, running the flight autocheck-lists and admiring the efficient software. Behind them, the hatch clanked shut and lockbolts squeaked as they were dogged home. Another minute and you could hear the outer airlock door thump shut. They were all alone.

Pories looked up and watched as the crew access arm swung away. Yep. Alone. Won't be long now. He glanced to his right. Shit. Eigenveidt was reading some kind of paper-back book. He squinted. Shit. *Rabbit Ruminate,* by John Updike. I guess since he's among the immortals he gets to live forever. And Heather April Ferguson, staring dreamily at the sky, was gently picking her nose.

Where the fuck do they *find* these people? Still, she was supposed to be a good mission specialist, at least by NASA standards. Tops with the OTV onboard computer. Fully checked out in on-orbit mating procedures. Hmm. I won-der if I'd like to find out. She must have a nice, tight little cunt. . . . He watched, incredulous, as she dug something out of her nose and placed it between her lips. Ookh. He looked away. Man. I guess not.

There was a distant whine as the service tower was cranked back out of harm's way. Not long now. That was part of STS-B's money-saving features. Not only did they get all of the parts back, they didn't have to refurbish the launchpad. Everything was out of the way but blistered cement, capable of living through dozens of launches, and a bolted-down metal ring, about five hundred thousand dollars worth of scrap that would melt into crud when the shuttle lifted off. This *was,* of course, a dangerous moment. The rocket *could* tip over—if you could find a wind strong enough to knock over a two-hundred-ton object.

"Heads up, guys," said one of the pilots.

You could hear things *whining* in the spaceship, pumps and shit like that. Four, three, two, one, on our way . . .

The thirteen liquid-fuel engines went on simultaneously, eight in the booster and five in the orbiter, rugged, a generation more advanced than the old SSMEs. They weren't NASP scramjets, but they didn't have to be. They just worked, over and over again.

One. Two. Three. Full thrust. Hold down release, and just in time. STS-B(001) *Aldebaran* staggered into the sky, then seemed to pause, teetering, a little way up.

"What the *fuck*?" muttered Eigenveidt, looking up from his book.

"Big payload. Little bit of a problem," said one of the pilots. They were working their controls and the ship continued to climb, rolling away toward the southeast, passing right over fucking Lompoc.

Big payload, all right, as big as this ship could haul. You had to wonder where they'd found the goddamned bombs. Big ones, twenty-four-megaton gravity bombs, originally intended for the bay of a B-52. Ten thousand pounds apiece.

Pories looked out the window . . . Jesus. *Right* over the tops of the goddamned mountains! The sky outside began to turn dark quickly. The ship rolled suddenly, so that the Nevada desert was underneath, out of sight. "Staging," called a pilot. And, like that, the weight on them, not much to begin with, was gone. There was a harsh sliding sound and the nose of the big booster suddenly dropped out of their view through the forward windows, then the thrust began to build back up.

Long goddamned way to Florida . . . But it was the only other landing site capable of bringing in an automatic flyback booster. The thing would have to make a series of skipglides off the top of the troposphere, before coming in over the Gulf.

He looked over at Ferguson, who seemed to be finished with her nose. She was staring out the window at the black sky, smiling slightly. "What d'you think, April?"

She glanced at him. "Well . . . Okay, I guess. This is my tenth flight. . . . I like being in space better than getting there."

Tenth flight . . . That made her his equal in experience. Hmm. "Ever ride one of the old shuttles?"

"Sure. Noisy. Smelly."

How can you tell, with fingers up your nose? "Make you nervous?"

"Sure. A little. No more than this flight, though." She paused, staring at him, then said, "I don't like riding with these bombs, General. I don't like this whole idea."

"Well, shit. Why'd you agree to come?" You little Commie bitch.

She shrugged. "Someone's got to do it. I know how. Besides, it's my job. They call you, you go."

And she'd had the same briefings he had, knew about the lies, knew what they were going to do. Everyone has their price. Hers is rides into space. "What if you had to drop it on someone, not just an asteroid."

Another shrug. "That's *your* job, General Pories."

"Well, and if it *were* your job?"

"I'd think about it, I guess."

You'd think about it, you guess. What a hell of an attitude!

"Oh, and by the way. I saw the way you were looking at me before lift-off. If you've got any ideas about microgravity sex, I would suggest that you abandon them now."

"Yeah, sure."

The engines went off, and they were in space.

SRF Colonel-General Vladimir Semyonovich Ponomarev stood outside a translucent glass-paned door and smoothed down his mane of dark hair. Inside, the General Secretary would be sitting at his desk, waiting for the interview. This was the crucial moment; a moment history would, in all probability, never know about, but a watershed in time all the same. Even now the *Aldebaran* orbiter was approaching rendezvous; the events from now on would pay out at a quickening pace. Well, in I go.

Mikhail Sergeevich stood and greeted him warmly, shaking his hand as only a master politician can. "So, Volodya, have a seat." He himself slid into his chair and rocked back. "How are the grandchildren?"

"Fine, Misha, fine. They grow like weeds; but of course you know that."

"It looks as though our plan has come to fruition. Wren is playing into our hands by sending those little space tugs; what publicity! And have you seen any of the End-of-the-World thing on CTN? It's excellent, just excellent. I have a report from an operative in some outlandish place, Tallahassee, Memphis, one of those, that indicates people are buying up commodities so they can leave their low-lying homes when the time comes. The backlash when the 'danger' evaporates will sweep those Republicans out of office once and for all."

Ponomarev sat forward against the stiff expanse of his uniform. The man *still* didn't know; the KGB had been virtually abolished in the early nineties, and the party had never recovered its espionage abilities. Fortunately, the military had its own spies, though, spies who had discovered what the actual mission of the OTVs was. "Wren is totally out of control. He has already lost the confidence of the American public. Even the old jokes are starting to resurface. No matter what happens to Sinuhe, at least you were correct in predicting the result in America."

Gorbachev gave him a steady, critical look. "Tell me, Comrade General. Your fingers are longer than mine. Can they really be so stupid? His military, I mean. Surely they must have come up with some plan to stop us."

Ah. He *had* heard something. But how much? "There is no doubt that some plans were made within the office of the Joint Chiefs of Staff. Extravagant, impossible plans. But they are impotent. President Wren is being totally honest with us. They will monitor the deceleration as best they can from mated OTVs; but their hands are tied by their foolish limitations."

"Good. Then everything will work out the way I envisioned. And since it looks as though we'll actually be able to get the asteroid into Earth-orbit, well, that will be frosting on the cake."

Ten days from Earth. Seventy-five days from Earth. It depended on which way you went. To match the orbit of Sinuhe, they'd had to follow the long, slow route, moving outward toward Mars then looping inward along a carefully plotted trajectory that would carry them to rendezvous. There had been a few hair-raising moments: a medium-size solar flare had erupted only twenty days out, forcing them to spend a day and a half inside the shelter, but on the whole they'd spent the time working profitably, exercising according to Chishak's regimen, and sleeping.

Tonya was peddling hard on the veloergometer, breathing deeply, feeling pleasantly high from the natural opioids in his system. Damn it if this wasn't as good as liquor! And without the unpredictable side effects. His world had swung about once again, and, now, things seemed well under control. In the absence of any contact with Darya, an optimism had ballooned in him, and his view of things had taken on a burnished, devil-may-care luster. He was proud of his inner changes and vowed that he would never again succumb to the pernicious weaknesses that whispered to him. Of course, realistically, he knew he'd made this vow before; but things, at last, were different now. With a woman by his side he would be able to be strong.

Volodya and Seryozha were manning their stations, preparing for the relatively short burn that would match speeds with the asteroid. Tonya watched them work, pushing with his legs, pushing until it felt like his thighs would burst. A sense of hominess flooded into him like *déjà vu*. The fears of the past were borne away on the current of lethe. *Molotochek* was home.

Lyova slipped through the hatch to Tonya's right, looking concerned. "Tonya," he said, "I think you've done enough biking for today. Remember that the tonus of your muscles is being augmented by the inductors; right now you're just wasting oxygen and food."

"Yeah?" Another addiction? Perhaps it was turning out

that way. All right, he would stop; show them that he could exercise or not, that his will was in control. He began to slow down. "If you say so. My goal is to walk away from the landing strip under my own power."

"Yes, well, we shall see." Chishak watched as the jags on the wall-mounted oscilloscope over the bicycle widened.

"There it is." Volodya sat back and regarded the star-filled screen on his lower monitor. Amidst a scatter of dim lights, the asteroid, only slightly brighter, was unremarkable, but then it was still more than seven thousand kilometers away. Such a small object had been invisible even through the refurbished Hubble Space Telescope for most of its solar orbit, and had been monitored only through the continuous radio signal from the control node they'd left. It was a relief to find it in the right place, despite all the assurances from the ground.

Tonya came over and stared at the screen. His sweat, trapped under the fabric of his shirt, was hanging on him like a second, irritating skin, and he pulled the shirt off to let it have a shot at evaporating. Well, there it was.

"That's your highest magnification?" asked Seryozha. "Hell, it *is* small, isn't it?"

Tonya smiled at the man's surprise. "Small, yes. But important. Disproportionately so."

Saarmula shook his head, noticing that the asteroid was moving relative to the stars behind it. "I still don't believe it."

Manarov turned and beheld the pilot, whose face was bland and buttery. "What don't you believe?"

The Estonian turned back to his keyboard. "I am afraid this may sound like blasphemy, but I just can't see a future in which this tiny bit of nickel-iron will play a role. Space will never become self-sufficient, not within our lifetime, or our children's. This is just a stunt, like all the others. An impressive stunt, I will concede, but a stunt nonetheless."

Chishak came forward from where he had been winding induction bandages. This was interesting. The man had been quiet enough during the trip out; and Lyova imagined that there was some kind of nationalistic barrier keeping them apart. Now he was finally going to reveal a few of his real thoughts. "You have an extraordinarily impressive record in LEO, Comrade Commander. I would have thought you would be just as gung-ho as the rest of them."

Saarmula detached himself from the Velcro on his bench and floated upward, turning to face the three of them. "Comrade Doctor, my motivations are not so simple as you would imagine. I was only a child during the Afghan action, but I wanted very badly to be a fighter pilot. I watched with regret as my people moved toward separation from the USSR in the time of troubles, knowing that tiny Estonia would never have an air force of its own. I have always moved against the tide of history, I suppose. As you probably guessed, I was initially chosen for the cosmonaut corps as a token in the game going on between Moskva and Tallinn. I resented the fact, but I went anyway. Space is not a means to an end for me. It *is* the end. I feel that the more we pin our near-term hopes on missions like this one, the greater the disappointment will be and the stronger the backlash. I have not spoken of this earlier, for obvious reasons."

Volodya marveled. Such a speech from this quiet, formal man. And so wrong-headed. "Your opinions astound me, Seryozha."

Tonya brought a hand to his cheek and rubbed against the grain. "I think I understand what you're saying. But, my friend, we cannot know what is possible until we try."

Manarov shook his head. "It is a funny thing. We each develop the idea that we know enough to evaluate those things which we see. No matter how little we actually *do* know. The future is not an open book. One must be an optimist."

"Well, as you say. All this is just my opinion. It does not affect my performance."

Lyova started back to the rear of the cabin, smiling to himself. "Comrade Commander, have you ever heard of cognitive dissonance?"

In the monitor, Sinuhe was once again swelling significantly, bright and curved like a sickle, swallowing stars down its capacious maw. Manarov and Saarmula had performed a perfect burn, and they were once again in the purview of the little chunk of metal. On the monitor, it looked very much the same. Tonya studied the familiar features, etched into his mind from all the photoanalysis he had supervised. The silicate spur, half in shadow, bulged up like a growth; and he could just make out the sinuous split of the Grand Groove. An image of the internal structure came to him, and he wondered how the explosion had changed it. The detonation site was invisible in darkness, though, and would not peep out for three and a half hours.

Adventure? He thought. This time it wouldn't be new. There would be no breathless exploration. Just a job to do. But a damn important one.

Arthur Pories floated behind the aft end of space shuttle *Aldebaran,* 1,024 miles above an enormous, cloud-mottled Pacific Ocean. Over the orbiter's mantalike starboard wing, space station *Eisenhower* was silhouetted against the sharp curve of the Earth's horizon. It was a silver wagon wheel, twelve-spoked, drifting at an angle in its orbit. There were gaps in the rim yet, hence the lack of spin, and the incomplete main battle platform was a minute girdery shell a half mile further out. He signalled to Ferguson and twisted a control on his Manned Maneuvering Unit to move closer to the big clamshell doors on the protruding hump of the cargo pod.

He let himself pause for a moment to enjoy the view. What a pity they couldn't have put it in a polar orbit. An oversight. All the other SDI modules went polar, hurled southward from the California coast by massive STS-C heavy-lift vehicles . . . but the principal components of *Eisenhower* had been designed wrong, too heavy to do without that little added thrust from the Earth's rotation. Still, a fifty-six-degree orbit was good enough. It was what the Soviets used, and, with the geo-stationary relays, the crew of *Eisenhower* and their ever-vigilant robots could watch and act in plenty of time.

"I wish we had one of those." April Ferguson's voice was tinny in his earphones, depersonalized. Pories nodded contemptuously to himself. I'll bet you do. *Freedom.* What a joke. A good idea to begin with, perhaps, but doomed from the start. He had watched as the little piece of flotsam had been steadily downsized and underfunded since its inception in 1984. With the lessons of *Challenger* fresh in memory, Congress had repeated its earlier mistakes exactly. Finally the ridiculous 1989 proposal for a four-man space station—even the diehards started to see what was happening. That had been the beginning of the end: when the Europeans and Japanese threatened to drop out and build their own station, the international concept had finally come to the fore. Before you knew it, DOD had been kicked out. . . .

It had been a good thing, too. SDI was coming into its own at last. With the Russkis' propaganda successes, the military picture looked bleak indeed. But the threat of ballistic attack from the third world, from things like madman Qaddafi's Islamic Bomb, had come to the rescue in the proverbial nick of time. With some judicious grease here and there, the money had begun to flow again. Everybody tried to get into the act; and, with the proliferation of new launch vehicles, even Commerce had gotten its own program before long. Of course, their station was just a stupid man-tended canister, but what the hell. . . .

"Here it comes."

Pories looked back at the ship and saw the big doors on the end of the cargo pod were slowly cranking open, exposing a deep red-lit cavity within. Okay. Time to get to work. "How you doing, Freddy?"

Back on the shuttle's cramped flight deck, Freddy Eigenveidt floated before his teleoperator console, watching the numbers flow. "Looks good, Art. Stand off while I back her out."

"We're clear."

A square box mounted on the ceiling of the cargo pod suddenly popped open. A little running light began to wink, white-then-red, and the cylindrical Telerobotic Service Vehicle slid from its garage, propelled by ejection springs. Arms still folded, it floated out a few meters, then thrusters twinkled and it came to a stop. "How's she look?"

"Intact, Freddy. That's all I can tell you."

"Good enough." The thing's four arms opened, making a robotic swastika, and began to unlimber, going through test routines of their own. The little bastard was a good piece of technology, a fine mix of AI and remote control that let you do what you wanted but kept you from fucking up. Only the steadfast opposition of the astronaut corps had kept the things from replacing the manned EVA altogether.

"Right. You pull the, uh, cargo out. We'll see to the OTVs."

Pories turned in place, using the MMU's thrusters, and looked out into space. About a hundred yards from *Alde-*

*baran,* four flying pancakes hung in a tight little cluster above the Earth's limb. The Orbital Transfer Vehicles, squat disks fifteen feet in diameter by four feet thick, were all that remained of the Space Transportation System's "space tug" option. They were mostly just a platform riding on engines and fuel tanks, with a sophisticated avionics package, intended for orbit-to-orbit service runs. NASA had two of them and DOD had, six. Of course, there *were* two manned foray cabins, but mostly the whole idea was pathetic. They were used primarily to ferry Telerobotic Servicers back and forth between here and geosynchronous orbit, along with occasional "inspection" teams.

Then, prior to this Sinuhe thing, there had been the Idea. At a mini-summit eighteen months ago, Wren had agreed to a bit of self-serving space diplomacy: Since, theoretically, two coupled OTVs would be able to deliver a manned foray cabin to lunar orbit, it should be possible for a tiny crew to visit the Russian station *Mechta.* Bullshit.

From a nearer perspective, the OTVs looked more complicated. Pories flew his MMU over to the dorsal surface of the OTV—the "top" he supposed it was, since that was where the avionics package was—and thought out the sequence of tasks. Ferguson came up behind him. Simple enough, guys and gals. "Okay April. Let's do it. I'll take one and you take two. Odd's the bottom, even's the top." She pulled the special tool out of her MMU's utility box and quickly detached the control panel, then carried it to a safe distance. The vehicle's thrusters were in four "quad" units located at the cardinal points of the disk, and now they flickered as she manipulated the controls, rolling the OTV to a proper orientation.

"You ready?"

"Yep."

She worked the controls, firing little bursts, slowly orienting the disk until it was exactly parallel to the second nearest, almost touching. "Good enough." Mating two OTVs looked easy on the books, but, as with most space work, wrestling these two massive hulks together, getting the male and female alignment units to fit, was a complicated business. When it was done, they began throwing manual latches, Pories working clockwise, Ferguson the opposite. When it was over, she reattached the control panel. "Okay. Now the other one."

Back aboard *Aldebaran,* Eigenveidt sweated over his task, the shuttle's pilot and flight engineer watching over his shoulder with some anxiety.

"Jesus, Freddy. Look at the bastards!"

On the TSV's video screen, the huge bombs could be seen cradled in the cargo pod, resting in the arms of a rusty old bomb rack that had been stripped from the ruins of an ancient B-52. The bombs themselves were in pretty good shape, however, having gone through a complex refurbishment process. The casing had been in protected storage for thirty years and looked okay. The bomb trigger was new, as was the fusion package. Only the U-238 secondary fission jacket was the original, somewhat degraded, but good enough.

Eigenveidt stared at the things and wondered, What the *fuck* am I *doing* here? Treaties are meant to be broken, but this . . . You had to wonder what the brass was thinking about when they pulled a stunt like this. "I guess it's time to do it, guys."

"Yeah. Geez, they look a lot bigger than the X-ray laser triggers we put on the Polar LasSat System last year."

Freddy turned and looked at the pilot in astonishment. Yeah, sure. "If these things blow in orbit, the country underneath loses its electronics."

"Yeah?" The pilot looked out the window. "Hey, Argentina!"

The flight engineer, a short, muscular man, said, "I hear they've set up a tactical nuke factory somewhere in Patagonia. Maybe it wouldn't be a bad idea."

Eigenveidt stared at him for a minute. Could the boob be *serious*? "Bad idea. The only reason we have jobs is because these little shit countries are building bombs and missiles. The big guys won't bother us no more; but what if Morocco gets pissed off?"

And over the radio link, Major General Arthur Pories, age fifty-two, said, "Yeah? What if Alabama gets pissed off?"

Once again, Hermann Oberg sat waiting for President Wren. This time a private audience. A phone call from M. Krivine himself had put him on the breakfast Concorde flight across the Atlantic. NATO still existed, in a sense, though its ways were strange and devious. He rubbed a hand over his paunch, feeling a sickness in the pit of his stomach, a sensation not too dissimilar from the one gotten by eating too much Italian food. Pepper and sausage, that's what it feels like. The inside of his head was warm as well, and he felt slightly dizzy. The beginnings of a virus. *This is a bad day for me to be sick.*

He switched off his micro-TV and sank back into the chair. Surprisingly, the launch of *Aldebaran* had been carried live on the morning news, right alongside coverage of *Molotochek*'s rendezvous with Sinuhe. There had been two perspectives, one from a camera crew at the military reviewing stand five kilometers from the pad, the other in downtown Lompoc, dominated by scenes of crowds, shouting and laughing as the ship thundered by, twelve thousand meters up. Shocking, really. The Americans were back to taking chances with people's lives. . . . But then it had been the Defense Department which had been planning to launch an old-style shuttle with those crazy Fiberglas boosters. Had *Challenger* not intervened . . .

Coverage of *Molotochek* had been strongly negative, Earth and Moon looming in the sky, an extended review of the dangers and problems of the mission including never-before-seen films of Colonel Bronstein being killed, apparently taken by the narrow-angle cameras aboard the *Piazzi II* bus module. They even had translations of staticky radio loops from the cosmonauts, picked up by British amateurs. Chishak's panic was appalling.

The door squeaked open and Wren walked in, alone. Oberg stared at him, astonished. He was disheveled and . . . *old* looking! There were lines standing out from the corners of his eyes, bracketing his mouth, and his skin seemed pale and mottled. *What am I thinking? He's older than I am.* "Good morning, Mr. President."

Wren flopped down in a chair. "Morning, Director." He shut his eyes for a moment and stretched, sighing. "Okay. What's on your mind?"

Oberg began to sort things out in his head. *Push down the ranting German and the greasy Frenchman . . . Hell, I don't have a real American in here and the Englishman just won't do, not with this farmboy. Herr Journalist, Monsieur Diplomat? Old Boffin? Bah. A mixture would have to do.* A momentary trickle of surprise and enlightenment. *I'll* have to speak as myself. . . . "Well. *Aldebaran,* Mr. President. And *Molotochek.*"

Wren looked at him curiously. "What can I tell you, Mr. Oberg? The OTVs depart Earth-orbit this morning, or so I'm told."

"Mr. President, I know about the bombs."

"Bombs." Wren sat back in his chair, staring at Oberg expressionlessly. "No one's said anything about *bombs.*"

Bastard. But it would do no good to acknowledge his source. "Mr. President, we're alone here and I don't intend to mince words. I know for a fact that *Aldebaran* went up yesterday carrying two twenty-four-megaton thermonuclear warheads. I'm here to ask you—*beg* you—to cancel this mission. The risks are too great."

Wren folded his arms and, for once, could be seen to be calculating. Finally, he said, "Mister Director General of the European Space Agency: First, I have said nothing about bombs, or thermonuclear warheads. Second, the asteroid Sinuhe is headed straight for Earth and will be here in one week. The true magnitude of the risks involved is for everyone to gauge. Where were your Russian friends when this *estimating* was taking place?"

This was a side of Wren he'd never seen before. Perhaps I should have suspected. He couldn't have become president by chance, after all. . . . "The asteroid is aimed at an encounter point well to the side of Earth. Even after the braking charge detonates, the chances of an impact are small."

Wren smiled at him, eyes slitting. "As I recall, you told Congress the chances of the Russians getting it here in the first place were quite small. I think you told them the odds were Sinuhe would never be seen again."

"What I told them then was the truth, based on what we knew about the composition and structure of asteroids in general."

"Perhaps your formulas need further refinement."

Bastard. "Perhaps. But that is hardly the point right now."

"What *is* the point, Mr. Oberg? If, that is, there is one, other than that the United States spinelessly give in to Russian domination."

"Do you think the *Russians* don't know about your bombs?"

"No one, Mr. Oberg, *no one* has said anything about any *bombs.*"

Oberg sighed his exasperation, breath hot and somewhat foul. "It's too late for these games, Mr. President. By your actions, you are placing the world at risk. . . ."

"I am not the one who has done so."

Last chance. "Mr. President, in the beginning, I begged the Soviet government to abandon the folly of this project. They would not listen. Now I am begging you to abandon a foolish course. Transcend them. Show the world that your wisdom exceeds that of Mr. Gorbachev."

Anger suddenly flickered on Wren's face, then was gone. "Ask Mr. Gorbachev to abandon his course once again, for it is not too late. Let him transcend himself."

"But . . ."

"Good day, Mr. Oberg. I have work to do." Wren rose and stalked from the chamber, closing the door behind him.

Oberg sat in his chair for another little while, eyes squeezed shut, feeling the sickness wax and wane in his gut. Failed. That's the end of it. I give *up.* Whatever happens will just have to happen. If we are destroyed . . . Fuck. We *deserve* this!

He got up and walked out of the room, head spinning, wondering if he should go to a doctor. No. I have a flight back to Brussels in three hours. I've got to get out to Dulles. I'll be back in my office by suppertime. Home . . . Home. Nothing there. I wish I were married. . . . No one to comfort me when I'm ill. He thought of his plump mother, dead now for almost twenty years.

No one. Nothing but my goddamned work.

Floating with his comrades on the cramped flight deck of space shuttle *Aldebaran,* Arthur Pories stared fixedly toward the eastern horizon. The Moon, in three-quarters phase, stood just above the precise blue world-edge. In the near distance, two loaded OTV packages drifted, glittering specks, hardly visible, picked out by sunlight. He stared at them and listened to his headset.

"General Pories."

"It's me, Mac."

"Yeah." The voice was crackly with static, there being an

electrical storm over Colorado Springs. "Four minutes to ignition."

"Right." He reached out for the portable console clipped to the bulkhead and put his hand on the ignition trigger. Ground was doing it, of course, but he was the manned backup. Good old Air Force. There'll always be a man in the loop.

April Ferguson stood back, watching things transpire. The vista out the windows filled her with the usual wistful, unanswerable longing. To be in space, to walk on other worlds . . . "Not in vain, distance beckons . . ." She had, of course, subjugated her feelings to responsibility before; many times. This was merely another job. Anger stirred within her, tinged with red horror, at these military men around her, playing their little games with the trillions of dollars of wasted hardware. We've spent our future. This is it.

"Two minutes, General."

Pories's hand tightened on the lever. "Right." Eigenveidt bobbed up to the port, partially blocking his view. "Get back down, Freddy, you're in the way."

"Sorry." Freddy Eigenveidt was thinking about bombs and asteroids, and his grandfather, who'd come to Alabama from Germany via Texas more than a half century ago. Geez. The fucking *bomb* is almost that old! You had to wonder how the old bastard would feel about this. Probably okay. He and his cronies, dreaming about spaceships, hadn't hesitated to build ballistic missiles and launch them at English civilians.

"Sixty seconds, General."

"Right."

The pilot and flight engineer were huddled above their consoles, watching. "Hey," said the flight engineer, "you suppose we'll be able to see it from the ground?"

"Don't know. What chu spose it'll look like?"

Arthur Pories felt a little lift of surprise. I hadn't thought . . . Let's see . . . Yup. North America would be in night, about a hundred thousand miles from the asteroid. It would make a bright little display indeed. . . . Maybe even visible in daylight? Hmm. No. Probably not. Too bad. Russians'll miss it . . . No they won't. At least, not four of them . . .

"Thirty seconds, General."

"Right." That bothered him a little bit. Those boys were going to get killed. Don't know their plans, or where they'll be . . . But the odds were they'd be *on* Sinuhe when the first OTV blew. Brilliant white light. No bang. Just white light and a quick trip to Commie Heaven, where they'd sit at the feasting table between Marx and Engels, among the blessed martyrs of socialism. . . .

"Ten . . . nine . . . eight . . ."

Fuck. Counting down already. His intestines seemed to draw together.

"Three . . . two . . . one . . ."

Silently, in the distance, the thruster quads of the OTV clusters sparkled, throwing off gaseous exhaust. The mated disks seemed to hang there for a long moment, rockets glittering, then, with hardly any sensation of motion, they began to grow smaller, rising in their orbits. Smaller, smaller, smaller. Gone. Lights out.

"Whee!" said Freddy Eigenveidt. "And awaaaay we go!"

Very strangely, Arthur Pories felt sick.

"What's the matter, General?" asked Heather April Ferguson. "You don't look happy."

"Uh. A little motion sickness," he muttered. But . . . he knew what was wrong. And what was right. And what the difference was. Too late now.

Dallas Milam stepped off an even cadence across the rubbly pale-yellow rim path, feeling the incipient sweat evaporating in the pure, hot sunlight. To his left, a great, obscenely circular hole had been torn out of the Earth, wider than his eyes could encompass without scanning. He took it all in with equanimity, ignoring the small part of his mind that wanted to run away. The winter desert sky was cloudless and crystalline and a warm, pumice-sweet breeze jiggled the sparse grasses that grew here and there—no doubt an adiabat sweeping down from Flagstaff. He stopped before an angular, house-sized boulder that had been heaved up here by the impact and studied it with care. Meteor Crater, Arizona, was, in all probability, as close as he would ever come to this sort of thing, and he never tired of the explosive scenery.

Damn it, though! John should be here doing this. But they'd had to open him up again, this time for a gall bladder. He looked at his watch. Twenty minutes to the damn interview. Well, they paid him a fucking fortune and he was going to tell them what they wanted to hear. There was no sense in trying to explain things. The few interviews he had given as CRAF project head had taught him one important lesson: Science and media did not mix. It was like being mugged: you give them what they want and act polite and maybe you won't get hurt.

Warren Runtibbie scrutinized the jagged periphery of the crater through a forest of cameras, lighting stands, and technicians, and said, "Where in the hell *is* he?"

"I don't know, sir." Johnson, location's best boy, tried to look concerned. "Doctor Milam said he'd be back in ten minutes."

Runtibbie noted the time on the nearest large-screen monitor. "Yeah, fuckhead. That was over fifteen minutes ago. Get out there and personally bring him back within five minutes or . . . else" The best boy stared out, suddenly bewildered and forlorn. It would take at least an hour to walk around the thing. "Yes, sir," he said, and started off.

"No need for that." Milam's hoarse, unpleasant voice came out of nowhere, and he appeared just as suddenly. Runtibbie glowered at him. "Stay *put,* all right? We're four minutes from air time."

The JPL scientist nodded, grinning. "I'm ready whenever you are."

"We're doing something about his voice, right?" Runtibbie returned to the portable and read silently the last question on the prelim script. Reluctantly, he pressed the transmit key and closed his eyes to gather strength. Live reports, bah! Still, he had to admit, there was a certain electricity that came across. And apparently he did them pretty well. They kept giving him more and more time on-air. This End-of-the-World thing helped, of course. Warren Runtibbie, science correspondent, CTN. It sounded good.

"Two minutes, Mr. Runtibbie." He got up and wardrobe and analog makeup descended on him, doing their little jobs. When they stepped back he was appropriately cool and dapper in the old-fashioned dark suit, chosen to stand out from the whitish-yellowish crater. He put on his own lapel mike and went to the small, flat area they had chosen for the interview. The scientist was carefully escorted to his spot and pointed at camera one. Milam, neutral and bland-looking in his khaki shirt and pants, would wash out to nullity without considerable enhancement. At least he was an athletic type; not like the dumpy pudges that seemed to be proliferating everywhere.

On the monitor, an infomercial was winding down, counting down to zero. He struck a noble pose, wishing for the handheld microphone of times past. That was the hardest fucking thing to figure out—what do you do with your hands? He opted for the traditional position, slightly bent arms, hands cupped. The complex, evolving, black-blue and white logo materialized in the center of the screen, Earth passing through a series of hoops, sharp 3-D abstracts circling and breaking apart, and, after a bright danger subliminal, a dagger stabbing into the heart of the U.S. mainland, crisp, red letters in a pseudo-Russian font came from out of eclipse:

CTN SPECIAL REPORT
SINUHE
THE END OF THE WORLD
Hour Eleven

Lyle Marlowe metamorphosed into the image, which shattered behind him. He was sitting at a small desk in front of a warehouse-sized room full of busy people. It looked like the old-fashioned conception of a newspaper office, as it was supposed to. He looked up from a blank piece of paper, expressionless. "CTN's special report on the End of the World continues. This just in: CTN has learned that President Wren has given the order to launch the observation satellite from space station *Eisenhower*. We will have a live report from Gary Jensen at Mission Control in Colorado Springs. But first, science correspondent Warren Runtibbie and an interview with Dallas Milam, project head of the U.S. Comet Rendezvous Approach Flyby Mission and authority on asteroids. This report comes to you from Meteor Crater, where, several thousand years ago, a much smaller asteroid hit the earth. Warren?"

"Two, one, you're on." Runtibbie saw himself looking grim. "Good morning, Lyle. I am here at Meteor Crater, Arizona, with Doctor Dallas Milam of the Jet Propulsion Laboratory. Good morning, Doctor Milam."

"Good morning, Doctor Runtibbie."

Was the asshole trying to be *funny*? "We stand here at the brink of this stupendous crater that many thousands of years ago was caused by the collision of a small asteroid." He gestured clumsily. "I'd like to ask you, Doctor Milam, how does it feel to look at this crater, knowing what you know about the way it was formed?"

"I feel a sense of wonder and awe at the tremendous amount of power that went into the explosion that formed Meteor Crater. As a scientist, my curiosity is piqued: I want to understand just what happened here so many years ago."

"I see. Just how much power was that, in terms the layman can understand?"

Milam smiled, inappropriately. "At least a hundred times more powerful than the Hiroshima bomb. It was a mighty blast, that's for sure."

Runtibbie blanched. "And you say this was caused by an object only eighty feet across?"

"I didn't say that, but, yes, that's a good guess as to its size."

"And how big is the asteroid Sinuhe?"

"Oh, it's much bigger. Since it is made of metal, it's much more massive, too. Maybe thirty to forty times as massive."

"That is incredible, isn't it, Doctor Milam, that the Russians would trifle with such a potential disaster in the making? Forty times bigger than *this*? Are we talking about a crater *forty miles wide*?"

"Well," said Milam, "I didn't exac—" He paused. Where have I seen this before. Some guy with rabbity teeth . . . Oh, well . . . "No, not more than five or six times as big as this one."

"Well, Lyle, there you have it. Our world faces a disaster of unprecedented proportion just a few short hours from now. Whether or not we will be here tomorrow is a question that I hear more and more. Let's take one more long look at this giant crater and think about the asteroid Sinuhe, poised just a few thousand miles over our fragile and beautiful planet."

Marlowe's image appeared in the upper corner of the craterscape. "Thank you, Warren. Could I ask Doctor Milam a question?"

"Certainly, Lyle."

"Doctor Milam, where will you be fifteen hours from now?"

Another weird smirk. "I am touched by your concern, Mr. Marlowe. I will, of course, be watching you on TV."

# CHAPTER 9
## *May 8, 2003*

Anton emerged from the airlock hatch, stepping into the cool blush of earthlight, and stopped for a second to look around. They were on a short time line now, this EVA into Sinuhe's brief night necessary to prepare for the operations to come. He looked down at the asteroid, and, somehow, the reflected light from the bright globe 350,000 kilometers away made the pitted surface look like new-fallen snow. The landmarks around the docking mount hadn't changed, and, yes, there were the little, toadstool-like antennae from the radar experiment. It was . . . very much like a homecoming. Out there beyond that slope, he had come to terms with space and, perhaps, with his own place in the grand universe. He shook his head, feeling the padding and phones against his ears. It seemed like another lifetime.

Volodya's voice crackled gently in his ears. "Time to go, Tonya." He'd been allowed to have his moment, but now it was time to move. Crawling from handhold to handhold, Anton climbed to where the CMUs were stowed. Again he stopped. The Earth, small but overwhelming, hung high above the distant end of the fuel tank, looking down like a Technicolor version of the somber moon. As he watched, the sun, peering above the nearby horizon, caught the gold-colored binding ring at the top of the cylinder with a blinding shaft of light, washing out the sky. Dawn. He pulled down his dark outer visor and moved on.

As they put on their flying machines, the rays of the sun crept down the tank, providing more and more illumination. Finally, Volodya stepped free and soared up, catching the sunlight and dazzling like a flare. "So," he said, "Let's see what happened."

The planetologist finished strapping himself in and reached out to the steering mechanism. He took the specially designed radiation detector and mounted it in the special housing. "Here I come."

The bombs had been detonated about a third of the way around the asteroid, in a depression that, from some angles, resembled a gently sloping valley. Here it was almost midafternoon, and, as they topped a rise, their shadows shot out to mingle with those of the myriad cracks and craters. Where the bomb had been set off, there was a shallow circular crater perhaps twenty meters across, something like a large swimming pool. Within the collar the metal was bright and shiny, clearly iron or one of its twins, scoured clean of markings. Melt-waves marred the perfect smoothness of the surface, making it look even more like some kind of pool.

"So, no structural damage," said Manarov.

"No, as I predicted. Just some scouring and melting. Sinuhe's a strong little fellow."

They approached the crater carefully, Anton monitoring his counter. The radiation count rose steadily, until they were directly above. Here, despite the protection of their suits, they were absorbing a dosage of a couple of dozen rems per hour, high but hardly alarming.

"Well," said Serebryakov, "except for a slowdown in rotation rate, and this little technobleme, it's as good as it ever was."

Volodya scanned the high horizon, where the earth, following them, had appeared. The famous horizon effect worked even here on this tiny rock, enhanced, no doubt, by the difficulty in telling distances from the irregular, random-sized landmarks. *Rodimir* looked huge, and, it seemed, the cloud-mantled North American continent accounted for a good percentage of it. "Okay, Tonya. Now we see if the control node survived just as well. . . ."

Space, 1999. Where have I heard that phrase before? A muffled shrug, hidden by the spacesuit.

Volodya floated in the open hatch of *Mir*'s principal airlock, looking out into the night, at the stars, at *Mechta* and the Earth's dark limb. The secondary space station was picked out by floodlights and he could see men bobbing around on the hull, working. Gripping the edges of the hatch, he gave himself a little push and drifted out into the airless void, safety line unreeling behind him.

The two stations were connected by a Brazilian monofilament tether, which could be seen like a thin rod extending from *Mir* and disappearing in the darkness. So. There it is. Our first step on the way to the Moon. The whole business had an air of unreality about it. We can't be going. Not after all this time. But the lunar orbital station was almost finished and the first Lunar Transport Vehicle, *Molotochek,* was undergoing final assembly in the big Energiya Integration Building at Baikonur Cosmodrome's main technical zone. It would be launched in a few weeks, minus its command module—just the propulsion unit and integral avionics packages—for on orbit checkout. A little while later it would embark unmanned on the task of bringing *Mechta* to the Moon.

He clipped his pulley mechanism to the tether and tightened down the clamping arm, then detached his safety line from its carabiner. Cheap. Sort of like in a 1950s science fiction epic . . . But the Cosmonaut Maneuvering Units were extremely expensive, little spacecraft in their own right, and there just weren't enough to go around. Sure, everyone could have one. But then we wouldn't be going to the Moon this year. He triggered the little electric motor and the pulley began swiftly hauling him along the line, *Mir* drawing away, *Mechta* growing larger before his eyes. When he got to the other end, at the temporarily installed tether station, he clipped *Mechta* to his belt and unhooked the pulley.

"Manarov?"

"Krivak?"

"Welcome to the Dream." Cosmonaut Krivak came toward him, crawling along the hull, grabbing handholds, bobbing to the left and right. He clambered to a stop beside Volodya, raising his sun visor, grinning out at him through clear, somewhat scarred Plexiglas.

Volodya grinned back. The Dream. Yes, that pretty much covered everything. Mankind's dream of the ages, dominating the dreams of technical men over the last century and a half . . . "Someday we'll unearth the whole offense, from Tsiolkovskii until now . . . find out what has driven an entire culture mad. . . ."

"What?"

"Nothing. A paraphrase." Driven us mad indeed. These dreams were bought with the blood of millions of *zeks* and bread from the mouths of a long lifetime of Soviet children. . . . But we have them!

Memory was a clue. What was I? Ten? Maybe eleven? "As I went strolling on the Moon one day . . ." Grainy television images, barred with conversion lines, of gray-white Americans behind opaque gold faceplates, bobbing about on the dark lunar sand, silhouetted against a gently rolling horizon, outlined against a pitch black sky . . . While far, far below, Pavel Popovich died of a stomach ulcer.

This was bought with my freedom. Fine. What's that coin really worth? Is there a Russian worse off than some pathetic *nyegr,* starving in the gutter of Ronald Reagan's capitalist paradise? Hollow words. He knew there were a million Russians, no, endless *millions* of them, who would argue with him, leap up to punch him in the nose. But we've got it now. And the dream has survived.

Gripping the nearest set of handrails, he began pulling himself along toward the work site, humming softly inside his helmet. Yes, that was it. The Dream . . .

Morning again. On the surveying trips they had tended to move parallel to the terminator, keeping the sun within the same quadrant of the sky. Now Tonya realized that moving back and forth parallel to the "equator" quickly exploded the illusion of planethood for the tiny asteroid. A hundred yards made the difference between day and night. The EVA had been planned to maximize daylight time at the control node, and, here, the sun was just coming up. The node was a large metal box like a garden shed sprouting a V of solar panels and a midsize parabolic dish antenna. It sat silhouetted at the end of a long, thin streak of shadow. In the slanting sun it was difficult to make out any details.

His earphones sizzled: "Tonya. I still don't see any sign of the cables."

"The explosion must have broken them off."

"Well, yes, it was supposed to. There were breakaway connections about twenty yards from the controller. Unfortunately, it doesn't look like they worked."

Tonya by now was almost beginning to anticipate

Manarov's style of flying, and they executed a controlled pounce, nearly in formation, coming to an almost-stop just a few meters from the node. Hidden within its own shadow, the box was almost inscrutable, but as they eased closer, a dark, ragged opening could be made out about halfway up.

There was a palatal hiss over Tonya's radio, like strange static. "Shit. The node's connection box was ripped out. Look at that hole." Volodya sidled close enough to grab on to a handhold, and pulled himself down directly in front of the machine. It was true. All that was left of the electrical box was a piece of bent metal and a few partially stripped wires. "It's a miracle that the thing didn't stop functioning altogether. If it *had* shorted, well, the mission would have come to a stop right there." As he studied the junctures carefully, he suddenly remembered an American astronaut tripping over a length of cable and ripping it out by the roots: right there, the end of a five hundred million dollar lunar experiment. "Well. It looks as if we may still be in business. All the wiring broke off near the box, and it doesn't look as if there was any internal damage, but we're going to have to work fast. I'll go back to the ship and get the connection box from the duplicate. While I'm gone, run the diagnostic program and download the contents of the computer. I don't have to tell you how . . . Christ! Look at that."

Tonya looked. The full Moon, swollen to almost twice the size of the Earth, was peeking over a broken plateau like some one-eyed, leering giant. A sideways Moon, dominated by Crisium and the foreshortened Serenetatis. They stared at it, awestruck. Sinuhe was already sweeping by the Moon's trailing hemisphere on its way to Earth. "Damn," said Tonya reverently. "We're really here."

Manarov shot up into the sky, spreading a tiny haze of dust that settled almost instantly. "A sign of how short the time grows. Get to work." He flew off on a high trajectory.

Volodya took the quickest route back to *Molotochek:* instead of trying to follow the curvature of the surface, he simply jetted to a high enough vantage point and took a line-of-sight trajectory. In the distance, perhaps thirty meters from the ship, two anomalous bright spots were drifting, set apart by the obviously connected shadows that they trailed. Chishak and Saarmula, apparently sight-seeing. Furious, he changed course and headed toward them. When he was close enough to establish some sort of visual contact, he opened his radio channel.

"Why have you left *Molotochek* unattended? Is there some sort of emergency?"

One of the spacesuits raised a hand and wagged it back and forth. "Volodya," the voice belonged to Saarmula, "Lyova was showing me around. Nothing to get upset about. The Dozhdevik is capable of regulating the ship's interior."

Manarov had a brief vision of Bronstein holding up the guideline book, pointing to the sentence, "A spacecraft shall NEVER be left unattended, under any circumstances, without a direct command from a ground officer." A silly rule, or so it seemed, now that virtually everything could be automatically regulated by the computer. But he had taken it seriously, almost to heart. "It's no skin off my neck, Seryozha, but you're taking a real chance. Suppose Capcom gives a call?"

"It's my decision, Volodya."

Volodya hung for a moment in silence, watching the two of them. "So it is. However, we do have an emergency here. The control node is damaged and needs a replacement component. That means that we must—"

"I understand. Lyova and I will start to unload the bombs."

By the time he returned, Tonya had determined that the computer was functioning nominally and that the node, except for the obviously damaged connection box, was in perfect working order. Manarov positioned himself carefully in front of the machine and fastened his suit straps to the matching clips on the node for extra stability. That done, he pulled the replacement box out of his sack with one hand and a pair of snips with the other. Tonya, floating lazily a few meters away, was watching the Moon rise.

Sirje Saarmula examined the series of numbers scrolling up in the text box inset in his CRT's analog gauge simulation. He looked again at his flight engineer, who had stopped typing and was watching his monitor. "Are you ready?"

Volodya looked over, numb-faced. "Ready when you are. The new figures only change our position by about fourteen meters. I've advanced our burn to sixteen-ten-thirty in, on the mark, twelve minutes, fifteen seconds. Mark."

"All right, Volodya, breaking dock. Here goes." He trackballed to the AUX icon and pulled down a menu, then clicked on the Docking Operations screen. The pseudoanalog graphics were replaced by a detailed representation of the spacecraft and asteroid, surrounded by picturesque icons. He clicked on Undock and then manually flipped a switch on his console. *Molotochek*'s hard dock winch unwound with a barely audible *fft,* but he felt no change in the spacecraft. "Hard dock broken." He flipped another switch, and, although nothing appeared to change, they were free, flying alongside the asteroid. Before *Molotochek* could fall, Saarmula grasped his controls and pulled back. Thrusters responded, and the separation graph began to spread. Five meters. The cheesy surface began to recede in his video monitor, and a large, dark rectangle appeared: *Molotochek*'s shadow. Ten meters. Twenty. He shut it off. It didn't take much to reach escape velocity. Slowly the asteroid dwindled to its distant, irregular aspect. On the video monitor, star images began to come out.

It took another three minutes to orient the craft in the correct direction for the separation burn. There was a maximally effective way to do all this, and Saarmula liked to do things in the optimum way. The gravity of Earth and, to a much lesser extent, the Moon were already being felt and things were more complicated.

Volodya watched his numbers. For the most part, the hurry that had gotten him through the node repair and bomb placement was gone now, replaced by the internalized set of responses to the machinery that he had built up through the years. Machine-boy, he thought. The description had been inappropriate for poor old Bronstein. When it came right down to it, he had died of humanity, plain and simple. And Saarmula didn't fit, either. They seemed somehow to maintain their exaggerated, emotional sense of self despite the rigors of spaceflight. The Estonian still was unreadable, and the gross violation of regulation on Sinuhe made him all the more incomprehensible. A wanton machine, maybe. But, in a pinch, he could be trusted. He guessed that, in the end, that was all that really counted. The numbers commanded him, and he said, "Three minutes."

Seryozha jerked a thumb back at the living quarters. "Shall we warn them or let them go flying?" He smiled facetiously.

Volodya switched on the intercom, shaking his head. "Tonya? Lyova? Time to get into your acceleration cots." Perhaps we *should* let them go flying. Volodya shook his head; his job should not include mother hen duties. The two appeared at the hatch and crowded through at the same time, quickly strapping in.

The burn was over before they had a chance to accommodate themselves to the familiar noises and inertial forces. In the video monitor, Sinuhe was already being lost among the stars. Volodya switched to the view from his navigator scope, and a newly reconstituted asteroid began to shrink much more slowly. He watched it for a moment and then referred back to the numbers.

"Speed relative to Sinuhe twenty-two kilometers per second. Separation five hundred forty kilometers. Looks perfect."

Tonya, unstrapped, sailed up, stopping himself against the forward hatch cover. "How long until the detonation?"

More numbers fraught with meaning. Volodya studied his CRT. "About half an hour."

Saarmula grinned. "We don't want to be nearby. We'll get a good bang at twenty thousand kilometers, but not enough to hurt anything."

Suddenly the encoded TTY made its tinny ding. "What the? . . . Volodya?"

Manarov entered his response code and the amber words appeared, scrolling up to fill the corner of the screen.

GLAVKOSMOS MISSION 04-M-17B
08 MAY 2003 / 16:22:00 MST
CREW OF MOLOTOCHEK ITV

RED ALPHA

TWO MATED UNITED STATES ORBITAL
TRANSFER VEHICLES LAUNCHED FROM
VICINITY OF EISENHOWER ON
COURSE FOR SINUHE FLYBY.
ESTIMATED TIME OF FLYBY 16:55:00 MST.
OBSERVE BUT DO NOT INTERFERE.
NEXT MESSAGE 17:00:00 MST.

Saarmula sat back. "What do they mean by 'interfere'? Just how in the name of Christ could we interfere?"

"Beats the hell out of me." Volodya turned back to his console. "We can probably pick them up on our radar. Let's see, they should be about . . . there. Huh. There they are, all right. Moving pretty quick for tugs."

Anton corkscrewed down and caught himself in a position to look at the radar output. "What in the world can the Americans be thinking of? They won't be able to recover them after the flyby, not at those speeds. What a waste."

Volodya rubbed his mouth with his fingers. "Mmm. And they are going to be awfully close to Sinuhe during the detonation. I sure hope they are EMP-hardened or they won't even get the information they were sent for."

"All their stuff is hard, Volodya," said Seryozha. "From what I understand, the new microchips can take huge surges without being damaged."

"It'll have to be *very* hard at that range." Manarov started typing. "Well, let's get this can turned around. I'm going to acquire the node's signal."

Lyova, feeling useless, floated just below the ceiling. Things, he thought, are just moving too fast.

The on-board computer of USAF OTV-2 knew who and where it was. Drifting between the stars, its sensors scanned the heavens, there, the Earth, the Moon, distant *Eisenhower,* nearby Sinuhe, the rock of heart's desire. . . : A little less than one kilometer away, OTV-1 flew on a parallel, slightly convergent course. OTV-2 twinkled its thrusters briefly and full parallelism was reestablished. OTV-1 would reach Sinuhe a full nine seconds before -2, commit its act first. Bomb one would shatter the rock, bomb two would scatter the fragments.

Of . . . me. OTV-2's on-board computer was based on a Texas Instruments 99048-4C microprocessor and 4096-bit data bus, the heart and mind of the autonomous SDI modules. It wasn't consciousness, exactly, but . . . the programmers had concentrated on making an obedient yet autonomous machine. The paths of the rule-based AI sieves were very complex indeed. Do what you're told. If the situation isn't covered by canned instructions, figure out what to do and do it. The programmers were very good, but they couldn't think of everything. The compulsion was: Do *some*thing. The end result was a slightly unpredictable effect, the hallmark of a primitive intelligence.

What is that?

Sensors converged on the unknown object, floating a few thousand kilometers away from the flight path. Satellite, large, cryogenic. Extensive telemetry following the standard Soviet encoding scheme. Translations picked up engineering data from the vehicle and a real-time voice downlink channel. Hmm. OTV-2 knew that some vehicles were manned, but it didn't know how to tell which ones. In any case, the programmers' safety flags had not been set up with nuclear weapons in mind. The OTVs were primarily interested in being careful around spacesuited EVA situations. These people, if people they were, were remote from the locus of activity. Though OTV-2 knew to be careful with chemical energy, it had no knowledge of nuclear explosives. The concept of EMP was restricted to large cryomagnetic devices.

Signal from OTV-1: arming. Okay. Nine seconds, then arming as well. OTV-2 searched along its future path. All was well. It tried to search for a post-encounter path and found nothing. Very well: OTV-2 and its on-board computer will be consumed in the explosion. Me . . . *ME!*

The asteroid was thirty seconds away. Twenty-one seconds in the future, OTV-1, directly behind Sinuhe, would explode. Nine seconds after that . . . Me.

At twelve seconds to encounter, OTV-1 disappeared from view. Very well. Three seconds. Suddenly there was a bloom of bright light from behind the asteroid, nothing the sensors couldn't handle though. Odd. It should have been *much* brighter than that. Hmm. Obviously, OTV-1's warhead had failed. That puny explosion could be nothing more than the bomb trigger mechanism, and going off prematurely at that.

Tick. Tick. Tick. Nothing more. Apparently, OTV-1's bomb had failed to explode. This would have a severe and complicating impact on the mission. Surely there must be some change required in the plan. Down the sieve. A rule: Complete your mission, regardless, unless instructed by an external abort code. Very well. OTV-2 steered toward the surface of Sinuhe. One bomb would have to do the work of

two. Since the object was to shatter *and* scatter, proximity
would have to be maximized.

But, it's . . . me!

A moment of intense regret, then count

Five count

Four count

Three count

Two count

One . . .

The bomb worked.

# CHAPTER 10
## *May 8, 2003*

It was a beautiful May night, with the temperature well above freezing. Jack Mozingo, feeling the weight of his hibernation fat hanging over his belt like an apron filled with rocks, stood on the little hill he had made his own as a boy and looked down on the town of Nome, a scattershot of twinkles. "Come on, boy, you can do it, here, away from the noise." His dog, a small, brownish spaniel named Randy, scratched among the low, bare bushes and tried to find just the right spot.

This End-of-the-World crap had really gotten hold of his family. Marsha had taken the day off work and was glued to the TV. He'd had to make his own supper, and it'd turned out lousy, somehow overmicrowaved to the point where it was either leathery rubber or rubbery leather. He burped, getting another peculiar taste of shrimp. Randy was still looking. Goddamn TV. Ever since they'd gotten the new HD screen no one ever did anything but sit and watch like zombies. The HD had a lot going for it. Crisper picture, three fairly realistic-looking dimensions. But this, reality: The air smelled good, too. Made you feel younger. And who knew, something not completely homogenized might happen. "Ready yet?" Damn, it was a little chilly. His eyes were getting adapted to the dark, and he let his gaze travel across the dark sky, a befuddling number of stars spread out like low-res mist. You didn't see the stars on TV very often. "Oh, come on, we—"

What was that? He looked over to the west, where the sun set over Norton Sound. It's getting brighter. Shit. What is this, an atomic war? I thought I didn't have to worry about that anymore. Jee-sus. Maybe it *is* the End of the

World. What were they talking about? Oh yeah, an asteroid, hitting the Earth. Could this be it?

The light grew brighter, higher, casting a reflection on the sound. It had some shape now, a swollen flame forming in the sky. He looked around him on the ground. Randy was nowhere to be seen, and the bushes were casting long, skeletal shadows. Christ! It became blindingly bright, filling his eyes, but completely silent, like a ghost.

The thing seemed to wax violet, hurting, like it was burning a hole into his head. He turned away. It was *too* bright. Down below, you could see everything, as clear as noontime in the summer, the sky a funny color of gray, the clouds lit from beneath. The streetlights had gone out, and people were coming into the streets. He wondered if Marsha would come out. He couldn't see her.

In a moment, it began to wane again, turning yellow, then red, a glowing coal in the resumed blackness of night. He stumbled down the hill, running full speed for home.

The four of them were jammed into *Molotochek*'s flare shelter, hearts thudding softly as they waited. Time for curtain on the last act. It was a calculated risk, being here. They'd sealed the hatch and pressurized the capsule, but the tunnel had been left unflooded. There shouldn't be much radiation, in fact they should have been able to stay in the command module . . . but you just never *knew*. The control remotes were activated and the navigation scope's image of Sinuhe was a bright and shadowy figure in the shelter's lone viewscreen.

Odd. I *really* wish we could watch it out the CM porthole. Volodya smiled in the dimness. We probably could. It won't be *that* bright, not at this distance, and the window is ultraviolet opaque. . . .

"What's that?" asked Saarmula.

There was an angular irregular shadow moving across the sunlit surface of Sinuhe. Volodya squinted at the bright speck above Sinuhe's limb. Has to be one of the American OTVs. Fucking closer than they said. "They're going to lose those things." He glanced at the control panel's digital readout. Two seconds. "All right. Here it comes." They all tensed, ludicrous under these conditions, but inevitable.

Suddenly the viewscreen went black as the ship's optics protected themselves. Pulse. The screen came back on and a brilliant globe of light, black-cored by the camera, was swelling beside the asteroid.

"Gaseous debris front in twenty seconds," said Saarmula. "How are the electronics?"

Volodya scanned his instrument panel. "Everything looks good. . . ."

And the viewscreen went black again. The instrument panel lights went out and the digital readout died.

"What happened?" It was Serebryakov, his voice high and thin.

"Uh." Volodya reached out and tapped a couple of switches. Nothing. "Ummm . . ."

Abruptly, the lights in the flare shelter went out and a fat spark jumped somewhere in the darkness. Saarmula said, "Oh, shit." And, under that, someone could be heard to whimper softly. Chishak.

Manarov activated the emergency battery backup and the flare shelter's low-wattage red engineering lights came on. Four blood-colored faces stared at the control panel, but the screen, along with the instrument panel, stayed dark.

"Fuck," said Serebryakov, "what's going *on*?" He was staring wide-eyed at Volodya: Tell me *something*, man. Anything!

Volodya let out a breath, looked at his wristwatch, and sighed. It seemed to be working. "Two seconds." And one, and . . . *Molotochek* bucked slightly as the shock from the steering charge went by. Now then . . .

Another second or two . . . Uhh. And they were flattened against the flare shelter's walls as the ship went into a sudden, hard spin. The engineering lights went out and where the earlier burst had been there was a bright electric arc that illuminated the inside of the capsule like a strobe. Chishak screamed, *"Nooo . . ."* and then the arc snapped off, metal glowing dull red, fading fast, where it had been.

Son of a bitch. The manual controls are in the CM. . . . Volodya stirred in the darkness, levering himself away from the wall, rummaging for the tool kit he knew was there, with its tiny flashlight. "We've got to get *out* of here!" he said.

"Hold it!" That was Saarmula. "What do we know about the external environment?"

Volodya shined the light at his face for a moment, reading a wan but controlled expression, then pointed it at a manual gauge on the inside of the capsule egress hatch. "We know there's still full pressure in the tunnel." *And be damned glad we didn't flood it.*

"Right. You know damned well that's not all I meant."

Volodya put his hand on the hatch sealing-lock lever. "I know. Look, there's an EVA suit in the tunnel. . . ."

"That won't afford much protection."

"No. In fact, I don't think we should bother. The ionizing radiation has come and gone, as has the neutron pulse. Bomb debris can't get through the hull, not alphas or anything on that order. There won't be any induced radiation. . . ."

"We may have to eject. . . ."

"We're dead if we do. *Molotochek* was trajectoried at a five-hundred-kilometer hyperbola. 'Just in case.' "

"No reentry, then."

"Nope."

Saarmula sighed, seeming to grow calmer with the escaping air. "All right. Let's get out there then."

Volodya started to crank the lock lever.

Serebryakov, stunned, still flattened to the capsule wall, listened to the terse and cryptic sentences of this exchange with growing bewilderment. *I just can't understand what's going on here.* His eyes were stinging. "What are you talking about? Our bomb just wasn't that powerful. . . ."

Volodya stopped cranking and turned to look at him, his face lit from below by the flashlight, looking like some hollow-eyed evil spirit. *"Our* bomb . . ." he said, and resumed cranking the door.

"Our bomb?" Anton felt something sinking in. *Our* bomb. *Good Christ . . .*

"It was a cold, cold war . . ." whispered Chishak. "They regretted losing us as the Enemy."

Anton nodded slowly to himself, listening to the harsh ratcheting of the hatch mechanism. *Of course. The doctrine of capitalism implies competition—between men, between companies, between nations. And without it there is stagnation . . . a little death of sorts. You can't win, if there's no one to beat. . . .* The hatch popped open with a soft sucking noise. It was dark in the transfer tunnel as well.

Volodya pushed the hatch open the rest of the way and crawled through, shining his light around. "No damage."

It felt really odd as he crept along the floor to the next hatch, at the other end of the meter-wide passageway. *Gravity,* or rather its inertial-frame analog, was holding him down, but some force kept plucking at his back. He illuminated the hatch environmental gauges. "Full pressure in the living quarters. I'm going in."

"Right behind you," said Saarmula. As he crawled he marveled at the sensation. *Almost a tenth-g! We must be spinning like a top! Shit. I wonder if the solar panels are gone?*

Volodya cranked the second hatch-lock lever rapidly. When the rubber gasket seal popped open, red light flooded in. "Engineering systems still operative." He pushed the hatch open the rest of the way and stared. There was junk all over the room, food packages dumped from storage units, equipment, puddles of water and whatnot, all of it plastered to the walls. And there was a strong organic smell . . . evidently the zero-g toilet had undergone some kind of active cycle during the . . . event. Somewhere, under the shit, was the faint, building smell of ozone.

"We'd better check for fires. . . ." He pulled himself forward by the hatch rim and swung his legs out. "What a goddamn mess." He straightened up, and suddenly was plucked upward, falling onto the ceiling.

Saarmula crawled through after him and crouched down by the floor, looking up. "The ship's centerline is about at crotch level."

Lying on his back, draped over a vent pipe, Manarov grunted, then rolled over slowly. No wonder things were scattered about. He hadn't fully understood what was going on. *A worse mistake than Slava ever made.* He crawled slowly toward the porthole, climbing over pipes and loose cabling, then down the wall to the window. The universe was flipping by steadily, black sky punctuated by a region of bright, fading red light. He tried to squint into the mist as it went by again. Somewhere, in there, lay Sinuhe. The scene reminded him of the bloody enhanced-color images of Comet Halley sent back by the *VeGas,* but the scene was going by too fast for the accumulation of meaningful detail. It would have to wait. At least the port solar panel was intact, protruding from its place on the side of the CM.

He crawled over to the propulsion control-room hatch, followed by Saarmula. The other two men were just crawling out of the flare shelter's transfer tunnel, staring about at the wrecked room, horrified. "Shit," whispered Serebryakov, making his way over to the porthole.

Volodya looked at the gauge on the hatch. "All right." He cranked open the mechanism and they went into another red-lit room.

The shambles here was less intense, just because there was less to fly around. He made his way to his workstation, while Saarmula went to the left-hand seat. "Right. Engineering is on, so we can do standard control power-up from battery." He reached out and flipped the appropriate switch. The red lights flickered, then, section by section, the control panel lights came on, needles of gauges stirring as power fed back through the system.

Saarmula could be heard to sigh softly, a sound of enormous relief. "Good enough," he muttered.

"Right. Now we've got about two hours to see if we can straighten things out." Volodya scanned the instruments, then looked at his overhead panels. "Son of a bitch. All the breakers are tripped."

Saarmula nodded slowly. "That's a good sign as I recall."

"Yes." He reached up and reset the first one in the top row. The ship's principal lighting came on and the engineering lights went out. In the bright yellow-white of the fluorescents, both men looked a good deal better, less frightened and drawn. "So."

Volodya reached out to the power-center circuit-breaker panel and reset six more switches. "Main power bus reactivated."

"We've been lucky," said Saarmula.

"Goddamned lucky." Volodya reset the switches for the reaction control system.

When the system's ready lights came on, Saarmula reached out and grabbed his joysticks. "Good enough. I'll stop this roll now. You finish putting things back together."

As the thrusters began to thump and hiss, Volodya turned his attention to powering up the Dozhdevik computer system. Its screen came up garbled and flickering, and he thought, Damned lucky, all right . . . But lucky *enough*? We'll see.

·     ·     ·

September 15, 2001. Volodya stood in Payload Assembly Engineering Bay No. 6 of YKK-MIK, the Shuttle Checkout Facility of Baikonur Cosmodrome. In the Shuttle/Energiya Integration Bay behind him, an unmanned payload canister was suspended on a platform above the railbed below, waiting for a fully assembled booster to be brought on its erector/transporter from the nearby Energiya-MIK facility and slid underneath. The canister's payload doors yawned open, waiting for their passenger.

Before him, standing upright on its payload truss device, was Lunar Landing Vehicle (Interim) *Oryol*. Nearby, riggers were preparing the strongback attachment that the overhead bridge crane would use to tip the little spaceship on its side, then lift it into the canister payload bay.

Little. These were relative terms. At eleven meters tall, *Oryol* towered over Volodya, stacked like a high-tech three-layer wedding cake, with an outsize decoration on top. The lowermost tier was the descent stage, simply a fat sideways disk, mostly fuel tanks, with four squat landing legs. Underneath, the protruding snouts of the four big engines pointed slightly away from one another. The middle tier was the smaller disk of the descent stage instrument unit, a casque of batteries and avionics, with three solar panels folded accordion-style into their mounting brackets. Once on the surface they would be extended out to lie on the ground. Above that, the ascent stage propulsion unit was four bright spheres bolted together in a truss-work, the two ascent engines peeking out through an open space below. And finally . . .

You had to laugh. There it was again: The manned section of *Oryol* was built from *Soyuz* components: the cylindrical life support system, the bell-shaped reentry vehicle, the spherical airlock compartment with the docking ring. The differences were few: no solar panels, for they would be relying on batteries for the brief ascent; no heat shield, either. This ship would never come back to Earth. From the airlock hatch, ten meters up, Zarkov, Artyukhin, and Serebryakov would have a long climb down.

Volodya closed the cover on the clipboard he was holding, the checklist completed, and turned to the technician at his side. "That's it then, Sasha. Everything is ready."

Sasha Pilyugin put his hands in the pockets of his crisp,

white lab coat. "I guess so. But then, I don't have to fly in her." He glanced over at Manarov. "And neither do you."

Volodya tucked the board under his arm and stared back, curiously. "I'd give a great deal to be on board when they take her down, Sasha. You know that."

"Maybe so. But I still think this is a stupid idea. We should wait for the LLV(M). What's to be gained by this?"

"Four years. Maybe five."

"Right. And maybe ten years to be lost! Volodya, this ship is untested! You know about the ambiguous combustion stability results in the prototype ascent engine. What if they can't get back?"

"What if? Chelomei Design Bureau says the problem is beaten."

" 'Chelomei says . . .' You want to stake *your* life on *that*?"

"Isn't that *just* what we do, every time we go up? In this instance . . . I'd be more than willing to."

Pilyugin turned to stare at *Oryol* again, silent for a little while. "Well. Maybe I would be, too." He turned back to Manarov. "How soon?"

"We're going up to *Mir* on October first, then leaving for *Mechta* on the fifteenth. If all goes according to plan, *Serpachek* should be dispatched with *Oryol* on the twenty-fifth. Landing is scheduled for 7 November, 2001."

"Happy anniversary," Pilyugin held out his hand. "Good luck, Volodya, I wish you could take her down, too."

He took the hand, pressing it gently. "Maybe some other time." He turned and slowly walked away across the concrete, toward the external access door. Maybe some other time. Maybe so. And maybe I *don't* wish I was flight engineer of the LLV(I). Hell. The time will come. LLV(M) will be ready sooner or later. No later than 2006, they keep saying. And then? Then, what? LLV(M) is designed as a reusable Mars lander. . . .

They keep saying 2010. And I will be forty-nine years old. Mars. Time to go.

It's just *not* out of the question. Not out of the question at all.

He walked away into bright desert sunshine.

·     ·     ·

Anton floated in the middle of the dining room, fire extinguisher held crosswise before his chest. There was a big spurt of foam clinging to the side of the refrigerator apparatus and on the bulkhead beside it. The last gray curls of smoke were drifting in all directions, dispersing on the air currents. In the background, thrusters were still bumping softly but the sense of inertial pseudogravity was gone. "I guess it's out." His heart was hammering in his chest, making him twitch in midair, had been for many minutes now. Christ! What's happening to us? "You see any more smoke?"

Chishak was twisting carefully in the air behind him, scanning the walls of the ship, looking at places where he knew there would be hidden wiring. "No. Nothing. That must have been the only one."

"Smell anything?"

"Just our shit, Tonya." Chishak kicked off from the side of the table and glided back to the *ubornaya* waste management unit, stopping himself with his hands against the outer frame. "Tkhah . . . There's a solid globe of stink here." He slid the folding vinyl door open and looked in. *"Fuck . . ."* There was awe in his tone.

Serebryakov drifted up and looked over his shoulder. The zero-g toilet, always a temperamental item, had, under stress, burped once, bringing up its dinner, several days worth from the look of it. There must have been some force to the explosion, for the semidried waste material, shit, chemicals, and who knew what, had been thrown onto the opposite wall, making a big star pattern, many-hued, but dominated by earth colors. Little fragments were beginning to break loose and drift about the space within.

Chishak shut the door and latched it. "So much for that."

"What if someone has to go?"

Lev grinned. Even at death's door . . . "We have an emergency supply of sticky-bags around here someplace." He pushed over to his bedroom and looked in. There were no signs of fire, but everything had broken loose. Most of the room's contents were balled up, drifting as a single mass up near the ceiling.

Impatient to find out what was happening now that he had done his job, Serebryakov headed forward into the propulsion control room. The smell of shit disappeared abruptly as he went through the hatch. Interesting. The little brown molecules hadn't had a chance to diffuse this far yet. Saarmula was up in the airlock module, poking around, holding a fire extinguisher in one hand; Manarov was seated at his console, staring at the Dozhdevik's display screen. "Status?"

Volodya looked up at him. "The ship's more or less okay. We'll get home. . . . The worst thing is our navigation data's gone from the computer. Something's wrong with the CPU, as well, but I don't know what. We can live without it, for a mere retrofire to low Earth-orbit. . . ."

Anton went over to his acceleration station, where he habitually stored the DEU when not using it. It was still tied down and its bright plastic case appeared to be undamaged. All right. He untied it and popped the case open. The screen and keycaps lit up with their normal display. So. There is some truth to Saarmula's statement. He pressed the keycap labeled AUTOCHECK and the screen shifted through a number of changes. ROM, RAM, Bubble, PROM-port, CD-RAW, BUS-path, driver cards, motherboard integrity . . . All okay. The thing was tough.

He looked up at Volodya. "Maybe we won't need to. The DEU still works fine. And everything you ever loaded to its memory is still in the bubble."

Manarov floated back to him, bumping his hands on the overhead to stop, feet swinging down to the floor. "Then the navigation data's in there, since I was using it for the math. We can rig it to run controls through the Dozhdevik's data bus in about ten minutes. . . ."

"Well . . ."

"What's wrong?"

"Volodya, what about the asteroid?"

"We'll have to leave it. The mission's shot."

"That's not what I mean."

Manarov looked at him, face expressionless. *If I wait, he'll say it.*

"Volodya, that was a pretty big explosion. Where's Sinuhe *going*?"

Uhh . . . "Not to Earth-orbit, certainly. Probably back into space somewhere, where we'll never see it again. But . . ." *Right.* "We'd better find out. Sirje! See if you can raise Mission Control, please." He turned back to Anton.

"Let's see if the telescope still works, and the main rendez-vous radar. That might tell us enough. . . ."

Saarmula palmed the trackball in small, scooting increments, looking at the downloads from the internal self-check of the electronics. As Volodya had said, most looked undamaged. The high-gain X-band antenna they'd been using for voice communication appeared to be completely out. The low-gain S-band, however, was perfectly functional but improperly pointed. Well, they wouldn't be looking for an S-band downlink, but some bright techie would figure it out. Click on S-band, click on Manual Override, click on Voice Com, click on Input Parameters. Let's see now, ascension forty-seven, azimuth eighty-nine. He watched the graphic readout from the antenna; slow peaking, lock on. Got it!

He put on his headset. Nothing. "Testing. Testing. This is *Molotochek*. Repeat, this is *Molotochek* sending on the S-band. One two three four five six seven eight nine, hello, hello, is anybody out there?" Nothing.

Volodya and Tonya were working feverishly, the former at his workstation keyboard, the latter trailing from the long cable connected to the DEU, hanging at midcabin. They ran through a series of subprograms, dumping them from the Dozhdevik into the DEU to be analyzed, translated, and implemented. Life support, at least, plus some of the basic electronics, would have to be run from the DEU before the ship computer could be disabled.

Manarov retrieved the tool kit from a small bin on the bulkhead and took out a large Phillips screwdriver. He tackled the sheet-metal screws on the enclosing panel first. Soviet engineering didn't skimp on essentials like screws, and there were at least twenty holding the panel in place.

Anton marveled at the man's skill under pressure: even under normal circumstances he couldn't unscrew a screw without slipping out of the slot three or four times, but this screwdriver spun like a gyrostablized power tool. Shortly the partition folded back to reveal a tangled mess of wiring.

Volodya leaned back and said, "Well, comrades, at last we see the ghost in the machine. Seryozha, switch over to manual control. Tonya, I'll need you to help me with these."

It took a good fifteen minutes to patch the DEU into the

Dozhdevik primary I/O controller card, clipping the wires from the sliced-open serial cable directly into the corresponding plugs with little plastic clips, Skotch-Loks manufactured under license in Lithuania. It was crude, but it would work, after a fashion. "All right," said Volodya. "Here we are." He put the DEU down over the hole and fixed it in place with a fat piece of fiber-tape, then motioned to Anton.

After pressing the key, Tonya said, "The emulation's working."

Volodya looked tired. "I guess it should. It's magic, after all. Thank God the Dozhdevik is such a primitive machine."

The navigation scope, at full magnification, was not helpful in piecing together what had happened to the asteroid. At this range, it was only a slowly variable point of light, spinning with a period of about thirty-five minutes. Their infrared telescope seemed to indicate that it was hotter and slightly smaller than it had been. Tentatively, Volodya began to turn *Molotochek* back toward the asteroid, vaguely feeling the tug of an unknown compulsion.

On the headset, Saarmula could hear a phased whistle sliding up and down the musical scales, whooping and stuttering. He was reminded suddenly of himself as a boy, tuning his shoddy shortwave radio trying to pick up the jammed signal of Radio Free Europe. Even from Tallinn, considerably west of the main jamming transmitters, it was never easy, and he spent more time listening to the ethereal music of shortwave interference than the transmissions themselves. You could get to like it, like the smell of gasoline. Techno-nostalgia. Speaking of smells. The acrid odor from the exploded toilet was becoming nauseatingly omnipresent. He tried not to breathe through his nose. He would try the radio again. *"Molotochek* on the air. Come *on,* dammit. How long will it take you to figure out—"

There was a sharp series of musical popping sounds, growing louder as they rose in frequency. "—terr . . . terference . . . diation effect."

Seryozha turned to the others. "I've got 'em." He switched over to the speakerphone, which emitted a series of blatts and squeals. He looked noncommittally at Manarov, wrinkling his nose, and said, "I guess you should try to talk to them."

Volodya listened carefully as the radio snarled in his earphones. Over machine-gun static, an unidentifiable voice was saying, ". . . unable to copy your engineering telemetry . . . ," a swirling hiss-sputter-whine drowned it out briefly, then, ". . . your report good enough. Ship seems serviceable. Do you copy that, *Molotochek*?"

"Understood, Capcom. We are able to continue the mission."

Snarl, snarl, *grind* . . . The earth's Van Allen belts were inflated with bomb debris and excess radiation. The loud buzzsaw suddenly declined to a fluttering hiss, punctuated by faint burps. ". . . radar-track computations are complete. Your perigee now eighteen hundred kilometers, ground-track over southern Indian Ocean at forty-seven-degree inclination . . ."

"What about Sinuhe?" The static swirled up like heavy snow as he spoke. "What about the *pieces*?" The urge to shout uselessly into the microphone was overpowering.

". . . getting to that. They are both, repeat *both,* headed for Earth impact. Large fragment trajectoried to North Atlantic, probably southeast of Greenland. Small fragment targeted for somewhere in western Europe, probably southern France . . ." The static went squeeooorrr . . .

Volodya found himself staring at an equally expressionless Saarmula. Southern France? Maybe on the central massif, where the French kept the last land-based scraps of an antiquated *Force de Frappe*? He tried to picture the bright-green countryside, sun-dappled meadows and the like. The scene was dominated by a towering mushroom cloud, by a vast and darkened sky. He turned and looked back at the other two men, floating by their stations, listening over headphones.

Serebryakov said, "This is it then. The little one will flatten France. And the big one will wreck the earth's climate."

"Fuck . . ." whispered Chishak, closing his eyes. Inside his eyelids, a crystal clear movie of Chernobyl began to play, pall of black smoke rising to blot out the sun, helicopters flitting about like helpless gnats, men dying as he watched.

"I guess so." Manarov turned his attention back to the roar in his headset. "Understood, Capcom. Both pieces will impact Earth." I hope *Mir* will be on the other side of the

Earth when it happens. Not that that would do any good. The ocean impact could jet debris back to orbital height.

". . . calculations are running on the Cray, almost completed. Perigee braking charge on surface of Sinuhe probably not intact. Your spare charge being factored into calculation . . ."

Factored in? What the hell were they talking about?

"My God," said Saarmula.

Right.

"But," said Anton, "the big piece is *tumbling*. How the fuck are we going to . . ."

Volodya sighed. "Don't know. We'll have to *talk* about this."

"Talk, my ass," said Chishak. "They're ordering us to die."

"Maybe so," said Saarmula, "or we live and millions perish."

Volodya said, "Understood, Capcom. Call us when you've finished the calculations. We'll discuss our options up here and see what we think is possible." He pulled off his headset and floated up from the engineering station. "We have some thinking to do. Lyova, could you see if any of the sandwiches have survived?"

Serebryakov gave the man an astonished look. He wants to eat, at a time like this? With that smell? He nodded slowly. Perhaps it will help us to think. Suddenly, the specter of his death seemed remote but certain, like a storm darkening the horizon.

Mikhail Sergeevich Gorbachev tapped the table with his pen until the talking subsided. He felt weary, and as old as his age. Around the table, the familiar faces looked at him as if he alone could put right this terrible situation. His sparring partners, friends, if that wasn't stretching the word too far. People who, like himself, had been attracted to power and influence. Perhaps even occasionally moved by true Soviet altruism, a desire to see mankind transcend its petty economic nearsightedness. Who knew how they *really* regarded him? When you got down to the nub of things, who really cared? He caught a familiar glance from Ponomarev, and acknowledged it with a nod. The bastard had known, he was sure of that.

"Good afternoon, comrades. I have called this emergency meeting of the Politburo for obvious reasons. You have all been briefed on the disaster in space that has unfolded today. The Americans have done the unthinkable. After all these years of pulling back, we are once again on the brink of war. Fortunately, not the horrible European war that was envisaged for so long. But one almost as bad, with the potential for unlimited escalation. My friends, as I have been saying for fifteen years, we must do everything possible to avoid this war. I have sent a note to President Wren expressing my sincerest—"

Ponomarev slammed a fist against the glass of his inset monitor, producing an odd, hollow sound. "Wait a moment, Mikhail Sergeevich. This is not a situation in which we can simply have our tea and cookies and declare everything to be right again. The United States has engaged in a coldblooded, unprovoked attack against our country. Even as we speak, the asteroid and its offspring are heading for Earth impact. Surely we must respond quickly or they will continue their bold aggression."

Gorbachev nodded. Of course this is going to be their tack. "Oh, we shall respond, Comrade General. The question is, just how should we respond?"

"The moment is rife with opportunity," barked Guptev. "They have transgressed, violated every convention of international law. We have a right to respond."

"I agree," said Yuvash, a bloated, phlegmatic Moldavian who rarely contributed anything. "*Eisenhower* is the obvious target. Their obnoxious Star Wars program will be forever silenced."

"An eye for an eye," said Blok melodramatically.

Gorbachev smiled as warmly as he knew how. "Come, come, my friends. The fate of the asteroid is not yet fully known. The stalwart crew of *Molotochek* are closing in, preparing to divert it back into space. The small piece that was knocked off, no bigger than about forty meters across, *will* hit, somewhere in the sparsely populated Pyrenees. This will be a misfortune, certainly, but it is hardly worth starting a war over. Let the Spanish and French seek redress."

Vacillation. It was always hard to get one's mind around this concept of global war; most spoke from the gut, from the atavistic past. How did one speak to that part of people?

Ponomarev cleared his throat. "Comrade General Secretary, you have presided over the disarmament of our great union. You have made concession after concession both to the West and to the hooligans who want this country to return to the days of Rasputin and his friends. We find ourselves, after eighteen years of continual retreat, without direction, rudderless, unable to even commit ourselves fully to socialism. And, I submit, it has been your weakness that has brought us to this state. It is time to turn away from *perestroika* and weakness. Come, my friends. Back to the glorious past . . ."

Guptev grunted. This was too much. Ponomarev had overplayed his hand. Even idiots like Blok knew there was no going back. Gorbachev waited for it to sink in, then casually presented his plan. "Well," he said. "We have seen what an overly emotional response can bring. What we need to do is prepare a rational response, rationally evaluate the pros and the cons. Move forward, not backward."

Someone said, "Hear, hear."

"I suggest that we secure all our land-based forces immediately to prevent any local incidents which might arise because of the strong feelings on both sides. At the same time, the strategic forces of the Red Fleet should stand out to sea, ready for whatever response is . . . needed."

Ponomarev's face began to darken ominously.

Gorbachev, ignoring him, continued. "Should the unthinkable happen, should the asteroid somehow land in the Soviet Union, it is obvious that we must respond quickly and in kind, in order to make our point. *Eisenhower,* of course, is vulnerable, and is an appropriate target in many ways, but it may be too small." He took a deep breath and looked squarely at the general. "If Sinuhe strikes, our submarines will have to unleash their vengeance on the United States." That got a surprised look from Ponomarev. "However . . . as things stand, our country will not suffer any devastating impact. The United States will suffer such a loss of prestige, no matter what happens, that it will falter and sicken as a society. I did not want it to happen this way. I did not anticipate that they were capable of such great stupidity. But in the end it will be the same. We will win without striking a single blow."

The vote in favor of the general secretary's plan was unanimous.

When it was all over, Ponomarev motioned Gorbachev aside. "Well, Comrade General Secretary. When the inevitable comes to pass, I *will* hold you to your word."

Gorbachev looked at him somberly. "Never fear, Comrade General. If it comes to that, history will keep my promises."

Time was making the signal get better as Earth's radiation belts and ionosphere started to calm down. Popovich, taking his turn at Capcom, sat before his console in Mission Control at Zvyozdnii Gorodok, staring at the microphone. All right. What do I say? I have to tell them something. But what? He was dreading the words he knew he couldn't put off any longer. Speak then! "Umm . . . Sorry it took so long to figure out what you were doing. All hell is breaking out down here. Do you know what happened?" His voice was strained almost to the point of breaking. "Those goddamn . . . Yanks sent up thermonuclear weapons. It's . . . an appalling mess. . . . Whatever their intention, it didn't work. The asteroid broke into two pieces, both of which are going to hit the Earth."

The voice over the loudspeaker, filtered through dense static, sounded a bit like Saarmula. "We know."

Popovich sighed and took another breath. "Well. Glad to hear that. We, uh . . . have a plan down here . . . but I'm afraid you aren't going to like it."

Another staticky voice, possibly Manarov. "A plan?" There was a fuzzed-out pause, then, "Go ahead."

Oh, God damn it. Why does it have to be me? "If . . ." Shit. The words came tumbling out: "If you can get back to the big piece quickly enough, there's a chance that you could still divert it with your backup bomb. We're working on the particulars."

Another brief pause, then a third voice, clearly recognizable as Dr. Chishak. "What . . . aren't we going to like?"

Popovich started to say something, stuttered, started again. "Once you match courses with Sinuhe Major, it will be extremely difficult for you to pull out of your dive. Atmospheric reentry will occur. Look, none of this is definitive yet. You may be able to get away with as little as fifteen g's. Think about it. But think about it fast." There, it was out. A hand fell lightly on his shoulder and he looked up. Dunaev.

"Let me have the microphone, please." When Popovich had handed it over, the director of Glavkosmos stared reflectively at it for a moment, then shrugged. Nothing to do but speak the piece as instructed. "This would be an encoded transmission, except it's clear that your TTY isn't working. This is a Red Gamma message from the general secretary himself. Quote. Stop it if you can. Save the world from its folly. Unquote. End Red Gamma message."

Aboard *Molotochek*, listening to the words, Saarmula felt enveloped by an air of unreality. He looked around at them all. "So . . . Do we have a choice?"

Volodya followed his gaze, wondered at the blanching Chishak and at Serebryakov, eyes closed, shaking his head slowly. Now we find out the relative virtues of old and new. "Fifteen g's isn't so bad. Although I would guess that's a low estimate."

Tonya opened his eyes. The cabin looked unnaturally clear and bright. "The longer we take to decide the worse it will be."

"I don't have enough information to make any sort of informed decision." Lyova, who had looked other people's death in the eye so many times, now looked, indisputably, at his own. It was a rancorous, ugly thing, in a way not a part of him at all. However, "I say that . . . we have to do it."

Seryozha smiled, looking suddenly haggard. He brushed his hair back as he habitually did, and it fell into place. "Then I suppose it's unanimous."

Volodya started up the navigation control program on the DEU, noticing the different fonts and resolution used by the machine. He activated the wedge routine which substituted arrow keys for the Dozhdevik's trackball, and began to upload the newest positions for *Molotochek*, Sinuhe, and the Earth. Factoring through the mathematics quickly, using the routines they'd written during the break in communications, he produced a preliminary transfer orbit that could be refined on the fly. When the course was laid in, he called up the Main Engine menu and started a countdown.

"Everybody in positions, please." Again a faint trickle of annoyance. Silly. "On my mark, exactly one minute till main engine ignition. Mark."

Anton once again fastened the straps across his chest and

waist. The cloying, foul smell of the toilet worked at his resolve, made dignity impossible. He remembered Poe's short story about the Norwegian whirlpool. "The Maelstrom," it was called. An image of diving into the horrible clutch of the water to retrieve, what? a little bit of flotsam. And looking up from beneath the surface of the sea, being hopelessly pulled down. Sucked down. We all have to die, he told himself. All of us, sooner or later. It is not as though I am anything special. I die—a baby is born, like in the song. The equation is preserved. Nothing lost, nothing gained. Bah! This really *is* useless. A sardonic self-pity bit at his guts.

The engines lit off like distant thunder.

Sinuhe loomed once more in the video screens, looking substantially different. The burn to match the asteroid's course and speed had been executed perfectly by the DEU, and they were tracking with it to a precision of a few centimeters per second.

Tonya, drawn by an almost morbid curiosity, examined the asteroid closely, trying to quantify the changes. The DEU was too busy to act as image enhancer, so they had to make do with the raw television. Much was hidden, but much could be made out. It was obvious that the silicate spur had been broken off by the impact, leaving the narrow end of the asteroid flat, dominated by jagged fractures. A large section near the wide end had been fused and melted by the heat of the explosion, in many places rendered almost smooth. The smaller craters and cracks had been, by and large, melted away. Only a few large, shallow circles, like eyes, evidenced themselves.

The asteroid's spin rate was truly impressive, and even with the reduced roughness it was easy to make out details being gorged down by the terminator. In addition to its stately, nearly imperceptible ten-hour day, oriented around the long axis, a short-axis component, a tumble really, of maybe thirty-five minutes had been added. What did that translate into? Let's see . . . if it were a sphere . . . he felt a twitch of resentment. A little more than two kilometers an hour? I could outcrawl the terminator!

He remembered the detailed analysis of the fast rotators he had done for Carla's paper, so many years ago already. A few largish asteroids rotated faster than two hours, but now there was one with a period shorter than an hour. Then again, this was the only one that had been hit by a thermonuclear weapon. Hardly the result of a stochastic process, unless that was what you considered human history to be. . . .

Tonya continued the calculations in his head. Son of a bitch! "I hate to bring this up, but the asteroid's centrifugal force at its surface is greater than its escape velocity. Anything not anchored to it will be hurled off into space."

Manarov considered the implications. "Damn it . . ." He squinted at the TV image and said, "The control node and docking unit are both gone, as well. . . . It was too much to hope for, I suppose, that this would be easy."

"Nothing," said Saarmula, his voice flat, "is ever easy."

"But it could be worse." Volodya smiled thinly. "We don't have to land, after all. Just a little station keeping operation, that's all. Seryozha pilots the ship while the rest of us go out and plant the bomb."

The rest of us . . . Tonya shivered. "How're we going to keep it on the ground?"

Volodya shrugged. "We still have the piton gun, and the big screws, and plenty of steel cable. . . . You and I will dog it down while Lyova holds it in place. . . ."

"Wait a minute . . ." whispered Lyova.

The others looked at him, taking in his ashen features. Finally, Saarmula asked, "What is it?"

"What happens when we set off the bomb? We won't be able to get away. . . ."

Get away . . . Do I, wondered Tonya, want to see a five-kiloton fission detonation close up? The image clutched at his chest.

Manarov scratched at a whiskery chin. "Well . . . we have to do it. I, uh . . . guess we'll solve that one when we get to it. . . ." Go ahead and lie to him! He doesn't know we'll *have* to stick around so we can set it off at the right time. . . .

"Shit," said Saarmula. "Let's get out there and get this over with."

Over with? Tonya played with the words, hearing their ominous meaning. So *this* is the way it happens. One step at a time. Calm. Mechanical. Down the whirlpool. "All right." No one heard his reply.

While the ship was flown to within a hundred meters of

Sinuhe's principal spin axis, Manarov prepared his EVA suit quickly, noting the dirt and scrapes from his previous jaunts. Tool case, as before, nothing missing. He stepped into the suit's entry hatch, thanking some unknown god of technology that the Russians hadn't been saddled with the awkward pressure changes necessary for an American EVA. What a fate! To get the bends in space, of all places. He slid his arms in through the stiff collars until his fingers were snug inside the sausage-fingers of the gloves, and looked out through the scuffed, reflection-pocked visor. Here we go again, he thought. Tonya closed the rigid backpack behind him and locked the release handle. He turned to where Tonya and Lyova had crowded into the airlock, struggling to suit up. "Let's go. There can't be much time."

Chishak, thrusting his head through his suit's neck-ring pressure bladder, stared at him resentfully. Not much time? No, damn you, there never is. . . .

In a little while the three of them, CMUs donned, were floating by the ship's storage bins. *Molotochek* seemed to be hanging nose down above a Sinuhe that pinwheeled slowly through the heavens, drawing ever closer to a bloated Earth.

Maneuvering by little putts of gas from his backpack, Volodya clipped the snaplock on the end of his cable to one of the D-ring handles on the five-kiloton tactical demolition charge, then carefully checked the integrity of Serebryakov's connection. Good enough. Though he tried to breathe slowly and evenly, his breath was whistling through his nose at a quickening pace, an annoying spot of fog tending to form in the center of his faceplate. "All right, you know the drill, Tonya. On my mark, back off at about thirty degrees from my attach point. When I count down to turn, add a ninety-degree vertical vector. Stay with us, Lyova, but keep clear until we reach the detonation site." They'd decided to place their last warhead in the middle of the broad end of the asteroid, at a position that would, theoretically, pass through the line of the rock's trajectory every thirty-five minutes.

"Understood." Though this should have been Saarmula's job, in the current emergency, Anton's vastly greater EVA experience counted for more than rank and training. He found himself marveling at his sense of calm. *Here I am again. And again.* Bathed in bright sunlight, the rock around them gleamed under a black and featureless sky, patches where metal had run molten reflecting brilliant highlights.

"Four. Three. Two. One. Mark." Volodya tugged on his joystick, building up X-translation delta-V. "Three. Four. Five. Release." *Molotochek* began to recede. "Four. Three. Two. One. Turn." He thumbed the button on his right-hand joystick, adding a Z-translation vector. "Seven. Eight. Nine. Release." Now they were rising from the ship's hull at a sixty-degree angle. . . .

As the ship grew smaller, the Earth, behind it, brilliant blue-white, flooded the scene with a cold, colored glow. The nightside of the asteroid was no longer dark, bright features reflecting blue-bright. Detached, Volodya regarded the spectacle. *Interesting. Winter has already receded far into the Arctic. Only Canada and northern Siberia are still snowy. Hard to believe we're midway between vernal equinox and summer solstice already.* The Greenland glaciers and a portion of the sea ice threw off searing reflections into space, and perpetual daylight was illuminating the pole. He let his imagination trace the line of the midnight sun around the world, then measured the distance down to Leningrad. *Well. White night season is not so far away after all.* . . .

"My God . . ." Anton's voice whispered in his earphones. "It's *huge.* . . ."

"We're a little more than an hour and a half out. Maybe forty thousand kilometers." The bare fact of the number struck down into his numb core. *Forty thousand kilometers. If you stuck the Soviet Union on end it would reach more than a quarter of the way out to us. Bizarre image.* He felt a tug on the outside of his suit as the cables went taut, and looked down. The bomb was pulling away from *Molotochek,* slowly swinging into the line of their trajectory, itself changing direction because of the momentary inertial drag. *Good enough.*

Lyova's voice, hesitant, asked, "Am I imagining things or can we actually see it grow?"

"We're . . . moving very fast now." *In a little while, if they did nothing more, Sinuhe would tear into the atmosphere over the North Atlantic at something like nine kilo-*

meters per second. Try to imagine it, Volodya! But he couldn't, not really. Inertial force rising, atmospheric gases thrust aside, ultraviolet light and hard X rays throbbing from the plasma bow-wave. Plunging into the sea, plumes of live steam and molten rock/metal splashed back into outer space, a hard rain of tektites in China. Tidal waves obliterating New York, ravaging the west coast of Ireland, the South Atlantic splashing up onto the ice of Antarctica. You could think those things, yes, but imagine the reality? Imagination would have to do: in all probability, he wouldn't live to see the reality.

No. It's me . . . *me* going down into the black hole of oblivion. . . .

The ground was rising underneath them now as they swept over the jagged fractures of the asteroid's "nose," where the little rocky spire had been blasted away. It was out there somewhere, tumbling in space, headed for a rendezvous with the south of France. Visions of a green and sunny clime rose once again. The latest communications from the ground were a little more precise. Near Bordeaux, they said, or perhaps up in the Pyrenees. I wonder if they've given warning? He pictured bathers, swarming out of the sea. Shark! Shark! Nowhere to run to, though. You couldn't get away in only an hour. And what if you ran in the wrong direction?

The ground was falling away again, becoming smooth and watery in the harsh azure-white light. No terminator? The rock is turning under us. Now, the smooth broad end of the asteroid approached. Time to go.

"Brake on my mark. Four. Three. Two. One. Mark." Their hands twitched at controllers and thrust began whispering through the CMU mechanisms. The bomb slowly swung under them in its V of cabling until it had taken the lead. "Nine. Ten. Eleven. Release." They were falling slowly toward the ground, the bomb striking first with a gentle bounce, then they.

They reeled in the cables as Chishak drifted closer, handling his CMU with a surprising skill. The bounce off the surface of Sinuhe carried them out a few meters to a quadruple rendezvous. "Just hold it steady, Lyova. The ground will be moving very slowly under you. Just keep it drifting in the same direction. . . . Don't let the cables go taut 'til I tell you. . . ."

Still gripping his CMU hand controllers, Chishak moved in under the warhead, until he was almost touching it. Wait, the voice whispered in his head, wait until you see the direction of the drift. Then . . . just a little nudge . . . Don't screw up, Lyova. Not *this* time!

Volodya pulled tools from his belt and began sorting through them, handing them to Serebryakov one at a time. Spanners, eyebolts, cabling, the radio detonator package. No time to fool around. If this thing is detonated in less than one hour, its energy will not be sufficient to deflect Sinuhe from its course. Bad luck. If the blast was too late, or exploded at the wrong moment, France would still be saved, but the rock would come down nonetheless, on hapless Poland, or maybe Moskva. . . .

As they set to work, Anton handing him eyebolts and bracing him while he screwed them home, cold reality ticked away in his head. You know what happened. There's too little time. You've ridden the edge of the envelope too far, Volodya. *This* time you're going to die.

"All right." He threaded the last cable to its eyebolt and began spinning the turnbuckle. "Let it go, Lyova." The warhead crawled closer, until it was dangling a couple of meters up. "Good enough. Let's get back to the ship and see if we can do something about surviving this." He lifted off, reeling out control wire as he went, flying backward, watching it drape across the distorted metal of Sinuhe.

Survive? As they moved over the landscape, Anton watched the Earth as it moved through their sky again. It seemed improbable.

The sweat was clinging to Volodya's scalp in thin, undulating sheets as he wriggled from his spacesuit in *Molotochek*'s airlock. Once free, he paused for a moment to sweep the moisture from his forehead, sending it spinning across the room to splatter on the padded bulkhead, a dark pattern that would slowly evaporate in the conditioned air of the spaceship.

From the propulsion control room, Saarmula shouted, "Hurry! Less than fifteen minutes now!"

Hurry. Yes. All the decisions were made, the control cable attached to one of the ship's external electrical connectors, *Molotochek* itself backed away to the full kilometer length of the command wire. . . . Hurry.

Volodya made a formless wish that things could be different; that they could still retreat to safety. . . . He dropped the thought. There wasn't time, there wasn't fuel, there wasn't even residual computer power. The controller latched to the bomb was no more than a detonation sequencer. The computer that had run the original detonations was . . . part of a dissipated plasma cloud, or melted seamlessly into the asteroid. In any case, the detonation command couldn't travel intelligibly any distance through the tortured exosphere.

He slammed the door to his spacesuit and dove through the entry hatch of the control room, grabbing his seat back as he flew over it, flipping, feet down on the deck. Saarmula was buttoning up the control station, throwing circuit breakers, shutting down all unnecessary systems, rendering them as EMP-proof as was possible with Soviet technology. Serebryakov was in the rear of the chamber, securing loose objects.

"Chishak?"

Anton looked up briefly, his face a pale oval in the fluorescent light. "Powering up the flare shelter."

Volodya clambered into his seat at the flight engineer's station and secured the seat belt. Things were a shambles here, wiring everywhere. They'd reconnected a few elements to the Dozhdevik and set it up to act as the bomb's controller node, a last act of grace for an obsolescent technology. The decisions were made. Now . . . nothing but an end to all things. He began typing on the Dozhdevik keyboard, making final adjustments to the little program that would send a signal out through the long wire they'd looped around Sinuhe's. A very simple program. When the sun and Earth sensors said the bomb was pointing along their orbital trajectory, wait one-half second, then blow the charge. It would probably work. Calculation on both Mission Control's Cray and the DEU *had* said the explosion would drop Sinuhe into a tall elliptical orbit, eight hundred by twelve thousand kilometers.

And us? He finished typing and clicked back to the standard graphical user interface. His program's icon, a little stick of dynamite, stood alone in the center of the screen. What about *us*? Well. The bomb was about as far from *Molotochek* as it could be, the bulk of the asteroid between them and the explosion. . . . Maybe so. And a cold inner voice said, You'll find out, won't you? True enough. He double clicked on the icon and the word RUNNING appeared in a conversation box underneath it. In the upper right-hand corner of the little gray screen, six hundred seconds began ticking off. "Ten minutes," he said.

Serebryakov snapped the pebble-finished case of the DEU shut, tucked it under his arm, and went aft, through the living quarters hatch. Saarmula reached up and flipped the final circuit breakers that would shut down most of the flight engineer's station. "Let's get out of here."

Volodya patted the Dozhdevik's case. Goodbye, comrade. Your death is coming. Even if the ship survived, even if the men survived, the explosion's electromagnetic pulse would reach around the asteroid, through the ship's hull, and kill the little computer. He checked everything one more time, and satisfied, unbuckled his seat belt. Quickly, he placed one booted foot on the control panel and dove aft, through the hatch and onward. Four minutes.

The other three were already in the solar flare shelter, strapped into their acceleration couches. The control panel, situated above the couch that Volodya had been using as a bed for much of the past year, was already lit up, its digital readouts active, its little TV screen alight. Volodya slid into his bunk and began securing its straps.

"One minute," said Saarmula.

Volodya glanced at the control panel, where a timer had been set. Fifty-eight seconds. He looked around at the others, three pale faces staring down at him, beaded with cold sweat. Nothing more to be said. Goodbye, goodbye, goodbye. Here we go, comrades, into the twilight land of posthumous heroes. Maybe so, maybe not. We'll know shortly.

"Thirty seconds."

I could do without the countdown, thought Volodya. Selfless, heroic cosmonauts to the end . . . But he felt angry with himself. I may die in a fraction of a minute! Why can't my thoughts be more . . . noble? There was no answer.

"Ten seconds."

Then, an answer. I am merely a worker. It's the world about me that has nobility.

"Five seconds."

Apropos of nothing, Volodya said. "Five kilotons. That's not so much."

And Sirje Saarmula said, "Zer—"

BLAANGG!

Something shoved them hard into their acceleration couches and the solar flare shelter's lights went out for a moment, then came back on as a backup system kicked in. The universe vibrated around them with a slow amplitude . . . oomm . . . oomm . . . oomm . . . dying down over a period of about ten seconds.

Volodya looked over at his control panel. The instruments seemed to be working, but the TV screen, hooked to an outside camera, was dark. He looked up at the others and they sat, silent, listening as the vibration slowly sank below their threshold of awareness. He let out what seemed like a held breath. "Well. We're still alive." So far . . .

Serebryakov laughed softly, an almost hysterical sound. "So we are."

As they unbuckled their straps, Saarmula said, "Alive. For now. Let's get out there and see what the damages are." We've got to be moving through a cloud of bomb debris right now, next to a big rock moving along an altered trajectory. . . . He hoped they wouldn't run into Sinuhe before he could reach his controls. Alive for now, he thought. Yes. But with an enormous range of potential futures. Maybe they'd saved the day. But . . . maybe not.

There was little enough time to tell.

With the video system out, there was only the simple but efficient porthole for visual reconnaissance. As Tonya peered through the glass, Sinuhe, silhouetted against the enormous circular earth, still rotating, was bringing a fading red crater into sight. A dark haze that slightly obscured a wide splotch of planet was rapidly dissipating. The asteroid was a little less than three kilometers off, slowly drifting away. It was magnificent and terrifying at the same time.

"Can't tell if it worked or not." Seryozha stared at the strange skyscape, frozen by apprehension and wonder. He started for the propulsion control room. "Only one way to find out."

Following him through the hatch, Manarov said, "We'd better be quick. If we have any hope at all, it's to follow Sinuhe's lead, see if we can get high enough to miss the denser parts of the atmosphere. But at this point anything we do is pretty useless."

Saarmula was throwing switches, bringing systems back. He had never given in to hopelessness before, and he wouldn't now. "Well," he said, "this is going to be tough with only empiric astrogation techniques. . . ."

They quickly clipped the DEU's I/O cable back in line. Manarov hit the WAKE key, and, to his great joy, the ship's systems came on again, little the worse for another EMP. "We lost very little."

"Video?"

"I can't tell. . . . Looks like the connections are intact, but . . . no response from the vidicon . . ." He shrugged, reaching out to flip on the radio communication subsystems. "Maybe the cameras were too soft . . . radar's all right though."

"That's good enough for me." Saarmula strapped himself in and reached out to grasp his two hand controllers. "Throw the radar display up on my lower CRT. I'll start us in the direction of Sinuhe. And see how the radio's doing."

As Manarov complied, the radio's speaker came on with a strangulated yodel that quickly shrank to a warbling moan. Nothing like a voice could be heard, and Volodya checked the radio controller. All correct. The ionosphere had been bathed in hot radiation once again, and was in no mood to let messages through.

Floating up behind him, grasping the back of his chair as the OMS thrusters began to thump and hiss, Serebryakov listened to the radio noise with regret. It would be a shame to die without knowing if their sacrifice was in vain. The sussurus of static got louder then, punctuated by a series of rhythmical clicking pops . . . Jesus. Visions of recording sessions in Max's room. This sounds like the static off a dirty old LP, with fuzz on the needle to boot. . . .

"Volodya?"

Manarov lifted a hand. "Just a minute." He studied his console, leaning close to eye several gauges, then reached out to touch Saarmula's shoulder. "The ullage ignition system for the main engines is dead. Can you make it on OMS alone?"

The pilot looked at his readouts, then up at the analog radar display, bright-blue lines against a black background. "Well, I guess . . . I guess I'll have to."

"Volodya."

Manarov looked up at him with something akin to irritation. "What?"

"The DEU's pattern recognition routine—couldn't we tie that into the com signal to filter out some of this garbage?"

"What do you mean?"

Serebryakov looked at the flight engineer, then down at the DEU. "The radio noise. I mean, if it has pattern recognition routines specifically designed to enhance old recordings, I don't see why it can't differentiate between voice and static."

"Voice and static? Uhh . . . right." The abrupt topic change was an aggravation, but . . . this was important. Laying his hands on the DEU keyboard, Manarov multitasked the object linker and brought up the icon array, deftly choosing the correct modules. "Input line twenty-eight being analyzed." The DEU's voice sounded vaguely smug. "Pattern search. Correction algorithms. Signal decoded."

"—read me, *Molotochek*. This is Mission Control. Can you read me, *Molotochek*? This is Mission Control." The voice was vague and unmodulated, certainly not perfect, but it was a voice, and understandable. Saarmula put on his headset and said, *"Molotochek* here. We read you, Mission Control. Can you hear us through this static?"

"We can barely make you out. Our preliminary radar plot shows Sinuhe redirection was a success. The asteroid is now headed for grazing atmospheric entry over eastern Europe. The parameters say contact no farther west than Berlin, no farther east than Minsk. Looks like it'll skip off the atmosphere and return to space. Can you hear me?"

"Yes. We can hear you."

"Congratulations."

"What about *Molotochek*?"

"Well . . . It doesn't look good. Recommend you minimize speed relative to Earth and eject escape capsule for emergency reentry. If you do this immediately, there's a chance you'll survive. Our current projection is that you will experience twenty-eight g's. Repeat, twenty-eight gravities. There is some possibility that the heat shielding of the capsule is not currugul zrrunurr zzahzzzrzrzrzrz." The voice had been losing definition for seconds, now it lapsed into incomprehensibility, then silence. The DEU said, "Pattern lost. Continuing to search."

Floating in the CM-PCR entry hatch, Lyova said, "Resistance to the potentially lethal effects of high g-forces varies quite a bit from individual to individual. Cases of people surviving about twenty-five g's are not unknown, although there is frequently considerable damage to the more sensitive parts of the body, such as the eyes and brain."

Twenty-eight gravities . . . Closer and closer. Step by step. Tonya felt his blood running cold, driving cold sweat onto his forehead and back. He tried to picture the reentry force, five times more powerful than the centrifugal simulator, which had squeezed him down like a horrible, invisible vise, cutting off his breathing, turning the world first dim red and then black. Five times that was death. "Why don't we just turn everything off and die of asphyxiation?" That didn't sound very pleasant either, but at least it was quiet, nonviolent.

That brought a bark of laughter from Manarov. "We couldn't possibly suffocate in the time we have left."

"You can use the piton gun if you want to commit suicide, Tonya," said Saarmula, sounding angry. "I prefer to take my chances, slim though they may be. Strange things happen. I have talked to pilots who have survived air crashes when there was absolutely no possibility of survival. At least we should let God have his chance."

Chishak gave him a withering glance. "God? That's the problem with you all in the West. Your civilization was never purged of superstition, as ours was. Please don't refer to your god in regard to this situation. I consider it in extremely poor taste."

Seryozha stared back, uncertain. In his heart of hearts he *did* find the religious answers rather pathetic, ludicrous even. But they were comforting. Perhaps he should have spent more time reading about theology and comparative religions. Lutheranism could hardly be called the most probable set of beliefs. "It's all moot, anyway," he said. "We shall shortly see whether there is any truth in the superstitions, as you call them."

Volodya leaned back in his chair, lacing his hands behind his head, falling into an artful pose of relaxation. "Don't be a damned fool, Seryozha. Death is just . . . death."

"Shut *up!*" hissed Anton. "It's bad enough I have to die now without listening to . . ."

"Right." Volodya laughed again. "Just drive us to the asteroid, Seryozha. After we're dead we'll . . . compare notes."

The thrusters hissed on, long, sibilant blasts punctuated by even longer silences. They all stared at the image on the CRT, the speckled blue shape of the small body renewing itself every few seconds, brightening and fading with the impulse sweep.

Volodya watched it grow, admiring the combination of angularities and curves, feeling an idea try to construct itself out of fragmented parts. There was something about Sinuhe's shape . . . what *did* it remind him of? With the silicate spur blown away it was somehow more regular, blocky, fat at the bottom, smoothed off by repeated doses of nuclear fire, tapering a bit toward a ragged summit, where the spur had been. Hmh. Odd. Almost a *bell* shape . . . He smiled unpleasantly to himself. Well. Wouldn't you know it. Sinuhe Major was shaped more or less like a *Soyuz* reentry vehicle. Of all the unfortunate . . .

He felt the idea come together, stealing through him like a sickness. Oh, you thick bastard, *think!* Is this an idea or isn't it? How the fuck can I *tell?* He cut off the inner argument with a metaphorical wrist-chop and turned to the others. "I have an idea. A slim chance, perhaps." The three faces turned toward him with identical expressions of alert attention. "It might be possible to survive the skip in the wake of the asteroid, using it as a heat shield."

The faces softened. Incredulity gave way to puzzlement. "Is that possible?" asked Tonya.

"Who knows? It depends on so many factors. Theoretically we can figure out where the center of the plasma cone will be. If we move the ship there, tie it down securely, it should provide enough protection. But there are no guarantees. The asteroid is tumbling, after all. I . . . just don't know if it will stabilize or . . . what will happen. . . ." The idea was taking hold of him now, driving his enthusiasm. If it worked, it would be . . . truly wonderful. If it didn't work . . . what the hell. Dead is dead, after all.

Tonya was bobbing about, shaking his head, rubbing his hands. Was it truly possible that they could be snatched from the jaws of death by this unlikely plan? Part of him wanted to hide, and just let what happened happen. But that part was dwindling in the face of a course of action, no matter how threadbare. Was death really an alternative? "Let's do it." His voice sounded so certain, convincing. He imagined the whirlpool spitting him out, inedible.

Chishak clicked his tongue thoughtfully. "It seems like the only choice."

Anton hit the DEU's return key with his ring finger and tilted his head up. A conversation box that said WORK-ING appeared. Since the machine's processors were still mostly taken up with regulating *Molotochek's* various systems, it would take quite a while to produce a result. Video images as well as Sinuhe's tiny gravitational effect on the spacecraft were being integrated into the previously done highly accurate shape and mass profile. He looked over at Saarmula, who was staring into space, vacant eyed. They were moving in tandem with Sinuhe once again, Chishak and Manarov in the airlock, suiting up. As soon as they had calculated the proper spot, had flown *Molotochek* there, they would go outside and begin the dangerous and ungainly task of tying it down.

He waved a hand at the commander. "Hey. Are you all right?"

Seryozha's eyes refocused, and he looked over. He smiled self-consciously. "Sorry. Just thinking."

"There's a lot to think about."

"Tonya, I'm sorry this had to happen."

Serebryakov cocked his head, grinned. "No kidding."

"No. That's not what I mean. You're a newlywed. Volodya has a wife and two children. Lyova a wife. I have never been able to make a connection like that."

You, too? Empathy flooded through him. This he could understand. "It's never easy."

"So. Perhaps it's just being romantic to expect that a woman would change. Because of love."

Now Anton was confused. This was far from the hard realities of here and now. "I don't know what you mean."

"We never understand until it is too late."

Well, that may be, but . . . He sighed to himself. He thinks we're going to die in a little while. Who knows what's going on in his head?

The conversation box disappeared, catching his attention, and the program seized half of the screen for its graphic output. Three grid-covered images of the asteroid appeared, viewed from the X-, Y-, and Z-axes. Below this, there was a high-resolution video-based map of the region around Sinuhe's small end, with a green ovoid at its center —the area of maximum safety. He called up the computer's redirection object, and, after a series of fill-in-the-blank type questions, sent a print-screen request. Would this work? He flung himself out of the chair, arcing up to the ceiling and back down in front of the communications center, where, next to the encoded TTY screen, a small, medium-resolution Fax machine was starting to light up. Seryozha watched in rapt interest. It whirred and the white edge of paper started to come out. It *was* working. The DEU's screen, at a somewhat lower resolution, was being duplicated on the paper. They would have a map.

When the Fax had finished, Tonya went up into the airlock, crowding between the two spacesuited men to the small starboard porthole. He looked out, hoping to get his bearings quickly. Sinuhe was a dark shape hanging in front of the staggeringly beautiful cloud-and-sky disk of the earth. "Ready."

Thrusters thudded, and Sinuhe began to grow until it covered half the globe, becoming a smooth blue-green-gray landscape with a curved horizon. "Okay, Seryozha, down and to the left." Thud. Thud. "Over to the right a little." Thud. Tonya held the map up, straining in the dim light of the airlock, finally recognized the distinctive pattern of little ripples that matched the green zone. It didn't seem very protected.

"This is it."

Saarmula leaned forward and grasped a joystick. "All right. Volodya, we're going in." As the thrusters hissed again, Manarov sealed the airlock hatch behind Serebryakov and began his decompression sequence.

They opened the hatch just as Saarmula began his station-keeping operation, drifting along in a weak sort of forced orbit that kept them opposite the slowly moving edge of Sinuhe. As soon as they were out, they noticed the few fractional percentage points of gravitylike inertia. Chishak made a sudden lurch to one side and began to slide down the hull, a slow motion parody of a fall. He finally got hold of the storage bay flange and stopped himself.

"Christ, don't fall off, Lyova! We'll never see you again. . . ."

Clinging to the CMU bay, Chishak tried to catch his breath. Never see me again? My God . . . reentry in a spacesuit! Would anybody see my little meteor, maybe make a little wish? Beyond the curving hull, the great arc of the Earth was so large that he had to turn his head to see it all. "Good. No problems so far."

Teetering on the edge of the abyss, they struggled into the CMUs. When all was ready, Volodya let go, floating free, compensating for the inertia with a little hiss of cold gas. "All right, then," he said. "Down we go."

Time was running out. Volodya attached the last of the cables and tightened it down securely. *Molotochek* was nestled uncomfortably against the uneven surface like a gigantic beached whale, or, with all the cables, a robotic Gulliver in some grim, metallic Lilliput, the arms of its solar panels neatly folded against the sides of the command module. They could run on battery power for this little while.

In the end, the tiny centrifugal force hadn't been that much of a problem. They'd bound the command module to the ground, driving home the last of their big screws, threading them with all their remaining cable. Damn. The propulsion module's endless long meters of almost-empty fuel tank, terminating in the engine bay, with its now useless rocket motors, was unsupported, protruding from the irregular surface at a slight angle. If you looked carefully, it seemed to bow, but . . . it was probably illusion. *Molotochek,* like most Soviet hardware, had been designed to be picked up by a strongback crane under full one-g conditions. This less-than-one-fifth-of-a-Newton load must be all but unnoticeable. "All ready here."

Saarmula's voice said "There's no more than twenty minutes. You'd better get a move on."

Volodya looked around. Where was Lyova?

Lev Mikhailovich Chishak, surgeon, space doctor, Frontal Aviation captain, floated in his little infrastructure on the edge of the abyss. At fifty meters over the surface, Sinuhe was only peripherally noticeable beneath his feet. The Earth, wider than two outstretched arms, hung, no, flew above him, spread out in infinite cloud-swirling Cinemascope. If this was the road to oblivion, it was decked with glory. As at the asteroid many months earlier, something was blossoming in him, making all the cares and pain that swarmed across this expanse of sky below seem tiny and insignificant. His own life, made up of so many small skills and habits, such tiny pleasures and puny injuries, simply was not important here. His first memory, of falling through the thin ice on the Kachovskoye Reservoir, started playing in his head. Falling into the icy water, clutching spasmodically at a chunk of ice, churning the water with his feet. He called out as loud as he could, but managed only a terrified croak. Was he really sentient then? If he had died, would he even have noticed? Mama had never come, and he had somehow managed to climb up onto the shore. Where had she been? It was a question that had remained unanswered for more than thirty-five years.

What *had* his life been? After his grandmother had died, and he had joined the Pioneers, things had moved at a quickening pace. Lenin. Girls. Komsomol. Medicine. Natasha. Chernobyl. Space. And now death. A life reduced to seven or eight words. Had he saved a thousand lives? That would be eight-thousand words, at best; less than a short story. Frustration, fear, anger vanished like the words that they were. Chernobyl, that ragged obsession, suddenly evaporated. *This* was something, *this* now, *this* moment, *this* cosmos spread out before him like a canvas. A moment of life, sweet as the jam at the bottom of a glass of tea, intense, sense-flooding. Wide-eyed, he tried to encompass it all, and almost succeeded.

"Chishak. Where the fuck are you?"

"Over here. I never dreamed I would be able to see so much."

Damn it. Volodya came up slowly, watching the tiny white figure floating before the magnificent backdrop of the earth. He paused. The burgeoning, irrepressible self machine scanned and digested and wanted more. So many things I'll never see, he realized. In all likelihood, the end was at hand. I'll never set foot on the Moon, much less Mars. He tried to imagine what it would be like, to step out onto the frigid, boulder-strewn duricrust and stare up to where Phobos and Deimos decorated the burning salmon sky. Well. That moment will be left to someone else. Sinuhe was all there would be, but it was much, much. Tiny vignettes, moments from the exploration of the asteroid, appeared in his head almost side by side. Firsts. Moments experienced by no previous human being. Moments indubitably his own. I guess . . . that will have to be enough.

And there were the moments shared with everyone else. Human things, the love of a woman, children, eating, sleeping . . . And Shutka, her face so close it made his eyes cross. Strong regret welled up inside him. Well. This moment would have come anyway . . . someday.

He was up beside Chishak now. Lyova, for whom he had felt mostly indifference, tempered with an angry fear. Doctors made you dead. Silly, such an atavistic reaction. Here was another man, not even a real cosmonaut, facing the same short future as himself. What must he be feeling? Did it matter? No. "Get back toward the bow. We're going to blow the instrument unit latches."

Inside, Saarmula had the vaguest feeling that he was hanging head down before his control panel, suspended by the lap belt. It was the tiny effect of the centrifugal force, very slight, but much stronger than Sinuhe's gravity had been, plucking things upward, depositing them on the ceiling. A stylus that he'd absentmindedly left hanging in the air began to drift slowly "upward," along the ship's reference vertical.

One more thing that must be done. They had decided to uncouple the CM, which was located at the center of the safe area, from the engine compartment and fuel tanks, which were long enough to reach the rim of the fracture zone. The crew cabin and life-support system, securely tied down, would stay put. He grabbed the stylus and shoved it in his pocket, then, a bit panicky, pulled back the clear plastic box covering a red, spring-loaded T-pull. He grasped the T, curling his fingers around the warm metal, and twisted. A big red light on his main panel began to flash, and a buzzer began to sound. Slowly, he pulled it out, feeling the ratcheting mechanism click. The rod came to the end of its track and there was a loud, hollow pop.

Outside, Manarov watched closely as the ring of hull material just below the flare shelter's water tank was suddenly enveloped in a puff of dense smoke. "Looks like a good separation. All explosive bolts fired. It's . . ." He stopped suddenly, surprised.

"Look at it," whispered Chishak.

Slowly, very slowly, the hull behind the command mod-

ule began to buckle, wrinkling across its width above, separating below, down near the surface of the asteroid. What
had been an illusory bend became real, the engines lifting
toward the dark sky. In their earphones, Saarmula's voice,
raspy with fear, shouted, "Volodya! What's happening?
There's a loud groaning sound. . . ."

Manarov sighed, remembering that long ago day above
the moon, and the swiftly opening steel flower of the radiotelescope. "The propulsion module is dropping away, Seryozha. The centrifugal force. It's . . . beautiful."

Towering above them, the fuel tanks twisted free and
lifted majestically away into the night, a thin green cylinder, shrinking, dropping away, the neat Cyrillic characters,
*Molotochek,* gone forever.

So. That's it, then, thought Manarov. All over but the
dying. "Time to go inside," he said.

They went.


Tonya was at the large porthole again, watching the
Earth set. Saarmula was in the airlock, helping Chishak
and Manarov out of their suits.

The Earth was mesmerizing him, taking him away from
the myriad buzzes that flooded his mind. An excellent
method for self-hypnosis—just dangle the Earth from a
string and say the magic words, concentrate, concentrate.
The freezing fear was totally gone again. What was he, a
goddamn merry-go-round? Up and down, up and down,
through an ephemeral repeating cycle of control and emotion, with no rhyme or reason. Forever at war with something that was not-him, outside, deeper. The giver of fear
and anger. As the skip approached, it seemed to be hiding,
so afraid it had become a vanishingly small blot of ink. Like
Ouroboros, self-eater. Well, he would not miss it.

A sudden insight. It was himself as an infant, wailing
and wailing for no reason, calling the universe down to
rescue him. For a while, it did, in the form of his mother
and Baba. But he had to grow up, face the fact that the
world around him was cold and inhospitable; alien, even. It
did not care at all about what happened to the little, unhappy boy. And never would.

So now, this world was calling him to his doom. After
such a short time of moving about, he would be snuffed out
like a candle. Like a shooting star, there was a song about

that. And he would literally die as a shooting star, as well
as figuratively. What an odd thing.

Was he growing up now, on the edge of oblivion? Was
that what adulthood was, understanding one's self a little?
He had speculated about it many times —acceptance of
the cruel fate imposed on you from above, that was adulthood. But it wasn't like that at all. Adulthood was self-
knowledge. And he had needed to die before he could
partake of it.

Too bad.

Moe Schlossberg sat in his office at CTN Headquarters,
New York, watching television with a bland and unearthly
dread. End of the World. End of the World? How the fuck
did I let myself get involved with something like this? I
must be crazy. Must be.

On the big, wall-mounted flatscreen TV, Lyle Marlowe
squatted, pale and evil-looking, in the main news studio
downstairs, surrounded by projection matte-surfaces, talking endlessly. Over his shoulder, the great, slowly tumbling
boulder that was Sinuhe Major rotated in telescopic view.

". . . the larger body will contact the upper atmosphere
in only a few minutes. In this view, taken by long-range
cameras aboard one of CTN's asteroid-tracking Concorde
jets, you can plainly see the outlines of the Russian spacecraft *Molotochek,* trapped by the asteroid's death plunge.
One wonders just what could be going through the minds
of those brave cosmonauts as the end draws near. Perhaps,
like their Kremlin masters, they now regret the egotistical
errand that brought them to this fiery fate. . . ."

Fuck. I can't believe it. . . . Schlossberg felt an intense
itching in his lungs, a growing shortness of breath. God. In
his earphone, the voices on the remote team communications net were growing more excited.

". . . Got it! Got it! Remote one, this is track six. Our
radar plot shows Sinuhe Minor impacting somewhere in
the western Pyrenees."

*"Where,* God damn it! We've got to get *close!"*

"Fuck, I don't know. . . . Wait one, Remote, we . . .
Right! Remote one, this is track six. Refined radar plot
shows impact probability circle for Sinuhe is two point six
kilometers northeast of Roncesvalles, with a radius of five
kilometers."

"Good enough. *When?*"

"Wait one, Remote . . . uh . . . Eight minutes, plus or minus."

". . . fuckin' A! We can just make it!"

"All *right*! Go!"

On the big flatscreen, Lyle Marlowe was saying, "In a moment, we will have *live* coverage of the giant meteor impact expected in southern France. But first, this important message . . ."

Listening, Schlossberg's critical facility went on ticking over: idiot. Roncesvalles is in northern Spain. Well. Probably the *Roland* thing. He remembered the live fiasco on last night's show, when Marlowe had referred to the famous epic as "The Song of Ronald." MacDonald, no doubt . . .

A handsome woman came onscreen, holding up what looked like a giant condom with an enormous prong on its tip. "Have *you* been thinking of using a disposable douche?"

Oh my God. Schlossberg rubbed one fat hand across his brow. It came away covered with cold, sticky sweat. What the fuck am I going to *do*? How am I going to *explain* this? *Wir müssen leider sagen* . . .

The Marine HUE-9/C jetcopter bounced hard as it set down on a spring-bright meadow in the low mountains of the Franco-Spanish border, the pilot cursing as he hauled back on the throttles and flipping switches disengaging the engine from the rotor. God *damn* these TV people! Where does the government get *off* making us ferry them around? End of the fucking world my sticky brown asshole!

In back, Warren Runtibbie was helping throw open the cargo door. "Come *on*, dammit! We've only got *two minutes!*"

The technicians scurried about setting up equipment on the hillside by the helicopter, running cables to the transformer, running a power takeoff from the machine's engine electrical supply. "West! West, shithead! It's coming from the *west!*"

"This *is* west!"

"West is that way. You're pointing north."

"Oh."

"Hurry the fuck *up!*"

Runtibbie smoothed his hair, clipped on his mike, popped in his earphone and faced the camera lens. "Yes.

Good evening, Lyle. Yes, just a few minutes ago, we were informed that the smaller fragment of the asteroid, now known as Sinuhe Minor, will come to Earth just about a mile from this spot, Roncesvalles, the historic site where French national hero Roland was massacred, some thousand and more . . ."

He listened to the earpiece, pretending to react to a human face. "Safety? Well, it's hard to say, Lyle. The fragment is fairly small, no more than forty meters across, at best. We think a mile is probably a fairly safe distance—"

One of the sound technicians gibbered and pointed, jumping up and down, at the western sky. Runtibbie, angry at the interruption, spun to look. "My God! I see it! Yes, Lyle. What a magnificent sight!"

The cameras were elevated and, in his studio, Lyle Marlowe stared at the screen, open-mouthed with amazement. Over the horizon came an obese, glowing ball of light, brilliant white, leaving a yellowish trail of fire behind it in the sky, silent, growing larger by the second.

". . . This is *fantastic*, Lyle! I've never seen anything like it! It's moving so fast, yet there isn't even a *hint* of a roar, just the breezes sighing through the trees around us. . . . I . . . I . . . I feel . . ." He suddenly reached up and touched his face softly. "Weird . . . I feel . . . pins and needles . . ." His face seemed to brighten. "Lyle? It's . . . It's . . ."

White light.

Lyle Marlowe sat back in his chair and stared, slack-jawed, at the static pattern on his studio monitor. "Warren? Warren? We . . . We . . . We . . ." Get hold of yourself! This is *live*! He sat up, squared his shoulders and looked earnestly into the lens packet of the hot-camera. "We seem to be experiencing technical difficulty with the remote team at Roncesvalles, ladies and gentlemen. While we attempt to reestablish contact with Warren Runtibbie in France, I take you now to Joshua Bulwark aboard the cruise ship *Viking Empress,* covering the movements of Sinuhe Major from the mid-Atlantic. Josh?"

A small fat man in a rumpled suit stood on an undulating deck under a bright-blue sky, looking about nervously. "Right. Lyle? I have with me science fiction writers Wilson Martin and Miles Baggiagalopo, here to comment on the asteroid encounter. Gentlemen, what do you suppose could have happened at Roncesvalles?"

To Bulwark's horror, the two plump, middle-aged men looked at each other and *grinned* . . .

Moe Schlossberg, watching the shambles unfold in all its glory, could hardly breathe any more. Enough. Enough. I wish I could make them *stop*. . . . The phone rang and he answered it automatically. "Hello?" Shit. "Oh, hi, Jerry." Jerome Glickman was the president of the Consolidated Television Network. "Yes. I'm watching it. No. I don't know, Jerry." He listened to the snarling voice on the other end of the line. "All right, Jerry. I'll be up in about five minutes. . . . Okay. Right away." He hung up and sat, staring at his desk, trying not to watch the flatscreen any longer.

Well.

He opened his desk drawer and pulled out the little twenty-five-caliber automatic he kept there. Well. He popped the clip. Yes. Four shiny brass bullets. He snapped the clip home, clicked off the safety and pulled the slide, jacking a round into the firing chamber. Now then.

He put the gun down gently on the top of his desk and sat looking at it. Well. His breath was coming in tiny sips now and dizziness welled up out of nowhere, darkening the room. He tried to inhale deeply and failed.

*"Nu?"*

He picked up the gun and held it, dwarfed by his fat palm. His hand closed around the gun and he threw it across the room, right into the flatscreen, right into the middle of Lyle Marlowe's inhuman face, where it bounced off harmlessly, clattering to the floor.

So.

So. I guess I go upstairs now and tell good ole Jerry that I quit.

He got up, wheezing erect from his padded leather chair, and started slowly for the door. As he walked, his breath began to come easily again. He straightened up and, as he put his hand on the doorknob, thought, fifty-three. That's not so old. . . .

Rising from the big new aerodrome at Bayonne, climbing the valley of the Gave d'Oloron, ESA's Dollfuss Observatory, built into the hull of an A-366 wide-body jet, vectored

eastward across *Pyrénées Atlantiques,* cameras facing
southward. Somewhere along here, the calculations said, no
more than fifty kilometers south of the plane's ground
track, it would fall. Not knowing exactly where the impact
would come, the French government and news media had
tried to keep things quiet. The Spanish government had not
been so successful. The rioting in Pamplona was . . . impressive to watch. For that matter, so was the Spanish-
language news special being broadcast from Zaragoza right
now. There should be a promotion in order for the man
who'd come up with that title: "Adios Andorra."

Hermann Oberg stood with his head projecting into the
flight deck's observation bubble, rich-field binoculars
pressed to his eyes, facing westward and slightly to the
south, looking past the jet's tall tailplane. Any minute
now . . . The A-366 jostled a little, managing to extract
turbulence from the calm air, making him sway. The binoculars bumped into the Plexiglas, pushing the eyepieces into
his cheekbones. Ow. That's three times. I'll look like a rac-
coon before the day is through.

The events of the past few days had been madden-
ing . . . and satisfactory. Well, *Hermann Fettmann,* you
told them so. *Told* them! So you did. And this feeling is
cold porridge in your gut. What good does it do you? What
good will it do them?

If his careful calculations were right, the little bit of rock
plummeting into the borderland between France and Spain
would create an explosion of no more than 150 kilotons, no
greater than any one of the thousands of strategic nuclear
warheads still spread across the earth. No more than that?
Just imagine! Cold comfort to anyone caught by the blast.

A light in the western sky caught his attention, making
his heart quicken a little. And what about those poor bastards up there? What about *them*? He'd met Serebryakov
once or twice, at planetological conferences. A colorless,
faceless professional. The others were just pictures on TV.
I wonder what the outcome of all this will be? After it's
over, there'll have to be some sort of international . . .
readjustment.

The light in the west suddenly brightened and, from below, he could hear the voice of the official mission recorder,
speaking to his tape machine. "Sinuhe Minor reentry detected fourteen-seventy hours Universal, plasma sheath for-

mation altitude seventy kilometers, crossing the Spanish coast west of Santander, a hundred three degrees azimuth, reentry vector thirty-nine degrees . . ."

Readjustment, yes. Hah. Ironic. SDI is shot down by the Russians, just as was feared. Only America, in its anxiety, pulled the trigger itself. Oberg felt a momentary warmth of amusement.

In the sky, a fireball began to form, spreading a long, hot trail across the heavens. Steep, mused Oberg. Very steep. He tracked the thing forward in his imagination and felt fear tickle his intestines. Christ! Just north of Pamplona! A million people may die today. Wren and Gorbachev will have a fine time arguing who owes what portion of the bill for this day's work!

Sinuhe Minor overhauled them rapidly, so that Oberg had to turn slowly under the dome. Passing Santander, the thing went directly over Bilbao, laying a hypersonic boom down through the atmosphere that broke shop windows in the ancient seaport, sending crowds screaming into the streets. By the time it passed just south of tiny Sumbilla, it was entering the upper troposphere, releasing a steady roar. The remainder of the pallasite transition material was beginning to fracture under the stress of reentry deceleration, pieces flying off here and there, but the heart of the rock was still cold, protected by the bowshock of the plasma sheath, carrying the cold of interplanetary space downward to the Earth.

Hermann Oberg turned steadily as it descended into the mountains . . . down . . . down . . . He flinched as it hit.

White light.

A ball of blue-violet flickered briefly over the Pyrenees, then you could see the shock wave spreading across the landscape, a misty arm pushing over the ancient forests.

So. There it is. Where? Pamplona? No, a little north of there, I think.

The voice from below said, ". . . impact detected at Roncesvalles, Spain, fourteen-seventy-six hours Universal . . ."

So. Farewell, Roland.

As he watched, the landscape darkened, the fireball snuffed out, and a small mushroom cloud, tall, with a spiky little head, began boiling up into the sky. Fallout. Only dust. Nothing.

As the plane turned southward, nosing into the air above Europe's worst disaster since the firebombing of Dresden-Saxony, Hermann Oberg turned his binoculars back toward the western sky.

And now, he thought, for the real thing . . .

L. Aloysius Wren, forty-second President of the United States of America, sat at the head of a long table, alone in a closed room with his cabinet officers and principal advisors. His hands, pressed flat to the tabletop, seemed rather blotchy, irregular lanes of white cutting courses between islands of vermilion. Every now and again a brownish, discolored area could be found, faint, rather small, but there nonetheless, a homely little harbinger of mortality.

Up the line, all their eyes were focused on him, invisible beams of buck-passing converging on his head. At the foot of the table John-John Fingol peered back, sympathetic but helpless. God damn. *Now* what do I do? Wren sat back in his chair, slumping a little, folding his arms across his chest, tucking his hands into his armpits, creating the invisibility of absence. "Gentlemen . . ."

Pairs of eyes began breaking away, seeking out their soulmates in other positions on the table. Bastards! You got me into this! "Gentlemen, I need advice. That's what you're here for, I think. To give advice." Suddenly Fingol was looking down at the surface of the table, at his own folded little hands, avoiding eye contact. Why, you little *prick*! "Gentlemen, what are we going to do now?"

The silence, unbroken even by the sound of breathing, was quite unpleasant. Come *on,* bastards, tell me *something*!

Finally, Secretary of State Barnwell's expensive suit rustled as he leaned forward slightly, catching Wren's eye and bringing the focus of the room on himself. "Since the detonation at Sinuhe and the revelation of its source, my department has received over one hundred separate diplomatic protests. That's every embassy that counts. The others . . . probably don't know where the State Department is. . . ." He sighed, sinking back in his chair, lacing bony fingers together on the edge of the table. "Mr. President, I think, when this is over, you'll have to go before the General Assembly of the United Nations . . . and apologize."

"Apologize, my *ass*!"

Wren glared suddenly at the Chairman of the Joint Chiefs of Staff. "We won't have any of that *here*, General Nelson."

Barnwell glanced contemptuously at the man, who'd grown suddenly red-faced, though whether with rage or embarrassment it was difficult to tell. "As I was saying, this country will have to apologize to the world for its hasty, if well-intentioned, act of self-defense. Make the best of it. The Soviets had no business trying to place an asteroid in low Earth-orbit. When they did, we had no business trying to interfere. We should say we're sorry, offer to pay the Soviets for ruining their project, pay an indemnity for the loss of the *Molotochek* crew, and pay for any collateral damages."

"But . . ." began Nelson.

Secretary of Defense Romain Bensonhurst jumped in suddenly. "I agree with Arthur, Mr. President. Admit we were wrong, in principle *only*, and offer to pay the Russians for fucking them. If there's no damage from the projected ground impact, we'll get off cheap. Hell, ten, twenty billion dollars tops! That's just a percentage of what your predecessors pissed away on the savings and loan debacle alone!"

"God damn it . . ."

"Shut up, General!" Wren snapped. "Yes, I see your point, Ben. If we're lucky, we get off cheap, and we throw a scare into the world. I don't think Gorbachev will try something like *this* again. . . ."

Bensonhurst smiled with satisfaction. "Exactly. We have achieved our principal aim."

Listening to them, Brad Harveson felt vaguely sick. I can't believe I took part in this. Why didn't I quit, go public with this? Public opinion will turn against space exploration for *years* now, until it's . . . too late. "For what it's worth, I have offered NASA's full assistance to the Soviet space authorities in attempting to rescue the cosmonaut team, should it survive."

"And their reply?"

Harveson shrugged. "Mr. Dunaev hung up on me when I called him."

CIA's Jimmy Russell smiled wryly. "What could we do,

send our last OTV on a suicide mission? In any case, *Serpachek* is about to round the Moon for its own rescue attempt. If those boys live through Sinuhe Major's perigee —I guess it's supposed to be no more than ninety miles up as it passes over eastern Europe—my guess is we'll see them again about this time next year. Russkis ought to give one hell of a nice parade when they come home."

Wren stared at the man with astonishment. What the fuck did *that* have to do with anything?

"Mr. President, may I speak?"

Nelson *seemed* calm enough, his thin face pale and earnest, every pockmark standing out in its place. "Very well, General. I'm sorry if I was abrupt with you earlier."

"Mr. President, what makes you think the Russians will let you just *apologize*? You think they'll let you say 'oops' and walk away?"

"Why shouldn't they?" Wren was genuinely puzzled. It *ought* to work, after all. . . .

"Mr. President, Navy and Air Force reconnaissance flights indicate that in the last hour or so the entire Soviet strategic ballistic missile submarine fleet, every unit not in drydock for repair and refit or refueling operations, has stood out to sea. All the medium-range missile boats are headed for the East coast of the U.S. The long-range boats are making for the open Pacific."

"I know that, General. Mr. Gorbachev indicated it was a precautionary move, to protect the fleet from any impact by going for maximum dispersal."

"A nice excuse. I think they're preparing for a full retaliatory strike against our few remaining strategic forces the moment there's an impact anywhere in the world. Who would blame them now?"

Wren put his hands on his hips, looking exasperated. "Come now, General. We all know Soviet militarism died in Afghanistan. . . ."

"God damn it, Mr. President, pull your head out of your asshole! The heyday of fucking *glasnost* was ten years ago! In order for fucking *perestroika* to work a goddamned cult of personality had to form around *Gorbachev*! He's the canniest politician the world has ever seen; and you're fucking falling for him, hook, line, and sinker."

Wren was shocked. "General *Nelson*! How *dare* you speak to me . . ."

Nelson's eyes shifted to one side and he put his hand to one ear, seating the earphone more securely. "Wait one . . ."

The room fell silent, everyone appalled and baffled.

Nelson's hand fell to his side. "Satellite imaging reports an impact and explosion, one-fifty to two hundred kilotons yield, along the Franco-Spanish border, a little north of the city of Pamplona. Casualties are . . . likely."

Wren crumpled forward, face falling into his suddenly cupped hands. "My God. Oh, my *God*! Why did I ever let this *happen*? What will people *say*. . . ."

Nelson bounced to his feet, face darkening. "Get hold of yourself, you little piss-ant! There's very little time! You have to release my weapons *now*!"

Wren looked up, wide-eyed. "Why . . . this is all *your* fault, General Nelson. Why . . . I believe you're relieved of your post. Consider yourself under arrest!"

Nelson's mouth popped open and his lips worked briefly. "Arrest?" His hand dropped to his holster, undid the strap, and he drew his service automatic, pointing it at the President. "My weapons! Now!"

Secretary of State Arthur Barnwell stood and stepped forward into the tableau. "Where the hell do you think you are, in the goddamned movies?"

General Daniel J. Nelson of the United States Air Force, age sixty-three, Chairman of the Joint Chiefs of Staff, stared at Bensonhurst for a moment, then looked down at his gun. The crimson color in his face slowly faded to normal, then his skin continued to lighten until it was almost translucent. "I . . . *movies*? No . . . I'm . . . I'm sorry. I . . ." He stopped briefly, looked around at the other men.

"General Nelson, please," said President Wren.

"No," said Nelson, "I am truly sorry." And he lifted the gun until its barrel was pointing at his head, then discharged a nine-millimeter hollow-point bullet into his right temporal lobe.

Manarov made the last adjustments to the ship's life-support systems, queuing the commands in through the DEU, then, task complete, leaned back a little from the keyboard. So much for that. All over now but the dying. Well. He put the thought aside, too late for that, and reached up to the circuit-breaker panels leaning out overhead.

Hmh. It was a good question which systems ought to be left on and which ones should be shut down in engineering-safe mode. The jettison and abort guidance systems were aboard the flare shelter, encapsulated. . . . He smiled, trying to imagine it. So Sinuhe Major falls too far into the atmosphere. What now, comrades? Shall we try to eject through the wall of the plasma cone and parachute to safety in our handy little *Soyuz*? Their destruction would be lost in the general conflagration of an incoming asteroid.

He began flipping switches, deciding, system by system, which ones would be temporarily indispensable in the event of their survival. Be a hell of a thing if we lived through the aerobraking event, then died because I'm stupider than a heroic cosmonaut ought to be. . . . Their last ground communication—best of luck, gracious spacemen—talked about *Serpachek*'s translunar trajectory. They'd go behind the Moon eighteen minutes after Sinuhe's fiery perigee, able, in that last little time, to select a proper intercept course . . . if necessary.

Serebryakov came floating through the aft hatch, bumping to a stop by the control panel, his face pale, features frozen. "Everything's secure back there. I've powered up the capsule and put it in standby mode."

Manarov stared at a last group of switches, considering, then shut down the electronics that operated the many little motors controlling *Molotochek*'s various antennae. If we live, we can go out and aim them by hand. "That's it up here, too." He began pulling the DEU's cables from their control panel sockets. Take it back with us. *This,* we'll need.

Looking at his watch, Anton said, "Five minutes?"

"A little less."

The forward hatch creaked as it opened upward. Saar-mula floated through, looking at the two men anxiously. "Is everything ready?"

Volodya nodded. "All set."

"All right. Not much time . . ." He thrust himself over the lintel of the control panel and headed aft, passing smoothly through the hatch. Chishak trailed after him, eyes wide, but otherwise calm.

Volodya watched the man depart, thinking, Good, good.

Terror under control. Functioning. No worse off than me. He turned to Serebryakov. "Shall we go?"

Anton stared at him for a long moment, small, glittering eyes shifting slowly back and forth. "Volodya . . . No. I'm . . . staying here."

Staying. Well. Manarov floated a little closer to the man, looking into his face for a clue. "What do you mean?"

"I've . . . reasoned it out. If the ship breaks up, the shelter will be no salvation. If we survive . . . Shit. I want to *see* this!"

So. Volodya nodded slowly. In truth, this is what I have been avoiding. It's the things I *see* that have meaning to me. Well, then, you've made me face it, comrade. "Go back and tell the others. I'll get our suits ready."

"Suits?" Anton seemed a bit surprised.

Volodya smiled. "In case we spring a leak or two. Hurry. There's not much time!"

"But . . . Volodya, you don't have to . . ." He stopped and took a closer look, then nodded. "Yes. Yes, I see." He turned and, tumbling in midair, kicked off toward the after part of the ship.

Strapped into his acceleration couch in the dim light of the flare shelter, Lev Mikhailovich Chishak faced himself at the edge of the abyss. And now, he thought, the time arrives, of its own accord. Say your prayers, hero, the church was legalized ten years and more ago. The humor, largely falsified in any case, had a bitter flavor to it. What did they call it in school, back in the old days? Yes. We expose superstition and religion to ridicule, that the new Soviet man may emerge from the womb untainted by the errors of history. Well, you little radical, what now? Say two Hail Lenins and make an Act of Contrition . . . Marx forgive me for I have sinned. . . .

A gentle force was tugging at him from somewhere, pushing him back into his couch, sliding him toward his own feet. His thoughts continued their tired whirl for a little bit, then, suddenly aware, froze in the center of the spiral. What? The knowledge was there, suppressed, hidden. What . . .

Saarmula said, "The point oh-five-g light has come on. I guess the aerobraking phase has begun."

Chishak's heart leaped slightly in his chest, a wave of cold, prickling sensations chasing about his abdomen as his thoughts derailed at last. Aerobraking begun . . . What do I say now? What do I think? He put one hand out and laid it on the wall. The thick, slick padding there was buzzing softly. The . . . *fire* is no more than a minute away. I . . . I . . . He felt tears begin to form in the corners of his eyes and crawl out on his cheeks. "I'm not *ready*," he whispered softly.

Saarmula turned from staring at the numbers on the little control panel to look over at him. "Yes," he said. "We're never ready. Not for these moments." He reached out and patted Chishak on the back of the hand. "Hold on, Lyova. This is it."

Manarov and Serebryakov were lashed to the port bulkhead of the living quarters, face down, feet toward the putative floor, heads pressed together so their helmets were touching, facing out through the porthole. They were, thought Volodya, like mariners in a storm, lashed to the mast of the sailing ship, or maybe bound to the great wheel, able to function, yet safe from the waves that washed over the deck.

"I feel like Odysseus," said Anton, "waiting for the Sirens' call."

Well. A more apt image than mine. Will we scream, I wonder, will we writhe and try to break free when death beckons?

Outside, Earth's bloated face peered over the horizon, terrifying. Slanting sharply up from Sinuhe's ground, it was flat now, blue and white, studded with clouds. Were it not for the black sky above, it wouldn't have looked much different than the view from a supersonic jet. You could see curvature on the horizon, but . . . Not enough. We're below orbital height. . . .

The wall shuddered softly under their chests and they began to sag in their spacesuits, weight forming, creating pressure at their crotches, on the soles of their feet. Theory. Well, there was that. Theory said they might get through it. They were sliding into the atmosphere on a nearly tangent line, too shallow for full reentry. . . . Reentry. Not for Sinuhe. It's never been here. . . . He dismissed the thought, concentrating on the solidity of what was to come. The rock would slide across the atmosphere, surrounded by the fiery sheath of its plasma cone, slowing appreciably, casting kinetic energy into the flames, then skip out again, back toward the depths of space, turning as it went, pushing whatever remained of *Molotochek* before it. I wonder, thought Volodya, if we did our arithmetic right? I guess we'll soon know. . . .

"Volodya?"

"Here, Anton."

"I just want you to know I . . . You've been a good comrade on these voyages."

Manarov nodded slowly, hidden in his helmet. "Thank you. I . . ." What to say in these last seconds. Something maudlin? "In the end, that's all we can be to one another. Good comrades. Trusted and trusting. You've fulfilled that role as well as any man could." That would have to be enough. He laid his head back in the helmet and watched the world rise beneath them.

As the ship began to shudder, reacting to the way Sinuhe began its bite at the air, Anton tried to put his thoughts in order. Good comrades? Only that? In the end, after everything they'd been through, Manarov was still a closed book. And is that a terrible thing? Maybe not. Maybe that's what we all have to be.

Outside, on the alien landscape of Sinuhe, a faint mist was beginning to form. Streamers of it were lifting over the metal horizon, whipping up into dark space. The thin air of the upper stratosphere was condensing beneath the asteroid's ram, beginning to heat, to break away into the shape of the cone. It's going up. A good sign. Maybe we're in the right place after all. Anton squinted hard at the surface of the Earth. Where are we now? He thought he saw the outlines of the Baltic not far away. Over Poland, maybe . . . right on track. The numbers said Sinuhe would pass just north of Moskva and climb back into cold black space over Siberia.

Good. Mama can look up from old, cold Mytishchi and see me die.

The shuddering began a steady increase, moving him around inside his suit, making his chin bang down against the inside of the neck ring, where soft crumpled padding took up the shock. He tried to hold his face steady, but it was no use. And . . . where is my fear? Gone. Gone down into the black hole of my life. Eaten by those same generalities that kill us all . . .

The world lit up. First it was just one long streamer of

fire, climbing swiftly from the horizon, bright, yellow-or-ange-red, mixing smoothly as it pointed, fingerlike, out into the darkness, unwavering. It stood alone for the barest second, then other streamers, tongues of flame, rose to join it, gradually closing off the sky with an incandescent wall completing a ring about their lives.

Suddenly, Anton felt himself transported back to another time and place, sitting in a dacha, just whose he couldn't remember, in the late fall. It was snowing in the darkness outside, a fire was lit, and he was sitting on the floor on a sheepskin rug, maybe seven or eight years old, staring into the flames.

It was a strange thing to notice, but behind the burning logs, with their yellow flames tinged by red and, here and there, bits of green, stood a little region of concrete, smooth, a bit dirty, not covered by fire. Sitting in the middle of that expanse was a tiny black fleck, roughly the size and shape of a spider. It was just a cinder, he knew, but . . . what if it *was* a spider? He imagined himself then, in that spider's place, looking out at him over the flames.

The light outside was becoming intolerably bright and the walls of *Molotochek* were singing with the fury of the storm. Fiery chunks were rising from the horizon, whipping by, leaping into space. There was . . . noise. You could hear it, crackling and twanging all around you. . . . And all at once a terrific rending sound. The landscape was flooded, briefly, with an even brighter light, yellow-blue, that seared his eyes, throwing shadows across the world, *outward,* toward the girdling fire.

Volodya was shouting something to him through the earphones, but it was hard to hear, overpowered by the real-world noise around them, a mere radio-buzz, insectile, unimportant. He strained to hear, inpatient with the distraction. What . . .

It sounded something like, *"Yaahooo . . ."*

In his agony, engulfed by the universal fire, Anton felt vaguely offended.

Mikhail Sergeevich Gorbachev and Vladimir Semyonovich Ponomarev stood on a Kremlin balcony together, staring into the bright spring blue of the western sky, waiting. "Somehow," said the general, "it seems appropriate that it comes on us out of this direction."

Gorbachev nodded abstractedly. "Strange, isn't it? We always wait for an invader to strike at us from the North German Plain, yet the only successful conquest of Russia in all of history came out of the East."

"It was that invasion that made us. Before that we were just . . . Slavs, primitives, lapping up cabbage soup with our bark sandals. Genghis Khan and his grandsons created Great Russia out of nothingness. Without them we would be no more than . . . Bulgarians."

The thought plucked at Gorbachev's imagination. A world without Great Russia, just little Slavic states sandwiched between the Polono-Lithuanian Empire and some Sinified Siberia. He could almost see it: Muskovy almost a city state, somewhere near Bolgary, a bit to the south of the mighty Novgorod Republic. . . . What a different world that might have been!

Ponomarev hissed suddenly. "There!" He was pointing at a place low in the western sky, down near the horizon, just above the Moskva skyline.

Strange indeed, thought Gorbachev. And here I was expecting it to come from the heavens. Inspecting the reddish dot, knowing it to be a small hillock, roaring into the sky above Poland at something like twelve kilometers per second, he shivered. Indeed, if it came at the angle I was picturing, it would descend upon us. In the end, the image of a thousand-megaton explosion detonating anywhere near Moskva was . . . imponderable.

In a swift succession of moments the dot grew into a bright smudge in the sky, swelling abruptly. Quite suddenly, their parallactic view changed and it was an orangered line in the sky, dreadfully silent, appreciably thick, looking a bit like a bright jet contrail, colored by sunset perhaps, or the firework-trail of a solid-fuel ballistic missile. Without warning, it was overhead, still silent, but they could hear shouting in the streets as people noticed something unusual in the sky. Perhaps they were waiting for it, thought Gorbachev, craning his neck to look straight up. After all, we no longer control the press. . . .

The thing was overhead for less than two seconds, crossing all of ancient Muscovy in an eyeblink, then arrowing away into the east, crossing the Urals, its fiery trail diminishing, fading as it rose back into the cold black depths of outer space. Watching it go, dropping toward the horizon, disappearing into the eastern haze, Gorbachev thought he could hear a distant peal of thunder. A sonic boom, coming down from the ionosphere? Improbable. Just my senile imagination, or some distant military jet. From somewhere, he remembered that the latest project of the Boeing-Yakovlev SST Cooperative was due for flight-testing some time soon.

Well, then. He turned to look at Ponomarev, smiling. "You see, Comrade General. It comes and goes, as promised, merely a light show in the sky. And now we have them just where we want them: not by the throats, merely by their collective balls, in a soft and suggestive grip. You wanted an end to SDI?" He pointed a finger dramatically skyward. "There it is."

Ponomarev looked at him, truculent, clearly struggling to suppress some outburst. "You think this is the end of it? No. It is merely one small move in the chess game. You are an old man now, *finished.* You no longer exercise control over the Soviet government, regardless of your personal popularity. I am chief of the military, a post *you* cannot revoke, and I have my own base of power. One day . . ."

Mikhail Sergeevich Gorbachev smiled very broadly. "Will you excuse me, Comrade General? I have a phone call to make."

Ponomarev felt a moment of bewilderment at this sudden distraction. What? Was the old devil gone senile at last? He followed Gorbachev in to his desk and watched as the man sat down and picked up one of his phones, the one connected to a good, old-fashioned *Nomenklatura* line.

"Boris? Yes, this is Misha. How are you doing? Yes, I saw it. Quite a show! Listen, you remember how you wanted to retire Ponomarev, put your own man in charge of the Strategic Rocket Forces? Yes, that's right. Well, I've decided to withdraw my objections. You can start putting through the paperwork. Right. Good day to you, Comrade President. I'll see you at the Foreign Ministry ball tonight."

Hanging up the phone, he smiled again, ever more broadly, becoming more grin than man perhaps, and said, "As you say, Comrade General, I am *such* an old man, and ready for retirement. In fact, I am quite ancient, almost eleven months older than yourself!" As he stared Ponomarev down, Gorbachev thought, What a pity. How does the old saying go? When you have a tiger by the tail you can never, never let go. And I am *so* damned tired.

John-John Fingol, breathing hard, stared into the expectant faces of James Russell, Romain Bensonhurst, and Arthur Barnwell. "Jesus, we looked everywhere. Oval office, family quarters, fucking *combed* the bunkers . . . It's no use. We can't *find* him!"

Bensonhurst shook his head sharply. "Damn the man. Well, we can't wait. There's got to be a speech before the nation, and right now, or this'll be one fuck-up that the party never recovers from. Can you imagine it? The U.S. will be a one-party democracy, just as the Russians are moving into a truly democratic phase."

Barnwell, horrified, tried to think of objections. But they were all based on paper morality, nothing that anyone actually believed in.

Fingol looked out through the window, at a growing crowd in the park across the street. "No choice. Let's get the speech written. Shit. A twenty-minute simulation won't be that hard . . ."

Russell smiled. "You know, I kind of like it. The first digital president . . ."

The vibration was growing less. Was that a good sign? Tonya stared into the glowing curtain of fire that now hid everything. And his weight against the wall seemed to be lessening too. But the temperature was becoming intolerable; twenty more degrees and they'd be in agony. He wished he had done a calculation to tell how long this was supposed to last. He looked again. The curtain was definitely receding, showing small, wispy gaps that shuddered and moved.

In his earphones, Volodya's voice was understandable. "The thing is stable! We're going to make it!"

He couldn't believe it. Yet the evidence was growing. A star peeked out in the upper reaches of the veil, then another. The sound, now something like a crackling moan, was almost gone. His foreboding was going away as well. If the computers' predictions were met, Sinuhe Major, aerobraked, would fall through a tall ellipse over the next couple of weeks. . . . Time enough! Time enough for *Serpachek,* with its cargo of bombs, to catch them and finish the mission properly. A little voice piped up from somewhere far away, pointing out that if *Serpachek* failed there'd be a second, certainly fatal, aerobraking event. . . . He pushed it away. Again, it appeared, this dark prophecy was not to come true. How foolish it looked in retrospect. If he survived this, he would probably die in his bed, a centenarian at least. The front of his spacesuit, wet with his sweat and compressed by his artificial weight, started to unwrinkle, and he pushed himself back within the constraints of the harness.

Volodya was starting to untie himself, pulling impatiently at knots that wouldn't yield. "It worked, goddamn it, Tonya. It worked!"

Anton shook his head, trying to compose something sensible to say. "I guess so." Words for the ages.

"Come on. Let's get out there. I want to see what happened."

A bit later, they flew up over the dark surface like blocky wraiths, searching out signs of what had happened to their little world. It was dark and starry, with just a trace of light from the great bluish-yellow arc that framed the sky like a rainbow. The sun was in eclipse behind the huge nightside of Earth; a sunset of sorts. In the immediate vicinity of the command module, the asteroid had changed little, but as they moved away, toward the leading edge, the surface began to show the deep regmaglypt structures where molten metal had been pushed back by the hot atmosphere. Further on, Sinuhe was slick and shiny, smooth as a mirror. They flew on, not exchanging a word, until heat began to overload the spacesuits' systems. Finally, they came to a vantage point where they could look back unimpeded at the receding Earth. Though it was night, a glittering webwork of light perfectly defined North America, and you could make out New York, Chicago, all the major cities.

Volodya hunched back in his suit, breathing in the tasteless air with relish, thinking that all his misgivings and philosophizing had been a foolish waste of energy. "Well, Tonya," he said, "do you suppose that we really are in orbit around the Earth, or shall we go sailing back out into interplanetary space?" He tried to pick out Cape Canaveral, somewhere halfway down the phallic peninsula. He thought he saw it. What a perversion their space program had become. A land of militarism and mighty confusion. Perhaps it would end, now.

Tonya shrugged, pulling straps with his shoulders. "An extremely elliptical orbit around the earth, I would say. Good news for Mikhail Sergeevich. But whatever happens to Sinuhe, we are marooned here."

"At least until they can get *Serpachek* after us. No more than a week or two."

Looking down at the receding Earth, Manarov said, "Well. It feels strange, Tonya. Being alive, I mean."

"Strange?" Anton thought about it and nodded slowly to himself. "Yes. I think I know what you mean."

Far below, lightning flashed over the Atlantic. In its fire danced Shutka's plump face, and that of slim, strong Darya Grazhdanina, and of all the world's people, alive once more.

# EPILOGUE
## *November 12, 2017*

Georgia Paar had weathered the years exceedingly well. She'd kept her weight down, and all the rest was easy: an unending succession of LadyTan tailored molecular cosmetics kept the skin unlined, the eyes bright, the famous horse's mane of hair the correct shade of beige, varying by season. It didn't hurt the director of the U.S. National Observatory on Mount Palomar to be pretty. The congressmen knew she was in their age range, a cute old bag at fifty-three, and it made them just a little more liberal with their handouts. A voice at her shoulder, faintly Dutch-accented, said, "Aha. Trust an astronomer to know where and when the good views are."

The years had not been at all kind to Maarten Hakluyt. Floating in the open hatchway of the *Rossiya*'s forward observation lounge, he was fifty-seven years old and looked a decade older still. The midsection had gone round and soft, the Vandyke was the color of steel wool, the skin lined and careworn. His face still had that mouselike presence, but the big glasses that had accentuated the look to an extreme were gone: microsurgical techniques had extended the Fyodorov methodology to cover most major eye defects. Indeed, the gray eyes were bright with a joy that waxed with each passing year.

Georgia smiled. "Hey, Maarty. This one wasn't hard to figure out."

Floating to her side, the director of Galileo Base, ESA's Lunar South Polar Optical Long Baseline Observatory, nodded slowly. "No, but you beat me here nonetheless."

"I don't get many opportunities like this."

Hakluyt clamped down on his speech mechanisms, not

wanting to hurt an old and very dear friend. He felt sorry for her. Since its hectic unification in 2005, the Federal Republic of Europe, under a dynamic and forceful President Oberg, had gone into space along a broad front, pursuing independent projects under the aegis of its transportation consortium with the Soviet Union. Funny how that had worked out. When the formal Boundary Treaty of 2008 had been signed, no one was surprised that the Baltics had joined up with the FRU . . . but the *uproar* when the Scandinavian states had joined the USSR! Some very amusing news commentary had resulted.

Isolationist America had had little part in what was to come. After Wren's resignation for health reasons in the summer of 2003, the situation under President McDermott, over the next five and one-half years, had simply . . . deteriorated. Two more presidents had come and gone and a third was rounding out his first year, yet America just sat. It was true they had a little laboratory space on Japan's Yamato Station, but . . . nothing. Maarten Hakluyt felt very sorry for Georgia Paar. He looked at her, eyes softening, and said, "You have a position on my staff any time you want it. You know that."

Staring out the window, she made her stock answer: "I know. Maybe next year." They'd had this brief exchange every year for the past five years, ever since he'd taken over at Galileo.

Hakluyt turned and looked out through the window, through the optically perfect glass. Cislunar transport *Rossiya* was the pride of Glavkosmos's fleet of five ships, their contribution as senior partner in the consortium to which ESA contributed three somewhat smaller vessels. Each of the great nuclear-powered ships, plying the spaces between Gorbachev Station in low Earth-orbit, Korolyov Station in lunar orbit, and the complex of bases around Promyshlennograd, could haul a dozen passengers and five tons of loose or liquid cargo. It wasn't really a fleet sufficient for the task, just a beginning. . . . But there were men approaching Mars even now, and work was proceeding in the massive bays of Tsiolkovskii Cosmic Shipyard on the major components of the *Volya,* prototype of a line of fusion-powered vessels that would fly outward to the Main Belt asteroids and beyond.

Staring out the window, Georgia Paar saw, and, as al-

ways, felt that she was seeing for the first time. Hanging in
its orbit, a little more than sixteen hundred kilometers
above Earth, near-Earth-Asteroid—she winced at the term
—5007 Sinuhe was eaten away. Soviet miners had been at
work on the great mass of almost pure metal for nearly
fifteen years, digging at it for the stuff of newborn space
industries. Pieces of Sinuhe Major were on Earth, mostly in
museums, but far more of it was incorporated in
Gorbachev Station and the moon's matching Korolyov facility . . . bits and pieces sawn off and towed away . . .
amounting to more than half of the original body . . . yet
most of it was still right here.

Hanging in space behind the remains of the asteroid
floated the great, triadic spinning wheels of Promyshlennograd, City of Industry, more than two kilometers in diameter, stacked four hundred meters deep, fountainhead of
the Soviet Union's spacefaring civilization, salvation of a
socialism that almost died.

Quite suddenly, Georgia Paar burst into tears.

The ship came thundering down out of a bright pink sky,
embedded in the streaming fire of a plasma cone. It
dropped along a curving path, aerobraking to subsonic velocity, trading in kinetic energy for thermal. At an altitude
of some twenty-seven kilometers, just as it swept above
Tharsis Ridge, heading eastward, the plasma cone detached
from the ablating surface and the flames blew out. The ship
was falling free now, sloping at a forty-five-degree angle
toward the red desert below.

The pilot consulted his gauges and, after a brief glance to
the right, getting his flight engineer's confirming nod, he
flipped open a plastic cage and threw the toggle switch.
There was a muffled bang as a drogue chute opened above
them, while, simultaneously, the aeroshell dropped off, falling away into the thin air below, lost. No matter; there
were five more of them waiting above, snuggled securely
against the structural framework of the mother ship. Six
landings, the program called for, six one-month surface ex-
cursions during an eighteen-month orbital stay.

Now the ship was falling vertically, no more than ten
kilometers up, the flat red landscape reaching up for them.
At another nod from the engineer, the pilot threw another
switch and the drogue chute was whisked away, only to be

replaced, amid a billowing, thumping clatter, by three great ringsail parachutes. There was a moment of heavy deceleration, then they seemed to be floating down toward a gently rolling prairie.

The pilot waited, watching, until the ground was no more than a kilometer away, then he threw a third switch. The ship dropped sickeningly out from under the parachutes and the ground jumped up at them again, eliciting a murmur of protest from the passenger. The flight engineer watched his dials for a fraction of a second, hand tense over the emergency abort lever, then, "Autoignition sequence complete!"

The main engines, four big hydrogen/oxygen rockets, caught with a rumble, deceleration pushing the three men back down into their padded seats once again. It wasn't much, less than a full g, but after seven months and more of weightlessness it crushed the breath from their lungs. The passenger shut his eyes, thinking, God, when *will* this end? . . . You'd think I'd get *used* to these things. . . . He smiled thinly. At fifty-one years of age I'm . . . unlikely to change. He shut his eyes and tried not to shake.

As the pilot gripped his control sticks, the flight engineer began a cadence of data, the edge taken off his flawless Russian by a slight, exotic, vaguely French accent. "Altitude four hundred meters. Twelve meters per second down, eighteen forward . . ."

The pilot twitched his hands and they could feel the trim little spacecraft shift under them.

"Two hundred meters. Five down, six forward."

The passenger looked up once and saw the red horizon rocking in the windows, then shut his eyes tight, fighting motion sickness, silently cursing his fears.

"One hundred meters. Two down, two forward."

Slowing . . . slowing . . .

"Fifty meters. Two down, one forward."

"Easy . . . easy . . ." whispered the pilot to himself.

"Ten meters. One down, one forward. Picking up some dust." Despite himself, the flight engineer was experiencing a sharp sense of dyspnea.

"Three meters. Point-five down, zero forward . . ." then, "CONTACT LIGHT!" he shrieked, and, reaching for the propulsion master switch, "All engines stop!"

The last few hundred centimeters banged out of existence, clouds of red oxide dust rising around them. They bounced once, twice, a third time, and then they were down, surrounded by a silence of many components.

Sirje Saarmula, citizen of the Federal Republic of Europe, employee of Glavkosmos, turned to his flight engineer, ESA's Bruno Monsaingeon, with a flushed grin, then he spoke into his microphone. "Hello, Earth; *Marineris* North Base here. *Nadezhda* has landed."

Only a little while passed, then the three Earthmen cranked open the ship's outer airlock door and watched as the metal-lattice stairs unfolded to the ground. They were standing bunched together on the little "front porch," silent, staring out across the broad red plain, a rocky, crater-pocked wilderness that plucked at them from under a cloudless pink sky. Finally, knowing that he was speaking for posterity, the pilot spoke: "The first man in space was a military fighter pilot; and the first man to set foot on the Moon was a civilian test pilot. Today we choose to break with that tradition, or perhaps to extend its direction. Today we choose to let a space scientist be the first to stand on a new world." He motioned to the passenger, who walked slowly and clumsily down the stairs, then hesitated. What, then, will *I* say? . . .

Anton Antonovich Serebryakov stepped out and placed his heavily booted foot squarely on the surface of Mars, marveling at the little dust wraith, then turned to look up at his comrades. Surely, he thought, the words will not come. . . . But they did, nonetheless: "Mother Earth," he said, "is the cradle of Mankind, yet one cannot remain in the cradle forever. Let it be recorded that today we took our first toddling steps into the childhood of humanity. The road to adulthood is a long one . . . but it is begun."

Soviet Deputy Minister for Space Vladimir Alekseevich Manarov stood with his hands clasped behind his back, gazing out the great three-meter observation window of Promyshlennograd Space Habitat's Grand Concourse, watching the heavens roll by. At this point in its orbit the spin-stabilized structure was perpendicular to the Earth and, by chance, a waxing Moon stood nearly overhead. As he stood, staring, pressed comfortably to the floor by the station's point-twenty-five-g, Tellus and Luna wheeled on stately courses, first one, then the other passing beneath his

feet. The stars were, unfortunately, contrast-washed out of
existence, but the sun was a disk of fire, even through the
window's strong filter looking like a portal into De Sitter
Space, infinitely hot, infinitely dense, the metastable source
of creation.

So. Here you are one last time, he thought, and old
Akhmatov is dead at last. Despite congestive heart failure
and a generation spent being tortured by stress-induced
gastroesophageal reflux disease, he'd lived to be seventy-
two, and . . . when did seventy-two start being old? Here
I am, fifty-six, only now promoted to the ground. He shook
his head slowly. Here I am. In another week, after a brief
vacation, he and Shutka would be back in Moskva. . . .

He glanced over his shoulder at the room full of people.
Yes, there she was, over by the refreshments, surrounded
by friends, slimmed down by some modern drug regimen or
another, but still . . . He smiled. She hadn't exercised
much over the past few months and would have a hell of a
time readjusting to full gravity. . . .

Back in Moskva. What will it feel like, after so long? In
ten days I'll be sitting down in Akhmatov's Kremlin office,
trying to make sense out of his computer's directory structure. Minister for Space. He tried to taste the words but
they were, as usual, flavorless. Well, even in the restruc-
tured Soviet Union, a full cabinet member, like someone on
the old Politburo, is a politician. . . . Three years to
go . . . and I know full well the party has no intention of
nominating Klimuk to stand for another term. They're
tired of his Byelorussian bullshit. . . .

"You still like looking at it after all these years, don't
you?"

Volodya made a graceful low-gravity pirouette. "Lyova!"
He held out his hand. "I'm glad you could make it! Good
to see you again."

The doctor smiled from under a thin gray mustache. "I
tried to talk myself out of it but, as usual, I failed."

Volodya nodded, looking at him critically. The interven-
ing years had not treated Chishak kindly. Despite every
opportunity offered by his friends, Lev had faltered again
and again. Even now, he was nothing more than the undistinguished head of the space medicine office at Baikonur.
He clapped the man gently on the shoulder. "I'm glad to
see you, in any case. This is like a little reunion."

Chishak smiled crookedly. "Yes. If Seryozha and Tonya were here . . . or we with them." He watched Volodya's expressionless face for a heartbeat, then went on: "I remember how much you wanted that for yourself. What did you call it? 'The Dream?' "

Still a cruel little bastard, aren't you? He turned away slowly, looking out into the blazing night once again. "I did call something that, didn't I? But it wasn't just the expedition to Mars, though I'd love to be aboard *Nadezhda* right now." He waved a hand at the view out the window, taking in half the universe. "No. This is the Dream; all of it. I dreamed of being first on Mars, but, in truth, my part in the drama has turned out to be . . . somewhat larger."

Chishak felt a sharp pang of disappointment but kept quiet, thinking, Some men are guarded by their dreams. . . . The next emotion he felt was envy.

"You've been over here for a long time, Minister. Are you expecting something?"

They turned to look at the speaker, then Volodya held out his hand. "I *am* a bit remiss in my duties as host of this celebration. Good afternoon, Mr. Vice-President. How is President Russell?"

Bradford K. Harveson, III, was a trim and handsome man of sixty-seven, good-looking in the multimedia fashion of American politicians, and he had high hopes for the year 2020. He shook Manarov's hand, knowing he faced his probable opposite number. "Paranoid and foolish, but he sends his regards nonetheless. We . . . talked about his coming, but he fears . . . Well. I wanted to come, in any case."

Volodya nodded. "I'm glad to see you. We can have . . . productive discussions, you and I."

"Agreed. It's too bad President Oberg can't be here."

"The Muscovites would miss the ceremonial. His wreath-laying every year at Gorbachev's Tomb has come to mean a great deal in my country."

Harveson nodded, remembering the occasion not so long ago when they'd taken Lenin away and buried him beside old Khrushchev. They stood shoulder to shoulder now, looking out into space. "You still haven't told me what you're waiting for."

Volodya smiled. "Not waiting. Watching." He pointed at

a spot in the darkness, just as light sparkled briefly. "Did you see that?"

Harveson nodded, suddenly haggard.

"It is 10228 Huluppu, a chondritic body of some ten billion metric tons, being steered by mass-driver to lunar orbit. It's to be our new fuel plant. When the *Volya* is flying, that's where she'll gas up for her first long jump."

"What's the destination?"

"Vesta, of course. Not a good choice, really, but it looms so large in our imaginations. . . ."

"God," said Harveson, "I'd trade places with you in a minute. . . ."

Volodya turned to face him. "So? You could have had all this."

"No. It just wasn't in the cards."

"Not in the cards? That's nonsense, Mr. Harveson. There are no fates. . . . It's like Lenin said: There are no rewards and no punishments, only consequences."

"What do you mean?" He had a premonition, but felt compelled to ask.

"In 1970, you had a twenty-year technological lead on the rest of the world, but you pissed it swiftly away. You know, Marx was right, in a sense, but for reasons he could never have anticipated. Your capitalism, whatever else it may be, denies the future. It has no underlying philosophical unity, no goal other than immediate personal gratification. A half-century ago, under inspired leadership, you had one 'brief, shining moment' of triumph, then you exchanged it all for military adventurism and backward-looking economics."

Volodya took a deep breath and turned back to the window, where a distant light was beckoning once again. "Money doesn't *dream,* you see, and now we will bury you after all."

# APPENDIX 1

# *Apollo—Aten—Amor*
# *A Fast Road to Tomorrow*

*Fellow Traveler* is a science fiction novel, intended to make a dramatic portrayal of an extraordinary adventure that is possible—though just *barely* possible—using today's off-the-shelf technology. The Soviet Union really could pull off the space spectacular portrayed herein, though it seems likely that they, like we, lack the political will to accomplish such a triumph. Why this should be is something of a mystery. The technology of interplanetary travel has been available to us for more than a generation, yet still we sit home. Why?

The other side of that question is often asked by the antiscientific know-nothings who dominate global politics. Why bother going? Because it's "there?" Nonsense. Human beings seldom bother doing anything, particularly a thing as expensive as space travel, unless there is a very compelling reason for doing it.

The authors of *Fellow Traveler* think there is a very good reason indeed for making the leap to becoming a spacefaring civilization, now rather than later, and have said so publicly at every opportunity.

Since the *Challenger* explosion, a national debate has arisen over the future direction of the American space program. Major positions have ranged from suggestions that the manned component of the program be canceled to the idea that the United States engage in a crash program to achieve some Apollo-like goal. Among prospace activists, there have been a bewildering variety of opinions and project proposals. These range from modest extensions of current programs like the International Space Station and Mariner Mark II to vast engineering projects such as space colonies and solar-power satellites. Since the release of the Ride Report, debate among enthusiasts has centered on the competing goals of a return to the moon, usually including a permanently manned lunar base, and a mission to Mars, most often in close cooperation with the Soviet Union.

Now that America is back in space again, the debate should be intensifying. Instead, politicians continue to talk in only the most general terms, refusing to deal with the specific goals and technologies that will be necessary to formulate a successful space policy. We seem to be returning to the same set of attitudes that caused the mess the space program was in at the time of *Challenger*'s demise. We *must* have explicit long-term objectives, underlying all else we do, for our shorter-term objectives to make sense.

It is essential to visualize the future of the human species on Earth to fully comprehend the importance of our long-term space objectives. If we do not accomplish the transition from an Earth- to a space-based society in the twenty-first century, then, as our fictional Mikhail Gorbachev states, it seems unlikely that the impoverished and desperate civilization of the twenty-second century will be able to do so. Even in the most optimistic scenarios, space travel plays a crucial part in the technological solutions that can save us from ourselves.

If we are to have a spacefaring civilization, we must have access to off-Earth resources, not so much for importation to the Earth as to supply raw materials for the deep-space industries to come. The Earth, with its deep gravity well, will never be able to deliver resources to space economically. Space will have to be self-sufficient. We must examine all possible space-based resources to determine the most usable ones, and this examination should direct and inform the choices we make in devising our policies.

The Moon, whose surface is in some ways like the basaltic ocean floor, is strongly depleted in the siderophile elements on which our industrial economy is based. Worse still, the Moon is quite dry and there is as yet no evidence that it possesses concentrated veins of minerals. Recent attempts to find signs of water-ice in the permanently shaded interiors of polar craters have turned up nothing, indicating that this most valuable of resources may be almost totally absent. Most lunar industrial schemes rely on using the readily available solar energy of space to process raw lunar soil in bulk for its constituent elements. While this is feasible, it is a bit like proposing to strip-mine the scablands of Washington.

And what about Mars? Its "Earth-like" regions, areas which have been somewhat geologically active and subjected to hydrothermal processes, will probably have abundant mineral resources. The poles are certainly rich enough in water. However, in many ways Mars is the worst possible candidate for a deep-space mining facility. It is very far away in terms of both mission energy and travel time and has a high surface gravity. In any event, our descendants, a thousand years down the road, will probably want to be living on a terraformed Mars. We would be making a poor decision indeed if we went out of our way to damage the place for expediency's sake.

It has been acknowledged generally by space development researchers that the most likely sites of accessible resources in the inner solar system are the asteroids. Foremost among their advantages is the fact that most asteroids are the collisionally shattered fragments of larger bodies. If they have minerals, they will not be buried "underground." Of comparable importance is the fact that they are small and consequently have negligible surface gravity. Most asteroids are so small that they might be transported to a near-Earth industrial facility more or less whole, using a technology only modestly more advanced than what is presently available. Science fiction stories detailing the necessary techniques have been appearing for more than fifty years.

The principal disadvantage of the Main Belt or Piazzi asteroids is that they are quite remote. A typical "normal" asteroid lies in an elliptical orbit somewhere between two and five Astronomical Units from the sun. In terms of both travel time and overall mission velocity, or "delta-V" as it is sometimes called, this makes them considerably farther away than either the Moon or Mars.

The asteroids of Main Belt IV, which are almost certain to be rich in minerals and to contain vast quantities of valuable volatile materials, are almost as remote as the moons of Jupiter. They are so remote, in every way that matters, that their potential will have to await the development of more advanced propulsion systems, perhaps generations in the future. In practical terms, we will have to *have* a spacefaring civilization before we can get at those resources, however much we need them.

Fortunately, there is an alternate target for our space program which has all the advantages of the Main Belt asteroids and none of their drawbacks. They are sometimes referred to collectively as the near-Earth asteroids. Several have made the headlines when astronomers have predicted their "close" approach to earth, 1566 Icarus and 1620 Geographos being the most famous. It is likely that small asteroids have collided with the earth in the remote past, and it has been speculated that one such collision caused the extinction of the dinosaurs at the end of the Cretaceous era.

These asteroids, whose orbits occasionally bring them into the vicinity of the earth, are divided into three categories. The Aten asteroids spend most of their time inside the Earth's orbit, but have aphelia beyond it. Apollo objects have the bulk of their orbits outside the Earth's, but have perihelia closer to the sun. Amor asteroids orbit entirely between the Earth and Mars, but can approach the Earth nearly enough (0.3 AU) to make them of special interest. It has been suggested that these Aten-Amor-Apollo asteroids be called the Triple-A's.

More than 150 of these objects are known at present, and it is estimated that there are at least ten times that number altogether. These asteroids display no common characteristics and in fact could not have formed where they are now. It has been demonstrated that they are most likely objects from diverse places in the solar system, brought to their present orbits by the perturbations of Jupiter. Their spectra show no systematic similarities and indicate a wide variety of physical types, probably representing a good sample population of small asteroids.

As might be expected, many of these asteroids are quite close in terms of delta-V, although travel time varies greatly depending on the orientation of their orbit relative to Earth's. Table 1 contains a listing of some of the close Triple-A asteroids, along with a number of other objects and "destinations" of interest for comparison.

## Table 1: Access by Rendezvous delta-V

| Name | Diameter (km) | delta-V (km/s) | Time (d) |
|------|-----|-----|-----|
| Low Earth-Orbit | 0.0 | 9.20 | <1 |
| Earth Escape | 0.0 | 11.18 | 3 |
| Geosynchronous EO | 0.0 | 13.40 | <1 |
| 1982 DB | 1.0 | 13.65 | 206 |
| Orpheus | 0.8 | 14.49 | 180 |
| Deimos | 15.0 | 14.70 | 259 |
| Luna | 3476.0 | 14.80 | 3 |
| 1980 PA | 1.0 | 14.81 | 750 |
| Low Mars-Orbit | 0.0 | 15.01 | 259 |
| Eros | 22.0 | 15.15 | 298 |
| Low Venus-Orbit | 0.0 | 15.54 | 146 |
| Ra-Shalom | 1.6 | 17.15 | 110 |
| Aten | 0.8 | 17.19 | 127 |
| Mars | 6786.0 | 19.15 | 259 |
| Jupiter Flyby | 0.0 | 19.97 | 998 |
| Antinous | 3.0 | 21.59 | 151 |
| Callisto | 4800.0 | 22.49 | 998 |

As can be readily seen, many of the bodies on this list, which is representative rather than exhaustive, are closer in terms of flight energy than the surface of Earth's own Moon. However, this characteristic is due to the shape and location of their orbits. And for the same reason, energetically close asteroids are often among the temporally remote. Table 2 illustrates this point with a representative compendium of flight times.

The problem of flight-time versus delta-V is an old one and often hard to understand. It is mystifying to imagine geosynchronous Earth-orbit being harder to reach than "escape to infinity" until one stops to consider the energy that must be spent circularizing the orbit of a GEO comsat. An ellipse with its apogee at GEO its not much less energetic than one with its apogee a billion light-years away. You just get there a lot quicker.

The Triple-A asteroids discovered thus far are quite small, ranging in size from 1036 Ganymed, at 40 km in diameter, to the 200-meter object 2340 Hathor. The remainder are elusive, either too small to be seen by the largest telescopes or simply not recognized for what they are, tiny spots of light lost in a field of stars. We know they are easy to reach, fulfilling one of our prerequisites for off-Earth resources. Can we say anything more about these nearby objects to gauge their potential?

Table 2: Access by Rendezvous Flight-Time

| Name | Diameter (km) | delta-V (km/s) | Time (d) |
|---|---|---|---|
| Low Earth-Orbit | 0.0 | 9.20 | < 1 |
| Geosynchronous EO | 0.0 | 13.40 | < 1 |
| Earth Escape | 0.0 | 11.18 | 3 |
| Luna | 3476.0 | 14.80 | 3 |
| Aristaeus | 0.8 | 22.23 | 91 |
| Ra-Shalom | 1.6 | 17.15 | 110 |
| Aten | 0.8 | 17.19 | 127 |
| Low Venus-Orbit | 0.0 | 15.54 | 146 |
| Hathor | 0.2 | 17.16 | 151 |
| Toro | 7.6 | 16.87 | 164 |
| 1979 XB | 0.8 | 24.26 | 164 |
| 1954 XA | 0.8 | 15.81 | 165 |
| Tantalus | 2.0 | 35.17 | 217 |
| Deimos | 15.0 | 14.70 | 259 |
| Low Mars-Orbit | 0.0 | 15.01 | 259 |
| Eros | 22.0 | 15.15 | 298 |
| 1981 CW | 2.6 | 15.10 | 319 |
| Anteros | 4.0 | 14.47 | 390 |
| 1980 PA | 1.0 | 14.81 | 750 |
| Jupiter Flyby | 0.0 | 19.97 | 998 |
| Io | 3630.0 | 24.24 | 998 |
| Callisto | 4800.0 | 22.49 | 998 |

Scientists have successfully matched the spectra of many of the Triple-A's with those of meteorite samples of known properties. On the basis of these comparisons, they have come to what they feel are fairly definitive conclusions about the compositions of these bodies. Some seem to be primitive undifferentiated material from the earliest history of the solar system. Others seem to be somewhat processed stony minerals from the bedrock of partially or completely differentiated planetesimals. A third group appears to have a large metal content, primarily nickel-iron, and could be from the heavy-element-rich cores of these bodies.

From the point of view of potential resources, both the carbonaceous chondrites (undifferentiated material from the colder parts of the early solar system) and the nickel-iron asteroids offer great promise. Many of the Triple-A's show the spectral signatures of Carbonaceous material, and probably contain carbon, primitive organics, and water, among other volatiles. At least two of the Triple-A's have spectra indistinguishable from those of the nickel-iron meteorites. Facetious estimates of their value range into the trillions of dollars.

The only solar system bodies this small for which we have a reasonable amount of direct observational data are the Martian moons Phobos and Deimos and the Comet Halley nucleus. Since many planetologists feel that the moons of Mars are "normal" asteroids which somehow got into what are decidedly unusual orbits, it may be useful to picture bodies somewhat like Phobos when talking about the larger Triple-A asteroids. The most general characteristics of very small bodies are governed primarily by impacts and have little to do with their composition. Asteroids which have spent most of their time in the Main Belt will have experienced a greater number of impacts, possibly so many that they are reduced to "flying rubble piles," all regolith and no core. However, nonbelt asteroids, like Phobos, seem to be reasonably intact.

We can assume that a typical asteroid will be a nonspherical object whose surface is saturated with craters. It may have ridgelike arcuate edges resulting from the impacts that broke it from an originally larger parent planetoid. This body will have experienced shock-metamorphism and fragmentation to a great depth, probably throughout the asteroid.

The amount of actual regolith covering the surface is open to question, but Deimos' is estimated to reach a depth of between one hundred and two hundred meters. Since impacts tend to overturn layers of material, the regolith will be composed of whatever was just beneath the preimpact surface. On very small bodies, much of the regolith will have been blasted away into space, but if the loose material is fairly thick then it will tend to travel "downslope" whenever a new impact or tidal interaction with a planet causes an asteroid-quake. Since it would pool in the bottoms of craters and wherever the surface was closer to the center of the object, topographic highs would be the best places for visiting astronaut-prospectors to find "bedrock."

The regoliths of most asteroids will share many characteristics with the surface of Luna, having been bombarded by the solar wind at a comparable intensity for a similar length of time.

Phobos shows many striations and pit-chains that have no counterpart on Deimos. It shows a brightening of crater and striation rims at low-phase angles that almost certainly results from the presence of finer textured material at these sites. On the other hand, Deimos has greater normal albedo variations and its craters are conspicuously filled with material. This would seem to indicate that Deimos has a weaker composition, but the photometric similarity of the two moons makes this argument difficult to sustain.

It has been proposed that the event that created Phobos' Crater Stickney stripped off most of its regolith, exposing the underlying material. However, Stickney is a very old crater, which requires the invocation of a scenario in which the regoliths of both moons were created during that hypothetical time when both were in the asteroid belt. Phobos would then have to experience Mars orbit insertion shortly after the Stickney event. Had the Soviet *Fobos* mission succeeded, new evidence might have been available to help explain the anomalies present on the Martian moons. The authors regret the failure of those two probes, whose success would have shown an increased maturity in the Soviets' thus-far unspectacular unmanned exploratory program.

There is also a distinct possibility that at least some of the Triple-A asteroids are "burned out" comets. P/Encke, a depleted periodic comet that follows an asteroidlike orbit, will be virtually indistinguishable from an Apollo asteroid when its volatiles are covered or gone. An asteroid with a very elliptical orbit, 2201 Oljato has been found to be associated with the sort of meteroid streams previously only found with comets. If there are, in fact, dead comets among the Earth-crossers, they would very probably be fabulous sources of water and other volatiles, as well as the primitive organic material needed for many industries. This sort of material may well become the petroleum of the next millennium.

A comet nucleus is a much more dynamic body than an asteroid, and would look very different. Fortunately, we have some close observations of this type of body to use as a model: Comet Halley.

As revealed by the several spacecraft that performed close flybys, Halley's nucleus is very dark, reflecting only about 4 percent of the sunlight that strikes it. It is an oblong body, roughly 15 km long by 8 km wide, in the same size range as the largest Triple-A asteroid. *Giotto* photographs showed a considerable amount of topography, including crater- and mountainlike forms. Dust impacts on the probes showed a chondritic composition, including magnesium-rich olivine grains and kamacite (nickel-iron), indicating that the nonvolatile components of Halley may not be too different from those of the carbonaceous chondrite meteorites and asteroids.

In fact, it may be difficult to tell a dead comet nucleus from a carbonaceous chondrite body, at least on the surface. Both are very dark with a reddish component in their spectra. Both are probably composed of the elements that dominated in the colder parts of the early solar nebula. Asteroids 1580 Betulia, 2061 Anza, 2100 Ra-Shalom and 1978 SB all have albedos in the 4 percent range—are they dead comet nuclei or carbonaceous asteroids? Only a prospecting trip will tell.

Ultimately, though a great deal may be said about the Triple-A asteroids, we can't be sure what resources they possess unless we can examine them in far greater detail than is possible with today's instrumentation. Even without direct, on-site examination by automated probes, we can discover more about these intriguing bodies through the use of equipment that should be available very shortly. The Hubble Space Telescope's planetary camera can be used to image possible candidates for further exploration. Although a high resolution image of some of the smaller bodies would require approaches within 0.01 AU of the Earth (an extremely rare event), some of the larger ones, such as 1978 SB, could be examined in detail. For even the smallest, refined spectral signatures and new photometric data can be gathered and evidence of reduced cometary outgassing can be sought.

It seems likely that new Triple-A asteroids will be found in the near future as well. If H. A. Zook of the Johnson

Space Center receives funding for his computer-monitored video motion detector, asteroids as small as 100 meters will be detectable out to distances of 0.5 AU, provided that motions relative to Earth exceed 10 km/sec. Such discoveries would round out our knowledge of the nonbelt asteroid population considerably.

And what about the near-term prospect of flights to the Triple-A asteroids, both manned and unmanned?

Getting there is relatively easy. Launch vehicles capable of sending large and sophisticated probes to the Earth-grazers have been available since the dawn of the space age. There is no reason why an early Mariner-class probe could not have been sent to one of these bodies during the 1960s other than, as always, lack of project funding.

And manned flights?

For the earliest missions, which would be Apollo-like "dashes" for prospecting and *in situ* planetological research, almost any off-the-shelf technology would do.

In the mid-1960s, Triple-A asteroid visits were proposed using two-man *Gemini* capsules propelled by prototype Rover nuclear rocket stages. In the latter part of that decade, it was noted that visits to Aten and (appropriately) Apollo asteroids were possible using unmodified Apollo/Saturn V hardware. Such expeditions were given serious consideration as part of the Apollo Applications Program, plans which were dropped when AAP, starved for funds, was reduced in scope to include only *Skylab*.

In terms of what is presently available, the Soviet Union is in the best position to make a Triple-A flight in the next decade.

A single Energiya launch vehicle would be able to send a *Salyut*-derived crew module weighing less than 30,000 kg on one of these relatively brief expeditions. Such a flight would be easier in all respects (and far safer) than a Moon landing. Though it seems unlikely that they will make the attempt any time soon, given the Soviet's understandably cautious approach to space exploration, they could do it as soon as the Energiya is considered reliable enough to be "man rated." If it came in the next few years, an asteroid expedition would completely overshadow anything that any other spacefaring nation might achieve. It would, indeed, be a *Sputnik*-class accomplishment, and it would be good preparation for the far more ambitious missions of the twenty-first century.

The United States is in a less enviable position, if for no other reason than that most of its space transportation system is as yet unbuilt. Even with the shuttle back on line, we still lack the means of reaching translunar trajectories with meaningful payloads. It would be possible to mount these flights with multi-component combinations of the proposed Orbital Transfer Vehicle, but we will probably have to wait for a heavy-lift vehicle of our own before we can attempt something so bold as a manned expedition to an Earth-crosser, much less a return to the Moon or mission to Mars.

One thing we must certainly note: An expedition to any one of the more easily accessible Triple-A asteroids requires nothing that we do not already know how to build. Because the required mission velocity is small, there is no need for an advanced propulsion system. Because the required mission times are short, there is no need for an advanced life-support system.

The benefits that make the Apollo, Aten and Amor objects so much more desirable than the moon or Mars as the principal goal of our near-term manned space program are based on speculation at this point. Can we justify sending men and machines to these tiny bits of asteroidal flotsam that litter the near reaches of interplanetary space? What will *we* gain?

We will gain knowledge. We will find a fair sampling of what the asteroids are like, for these are real asteroids, but as close to us in terms of delta-V as the Moon. If asteroids have resources, then these asteroids will have resources. And having reached them, we will know with precision what we must do to build the spacefaring civilization of the twenty-first century.

If these early and inexpensive flights show that the resources are there, then the nations of the Earth can safely make a commitment to more advanced missions, perhaps carrying automated fuel processing plants, perhaps carrying mass-drivers with which to move the asteroids themselves.

And perhaps some time in the second quarter of the twenty-first century, a small Triple-A asteroid will be towed to a factory complex at $L_1$(SE), as "close" to the

Earth as any cislunar Lagrange point, yet not defacing the night sky that we all value, and the industrial economy of that spacefaring civilization will spring into being in an instant.

## BIBLIOGRAPHY:

### ARTICLES:

1. "Harvesting the Near-Earthers," William Barton and Michael Capobianco. *Ad Astra,* Vol. 1, No. 10, November 1989, p. 24.

2. "Reconnaissance Mission to Near-Earth Asteroids," Luciano Anselmo. Paper submitted to Asteroids II Conference, 1988.

3. "Earth-Approaching Asteroids: Populations and Collision Rates with Earth, Venus, and Mercury," Eugene M. Shoemaker, Ruth F. Wolfe, and Carolyn S. Shoemaker. Paper submitted to Asteroids II Conference, 1988.

4. "On the Optical Detection of Meteoroids, Small Near-Earth Asteroids and Comets, and Space Debris," H. A. Zook. Paper submitted to the Nineteenth Lunar and Planetary Science Conference, 1988.

5. "Trillion-Dollar Asteroids?" No Author Cited. *Sky & Telescope,* July 1987, p. 11.

6. "Accessibility of Near-Earth Asteroids," C. O. Lau and N. D. Hulkower. *Journal of Guidance, Control, and Dynamics,* Vol. 10, No. 3, May-June 1987, p. 225.

7. "Near-Earth Asteroids: Possible Sources from Reflectance Spectroscopy," Lucy A. McFadden, Michael J. Gaffey, and Thomas B. McCord. *Science,* Vol. 229, 12 July 1985, p. 160.

### BOOKS:

1. *Meteorites and Their Parent Planets,* Harry Y. McSween. Cambridge University Press, 1987.

2. *Satellites,* J. A. Burns, M. S. Matthews, eds. The University of Arizona Press, 1986.

3. *Origin of the Moon,* W. K. Hartmann, R. J. Phillips, G. J. Taylor, eds. Lunar and Planetary Institute, 1986.

4. *Lunar Bases,* W. W. Mendell, editor. Lunar and Planetary Institute, 1985.

5. *The Facts on File Dictionary of Astronomy* (2nd ed.), Valerie Illingworth, editor. Facts on File Publications, 1985.

6. *Asteroids,* T. Gehrels, editor. The University of Arizona Press, 1979.

7. *Manned Spacecraft,* Kenneth Gatland, Macmillan, 1967.

8. *Dynamics,* A. S. Ramsey, Cambridge University Press, 1962.

9. *Assignment in Space,* Blake Savage, Whitman, 1952.

10. *Handbook of Chemistry and Physics* (various editions), R. C. Weart, et al., eds. The Chemical Rubber Company, annual.

# APPENDIX 2

## 2001 through 2003
## The Technological Surround

### SPACE STATIONS:

**Eisenhower [USA]:** Military station begun in 1998 on a 10-year construction cycle. Current permanent crew is 12, with 24-man construction teams in residence. Artificial gravity design. Eventual max crew configuration is 48. The irony of the name is, of course, that President/General Eisenhower is the one who warned us about the military-industrial complex in 1960.

**Freedom [USA, ESA, Japan, Canada]:** Multinational station begun in 1994 and completed over a period of 7 years with much squabbling. Single keel, zero-g design, max crew 24.

**Mechta [USSR]:** *Mir* base module in lunar polar orbit, to be manned intermittently by lunar landing crews, it was placed in lunar orbit in 2000 and first manned in 2001 by a survey team. A landing team was there briefly in 2002, before their mission was canceled in favor of the asteroid project.

**Mir [USSR]:** Soviet general-purpose station begun in 1986, reached its final configuration in 1994. Zero-g keel-less design. Max crew 24. Note that it has none of its original components but is the product of a gradual evolution.

**Zemlya [USSR]:** Planned successor station to *Mir*, it is a two-keel, zero-g design with a theoretical max crew of 48. Targeted for a two-hour orbit (1,076 mile), construction was scheduled to begin in 2004.

SPACECRAFT:

## 1. Ground to Low Earth-Orbit

**STS-A [USA]:** Original space shuttle first flown in 1981. Two flight vehicles are still operational in 2002. *Atlantis* and *Discovery* are still flying on a limited basis. *Columbia* has been retired and *Endeavour* was ruined by a bad landing in 1996.

**STS-B [USA]:** Shuttle-2 fully reusable design first flown in 1998. Two flight vehicles on line by 2002. The design is a fuel-integral, canarded delta-wing orbiter and remotely piloted fly-back booster. The two shuttles are named *Aldebaran* and *Bellatrix*. A third flight vehicle, *Capella*, is scheduled for delivery in 2003.

**STS-C [USA]:** Shuttle-derived (STS-A) heavy-lift vehicle first flown in 1995 to support space station construction.

**NASP [USA]:** DOD-operated transatmospheric vehicle first flown in 1994, restricted to use supporting Project Overlord (as the operational phase of SDI will be called). There are 6 flight vehicles, none of which have names.

**Kosmicheskii Korabl [USSR]:** Soviet shuttle first flown in 1988. There are eight flight vehicles: *Buran, Ptichka, Raduga, Taina, Lyzhnya, Poloska, Rodina,* and *Yamochka.*

**Energiya [USSR]:** Heavy-lift vehicle first flown in 1987.

**Hermes [ESA]:** DynaSoar-like 3-man space plane lifted by Ariane 5, first flown in 1997. There are 4 flight vehicles.

**HOPE [Japan]:** Unmanned fully reusable mini-shuttle first flown in 2000. The Japanese plan to fly a manned version some time around 2005, after which they will begin work on a national space station. In 2002, there are enough parts on hand to operate two vehicles simultaneously.

## 2. Trans-Orbital Vehicles

**Soviet Lunar Transfer Vehicle ("LTV").** Component system for moving cargoes between low Earth-orbit and lunar orbit. The propulsion module consists of a heavily modified Energiya sustainer core that can be refueled in Earth-orbit. Each vehicle is expected to survive 10-15 lunar round-trips before being broken up for parts and scrap. The first one

*(Molotochek)* was delivered in 1999 and made an unmanned test flight to the Moon and back. It was then used to deliver *Mechta* to lunar orbit in 2000. A second flight vehicle *(Serpachek)* was delivered in 2001, after which manned lunar landing missions were authorized. Cargoes include Salyut-derived command modules and LLVs. This vehicle is capable of making round trips to Mars. With inflight refueling, it can reach the Main Belt Asteroids.

**Soviet Lunar Landing Vehicle (Unmanned) ("LLV(U)").** Vehicles designed to transport cargo from Mechta to various points on the lunar surface. The lower stage is a standardized vehicle scaled up from the last Luna probe designs (XVI and later). Various cargoes include a *Salyut*-derived base station which will support surface stays by 6-man crews of up to 90 days (extendible by resupply flights) and such things as a planned Mobile Laboratory Vehicle.

**Soviet Lunar Landing Vehicle (Interim) ("LLV(I)").** Since the development of the LLV(M) has been delayed, the first several flights will be LLV(U)s adapted to carry cosmonauts in a *Soyuz*-derived ascent stage. This hybrid vehicle is referred to as the LLV(I). *Oryol* and its sister-ship *Lastochka* are the only complete flight articles to be constructed, though five descent stages are planned.

**Soviet Lunar Landing Vehicle (Manned) ("LLV(M)").** Scheduled for delivery in 2006, this will be a down-up reusable lander. Delays have been caused by engine reliability problems. An aerobraked version is planned as an eventual Mars lander.

**American "Space Tug" ("OTV").** Versatile small spacecraft capable of manned and remotely piloted missions in cislunar space. Its principal purpose is to make servicing forays to geosynchronous Earth-orbit, but a two-stage version can make a round trip to lunar orbit. There are enough parts on hand to assemble 5 flight vehicles, including two mannable capsules.

### TYPICAL EARLY SOVIET LUNAR MISSION

**Phase 1:** LTV is fueled in low Earth-orbit and mated with command module (day 1). 6-man crew ascends to *Mir* in shuttle and transfers to LTV (day 2). LTV takes crew to *Mechta* in lunar polar orbit (days 3-6).

**Phase 2:** Second LTV is fueled and mated to LLV (day 16). LTV delivers LLV to *Mechta* (days 17-20).

**Phase 3:** 3-man crew descends to surface in LLV (day 21). Research team conducts surface operations (days 20-23). Team ascends to *Mechta* (day 24).

**Phase 4:** Both LTVs return to *Mir* (days 25-28).

The fact that these early-style missions require two LTVs, coupled with the fact that the Soviets only had two vehicles at the time, explains why the first lunar landing mission had to be canceled when the Sinuhe opportunity came up. During later missions, safety rules would be relaxed so that eventually teams would be left on the lunar surface without a means at hand for evacuation to the Earth. The long delay between the ascents of the LTV and LLV(I), around 14 days, are due to the fact space station *Mechta* is in lunar polar orbit, and a convenient and energy efficient rendezvous may be made only when the station's orbit lies parallel to the Moon's orbital axis; that is, when its orbit bisects the face of the Moon.

# APPENDIX 3
# *A Glossary of Unfamiliar Words*

**Achondrite.** Stony meteor type displaying no chondrules that seem to result from igneous differentiation.

**Albedo.** Reflectivity on a scale of 0 to 1.

**Apparatchiki.** Minor bureaucrats of the Communist party.

**Arbat.** Artistic district within Moskva.

**Aspirantura.** Equivalent of a Ph.D. in the Soviet system of higher education.

**Baikonur.** The principle Soviet cosmodrome, analogous to Kennedy Space Center (Cape Canaveral). It is located between the towns of Baikonur and Tyura Tam in Kazakhstan, Soviet Central Asia.

**Breccia.** Composite material made up of broken rock fragments cemented together by fine-grained material.

**Brennschluss.** "End of Burning." A phrase used by early German rocket pioneers to indicate the moment when an experimental rocket's fuel had been exhausted. In modern parlance it refers to the moment when powered flight has concluded and the motors are turned off.

**Carabiner.** Clip-ring used in mountaineering.

**Carbonacious chondrite.** Stony meteor type with chondrules, containing carbon compounds.

**CMU.** Cosmonaut Maneuvering Unit, the Soviet equivalent of the U.S. Manned Maneuvering Unit. It is a propulsion unit for use by a cosmonaut making an EVA.

**CM-PCR.** *Molotochek*'s propulsion control room.

**CPSU.** Communist party of the Soviet Union.

**Dozhdevik.** *Molotochek*'s primary control computer. It is an illegal Macintosh clone.

**Dzhugashvili.** Joseph Stalin's real name. He was a Georgian.

**EMP.** Electromagnetic pulse. An after-effect of any large explosion (but particularly notable in nuclear and thermonuclear detonations) it sets up an extremely damaging induced current in electronic devices.

**EVA.** Extra-vehicular activity.

**Extractor rocket.** Rocket used to separate manned spacecraft from damaged or exploding boosters. Both the American space shuttle and the Soviet *Voskhod* were flown without these devices.

**Glavkosmos.** The USSR's main civilian space agency, created as a side effect of *glasnost.*

**GEO.** Geosynchronous orbit.

**Grazhdanin.** Citizen.

**Grazhdanina.** Citizeness.

**IKI.** Institute for Space Research. Scientific agency responsible for conducting planetary research.

**Intourist.** The USSR's agency for handling tourist affairs.

**Inverse-square law.** In spherical phenomena, a physical quantity varies with distance from its source inversely as the square of that distance.

**Isotopic dating.** A method of telling the age of something by comparing the ratios of certain elemental isotopes.

**Kandidat.** Soviet master's degree.

**Kapustin Yar.** "Cabbage Crag." A minor Soviet cosmodrome, somewhat analagous to the Wallops Island, Virginia, space center in the U.S. It is located on the Volga River, just south of Volgograd.

**Komsomol.** The young adult Communist organization. "Red Boy Scouts."

**Kopeika.** A penny.

**Kosmicheskii Korabl.** Cosmic ship, the Soviet term for "space shuttle."

**Krai.** An administrative district of the USSR.

**Kvant.** Scientific module for attachment to *Mir.* From "Quantum."

**Lebed.** Swan.

**LEO.** Low Earth-orbit.

**LPSC.** Lunar and Planetary Science Conference.

**LSS.** Life-support systems.

**Lunokhod.** One of the unmanned lunar rovers sent to the Moon by the USSR in the early 1970s.

**Monocoque.** A self-supporting hull, without internal bracing structure.

**Moskvich.** Soviet sub-compact car.

**Nomenklatura.** "The List." High-ranking Soviet bureaucrats.

**Nunatak.** In Antarctica, a mountain peak protruding from the thick ice.

**OAMS.** Orbital/Attitude Maneuvering System.

**Olivine.** Common silicate mineral containing magnesium, iron, and silicon oxides.

**OMS.** Orbital Maneuvering System. Thrusters on shuttles and *Korabli* for changing orbits, slowing down for reentry, etc.

**Pallasite.** Meteor type made of mixed metal and olivine.

**Papirossa.** Very harsh Soviet cigarettes.

**Pelmeni.** Russian *dim sum.*

**Pirogi.** Little filled pies very popular as appetizers.

**Plesetsk.** Soviet cosmodrome used for launching spacecraft into polar and other high-inclination orbits. Analagous to Vandenberg Air Force Base, in California, it is located on the railway line from Moskva to Arkhangelsk, in the Russian arctic.

**Pluton.** Pocket of magma that solidifies underground.

**Politburo.** Eleven-member group that guides the Communist party of the USSR.

**Regmaglypts.** Thumbprintlike distortions in the surface of metal meteorites caused by atmospheric friction.

**Regolith.** Fine-grained material. The "dirt" on the surface of other planets.

**Samfab.** Self-administered Soviet factory.

**Samfabkosmos.** Samfab responsible for producing much Soviet space hardware by the late 1990s.

**Samizdat.** Self-publishing by copy machine or written copy.

**Samkhoz.** Self-administered Soviet plantation.

**Sänger.** Eugen Sänger. German rocket pioneer, originator of the space shuttle concept.

**Schwachsinnigers.** Morons.

**Semyorka.** "Old Mark Seven." The original Soviet ICBM/ Satellite Launch Vehicle. Also known as R-7, T-3, ALV, etc.

**Silicate.** Mineral containing silicon. Rock.

**Soloshnur.** Bungee-style zero-gravity exercise machine.

**Strategic Rocket Forces.** A separate, coequal branch of Soviet military responsible for long-range rocketry.

**Sustainer-core.** The central portion of a side-staged rocket which keeps firing after the strap-on boosters have been expended. Examples include the Semyorka, Energiya, and the American Atlas rockets.

**Swedish Maulers.** Nuclear weapons whose force is directed linearly, with energy release focused in the kinetic form. Concept developed by Swedish scientists in the late 1960s.

**TAV.** Trans-Atmospheric Vehicle. Hypersonic aircraft such as the "Orient Express."

**Tminaya.** A kind of vodka flavored with caraway seeds.

**Tovarishch.** Comrade.

**Triple-A.** Near-Earth Asteroid. See Appendix One.

**TTY.** Universal abbreviation of teletype. Now taken to mean "terminal."

**Ubornaya.** Bathroom.

**Ullage.** Small pressure-fed rockets that ignite prior to main stage ignition in an orbiting spacecraft. Their purpose is to force the fuel to enter the engine turbopumps through inertia.

**Veloergometer.** Stationary bicycle.

**Vernadskii.** The Soviet Academy responsible for geochemistry and planetology.

**VfR.** *Verein für Raumschiffahrt.* The German Society for Space Travel, founded by Willy Ley and his friends in the 1920s. It trained Werner von Braun, who built the V-2 and, later, the Saturn V moon rocket.

**Vladimir Ulyanov.** Lenin's real name. Ulyanov took his new name from the Lena, his favorite river.

**Vzor.** An etched pattern in Soviet spaceship windows for accurate sighting.

**Widmanstätten pattern.** A crosshatched pattern caused in metal meteorites by uneven distribution of iron and nickel.

**Zek.** Forced laborer.

**Zelenist.** Member of the USSR's "Green" party.

**Zenit.** "Zenith." An advanced booster, successor to the Semyorka.

**Zheleznodorozhaya.** Railroad (adj.).

**Zil.** Massive Soviet limousine used by high officials.

**Zvyozdnii Gorodok.** Starry Town. Located in a suburb of Moskva, it is the main cosmonaut training center, where the Soviet equivalent of Mission Control is located.

"Barton and Capobianco prove themselves a team to watch out for." -- *Locus*

# Be sure to look for these other titles by the authors of *Fellow Traveler*

☐ **Iris** (28822-9 * $4.95/$5.95 in Canada)
by William Barton and Michael Capobianco.

Escaping an Earth ravaged by economic collapse, the colony ship *Deepstar* soars toward a dazzling odyssey of alien contact that begins in the heart of a rogue planetary system. "A virtually perfect blend of diamondhard scientific extrapolation and stylistically brilliant narrative."
--*Science Fiction Eye*

☐ **Burster** (28543-2 * $3.95/$4.95 in Canada)
by Michael Capobianco.

As the multinational starship *Asia* journeys through the near solar systems, contact with Earth is suddenly lost. Restless, young Peter Zolotin is sent on the mind-bending journey back home to discover the reason for this sudden radio silence.

Now available wherever Bantam Spectra Books are sold, or use this page for ordering

"Conflict enough to drive any two ordinary novels."--
*Analog*

# SHIVERING WORLD
# by
# Kathy Tyers

"A splendid read, both realistic and engaging."
--Lois McMaster Bujold

When Gaea Consortium offers Graysha Brady-Phillips a
tour of hazard duty on a raw pioneer planet she leaps at
the chance, even though her predecessor died--a victim
of either the savage weather outside the domes or the
fanatic population within. But Graysha isn't on Goddard
just to collect triple pay. She's trying to save her life.
The colonists' radical--and illegal-- science just might
offer Graysha a cure for the genetic disease that is killing
her. But Goddard's terraformers, pursued by the
Eugenics Board for gene tampering and battling Gaea
Consortium for their very survival, are suspicious of
outsiders--especially someone connected to the two
organizations that are trying hardest to destroy them.

The settlers think Graysha's a spy. Graysha thinks the
settlers are trying to kill her. They're both right. And the
fate of their planet hangs in the balance.

On sale now wherever Bantam Spectra Books are sold.

AN287 – 7/91